Lyn Andrews is one of the UK's top one hundred best-selling authors, reaching No. 1 on the *Sunday Times* paperback bestseller list. Born and brought up in Liverpool, she is the daughter of a policeman and also married a policeman. After becoming the mother of triplets, she took some time off from her writing whilst she raised her children. Shortlisted for the RNA Romantic Novel of the Year Award in 1993, she has now written twenty-eight hugely successful novels. Lyn Andrews divides her time between Merseyside and Ireland.

lyn
andrews

Mersey Blues

headline

First published in 1995 by Corgi Books
an imprint of Transworld Publishers

First published in this paperback edition in 2009
by HEADLINE PUBLISHING GROUP

9

ISBN 978 07553 5672 0 (A-format)
ISBN 978 0 7553 4188 7 (B-format)

Typeset in Janson by Avon DataSet Ltd,
Bidford-on-Avon, Warwickshire

Printed in the UK by CPI Group (UK) Ltd, Croydon, CR0 4YY

HEADLINE PUBLISHING GROUP
An Hachette UK Company
338 Euston Road
London NW1 3BH

www.headline.co.uk
www.hachette.co.uk

For my new daughter-in-law,
Fiona.

Acknowledgements

———•———

In writing of the police strike I have been much helped by A. V. Selwood's excellent and informative book, *Police Strike 1919*, (W. H. Allen 1978).

My grateful thanks also go to the Merseyside Police at Headquarters, Canning Place, in whose archives I was allowed to delve. Without the information gleaned from the reports, statements etc., *Mersey Blues* would have been sadly lacking in authenticity.

Thanks to my editor, Linda Evans, for leading me through the minefield of titles held by the British aristocracy.

Lyn Andrews
Southport 1995

Chapter One

———————

1919

IT WASN'T WHAT YOU WOULD call a perfect May afternoon, Mike Burgess mused moodily as he gazed out of the shop window at the row of grimy houses on the opposite side of Burlington Street. The narrow streets of dilapidated houses that ran from Scotland Road down to the docks were all the same: dismal, decaying and decrepit, despite the strenuous efforts of their occupants who waged a daily war against dirt, disease and poverty.

A few shafts of sunlight had managed to penetrate between the roofs and danced on the dusty cobbles in the road, but in the main, the air was oppressive, the sky overcast, and the grey clouds threatened a downpour before long. Business had been slack in the shop on the corner of Burlington Street and Vauxhall Road that had been run by his mam and dad for as long as he could remember. This afternoon Frank Burgess had taken the opportunity to go to the provision merchants in Canning Place, and Hilda, his mam, was putting her feet up for half an hour. Like all the small shops in the vicinity, Burgess's was open from eight o'clock in the morning until nine o'clock at night, which made for a long, tiring day. Mam wasn't getting any younger, and there were times when she looked old and careworn. He knew from experience that, once it had turned half past four, business would begin to pick up. People would be thinking of the evening meal and what groceries they had run short of. In this neighbourhood very few could afford to keep a larder stocked up. They shopped from day to day, sometimes from meal to meal.

Mike sighed, and his dark eyes filled with despondency. He'd never really wanted to work in the shop. He'd wanted to go to the Mechanics Institute after he'd left Our Lady's School in Eldon Street, at the age of fourteen. There hadn't been enough money, though. 'Maybe later on, lad' his mam had said then. But later on the war had come and engulfed everyone.

He swept away some imaginary specks of dust and polished the edge of the counter with a corner of the brown shop coat he wore. He was twenty-one, a man – and a married man at that – and this certainly wasn't what he had envisaged for himself after he'd been demobilized from the Army. Before he'd enlisted he'd been just a kid, not taking anything really seriously, and resigned to working in the shop. Now he was grown up, mature. It was hard to adjust to this monotonous routine, when hours were spent just waiting for customers, or in carrying out trivial tasks such as brushing the dried soil from the potatoes.

He'd not wanted to stay in the Army; he'd been wounded twice, and there were too many dreadful memories he still carried with him of the four years he'd spent in the trenches. Like hundreds of others, he'd lied about his age. He'd been sixteen when he joined up, seventeen when he'd been thrust into the horrors of trench warfare. That was when he'd left his youth behind. No, he'd had enough, he'd seen too much. There were too many friends he'd lost, too many men and boys from the neighbourhood who would never walk the length of Scotland Road again. When he'd first come home he had had no real plans, everything was too confused, so somehow he'd just slipped back into his old position, helping out in the shop.

The door opened and Mike became alert, thankful for the diversion and the company.

'Nice to see you Mrs Chatterton,' he said warmly, straightening up and trying to look efficient.

'You saw me this morning. You waved at me as I went past, you daft ha'porth! It's only folk of my age who are supposed to have bad memories.' Bridie Chatterton laughed. She'd always been a big woman, but she'd grown a little stouter with the years, and there were silver hairs now amongst the luxuriant dark auburn ones. She'd worn her hair pulled back in a neat bun for as long as he'd known her. Despite all the hardships Bridie had known in her life, she had managed to keep her easygoing, good-humoured out-look. It had made her very popular with the customers of The Black Dog, in the days when she'd served behind the bar there, before she'd married Edward Chatterton and had had Elizabeth.

Though the day was fairly warm, she wore her black knitted shawl over a paisley print cotton blouse and plain black skirt. She looked at him closely and frowned. 'Mike Burgess, you've got a face like a wet week, what's up with you now?'

He shrugged. 'Boredom I suppose. I never wanted to work in the shop in the first place.'

'Don't you let your mam hear you talking like that, lad. Trade isn't booming, money isn't showering down from the sky. She's paying you, it's a job, and they're getting harder and harder to come by.'

Mike knew he could confide in Bridie Chatterton with complete confidence. It was another attribute that had endeared her to the patrons of Red McClelland's drinking establishment. If it had been Lizzie Simcock, he wouldn't have opened his mouth. Lizzie was the local gossip, and would make it her business to ensure his mam heard every word he'd uttered, and not only his mam but most of the street as well.

'I know all that, and I'm grateful. It's just that I didn't expect things to be so . . . normal, so quiet after the war.'

'Oh, I see. It's the excitement you miss. Well, that kind of excitement we can all do without, and there are a lot of families around here who wish things were "normal" again. Count your blessings, lad. How's Abbie?'

Mike's frustration evaporated and he smiled broadly as he thought of his wife. They'd only been married ten months, and, until the Armistice, they'd spent very little time together, but he loved her passionately and had done since before the war. Abbie Kerrigan she'd been then. One of the large brood that Sal and Pat Kerrigan from number seventy-six had produced on a regular basis. Being a member of that boisterous, belligerent family had not endeared Abbie to his mam in the early days of their courtship. However, Abbie had proved herself to be quiet, reserved and courageous, for she'd trained and served in the Voluntary Aid Detachment in the field hospitals in France. The nightmarish memories that still haunted him were things Abbie understood and shared with him.

'Oh, she's great. She's still working at Walton Hospital and enjoying it. The ward sister is a bit of a tartar, but aren't they all? She says it's a joy to work there after the VAD, except for doing the night shift.'

'What's wrong with the night shift?' Bridie asked, glancing along the shelves behind Mike in case the sight of a certain commodity might jog her memory as to its absence in her larder.

'It's too quiet.'

Bridie looked startled. 'What a pair! As God made them he matched them. You'll come to yearn for a bit of quiet in the future. You wait until you've got a house full of kids driving you mad with their noise and antics.'

Mike became embarrassed. 'We . . . we don't want to start a family yet.'

'You might find you've not much choice in the matter. Babies don't usually wait to be invited. Look at me. I was forty when I had Elizabeth. A real surprise she was to everyone, and most of all Edward and me.'

Mike felt that this conversation was one that would have been better conducted by his mother. 'Well, we want to have a house first and a bit of money behind us.'

'What's the matter with the rooms you've got in Hopwood Street? It's better than having to live with your mam and dad or worse still, Sal and Pat.'

'Oh, there's nothing wrong with them, it's just that . . . we feel . . . that we'd have more privacy if we had a place of our own; a house we could really call ours. We're trying to save up.'

This was really being over-optimistic, Bridie thought, and said so.

Mike laughed. 'I don't mean buy one, we could never afford to do that. No, rent one.'

'I don't know, you young ones today. I was quite content to move in with Ma Butterworth and her tribe. We eventually got the place to ourselves when they all left and she died.' Bridie thought wistfully of the few short years she'd been married to Mick Butterworth, her first husband. He'd died of cancer when still a young man, leaving her with a baby to bring up. Inevitably, sadness replaced the wistfulness. It always did when she thought of Nancy. Her poor Nancy had been fated to follow her da at the age of eighteen. Even now, she thought bitterly, it was such a useless and terrible waste of a young life, ended at the hands of a back-street abortionist.

'What was it you wanted?' Mike asked, noting the mist of tears that had sprung into Bridie's eyes, and knowing she was thinking of poor Nancy.

Bridie sighed. 'Oh, just a quarter of tea and a jar of Hartley's raspberry jam. I give Rosie and Elizabeth a couple of butties when they get in from school. It keeps them going until tea-time.'

Mike grinned at her. 'They're spoiled rotten, the pair of them.'

'Ah, go on! Tell me that you never had such luxuries when you were their age. I seem to remember you having a permanently sticky mouth,' Bridie joked, her old self again. 'Now we've got three wages coming in, we can afford a few extras.'

Hilda Burgess emerged from the room at the back of the shop, a small, neat woman whose dark eyes missed nothing. She had a good head for business and a sharp tongue. In her younger days she'd also been accused of being pushy and snobbish; but time had mellowed her, and her heart was in the right place. 'I thought it was you, Bridie.'

'Mam, you're supposed to be having a bit of a rest. I told you I can manage.'

'I was, but I wanted to see Bridie.'

'What for?'

'Just to ask if you will pass these few bits in to Sal Kerrigan for me on your way home.'

Bridie adjusted her shawl and nodded. 'You're looking tired Hilda.'

'Well, none of us are getting any younger, are we Bridie? See, I've put them in this brown paper bag. Don't worry about the money. She'll settle up at the end of the week, as usual. Or at least their Joan will when she's hounded Pat long enough for the house-keeping.'

'I can drop them in,' Mike offered. Abbie nearly always called in to see her mother, who was confined to bed most of the time now. Dr Wallace had warned Sal that if she didn't rest the next stroke could be fatal. Nor would he take any responsibility if she wouldn't listen to or heed his advice.

'No, it's all right, Mike. I'll nip in and have a bit of a jangle with Sal, she gets fed up stuck in that bedroom all the time, and I've got half an hour before the kids get in. You'll want to be getting off home as soon as Abbie's finished her shift at Walton.'

When the door had closed behind Bridie, Hilda sighed. 'You go and have a cup of tea. I'll manage. I'm hardly likely to be rushed off my feet at this time of day.'

'Mam, you should be resting, even Bridie said you look tired. There's no need for you to stand – there's nothing doing.'

'There's no need to remind me that custom is scarce. Everything has gone up since the war. We'll soon be having to charge sixpence for a large loaf. I ask you! Folk will do without or go elsewhere, and our profits will go with them.'

'I know, and I also know that you really don't need me here, it would be a big saving for you if I got another job.'

Hilda could have bitten her tongue. As she'd told Bridie, no one was getting any younger, and that included Frank. He needed Mike's help to shift the heavy stuff. 'I wasn't complaining about you, lad. Don't forget we've got Chrissie's money too.'

'You mean what bit she eventually turns up after a big song and dance about it.' His sister Chrissie had always been a pain in the neck, he thought grimly. As a child she'd delighted in tormenting him and now, at eighteen, he knew she caused his mam many a restless night. 'Mam, I've been thinking a lot about what I'm going to do with my life.'

Hilda glanced at him sharply. 'And what have you decided? Jobs are harder to get now than they were before the war. The girls and women are sticking to their guns and refusing to give up the freedom and the wages they've had for the past five years. Not that I approve. A woman's place is in the home, unless she's a widow or forced to work to keep the family out of the workhouse.'

'Abbie and I have been looking at the papers every day.'

'And?'

'We've decided that I should look for something that's reliable, secure and pays a good wage.'

Aye, that sounded like something Abbie would come up with, Hilda thought. Always one with an eye to the future, always looking for a golden opportunity, was Abbie. Look how she'd managed to drag herself up and out of the pigsty Sal had called a home. She'd done well for herself, had Abbie: a good husband and a good job as a trained nurse.

'I hate to put the damper on things, but the only jobs like that are in the professions, and you've no chance. You've neither the education, the experience or the right background. We're working class. Lower your sights, lad, be realistic. And anyway, what job is secure these days? There's always something up. There's a general strike on in Glasgow right now, according to the newspapers.' Suddenly a thought occurred to her, one that drained the colour from her cheeks and caused her to suck in her breath sharply. 'Holy Mother of God! You're not thinking of going back in the Army? There's still lads in the King's Liverpool Regiment fighting those revolutionaries, those Bolshi something or other in Russia. You're not thinking of making a career in the Army?'

Mike smiled at her. 'No, Mam. I've had enough of the Army and enough of fighting. I've done my bit, and being wounded twice is twice too often. I won't risk a third time.'

Hilda sighed with relief. 'Then what?'

He shrugged, not wanting to reveal his idea, for he'd not even mentioned it to Abbie yet.

Hilda was exasperated. 'You don't know when you're well off. Go on and get a cup of tea, boil the kettle up again. Your da should be back soon with the cart. He'll need you to give him a hand.'

When he'd gone she glanced around at the stock without much pleasure. There were things on some of those shelves that had been there too long. She just hoped that Frank would remember what she'd said and not get carried away, or be induced to take stuff they couldn't hope to sell. Theirs wasn't a shop like Coopers in Church Street, where you could buy any amount of exotic and fancy food.

She rearranged some tins of Fry's Cocoa on one of the shelves, then went to the door and peered out. Burlington Street was fairly quiet at this time of the day. Only at the far end, beyond the bridge over the Liverpool to Leeds Canal, was there any sign of bustling activity. That was where Tate and Lyle's sugar refinery was, and beyond that the docks. Most of the kids were at school. The women were either doing the ironing, it being Tuesday and the day after wash-day, or they were shopping in town or Great Homer Street market where things were cheaper than at Burgess's corner shop.

She knew that what Mike had said made sense. They were hard put to pay him a wage, there had only ever been enough to keep one family on. Oh, they'd been much better off than most of their neighbours when all the kids had been small. Sal Kerrigan had never known from day to day how she'd be able to feed her family, or if she'd have enough money for the rent. Bridie, when she'd been a widow, had worked in two pubs – the Black Dog and The Green Man – going straight from one to the other. Lizzie Simcock had gone office cleaning and had taken in washing and mending, but often Mary Simcock had gone to school barefoot in summer.

Everything had changed with the war. The world had been turned upside down and old values, old traditions, had been swept away for ever. When the men and boys had gone to fight, it was the women and girls who had taken their jobs and kept the country going. And not just single girls, widows and old maids. Married women with families, and ladies from the upper classes, had gone out to work. They'd earned good money too, money of their own, a totally new experience for most of them; an experience that had given a lot of them ideas she didn't agree with. During the war things had got a lot better for most of the families in Burlington Street, at least in financial ways.

She pursed her lips, then with her foot she moved the cast-iron doorstop a bit to one side and went back behind the counter. Absentmindedly she began to polish the scales and the brass weights with a piece of clean mutton cloth. She wanted Mike to get on in life, of course she did. It was what every mother wanted for her children. By a lot of people's reckoning, Mike and Abbie were doing quite well. They had a couple of decent rooms in Hopwood Street. They had Mike's wage and Abbie's, until such times as she got pregnant. It was more than a lot of couples had, and maybe they should be content with their lot, for she couldn't see that there was anything in the way of a reliable, secure, well paid job in the offing at all.

Chapter Two

A S THE AFTERNOON WORE ON the customers began to trickle in. Frank Burgess arrived home with his purchases on the cart he always borrowed from the provision merchants, and which he took back as quickly as possible. It didn't do to put years of goodwill in jeopardy. The cart wasn't full and Mike had soon unloaded it, then he had filled up the shelves and was stacking small sacks of potatoes and coal in the yard when his wife interrupted him.

Abbie was a tall, slim girl with blond hair brushed neatly up into a roll that framed her face. She had the blue eyes and the pale, delicately coloured skin of her father's Irish forebears. She was smiling, pride and love for her young husband radiating from her sparkling blue eyes.

'Is that the time?' Mike exclaimed, catching sight of her.

Abbie laughed. 'It is, and you've got dirty streaks all over your face. Are you trying to convince me that you've been hard at it all day?'

He kissed her on the cheek and thought, as he did every single day, how lucky he was to have married her. She was twenty-three now, two years older than himself, but she was kind and generous, amusing, practical, hardworking, and a very attractive girl. Even the rather severe uniform of a staff nurse that she still wore under her coat didn't detract at all from the beautiful, curvaceous form beneath it.

'Have you been to see your mam yet?'

'No. I came here first. How much longer do you think you'll be?'

'I've nearly finished, but I've promised I'll stay until our Chrissie gets in. Mam doesn't look very well today and Chrissie can give her a hand later on if business gets brisk.'

'Providing Chrissie hasn't got other plans,' Abbie replied rather curtly. She had little time for her sister-in-law, who had never liked her, and who had tried, more than once, to cause trouble for herself and Mike when they'd been courting. In fact she'd once slapped Chrissie's face – at Nancy Butterworth's funeral. In her opinion, Mike's sister was a spoiled, selfish, self-opinionated little madam.

'I know she's no angel, but she can help out and that lets me leave earlier.'

'Oh, I know. I think I'll go and see Mam. I'll come back for you in an hour. I got an *Echo*, we can see if there are any jobs going, later on, when we've had something to eat.'

'It's been very quiet today, Abbie, and I've been thinking.'

'And?'

'Well, I have got an idea, but I'll tell you about it later. When we're on our own.'

She raised her hand and gently patted his cheek. 'You'd better get a wash before we go home, or the neighbours will think I'm carrying on with the coalman,' she joked.

When she'd gone, Mike heaved the last sack of potatoes onto the wooden pallet that stood against the wall of the house. He stretched and rubbed his shoulder, which usually ached after heavy work or when there was rain imminent. It had healed very well. There was no reason why it should do otherwise; he was a fit, healthy young man, the Army surgeon had impressed upon him, after the shrapnel had been removed. Yes, young bodies healed quickly, but many young minds hadn't healed at all. He knew lads who had been rendered speechless and witless by shell shock.

He looked up at the lowering sky and felt the first heavy spot of rain on his face. The idea he'd been toying with all afternoon took hold of him again and he wondered how Abbie would react. How everyone would react. It was a big step to take and one that wouldn't be universally popular with everyone he knew.

Abbie's cry of greeting as she pushed open the door of number seventy-six, her old home, was answered by her eldest sister, Joan.

16

'Oh, it's you. I thought it was a bit early for our Ginny.'

Abbie followed her into the spotless kitchen. It still amazed her, even after all these months, even seeing it day after day. It was a far cry from the days when the place had been messy, cluttered and thoroughly untidy. There had been nine of them then, all running in and out. Mam had been oblivious to the utter chaos that had always surrounded her, and was usually to be found sitting toasting her legs in front of the range, a mug of tea at her elbow.

Glancing around the small, pristine room Abbie felt a sense of loss, of disappointment even. In the past Mam had always been here, ready to dole out punishments or to kiss and hug away childhood upsets and scrapes. She'd always been their rock in the turbulent sea of daily life in Burlington Street, and she'd enjoyed that role, even though she'd sworn that she would sell her soul for some peace and quiet.

'I'll never get used to all this . . . tidiness, Joan,' she remarked as her sister poured her a cup of tea.

'And I'll never get used to Da's flaming untidiness and sheer laziness. He can't even be bothered to put his dirty clothes in the basket I bought out of my own money. It's not much to ask. He just drops them all over the place, and Ginny's no better. That room of hers is like Paddy's Market. At least our Bertie is tidy, when he's home. Cunard have strict rules.' Bertie Kerrigan was a bell boy on the *Aquitania*. 'And Rosie Chatterton still treats this house as though it were her

17

home. Mam's ruined them all. It's no wonder she's had two strokes, no one lifts a flaming finger.'

Abbie smiled wryly. 'All she ever wanted was peace and quiet, so she said, and now she's got it.'

'Don't you believe it. She drives me round the bend banging on the floor all day. I've threatened to take that flaming walking stick off her. Listen to her, she's at it again. She heard you come in.' Joan jerked her head towards the ceiling as a series of loud thumps threatened to bring flakes of plaster down on their heads.

'I'll go; sit and have your tea,' Abbie instructed, and Joan nodded thankfully.

Abbie found her mother propped up with pillows in the brass bed that completely dominated the room. It was a tidy room these days. Beside the bed was a small chest on top of which were a glass, a jug and a copy of yesterday's *Echo*. The bed was covered with a patchwork quilt that was crumpled and had slipped partly onto the floor. After kissing Sal on the cheek, Abbie took her hand and pressed her thumb against the inside of her mother's wrist, to feel the pulse. 'How are you today Mam?'

Sal jerked her hand away irritably. 'I'm fed up to the back teeth, that's how I am today!'

'It's no good getting all airyated with me, you know what Dr Wallace said.'

'He's a ruddy fool. He was just trying to put the fear of God in me.'

Abbie had smoothed out and tucked in the quilt.

'Lean forward while I fix these pillows. This bed looks as though you've been doing Swedish exercises in it, and you know Dr Wallace is not a fool.'

'At least when I had the bed downstairs in the parlour I could see what was going on. It's desperate up 'ere. It's morbid all this . . . this flaming silence.'

'I seem to remember that you were always saying you'd sell your soul for a bit of silence, and you know the bed had to be brought back up here because it got to be like Lime Street Station down there. Half the street in and out at all hours of the day and night. Da ranting and raving, Seb and all his mates tramping up and down the lobby, and Joan threatening to wash her hands of the whole lot of you. You were getting precious little rest and neither was anyone else.'

'Oh, I know, luv, but it's being stuck up here looking at the same four walls day in and day out, and madam down there laying the law down. I feel useless, finished, a burden. I'm like a lodger in me own 'ome.'

Abbie took her hand. 'Don't be having a go at Joan. She's only thinking of you, Mam.'

'She's got too much time to think, that's what's the matter with her.'

'That's not her fault and you know it,' Abbie said quietly, thinking of Terry, Joan's husband, who had been killed in the battle for Montauban.

Sal nodded; she was also thinking of Terry and of her two eldest sons, Kenneth and Norman, who had been killed that day too.

'Now that Terry's mam has passed away, you know

she'd like nothing better than to get herself a job and keep that nice little house in Everton spick and span, and perhaps go to the moving pictures once in a while. We should all be grateful for her help, Mam.'

Sal reluctantly agreed. Of course it was Joan who had influenced Abbie. Encouraged her to see that she could demand and get more from life. When Joan had married Terry and had moved to that oh-so-tidy house in Everton, it had opened Abbie's eyes to the sort of life she could expect, providing she, too, found a good husband who didn't waste his money on drink or gambling, the way Pat had done for most of his life.

'Has she told you that Da and Ginny are always going on and on at her to give up her house and move back here for good?'

'Jesus, Mary and Joseph! You see what I mean about being stuck up here? No one even bothers to consult me. Well, I won't have it. Much as she gets on me nerves, you tell her to take no notice of them. The pair of them have got her for a skivvy now, and they could manage if they tried. Bone flaming idle, both of them. She's not to give up her home, Abbie, you tell her that. When I've gone I'm not having her devoting her life to those two, tell her that.'

'I will, but I don't think she needs telling. She's digging her heels in and won't budge, thank God.'

Sal settled herself again and hid a yawn behind her hand.

'Why don't you learn to knit, Mam? It would pass

the time. Joan will teach you. Her ma-in-law taught her.'

An expression of keen interest crept over Sal's face. 'Oh, aye! Is there something you want to tell me?'

Abbie laughed. 'No there isn't. Why does everyone keep hinting and referring to babies and families?'

Sal looked disappointed. 'I suppose because everyone thinks it's about time you made me a granny, and I agree with them.'

'We've plenty of time yet, Mam.'

'You might have but I haven't. You heard Dr Miseryguts. I could pop me clogs at any time.'

'Now stop that. And if you think you're going to blackmail me that way, you're mistaken.'

'It's not blackmail,' Sal said huffily. 'You're the only one in a position to give me grand-kids before I start pushing up the daisies. Our Joan's a widow, Ginny isn't even courting, and our Monica is a flaming nun.'

Abbie shook her head. 'I'm sorry, Mam, you'll have to wait. Just think, though, it will be something to look forward to. Something to keep you going. Start learning to knit and by the time I do have a baby it will have a complete wardrobe. It will be the best dressed baby in the neighbourhood.'

'Oh, get out of here! I'm tired and you've got a home to go to. Fetch your husband, if Hilda's finished with him, and go 'ome. Bridie called in to see me earlier and so did Lizzie. Mind you, all she ever does is moan and complain, so she's not much company.'

'You fraud! You said you never see anyone.'

'I don't. A few minutes' chat is neither here nor there. Anyway, I'm tired now. I'll have a nap before yer da gets in and starts annoying me.'

Abbie smiled and kissed her mother on the cheek. 'I'll see you tomorrow. God bless.'

As she closed the bedroom door, the sound of Joan's voice and that of her ten-year-old brother Seb, came clearly from the kitchen. They were arguing, and a small group of scruffy boys were camped on the front step. She sighed. They'd always been a rowdy, acrimonious family, but they'd always been a close family too. She'd go and help Joan sort out whatever scrape Seb had got himself into now, then she'd go back for Mike. As she ran lightly down the stairs a frown creased her forehead and she wondered what he intended to discuss with her.

They had the two upstairs rooms in Hopwood Street. One they used as a bedroom, the other a sitting-room and dining-room combined. They had rented them as partly furnished from the Blakes, an elderly couple who no longer needed much space, as their family had long flown the nest. Moreover, the rent Mike and Abbie paid them was a very welcome addition to their budget.

Abbie took off her coat and hat. 'I'd best get changed before I start to cook.'

'I'll put a light to this fire and put the kettle on the gas,' Mike offered. It was a tiny bedroom fireplace, and was barely sufficient to heat the room in winter, but

Mrs Blake had provided them with a gas ring to cook on.

'How was your mam?' he called.

'Oh more or less the same as usual, a bit mardy. She hates not being at the centre of things.' Abbie came back into the room, a cotton skirt and a cambric blouse replacing her uniform. 'She was going on about us starting a family. Honestly, the minute you get engaged they want to know when the wedding will be, when you get married they start asking about babies! There's no keeping up with some people.'

'I know, I had Bridie Chatterton quizzing me.'

'Well they can quiz all they like, I want a bit of money behind me, for emergencies, and a house. I don't want to be like Mam, not a penny to bless herself with once the boys were born.'

Mike caught her around the waist and pulled her to him. 'Bridie said babies don't usually wait to be invited.'

Abbie laughed and extricated herself from his embrace. 'I'm starving and I want to hear about this plan of yours first, then I might consider,' she laughed suggestively.

She made a pot of tea and then deftly placed the sausage, black pudding and tomatoes in the frying pan on the gas, while Mike obligingly set the small gateleg table. He tried to help as much as he could for she, too, worked long hours.

Meals were so difficult to organize, Abbie thought ruefully. Only one pan could be used at a time, which drastically limited their choice. Sometimes Mrs Blake would let her use the oven in the kitchen, but she didn't like to ask all the time, she felt she was intruding. One of the good things about the Blakes was that they were not always popping in and out. Most of the other people she knew would do just that. On Sundays they went to Hilda's for their dinner, when her shifts permitted. It was a meal they both enjoyed, but she doubly so as she didn't have to cook it. She and Chrissie always washed up, though. 'There, that'll do nicely,' she said with satisfaction, placing Mike's plate in front of him, then cursing as there was a knock on the door.

'I'll get it,' Mike offered.

'No, eat your tea. I'll go.'

It was Mrs Blake with a letter that had come in the late delivery. Abbie thanked her.

'I didn't hear you come in, luv. I think I must be getting deafer.'

'Take care going downstairs Mrs Blake, and thanks.'

'Who's it from?' Mike asked, his mouth full of thick, spicy Cumberland sausage.

Abbie pulled a face. 'From the handwriting I'd say my sainted sister.'

'Aren't you going to open it?'

'Not until I've had my tea. I'm starving and I can't take a letter from our Monica on an empty stomach. Besides, I know what's in it. It's always the same, doom and gloom and pages of agonizing whether or not she did the right thing. Then more pages going on and on about how wicked she is to even have such thoughts. In the end I don't know who is more confused, her or me.'

'She's changing her mind about being a nun then?'

'I think if they gave her half a chance she'd be out like a shot. She doesn't actually say that, but I know her.'

'You should do, she's your twin sister.'

Abbie pulled another face. 'Don't remind me. She's tormented me one way or another all my life. The last time I saw her she was the relief nurse, she took my place so I could come home on leave. Talk about po-faced! It was really odd seeing her in that habit and having to call her Sister Mary Magdalene. Although she made a good choice of names there.'

Abbie mopped up the tomato with a piece of dry bread and chewed thoughtfully. In her teens, Monica Kerrigan had been as bold a piece as ever walked the streets of Liverpool. She'd given Mam no end of worry and then she'd disgraced and shamed the entire family by getting pregnant. She could still remember the rows that had followed as Monica had refused to say who the father was. Even to this day, no one knew. She'd been sent away to a convent to have the baby. The child had been adopted and Monica had returned, stating firmly that she wanted to be a nun. Abbie thought of her conversation with Sal, and wondered did her mam ever think of the grandson she already had, who was being brought up by other people.

Mike interrupted her train of thought. 'She was too young and she was probably browbeaten.'

'Now she's grown up, seen a bit of life while nursing in France and wants to come out. Well, she can get that idea right out of her head. It would kill Mam. You know how proud she is of her daughter, Sister Mary Magdalene, especially after the carry on out of her all those years ago.'

'Will you write and tell her that?'

'I will, and our Joan's got enough on her plate without having Monica descending on her after being defrocked or whatever they call it.'

Mike pushed his plate away while Abbie scanned the lines of her sister's letter.

'Anything new or interesting?'

'No, just the usual stuff, Sister Aiden did this, Mother Superior said that, Sister Agnes's brother's become a missionary priest in a place I can't even pronounce, and then "I pray to Our Lord for guidance every day. I ask Him am I serving Him properly or could I do more outside these walls? I ask His Blessed Mother" etc., etc. Well, she chose it, she can damned well stick it out!'

'You're a hard woman Mrs Burgess,' Mike laughed.

'I have to be with the terrible husband I've got, not to mention the awful relatives. Forget our Monica, what was it you wouldn't tell me until we got home?'

Mike leaned his elbows on the table. 'I don't know how you're going to take this.'

'Take what? Don't be so dramatic. You sound like someone from a pantomime.'

'Well, you know we said I should look for something secure and well paid.'

'Yes, and . . . ?'

'The only thing I can think of that comes into that category and isn't a doctor, a dentist, a solicitor or a teacher, is a scuffer.'

Abbie was stunned. 'You mean . . . you'd . . . you'd . . . ?'

'Join the Liverpool City Police. I will, if they'll have me. Is it really that bad? You look as though I'd told you I wanted to run for Prime Minister or be Grand Master of the Orange Lodge, if that's what he's called.'

'No, it's not bad at all. It just never occurred to me that . . . that . . .'

'That someone from Burlington Street would want to be a scuffer?'

The initial shock was wearing off. 'It is reliable, secure and they pay a decent wage, but . . .'

'But there are a lot of people who will just cut us dead. We've always more or less dished out our own sort of justice around here and I've never heard of anyone from the area joining the police. I know a lot of villains and they know me. No, Abbie, there will be a lot of folk who won't take to the idea with enthusiasm.'

'Will that bother you much?'

'No, as long as my family and yours are behind us.'

'I should think your mam and dad will be pleased, but I don't know about my da, or Harry O'Brien, or even Red McClelland at the pub.'

'Will you mind, Abbie? We'll probably have to move. They don't like you living somewhere they class as undesirable, that I do know.'

Abbie frowned. 'I don't know. How far away will we have to go?'

'Oh, not that far. Anfield, Everton, Walton maybe.'

She nodded thoughtfully. 'Not too far from Mam.'

'Do you think maybe your Joan would let us stay with her?'

Abbie thought for a few seconds. 'I really wouldn't like to ask her. You know how she treasures everything in that house. The front parlour is like a shrine to Terry with photos all over the place. And I think she looks on it as a bolt-hole, somewhere she can have peace, perfect peace. She's told me often enough, and I can't say I blame her after being at Mam's all day. Anyway, if we are going to have to move, I'd really like a place of my own.'

'I haven't even applied yet. Even now I might change my mind if there's going to be too much opposition.'

Abbie raised her chin determinedly. 'Mike, it's the best chance we have of ever getting on in life. The professions – doctors or lawyers, jobs like that – are just out of the question, but the police, that's different. They're respected by decent people anyway. You don't want to waste your life stuck in that shop all day, do you?'

'No, I've always hated it. The only thing is, how will Da manage?'

'He can get one of the lads in the street to help him. Pay him a few pennies. I can think of at least half a dozen who would jump at the offer.' She got up from the table and sat on his knee. 'Most people would get used to it. It's only the real hard cases who hate the police. Most folk are really only wary and suspicious, that's all. They're like that with anyone who has a bit of authority, the housing inspector, the sanitary man. There are a lot of people who are terrified of Dr Wallace. No, never mind the opposition, you've got to try for it.'

'Well, let's sleep on it, and if we still feel the same way in the morning, I'll go up to Hatton Garden and see if they'll have me.'

'Of course they'll have you. You're tall, you're bright, you were in the Army and you're honest, what more do they want?'

'I don't know, but we'll sleep on it.'

She gave a little cry as he pinched her bottom. 'That's all you ever think of, Mike Burgess!'

'How can I help myself when I married a wild, wanton woman?'

'Stop it! They'll hear us downstairs.'

'They won't, she's as deaf as a post, I heard her say so herself.'

'Oh, I'll be glad to have a place of our own,' she said, before his lips cut off the rest of her words.

Chapter Three

———•———

NEXT MORNING ABBIE HAD made up her mind. As far as she could see, it was something to aim for. It was the best chance they had of a decent future.

'Will you go and see them today?' she asked, drinking a cup of tea, hurriedly eating a piece of bread and jam, while making sure that she had freshly starched cuffs and apron. Today her shift started at eight and ended at eight.

'I'll ask Da for a few hours off.'

'Will you tell him what for?'

'I suppose I'll have to.'

'Tell him not to say anything to your mam just yet, they might not have you.'

Mike nodded, shrugging on his jacket and looking for his cap.

Abbie was horrified. 'You can't go looking like that! You'll have to come home first and change into your good suit.'

'Abbie, stop fussing and get off, you're going to

miss the tram, and then you'll have Sister on your back all day.'

She reached up and kissed him. 'I'll see you later. Good luck.'

There were already customers in the shop when Mike arrived, including Lizzie Simcock, who was complaining about the cost of everything. His mam still looked tired and his da looked flustered. Trade today appeared to have improved, and that didn't augur well for asking for time off.

His opportunity came when the shop was finally empty and Hilda had gone to put the kettle on.

'Is it really what you want, lad?' Frank asked after Mike had informed him of his decision and his plans for the future.

'It is, Da. I suppose the Army changed my life. I'm used to taking orders. Used to being always on the go and actually achieving something. Most of the achievements were bloody awful, though,' he added bitterly. 'It's a chance to make something of my life and Abbie's.'

Frank shook his head. 'There's a lot of folk around here who'll never speak to you again, you know that?'

'As long as you do and Mam does, that's all that matters. I've lost all my mates, one way or another. Tommy's in Canada, Jerry's dead, the rest I left buried in France.'

Frank smiled. 'Then get yourself up to Hatton Garden, lad.'

'What shall I tell Mam?'

'That you've gone to the council offices to see that housing feller again. That usually takes all morning and is usually a waste of time as well. No need to tell her anything else until you've been to see them.'

'Do you think she'll mind?'

'No, she'll be proud of you.'

'It could affect trade.'

'Not for long it won't. It'll be a flash in the pan. Get off with you now.'

Abbie was on S ward – men's surgical – which was mainly routine, but there were a few emergencies. She'd done her stint in Casualty and Out Patients, and even that had been very tame after the field hospitals. She was efficient and well liked by the patients and other nurses. Even Sister Marsden grudgingly admitted that. The Voluntary Aid Detachment had trained its nurses well, and they had more experience of shattered limbs and serious wounds than most other girls.

'She's got a right cob on this morning, Abbie,' Hannah Harvey whispered as Abbie clipped on the stiff white wimple.

'Oh, hell, what for?'

'Someone on the night shift left the sluice room untidy. She's livid. She's already had a steaming row with the Night Sister before she went off duty.'

'Then I'm going to keep out of her way as much as I can, although that won't be easy,' Abbie whispered back.

'Staff! When you and Nurse Harvey have quite finished your tête-à-tête, there are dressings to be changed. This is not a field hospital. We don't leave soiled dressings for days on end!'

Abbie bit her lip. They hadn't left dressings on for days, it had often taken the men days to get to the hospital, and Sister Marsden knew that. It just irked her that she'd been forced to remain at home, taking charge of up to six wards, to release her colleagues and most of her nurses for duty at the front. Hers had been a very responsible and important position, a great asset to the war effort, but she hadn't viewed it like that. Sister Marsden felt her skills would have been better employed in France. There were often cutting and derogatory remarks about uniform, preceded by such taunts as 'I know you wore tin hats and army boots and abandoned your cuffs and aprons, but I'll have none of that sloppiness on my ward!'

There were still soldiers on the ward, those who had been wounded in the last days before the Armistice, or those whose broken limbs refused to heal properly.

In a small side ward they had a very prominent young man. Richard D'Arcy was the eldest son of the lately deceased Lord Ashenden of Ashenden Hall. His presence in the hospital was a mistake, he should have gone to a much more comfortable and auspicious establishment. He had been badly wounded, and in the general chaos that had reigned at the Dover Reception Office, the Dowager Countess of Ashenden's instructions had been lost. His father had been dying at the time, and his mother had had so much to contend with that it was not until the funeral was over that she realized what had happened, that the 7th Earl of Ashenden had been taken to Walton Hospital.

She had duly arrived in a towering rage and had demanded that he be taken home to be nursed. While they agreed that it was not the place most suited to his high standing in life, all the specialists had persuaded the Dowager Countess of Ashenden that he must not be moved for at least six months. He had already been moved far too much, Mr Copeland impressed upon her. He should have been taken to a hospital in Dover, no matter how overcrowded they were. He had a bad head injury that had resulted in paralysis of the right side of his body, and were he to be moved the possibility of his recovery was less likely. His condition necessitated the highest specialized medical attention and diligent nursing. Should his condition improve at the end of this period, then he might be taken home.

Both Abbie and Hannah well remembered the arguments that day, and the upshot was that Richard Ashenden was moved to a side ward and provided with all the comforts and luxuries that money and a house like Ashenden Hall could supply. He was improving, but it was obvious that he would never, ever walk again. For the rest of his life he would be confined to a Bath chair.

It was almost two o'clock before Abbie was allowed

to have a break. She found Hannah already in the small, sparsely furnished nurses' sitting-room.

'I've got a banging headache. I could murder her sometimes, I really could. She's just that way out today, nothing suits her at all. It's not my fault that she spent the war here.'

Hannah sympathized, she'd had a tongue-lashing from Sister herself. 'Have a cup of tea and an aspirin.'

Abbie flopped down in one of the shabby easy chairs. 'I'm worn out already, I'll be dead on my feet by the time I get home. Oh, you've no idea what it's like, Hannah. Going to see Mam, then going home and getting a meal ready, doing the shopping and washing and ironing. I wish I had my own kitchen and scullery, I really do. I'm sick to death of fry-ups and so is Mike, but it's impossible to cook a decent meal on a single gas ring. Then there's the washing, I have to take most of it to Mam's.'

Hannah sipped her tea. 'I thought Joan helped you with all that.'

'She does, but it's not fair to expect her to do it all the time.'

'I suppose I am lucky, Mam does everything.'

'How is she getting on with her job?'

Hannah looked concerned. 'She hates it, but she won't admit it. I just wish I earned more.'

Abbie swallowed a tablet with a mouthful of tea. 'It must be hard for her. I mean she never went out to work when . . . well, before the war.'

Hannah concentrated on the pattern on her cup.

Her father had died a few years ago at the hands of her brother, Jerry. Poor Jerry had been dying himself of bovine tuberculosis that he'd caught when he worked in the stockyards over in Birkenhead. Abe Harvey had been a religious man, a real zealot, but with a terrible temper. She'd been terrified of him and so had her mam. It was Hannah's request to join the VAD like Abbie and Dee Chatterton that had started the trouble. Her da had refused, and Jerry had argued with him on her behalf. There had been a terrible row, her da had hit Jerry, knocking him to the ground, then Jerry had picked up the poker and had caught Da a massive blow on the head that had killed him. She shuddered at the memory. Oh, it had been a horrendous day. They'd taken Jerry to Walton Jail and he'd died there; but at least they'd been spared the anguish of a public trial, and Jerry had been spared the hangman's noose. They were memories she had fought hard to erase, but Abbie's words had brought them all flooding back.

Abbie leaned over and touched her hand. 'Oh, Hannah, I'm so sorry, I really didn't mean to upset you. I should have known better. I'm tired and all on edge. You see, Mike is thinking of getting away from the shop, trying for a decent job.'

Hannah had pulled herself together. 'Doing what?'

'I can't tell you right now, you see we want to wait until everything is definite. I'm not being awkward, Hannah, truly I'm not. I'll be able to tell you in a day or two.'

Hannah smiled. She was a pale girl with soft, light brown hair and wide brown eyes; she was also quiet and still a little shy with strangers. Just the qualities that Sister Marsden deemed suitable for a nurse to attend Richard Ashenden. Hannah Harvey wouldn't overstep the mark by making fatuous remarks or by being overly familiar. Nor would she repeat anything she heard, as many of her nurses would. She was the obvious choice and she was very efficient.

'I don't mind, Abbie. Is it a good job?'

'Yes, it pays quite well, but it does have some drawbacks and I'm not telling you anything more, so don't try to wheedle it out of me with that sly determination of yours. How is his Lordship today?'

'Don't skit him Abbie.'

'I wasn't, it's his proper title isn't it? His da's dead, so he's Lord Ashenden.'

'He's coming along slowly. He's much better than he was a couple of weeks ago. He's really very nice, not a bit snobbish. Very polite he is too, always thanks me, which is more than can be said for half of the lot in there.' She jerked her head in the direction of the ward.

'His mam's a real tartar, though.'

'Oh, aye, but she is better than she used to be. At least she's stopped calling me "Girl". Now I get "Nurse Harvey". That's an improvement. She used to make me feel about six inches tall.'

'Will he ever walk again?'

'You know they tell us nothing, but I don't think so.

They've only just got him sitting up, and only for an hour or two. You know, Abbie, I'm sure Mr Copeland doesn't even see me. He just seems to – well, look through me, as if I were a ghost.'

'Pompous old git!'

'Oh, I don't think he really means to humiliate me or anything, but he is very important, and Lady Ashenden must be paying him a fortune.'

'She can afford to.'

Hannah lowered her voice. Abbie was the only one she confided in, and that was because Abbie was her friend and she'd known her all her life. 'I don't think there is still a vast fortune. I overheard him telling his brother—'

'The loud-mouthed one who sounds as though he's got a plum stuck in his mouth?'

'Abbie you're awful! Anyway, he was telling him they may have to think about selling some land off.'

'Oh, stop it Hannah, you're breaking my heart. Half the people in this city live in slums, just scratching a living, not even a decent house to live in, me included.'

Hannah suddenly remembered something else she'd overheard. 'I just might be able to help you there.'

'How?'

'He has property.'

'I'm not going to live out in the wilds. Ashenden Hall is miles from Liverpool, miles away from Mam.'

'No, he has some houses near here. His brother was

saying they should sell them and some other property as well.'

'What use is that, Hannah? The day we can afford to buy a house is the day the Liver birds will fly off.'

'He might rent one to you though, it would be handy for work. Shall I ask him?' The thought made her very nervous, but she was willing to try for Abbie.

'Would you? Would you really do that, Hannah?'

Hannah nodded.

'What if he tells his mam or brother or sister? There'd be hell to pay.'

'I don't think he would. I told you, he's very nice. Shall I go now and get it over with?' Hannah offered, although her legs felt a bit weak.

'Oh, please. I've got to get back in ten minutes.'

'I'll ask him and then I'll try and have a few words with you later on, in the sluice room.'

Hannah's heart was thumping against her ribs as she entered the room. A bed with an ornately carved headboard, a tallboy, a marble-topped wash-stand and a bedside chest had all been brought from Ashenden Hall. So had all the bedding and the big, soft, white towels on the wash-stand. Nothing went to the hospital laundry, it was returned to the Hall and fresh supplies were always on hand. Silver-backed hair-brushes, expensive toiletry items, a crystal water jug and glasses and fine china had also arrived. Richard Ashenden was twenty-seven and had been a tall, slim young man. He had the D'Arcys dark chestnut hair and intelligent eyes. From his mother (a Parker-

Graham) he had inherited a high forehead, straight
nose and full lips. He was still trying to come to terms
with his injuries. He was also struggling with his grief
for his father and his brother Hubert, who had been
killed at Arras.

He had been trying to read, but his mind wasn't
really on Kipling's prose, so Hannah's entrance didn't
disturb or annoy him. 'It's not time for more
temperature taking is it, Nurse Harvey?'

Hannah pulled the window blind down a little
further. 'The sunlight's strong, that may be better for
your reading, Sir.'

'Thank you.'

'And I don't have to take your temperature until
four o'clock.' She began to pluck nervously at the edge
of her apron. 'Sir, could . . . could I . . .'

He could see she was trying to muster up the
courage to ask him something. She was a timid
creature, but she was efficient. She was also gentle and
sensitive, although that sensitivity he put down to her
youth and perhaps a lack of life's harsh realities and
experiences. 'What is it, Nurse Harvey?'

Hannah glanced at him from beneath her lashes,
wishing now she'd never mentioned the subject to
Abbie. 'It's a sort of . . . favour.'

'I had gathered that much.'

Oh, it was no use beating about the bush, she
thought. Best get it over and done with. 'I believe you
have some houses, Sir . . .'

'I have many houses.'

'Near here, I mean.'

'I believe there are some. You must have heard me discussing them with my brother.'

Hannah became flustered, her cheeks burning with embarrassment. 'Oh, no, Sir! I mean . . . I mean I did, but I didn't! I couldn't help it.'

'It's all right, Nurse. There's no need to get upset. My brother can be quite . . . animated at times.' Excitable, crass and extravagant were words more suitable to describe Freddie, and he wasn't being unkind. Freddie had been like that before the war. Being the youngest, he had been rather spoiled. He'd never had to fight either, it had all been over by the time he was old enough, something his mother had been very relieved about. One son crippled, one dead, and he knew the shock had killed his father. His mother had every reason to be relieved. The damned war had touched every family in the land, from the highest to the lowest. He smiled encouragingly at Hannah. 'And you were wondering . . . what?'

'My friend, Staff Nurse Burgess, well, she lives with her husband in two rooms . . . in someone else's house . . . and I —' she swallowed hard.

He smiled. 'And you were wondering if I could let her have one of those houses?'

Hannah became confused, wondering exactly what he meant by the words 'let her have'. 'Well, not to buy, Sir, they can't afford to do that.'

'No, I did assume that you meant to rent. Is that correct?'

'Yes, Sir, please, Sir.'

He remained silent; he had been intending to sell them off. It had been Freddie's idea. Ready money was getting a bit tight, so why not sell off some land and some property, he'd urged. He knew that if his mother found out that Freddie had been harassing him she would be furious. But because he'd been feeling too ill and dispirited to think deeply about the estate and its finances, he'd agreed; more to preserve the peace than for any other motive. Maybe he'd keep one or two of those cottages.

Hannah held her breath, not daring to look at him.

'Would you ask Nurse Burgess to come and see me?'

'Oh, Sir, I couldn't do that. Sister Marsden would kill us both if she knew I'd even asked.'

'Is she that much of a dragon?'

'She is, believe me,' Hannah replied emphatically. 'I was told never, never to ask favours of any kind or to be . . . familiar or outspoken.'

'Good God! Mother's instructions I presume?'

'Oh, no, Sir, Lady Ashenden had nothing to do with it. It was Sister.'

He sighed. 'All right then, tell Nurse Burgess she can rent one. She must see my urban property agent. I'll give you the address.'

'Thank you, Sir. It's ever so kind of you, it really is. Perhaps we can go after work, that is if you think it will be all right? That we won't be disturbing him?'

'See him whenever you like,' he replied, reaching

awkwardly with his left hand for the pen and leather writing case embossed with the family crest that was on the bedside chest.

'I'll get that, Sir, you're not to exert yourself, Mr Copeland said.' Hannah handed him the case and placed a carved wooden tray before him.

'I hope you'll be able to read this, it's very difficult to write. What time are you off duty?'

'Eight o'clock, Sir.'

'From early this morning? You were here when I awoke, that is a long day. I've recently noticed that you seem always to be here in attendance, so to speak.'

'I worked much longer hours and in far worse conditions when I was at number twenty-three General Camp Hospital, Zillebeke,' Hannah said quietly, twisting her hands. She had never had a real conversation with him before. She'd been afraid to, and he had been in a lot of pain until recently.

He was surprised. 'You were out there nursing?'

'Yes, Sir, until the Armistice.'

His eyes became filled with admiration. 'I admire your courage, Nurse Harvey. Things were not easy for you.'

Hannah looked him straight in the eye. 'It wasn't courage, Sir,' she said quietly. 'I . . . I wanted to help, and in a way it was a sort of escape.'

Again he looked startled. 'An escape from what? It was sheer hell over there, what possibly could have been worse?'

Hannah pulled herself together. She was talking

too much, becoming too familiar, and besides, she couldn't tell him what she had been trying to escape from. 'I'm sorry, I've taken up too much of your time. Thank you for your kindness, Sir.' She took the note and slid it into her pocket.

As the door closed behind her Richard Ashenden looked thoughtful. He'd been wrong in his earlier assumption. She had indeed experienced most of life's harshness and cruelty, and yet she seemed so untouched by it. But what did he really know about her? What on earth had happened in her young life that was so terrible, so monstrous, that she had willingly gone to those charnel houses that had been field hospitals? He closed his eyes, feeling exhausted. Any exertion seemed to tire him these days.

It was nearly six o'clock before Hannah managed to get a few minutes to confide in Abbie in the sluice room.

All afternoon Abbie had been unable to concentrate properly on her work. 'For heaven's sake start polishing those bedpans, or she'll go mad again. What a day! Did you ask him?'

'Yes. He said you could rent one. He's given me the address of his property agent. You've to go and see him.'

'When?'

'After work. He said it would be all right, you won't be disturbing him. Shall I come with you?'

'Yes please. Oh, Hannah! I don't care what it's like,

we'll take it! Oh, a place of our own at last, near here, which will save me lots of time and it's not too far away from Mam. I can get the tram up there! Oh, Hannah, thanks!' Her voice had risen with excitement, something they'd both been unaware of.

'Staff Nurse Burgess! Nurse Harvey! Where do you think you are? At a ladies' afternoon tea party? I have been watching you all day, Staff. You've been slap-dash, and if this behaviour continues then we'll have to see what Matron has to say about it! I do not approve of married women working, they lack dedication. They have too many things to take their minds off what really matters – the patients' welfare – and not what they are going to give their husband for his supper. And you, Nurse Harvey, you were in with Lord Ashenden for a long time. What were you doing?'

Hannah swallowed hard. 'He . . . he asked me to . . . to read to him, Sister,' Hannah lied, not very convincingly.

'Indeed? He's a highly educated man, Eton and Oxford I believe, so what on earth would he want an ignorant chit of a girl like you to read to him for?'

Seeing that Hannah was foundering and risking Sister's full wrath, Abbie replied, 'Didn't you tell me he finds it restful, Nurse?'

'Yes, restful,' Hannah repeated.

Sister uttered a snort which implied that she didn't believe a word of it, but was forced not to inquire from Lord Ashenden himself if it was true or otherwise. She couldn't risk upsetting him either if it were true. No matter what his reasons may be, she couldn't instruct Hannah not to read to him. She'd heard Mr Copeland telling Dr Forbes that Lady Ashenden was talking about endowing the hospital with a gift.

'Get on with your work the pair of you, and let there be no more of this nonsense!' she snapped.

'Thanks,' Hannah whispered as they both returned to the ward.

Abbie was smarting under Sister's words. 'It was the least I could do, but I'd better watch my step from now on. I knew there was a reason why she didn't really like me, now I know. But she's wrong. I don't spend all day thinking about what Mike's going to have for his tea.'

It was dusk by the time they walked out of the hospital gates but, tired as they both were, they quickened their steps towards Walton Park, the address Lord Ashenden had given Hannah.

It was only a short walk before they turned into the tree-lined road. The houses were quite big, four stories high, and there were six steps up to the front door.

'Do you think we should go around the back?' Hannah asked.

'No. Why should we? We're not tradesmen or hawkers.' Abbie pointed to a small notice on the gate that stated that all such persons should use the back entrance. She knocked firmly on the door.

A young girl opened it and when they'd stated their names and business she showed them into a small room off the hall. It appeared to be some sort of office,

Abbie thought, gazing around. The walls were lined with books on shelves and in cases. Papers and ledgers were strewn untidily across the top of a desk that was obviously much used, judging by the marked top and scuffing on the legs. A green leather chair stood to one side of the desk. Beside it there was a small table with a glass bowl, an old leather pouch and a carved pipe lying on its top. There were more pipes in a rack on the wall by the fireplace. Abbie wrinkled her nose at the pungent smell of stale tobacco that permeated the room.

It was about five minutes before a stout, middle-aged man appeared, looking none too pleased.

'Well?' he barked.

Abbie wasn't going to be put off by the likes of him. 'We've come about a house. In Smithy Lane. Lord Ashenden said he would rent it to me, he gave me your address and told me to come and see you.'

'At this time of night?'

'We have only just finished work. Nurse Harvey here is attending to his Lordship.'

'Well you won't be able to see anything much tonight. It's too dark, and besides, I can't go letting people have keys just because they come here with a tale about Lord Ashenden.'

'It's not a tale!' Abbie interrupted sharply. 'How else would we have known where to find you? How else were we even to know that you are Lord Ashenden's manager or agent or whatever you are? Give him the note, Hannah.'

Hannah duly handed it over, and they both had the satisfaction of seeing his suspicions confounded as he took in the crest and Richard Ashenden's tidy writing.

'You'll have to come back tomorrow,' he said at length.

'I can't. I'm working.'

'Then it will have to be the weekend.'

'I work weekends, too, but my husband will come tomorrow morning.'

He shrugged resignedly. 'Suit yourself. The rent is six and fourpence a week, to be paid promptly. My collector will call on Friday nights.'

Abbie nodded. 'We'll go and have a bit of a look around then now.'

'You won't be able to see much.'

'I mean from the outside,' she answered tartly.

He was right, they couldn't see much. He had called them cottages but they were not the pretty, thatched picturesque cottages found in the countryside. They were small houses, built in the shadow of St Mary's churchyard. The front doors opened onto the street. In the narrow lane there were two pubs called The Beehive and The Brown Cow, and a forge and stables at the other end, from which the lane took its name.

'They don't look up to much, Abbie,' Hannah ventured, trying to peer into a ground-floor window.

'Nothing that a bit of paint and a good scrub out won't put right. I think there's two rooms down here and there must be two upstairs.'

Hannah shivered. 'Won't you mind living next to the church and the graveyard?'

'No. Anyway there's probably a yard at the back, and a wall, and then the cemetery.'

Hannah shivered again. 'Suppose it's haunted? Maybe that's why he was going to get rid of them.'

'Oh, stop that Hannah Harvey! The others are occupied, well at least two of them are.' She didn't really care, she didn't believe in ghosts, and as for death and graves, she'd seen too much of both at first hand to fear them. 'I think it's great, four rooms, probably a scullery and maybe even a wash-house and whatever else there is, and it's ours. A place of our own at last!'

'Won't Mike have to travel if you live here and his new job is . . . somewhere else?'

'You can stop that, too. You're just fishing and you won't catch me out like that.' Abbie laughed as they linked arms and turned towards the main road. She gave the narrow cobbled lane a last backwards glance and sighed with satisfaction. A new home and hopefully a new job for Mike. It hadn't been such a bad day, despite Sister Marsden and her acid tongue.

Chapter Four

———◆———

MIKE STARED AROUND AT the cavernous waiting-room at Hatton Garden, the headquarters of the Liverpool City Police, usually referred to as 'the Garden'. It was dimly lit. The walls were half tiled, a couple of wooden benches were set against one of the walls and passages led off to the right and left from the centre of the room. A uniformed sergeant and a constable were engrossed in paperwork of some sort and didn't look up until Mike coughed.

'What can I do for you, lad?' Sergeant Gregory asked, good-humouredly. He'd only just come on duty and hadn't, so far, been harassed or annoyed by either his superiors, subordinates or the general public with demands that often sorely tried his patience and his temper.

'Well, I've come to ask how I go about joining.'

Sergeant Gregory studied him closely. He was an ordinary looking young lad, well turned out, decently spoken and about six foot in height. All important factors for consideration. 'Well, you'll have to write in at first, to the Head Constable. Then you'll sit an exam. Don't look so worried – they won't be expecting a genius – and then you'll have an interview. If you get through all that you're in, and you'll get two months' training before we let you loose on the law-abiding, and not-so-law abiding, citizens.'

Mike was perturbed. 'What kind of things should I put in the letter? I mean, I've never had to write a letter like that.'

No, he probably hadn't, Sergeant Gregory thought. By the look of him he'd been pitched into the war, and you certainly hadn't needed to apply for that. 'Were you in the Army or the Navy?'

'The Army. 18th Battalion King's Liverpool "Pals".'

Sergeant Gregory winced. His only son, George, had been in that battalion, and he'd died at Montauban, like hundreds of other Liverpool lads. 'You were lucky, son, to come through in one piece.'

'I know. I was wounded twice,' Mike informed him, and then instantly regretted it. They might not take him, knowing he'd been injured. 'Will that make any difference, do you think, Sir? It was only in the shoulder, it's fine now.'

Sergeant Gregory smiled. He liked the lad, he had an open, honest sort of face and a quietly confident demeanour. 'No, I don't think so. What did you do before the war, if anything?'

'I worked for my dad, he's got a grocery shop.'

'But now that's pretty tame?'

'I suppose so. I . . . I'm married, my wife is a nurse at Walton Hospital, so now I'm looking for, well, a career, I suppose. Do you think I stand much of a chance? Of getting in, I mean.'

'I don't see why not. You're young, fit, keen and married – that impresses them. They think a wife is a steadying influence. Any kids?'

'No, we've only been married for ten months.'

A young constable appeared from the long corridor on the right, and the older man turned towards him.

'Keys to the cells, Sergeant.'

Gregory took them from him. 'All the paperwork done, Miller?'

'Yes, Sir.'

'Then out you go, Miller. You don't get a tea break after every arrest, you've another five hours yet and I don't want to see you back here until two o'clock.' He turned back to Mike. 'So, where do you live then?'

'In Hopwood Street. We've got a couple of rooms, rented, like. We're hoping to get a house soon.' His heart began to sink, for at the mention of Hopwood Street the desk sergeant's expression had changed. 'I know it's not usual for lads like me, living around Scotland Road, to want to join the police, but there's plenty of good people there.'

'And plenty who cause us a great deal of trouble. Oh, I know the conditions are bad and nearly every other man is out of work, but that's a problem for the

City Fathers, nothing to do with us. We're just here to uphold the law as it stands.'

'Will we have to move somewhere else?'

'You will, and not only because the Head Con will say so. I can't see you being very popular with some members of the local community around there.' Sergeant Gregory wrote something down on a piece of paper and handed it to Mike. 'There you are, name and address to write to. Make sure you put in all your Army service and as much of your background as you think will be helpful.'

Mike took the paper and folded it. 'Thanks, Sir, I really do appreciate your help.'

'Well, good luck, lad. I hope I'll see you again.'

Mike shook his hand warmly, and as the older man watched him walk away he pursed his lips. He hoped he would be successful. He wasn't exactly from the desired background, but he knew men who'd come from humble homes and they were good coppers. He didn't doubt that the lad could cope with the job. Even a full scale riot such as those that often occurred between the citizens of Catholic Irish descent who lived in the Scotland Road area and those of Irish Protestant lineage who resided in the Netherfield Road area on the 17th March and 12th July, would be nothing compared to what that lad had been through. If anyone asked for his opinion, he'd speak up for the lad. Times were hard and were likely to get harder, the country was reeling in the aftermath of the war and its cost, not only in lives, but in money.

* * *

When Abbie got home, Mike was sitting at the table. Writing paper and envelopes lay before him and half a dozen screwed up sheets of paper covered the table top. He looked harassed. 'You're late tonight, Abbie.'

'I know, but I'll tell you why in a minute.' She kissed him and gave him a hug. 'How did you get on?'

Mike pushed the half-completed letter away from him. 'I've got to write in. That's what I've been trying to do, and it's not easy either.'

'Is that all they said?'

'No, the desk sergeant was a nice bloke. He was very helpful, told me what to write.'

'And what happens once you've written?'

'I have to go for an exam and then an interview. I don't know if they tell you there and then.'

'It's all a bit strange. Official, I mean. If you go for any sort of a job, you have a chat to the boss and he says yes or no, and that's it.'

'It stands to reason that they've got to be more thorough, more careful.'

Abbie took off her coat and hat. 'You must be starving, I know I am.'

Mike had returned to the letter. 'I'm not too bad. I had a bit of something at four o'clock, with Mam.'

Abbie looked irritable. She knew Hilda would now think she wasn't looking after him properly, there being no meal on the table for him. 'Put that away for now, we'll do it together later. Don't you want to know why I'm late?'

Mike grinned. 'Why?'

'Hannah Harvey has found us a house.'

'Hannah? How?'

'You know she nurses Lord Ashenden. Well, she heard he was thinking of selling off some houses, so she went and asked him if we could rent one. It was really good of her, Mike. She'd get into terrible trouble if Sister found out – we both would.'

'Where is it?'

'Smithy Lane. Just at the back of Queen's Drive public baths, around the side of the church. You know, St Mary's, Walton-on-the-Hill. They are just small houses, two up and two down, I think.'

'Didn't you go inside?'

'No, his Lordship's agent said it was too late. I told him you'd go tomorrow.'

'How much is it?'

'Six and fourpence a week, and the rent man calls on Friday nights. Oh, just think, a place of our own at last, and it's not too far from everyone here. It will be great for me, it's only a five-minute walk to work.'

'And it's a much better area for me. I mean, that sergeant wasn't very impressed when I told him where we lived. I told him that not everyone was bad, that most were good, hard-working people, when someone will give them a job that is. But I suppose I'll stand a better chance with Smithy Lane, Walton, on the letter, instead of Hopwood Street. I just can't get over Hannah, Abbie.'

'She's changed so much, Mike. It was the best thing

that ever happened to her, joining the VAD and getting away from home. She was always so quiet and . . . cowed.'

'It's no wonder, living in a house like that, with a da like Abe.'

Abbie sighed deeply. 'She's got poor Jerry to thank for getting her out of that house. I hope that wherever he is, he can see how much he changed Hannah's life, and for the better.'

'So, what time have I got to be at this place?'

'I think you'll have to call at his house, it's number eleven Walton Park, the next one along to Yew Tree Road. I can't believe it, it's like a dream. Tomorrow we'll have a house. A whole house. Let's finish the letter. We can post it and then go and see Mam and your mam and tell them all the news.'

'Abbie, it's ten past nine already.'

'Oh, I don't care. I'm so excited I couldn't sleep even if I went to bed early.'

'I'll bet you could.'

'Oh, stop that! No, I've got to see Mam and tell her, you can go to the pub for the last half hour with your da if you want to. Just let's get the letter done.'

The letter had been written and duly posted, and Hilda had been informed of all the news. Abbie had had the satisfaction of seeing her mother-in-law puff up with pride that not only did they now have a house, in a good area, but Mike was applying for a job that commanded respect. Frank had slapped his son on the back, kissed Abbie and had reached for his jacket and cap and said they must celebrate at The Black Dog. They'd collect Pat Kerrigan on the way up the street.

'I'll bet Hilda is giving herself airs and graces already,' Sal commented tersely after Abbie had finished communicating all the news.

'She's made up, I know that much.'

'She would be.'

'Mam, don't be like that.'

'Oh, it's just that she'll be running down there to see you by the minutes, "I'm going to see my son, he lives in Walton-on-the-Hill you know", and I'll be stuck here.'

Abbie sighed. Hilda had offered to go and help her clean the place and organize the move. 'Mam, if you like, our Joan and me will get a taxi cab and take you down there. Ginny can chip in, too.'

'Oh, so you've got money to chuck away on taxis now?'

'There's no pleasing you today, is there? No, I haven't got money to chuck away, but I want you to see our home and I'm not taking no for an answer.'

Sal grunted, not displeased about Abbie's decision. If Hilda Burgess was going, then she was too. 'I don't know how your da's going to take this police business, Abbie.'

'I don't care. I'm not interested, Mam. It's our future, not his. I told our Joan years ago, before Hilda Burgess's Christmas party before the war, that I wanted more from life than you've had. Da's led you a right dance, Mam, and don't deny it. All your life you've had to scrimp and save just to keep food on the table and clothes on our backs, and often you couldn't manage even that. You had to go out and clean offices at night, having done a day's work. Da's got a lot to answer for, it's mostly his fault that you're stuck here now.'

'Now, listen to me, girl, I'm not having you sitting there dishing out insults about your da. I can call him up hill and down dale, that's my right, he's my 'usband, but I won't have anyone else doing it, not even you.'

'Oh, Mam. You know it's true. When we were kids he was always in the pub or down the back jigger with Mo Cowley and that lot, playing pitch an' toss. You know that's where the housekeeping money always went. No, I want better than that and I'm going to have it, so you can start saying a novena that Mike will get in the police force.'

'It'll have to be one to St Jude then, for impossible causes. I don't know of anyone from around here who ever got in,' Sal finished tartly.

Frank had insisted on buying the drinks. The pub was quite full, and the three men nodded to all their acquaintances and neighbours.

'What are we celebrating then, or have you just escaped from the wives for half an hour?' Red McClelland asked good-naturedly, taking the money Frank was offering. 'Mind you, it's a lot easier for you these days, Pat,' he added.

'Not that Sal ever stopped him before,' Harry O'Brien remarked.

'Ah, give over, the lot of yez. She's a good skin is my Sal.'

'She's had to be,' Bert Soames muttered to Edward Chatterton.

'I 'eard that, Bert. An' your Maggie's life 'asn't been a bed of roses, with full an' plenty with you either.'

'Pat, you'd start a row in an empty house!' Frank intervened. 'Tonight we're celebrating.'

'Celebrating what, Frank?' Edward Chatterton asked, his tone quiet and well modulated. Even after all the years he'd been in Liverpool, there was no trace of the nasal Scouse dialect.

'Our Mike and Abbie have got a place of their own at last.'

'Dead posh address it is, too. Walton-on-the-Hill,' Pat added.

'But it's not a posh house, it's only a two up and two down like the ones around here,' Mike added.

'Well, it's a start, lad, once you get on your feet you might get something a bit better.'

'You'll need one a bit bigger if yer have any kids. God, I seem to 'ave spent all me life being tormented with kids. There was kids everywhere, not a room where I could get a bit of peace. Nor even in the privy, they'd be banging on the door or dancin' up and down on the roof playin' jumpin' the jigger walls.'

'It was your own fault, Pat. There was no excuse for having nine of them!' Mo Cowley laughed.

Pat didn't reply, nor was there any answering grin. He knew what was coming next and he didn't approve of what it was either. He was still a bit shocked.

'And that's not all, we've got something else to celebrate,' Frank announced cheerfully. Better to get it out in the open now, get it over and done with, he thought.

Edward Chatterton nodded to Red. 'Then we'd better have another drink. The same again for everyone, please, Red.'

Pat wondered morosely would it be the last time his mates stood him a drink. Would he now be ostracized?

Mike took a deep breath and glanced at his father for support. Frank nodded. 'I'm hoping to have a new job soon, too. I've just posted my application.'

'What kind of a job is it that you need to write an' apply for?' Harry O'Brien asked, looking puzzled. Normally you went to the Labour Exchange or direct to whoever it was you wanted employment from.

'The police. I've written applying to join the Liverpool City Police.'

There was a stunned silence. Pint glasses were clutched tightly, eyes widened and some mouths dropped open.

Bert Soames was the first to speak. 'You want to be a . . . a scuffer?'

'It's a secure, steady job, with a decent wage. There won't be any worries about being out of work.' Edward Chatterton's voice seemed to diffuse the tension. He was an educated man and much respected. 'There are hundreds of lads coming out of the Army, and there aren't jobs for them all, Mike. You've chosen well, it's a good career.'

'Well, I'm glad you think so, Eddie. You know how people around here feel about the scuffers!' Pat said acidly.

Many of the men had already turned away in silence. Billy Hodge and two of the MacNamaras from William Moult Street cursed openly. Billy Hodge spat deliberately into the brass cuspidor at the end of the bar. Mike ignored them, but it appeared that only his da, Pat, Edward Chatterton and Harry O'Brien were supporting him, and Pat not fully at that. But he'd expected this.

'I know how you all feel, we've always sorted things out ourselves around here, but there's no need to treat me like a leper,' he said loudly. 'You've all known me from a lad, and being a scuffer won't change me. I've only applied, they might not have me.'

'Best bloody thing if they don't,' Mo Cowley muttered, thinking that now he'd have to think twice about starting up a game of pitch and toss, for Mike Burgess knew all his haunts, and street gambling was illegal.

'Aye, 'e knows too effin' much,' Billy Hodge remarked darkly to his companions.

Red shot them a suspicious glance. The MacNamaras were cousins of the infamous Big Kevin MacNamara who'd been killed on the Somme, some said not by the Hun but by his own regimental sergeant major. 'If yer don't like the company, yer know what ter do – sling yer hook!'

'Get that ale down yer, Billy lad. We're not stoppin' 'ere with this lot. Coppers' narks, the lot of yez!' Marty Mac banged his empty glass down on the bar counter and made for the door, followed by his brother Fergal and Billy Hodge.

Harry O'Brien broke the silence. 'It will change you, lad, it's bound to.'

'Harry, the Army didn't. Well, not in that way.'

Harry looked at him and shook his head slowly. It would change him, they were a breed apart, were scuffers. Oh, some of them were good blokes, well respected, but never really liked. He'd often seen Sergeant Harris from Rose Hill cart a drunk from the middle of the road where he was endangering himself and the traffic, and shove him in a doorway when he should have arrested him. If they were all like Harris then it wouldn't be so bad, but they weren't. Put most of them in a uniform and they became power mad.

Most of the crime in the area had its roots in poverty but the majority of the scuffers couldn't or wouldn't see that. They didn't live in the area, it was considered unsuitable, so at heart they really didn't care. Of course there were a lot of real hard cases, it was a rough area, bordering as it did on the docks estate. No one could afford to move and folk had to be tough to survive here – often it was just a case of surviving. It couldn't be called living, gracious or otherwise.

Red McClelland had made his decision. Frank and Pat had been good customers over the years, Mike was a decent lad and he could see his point of view, even though he thought along the same lines as Harry O'Brien. 'Well, let's know how things go, Mike, and don't think you won't be welcome here.'

Conversation resumed slowly.

Frank took a swig of his beer. 'Well, that wasn't too bad, was it? At least no one has had a go at you, no one wanted a stand-up fight.'

'Aye, but look at the gobs on some of them. We might 'ave to change our alehouse, Frank.'

'Don't be so bloody daft, Pat! That's not the attitude to take at all.'

Edward Chatterton nodded. 'We can't do without the police, Pat. Anarchy would ensue and no one would be safe. They're usually fair-minded men, and they have a lot to put up with at times. I for one wish you luck, Mike.'

Mike grinned at Edward. He just hoped they would accept him, for he'd burned his boats now. Even if he didn't get in, there were men in this pub who wouldn't speak to him ever again.

Chapter Five

———•———

CHRISSIE REARRANGED THE LACE-EDGED, pin-tucked neckline of the pure silk nightdress on the mannequin and wished it was time to go home. She was bored stiff. She hated this job, even though she knew she had been extremely lucky to get it.

She'd worked in the General Post Office in Victoria Street during the last years of the war, sorting mail. She'd enjoyed it and had made a lot of friends, all girls and young women, for the only men left working there were old, like her da. But after the Armistice, the man whose job she had taken over had come back to claim it. It was a pattern that was being repeated all over the city, in all types of work, so when she'd applied for and got the job of sales assistant in Lingerie de Paris she'd been very relieved, for she'd tried all the big shops in Lord Street and Church Street.

She walked over to the door and glanced out into Bold Street, Liverpool's most exclusive and expensive thoroughfare where they had some very well-to-do, and even titled, customers.

Because it was a lingerie shop there were no window displays. Cream-coloured blinds covered the windows with the words Lingerie de Paris embossed in gold-coloured letters across the centre portion. She couldn't even look through the window and scrutinize the people walking past. She'd thought it would have been very glamorous to work with such gorgeous merchandise, but she'd soon found that it was boring. The shop was never really busy, as a lot of places were, and many of the customers were middle-aged women who did not want a slip of an eighteen-year-old girl attending to them, turning her nose up at the size of the directoire knickers or whalebone-ribbed corsets they wished to purchase.

Miss Unsworth attended to the old biddies, being an old biddy herself, Chrissie thought spitefully with the arrogance of youth. Oh, why hadn't one of the big stores like Lewis's, Frisby Dyke's or the Bon Marché, accepted her? There would certainly be more going on in places like that to interest her and make the day go faster.

'Miss Burgess, have you finished that inventory?' Miss Unsworth's clipped tones interrupted Chrissie's petulant thoughts.

'Yes, Miss Unsworth. I've put it on the table in the back room.'

'Then you can tidy the stocking drawers.'

Chrissie felt like screaming. She'd only tidied the drawers of silk stockings yesterday, and today they'd only had one customer who had purchased two pairs of fawn-coloured ones. She hadn't even asked to see any other colour. Moodily she bent down and pulled the first drawer open. The rows of off-white silk hosiery hadn't been disturbed at all. Her dark eyes became mutinous as she tipped the entire contents of the drawer onto the top of the counter. This was stupid, it was just making work. It was really only Friday and Saturday that they were so busy that it needed two of them to cope. Oh, she was going to tell Mam that she just couldn't stick it any longer.

The black dress with the neat white collar (the uniform of all shop assistants) actually suited Chrissie. It enhanced her finely drawn features and pale skin. Her thick curly hair, blue-black in some lights, was piled high on her head and held with tortoiseshell combs. She was a pretty girl and she knew it. At the moment life was as dull and as uninspiring as ditchwater she thought.

She'd had a few boyfriends, nothing serious, and Phillip Chatterton was always hanging around her, but she wanted some excitement from life before she had to settle down and get married. Once you were married all the fun seemed to disappear. She'd said this once to Abbie, who had given her what she had interpreted as a superior look, and had said she wouldn't think so when she fell in love. Fell in love, that was a joke! She hardly went anywhere to meet anyone to fall in love with. Mam was so strict about where she went, who with, and what time she had to be in for. She was eighteen, she'd be nineteen next month and still Mam treated her like a young kid. She had to be in the house by half past nine on working days and ten o'clock at the weekend.

She usually went to the Grafton Ballroom or to the Rotunda Theatre on Saturday nights with Polly and Ellen, her friends from the Post Office. But to have to be in at ten was so embarrassing. She never got to see the end of any show, and at the Grafton it was really mortifying to have to reply, if any lad asked to see her home, that she had to be in by ten.

The bell on the shop door tinkled. Even that had a musical genteel tone, unlike the harsh, shrill one on the shop at home. She looked up hopefully, glad of any diversion. The sound had also brought Miss Unsworth from the back room; she was smiling ingratiatingly at the girl who had come in.

'Good afternoon, Modom. May we be of assistance?'

Chrissie hated having to pronounce Madam as 'Modom', but was looking at the girl with undisguised envy. She'd never seen anyone so fashionable before. Nor had she seen anyone with a skirt so short, either. The girl wore a pale green linen coat over a dark green linen dress, and both hemlines were well above her ankles, showing slim, shapely calves, encased in cream silk stockings; and that wasn't all. Her light auburn hair was cut short, just below her ears, and covered by a small enveloping hat of light green straw trimmed with a large rosette of dark green ribbon. Chrissie drank in every detail of such novel and elegant fashion.

'Do you have any of these new combinations of a short slip and knickers? Cami-something or other I think they're called.'

Miss Unsworth looked shocked to the core.

Chrissie smiled at her discomfort. 'Could you . . . er . . . describe them more, Modom?' she asked.

'I'll leave you in Miss Burgess's capable hands,' Miss Unsworth said faintly and removed herself from the room, wondering what on earth had happened to delicacy and decorum in the modern generation.

The girl looked impatient. 'I don't know what they're called, a friend has a pair, she says they are wonderful, so comfortable. They came from Paris, so I assumed that as your establishment is called Lingerie de Paris, that you would stock them.'

Chrissie lowered her voice. 'They are very old-fashioned here, Modom. Corsets, chemises and bloomers I'm afraid.'

Lady Angela D'Arcy pouted with annoyance. 'I do wish you'd stop calling me "Modom" in that ridiculous manner. You make me sound like a dowager duchess in her dotage.'

Chrissie couldn't help herself, she hastily stifled a giggle. 'It's . . . it's the rules. What . . . er, what should I call you?'

'Lady Angela D'Arcy.'

Chrissie was taken aback. Indeed the few Ladies and Honourables she'd come into contact with *were* like dowager duchesses, and had been attended to by Miss Unsworth. 'Oh, right, er, your Ladyship. Is there anything else I can show you? I will try to see that Miss Unsworth does stock more of the modern lingerie in future.'

'Can you recommend anywhere else that might be forward-looking enough to have them?'

Chrissie thought hard, but could think of nowhere. 'Have you tried Henderson's, my Lady?'

'Yes. They looked at me as though I were mad. I suppose I was mad to think that shops in Liverpool would be so up-to-date.'

'We have just had some beautiful slips in, and in some very pretty colours,' Chrissie ventured. If she could tell Miss Unsworth that she'd managed to sell something to Lady Angela D'Arcy, she might not be so dismissive in future.

'Oh, I suppose I might as well have a look at them.' Angela D'Arcy was killing time. Shopping was something she enjoyed when she was in London, but she'd doubted that she'd find anything she wished to purchase here, she'd told her mother. The Dowager Countess of Ashenden had not replied. She'd never been the same since Hubert had been killed. Angela thought that since Richard had been so badly wounded and her father had died, Mother seemed to have aged terribly.

Chrissie spread three pure silk slips out along the counter. One was shell pink, one pearl ivory, the other an iced turquoise, all trimmed with exquisite lace. In fact they were so delicate and fine, and so expensive, that Miss Unsworth had told her not to touch them at all. She didn't care, not if she could sell one.

Angela fingered the ivory one. They were certainly lovely, and of the finest quality. 'Fine. Yes. I'll take them.'

'What, all of them?'

'Yes. What's the matter, don't you want to sell them to me?'

'Oh, yes, your Ladyship. They're a guinea each.' This amount she thought was sheer extortion, but as the young woman in front of her hadn't batted an eyelid, she assumed that money was certainly no object for the landed gentry. She wrapped them carefully in tissue paper and then in the gold-and-cream striped wrapping paper, then placed them all in a small, gold-coloured box.

'If you like, I will see that the new, what was it—?'

'A combination of some sort,' Angela supplied.

'—is ordered specially for you.'

'Oh, it doesn't matter, I'm going back to London next week. I should imagine that Harrods will have them. Thank you for the offer, though.'

Chrissie watched with envy as Angela D'Arcy pulled on beige kid gloves. Angela turned to leave, and Chrissie noticed that she had left a slim package on the counter.

'Your Ladyship, you've left this,' she called.

Angela turned back and took the package from her. 'Thank you, it's just a little something for my brother. He's in a ghastly hospital here. Walton, I believe it's called.'

'Oh, I know someone who works there,' Chrissie said, then wondered should she have spoken at all.

'Indeed?'

The word seemed to have been uttered as a question, or so Chrissie thought. 'Yes, a friend of mine. Nurse Hannah Harvey, she is nursing someone called Lord Ashenden. Would that be your brother?'

'Yes.' Angela was not in the least bit interested in who was nursing Richard, nor in any friends of this young shop girl.

'Can I . . . well, can I say . . . that I've never seen anyone who looks so elegant and fashionable, your Ladyship.' Chrissie was amazed at her own audacity.

Angela looked surprised and pleased. She'd been aware that her appearance had caused a stir. Wherever she went heads had turned, and expressions that ranged from the astounded to the frankly disapproving had been directed at her from both women and men. Her own mother had been shocked and horrified by the shortness of her skirt and hair. There had been a heated argument between them and she'd flounced out, but this little chit of a shop girl was gazing at her with open admiration.

'Well thank you. How nice of you to say so. I'm afraid there are not many people who share your view.'

'Oh, I think the shorter fashions are very . . . nice.' Chrissie had searched her memory but could find no other suitable word.

'They are certainly less restricting. My hair was so heavy, I frequently suffered headaches in summer.'

Angela looked closely at the girl, for the first time really seeing her. 'Do you know, you are a very pretty girl. You have such thick hair, it would suit you short.'

Chrissie's hand went automatically to her dark locks. 'Oh, thank you. I . . . I wish I had the nerve to have it cut, but my mam . . . mother . . . would kill me.'

Angela laughed. 'Find the courage. After all, the war has liberated us. Have it cut.'

Outwardly Chrissie simpered, but inwardly she quailed at what her mam would say if she did. 'I might do that.'

Angela laughed again. 'What's your name?'

'Christine, I usually get called Chrissie though.'

'Then goodbye and thank you, Chrissie.'

Chrissie nodded, her cheeks burning, her dark eyes sparkling. Fancy that! A real lady asking her name and calling her by it. This would be something to tell Mam and Polly and Ellen. She pinched herself. No, she hadn't been dreaming, and she clutched the three gold sovereigns in her hand.

'Modom has gone I see.' Clara Unsworth sniffed disapprovingly, and Chrissie thought about what Lady Angela D'Arcy had said about the word 'Modom'.

'Yes, Lady Angela D'Arcy has gone. She bought three of those new slips. I said we would order this new garment for her, but she said she's going back to London and she'd get it in Harrods.'

Clara Unsworth pursed her lips tightly in annoyance, cursing herself for a fool to have left someone so important, although very forward, in the hands of this chit of a girl. 'Good. I hope you were suitably polite to her, Miss Burgess?'

'Of course I was. She thanked me and asked me my name and said I should get my hair cut like hers.'

'Indeed! No doubt her Ladyship is a very "modern" person.' The word 'modern' was uttered in a tone that made it quite clear what Clara Unsworth thought of short hair and short skirts. What were things coming to when the likes of Lady D'Arcy fraternized with shop girls? What indeed were things coming to when the nobility asked straight out for a new style of knickers? Indeed, who ever heard of something that was a slip and knickers combined, and was short, too? 'Did you finish tidying those stockings, Miss Burgess?'

Chrissie almost glared at her. 'No, I'll do that now, Miss Unsworth,' she replied quite curtly, wondering if she would ever see young Lady Angela D'Arcy again.

She relayed the events of the afternoon to Hilda and Frank over tea. 'I couldn't believe it, Mam. She bought all three, just like that. Never even turned a hair. Three guineas! Three guineas, just like that.'

'Well, she must have pots of money,' Hilda answered.

'I don't think she really needed them, either. I don't know what on earth it was that she wanted. I'd never heard of it, and neither had old sour-faced Unsworth. She was dead shocked the way her Ladyship came right out with it.'

Hilda nodded her approval of Clara Unsworth's attitude, even Chrissie hadn't said 'knickers' in front of her father. This Lady what's-her-name sounded a right bold madam, titled or otherwise.

'It's her brother that Hannah's nursing,' Chrissie added by way of a further explanation.

'It's to be hoped that he's not as hard-faced as she is, or Winnie will get very worried,' Hilda replied curtly.

Chrissie ignored her mother's terse remarks. 'She said I was very pretty and that I'd . . . I'd suit my hair short, like hers.'

Hilda rounded on her. 'She said what?'

Chrissie bit her lip. She should have kept her mouth shut about that.

'You have your hair cut short over my dead body, Christine Burgess! You're still not too big to get a hiding, so don't you even think about it!'

Chrissie got up. 'Oh, there's no need to carry on like that, Mam. She was just . . . well, it was just her opinion. I'm going to see Polly and Ellen. I won't be late.'

'Don't you go saying things like that in front of Mrs Waring or Mrs Woods either, or they'll think you're a bad influence on those two,' Hilda called after her, thinking how much both Chrissie and Mike had changed over the last few years. Oh, the war had a lot to answer for besides the grief and loss. Standards were falling rapidly when even the gentry carried on like that young madam. Short hair, short skirts and absolutely no delicacy or sensibility regarding underwear.

As Chrissie crossed the road, Phil Chatterton came out from number eighty and she sighed irritably. She'd wanted to get to Polly's quickly to have a good gossip; now she would have to talk to him, she couldn't avoid it.

Phil was nineteen, a tall, serious lad with light brown hair and grey eyes. He worked in the offices of a shipping company, the same one where his father was employed. He was the elder of Edward's two sons, and had been twelve when they came to live in Burlington Street; he could remember his mother, Gwendoline. She'd come from a good family and had been devastated when his father had lost all his money and they'd come here. She'd been dying then, but none of them had known it. Within nine months of the move she was dead.

'Hello Chrissie.'

'Hello Phil, where are you off to then?' She wasn't really interested but no doubt Mam was watching her from the shop, and if she was rude to him or just walked on, she knew there would be more censorship. Mam believed in Doing Things Properly.

'Just off to see Vinny Burke, nothing very exciting. What about you?' Phil hadn't been old enough to fight, but Vinny had – he'd been a mutual friend of Tommy Kerrigan and Phil's sister Dee, who had emigrated to Canada after the war.

She shrugged. 'Only to see Polly and Ellen.'

Phil always became tongue-tied and he cursed himself for it. To say that he was fond of Chrissie was an understatement. She was beautiful, confident and spirited, and he always felt this singing in his blood when he was near her. 'I believe Mike's going to join the police, and they've got a house?' he said at length.

'News certainly travels fast around here. He's applied to join, but it's not definite. But they've got a house. Apparently Hannah got it for them.'

'I know. Bridie told me, she'd been talking to Mrs Harvey. Do you think they'll take Mike?'

'I don't see why not, although there's some round here who'll get a cob on about it. In fact I heard that Billy Hodge and Marty and Fergal Mac got told to leave the pub. Not that anyone would mind that, scum they are!'

'Well, Dad says it's a good career. It's got to be better than sitting in a stuffy office all day.'

Chrissie was becoming impatient. 'Stop moaning. At least you can sit. I have to stand all flaming day.'

'Sorry, I didn't think. I just meant that . . .' his voice trailed off as he desperately tried to think of something else to say to keep her with him for a few more minutes. 'I . . . we had a letter from Dee today.'

'Really? How are they?'

'Oh, fine. Tommy's got a few acres of his own now. I told you they'd been saving hard. Dee was always a great manager.'

'Well, she had to be or you'd all have finished up in the workhouse,' she replied curtly. She could remember the day the Chattertons had come to Burlington Street. They were all totally bewildered and utterly useless in the environment they'd been plunged into, except Deirdre – Dee – who was the eldest and who, at fourteen, had had to take on the running of the entire household. They'd been rich, they'd had servants. Dee had never had to lift a finger in her life before, so she didn't have a clue, but she'd learned fast, Chrissie thought grudgingly, and because of Dee's adaptability they'd survived.

'They are going to manage their own fruit trees this year. It will be hard, they've got a lot to learn, but they're determined to make a success of it, so Dee said.'

'That's great,' she replied flatly, hoping she wasn't now going to get a detailed account of what should or should not be done in the management of fruit trees.

'Chrissie . . . would . . . would you like to go to the Rotunda on Saturday night?'

'Oh, I'm sorry, Phil. I've promised to go to the Hippodrome with Ellen and Polly. It's Ellen's birthday, and Polly and me are treating her.'

He looked crestfallen and miserable. Trust him to have plucked up the courage to ask her on her friend's birthday. It never occurred to him that she was lying. He trusted people far too easily, or so Bridie was always telling him, but he never even entertained the suspicion that Chrissie would lie to him.

'Well, I'd better be going. I don't have much time. Mam insists I'm in early in the week.' It was something he already knew, but it still annoyed her. Oh, Mam was so old-fashioned, such a stick-in-the-mud. Still, she was looking forward to seeing the faces of her friends when she told them the tale about the visit of Lady Angela D'Arcy. She just wished she had enough courage to ignore Mam and have her hair cut.

Chapter Six

———◆———

ABBIE GLANCED AROUND THE kitchen of her new home and sighed. All she needed now was for Mike to be accepted and life would be perfect. The shorter distance to work meant so much to her, she could get far more done around the house, and it was more time she could spend with Mike.

He'd gone to take the exam and then the interview on Friday of last week, and each day they both waited in eager anticipation for the post. Of course she had plenty to keep her occupied, and she did go for hours on end not thinking about that letter, but there were times when it was all she did think of.

Mike had gone at the appointed time to see the house and had met her from work later that day. He'd had the keys in his pocket. He'd insisted on carrying her over the threshold and she had been laughing and crying at the same time. They didn't have much yet in the way of furniture, just the basics really. A bed, a sofa, a table and four chairs and pots and pans.

'It takes years to get a home together, girl, if you

ever do manage it at all,' Sal had said when she'd complained about the sparseness of the rooms. True to her word, she and Joan had brought Sal here on the first full day she had off. She and Joan and Hilda had scrubbed every inch of the place, Hilda bemoaning the fact that the kitchen floor was flagged.

'Damp, that's what it'll be in winter.'

'Not if she keeps a good fire in the range, it won't,' Joan had stated firmly. She was more than a match for Hilda Burgess these days. 'You've got two bedrooms, a front parlour, a scullery and running water. Oh, I know it's a bit of a bind having to share the yard and the wash-house, but what more could you ask for, especially at that price in this area?'

'I still think it would be better if you got some lino down on this floor. Our Michael's not used to flags.'

'I thought he would be well used to them, seeing how bad the conditions in the trenches were,' Joan had countered.

'He's not used to them in his home, is what I meant.'

'Well, lino's no use. It traps the damp all right but then it just rots away. Better to have peg rugs.'

'I'll brush it each day and scrub it once a week and with the heat from the range it should be fine,' Abbie had said firmly, so nipping in the bud a potential argument between her sister and mother-in-law.

Mike had said they would buy some furniture and a carpet for the parlour with his first week's wage, if he was accepted.

Abbie pushed the kettle onto the hob. She'd have a cup of tea before she went out shopping along County Road for something for their tea. She'd call and see if Ellen Hayes next door wanted anything. They were nice, the people next door. Ellen, or Nell as she'd told Abbie to call her, had come in the first day with some scones, and they'd got on like a house on fire, which was just as well seeing how they had to share some of the amenities. Mr Hayes was away at sea for nine months of the year, so it was either a feast or a famine, Nell had informed her. They had two little girls, Monica and Eileen, and Nell said she had to be father and mother to them. Of course Mr Hayes left an allotment, a set sum of money deducted from his wages and made payable on demand at the company's offices, so she was never without money, but occasionally she helped out in The Beehive when they were rushed, and when she could get someone to mind the children. It was a lonely life at times, but she was used to it now.

'Of course I could always go and see my sister-in-law,' Nell had said conversationally. 'She lives in Yew Tree Road.'

'That's posh.'

'Oh, aye. When Mam died the business was divided up between the lads. You see, the old man was a lot older than Mam, she was his second wife, he died first. I've got stepsisters and stepbrothers, but I don't bother with them much. Our Bernard gambled away his share of the coal business, but our Tom works at it, works

81

hard too. Leila's his wife, she's a bit of a scatterbrain. My other sister-in-law, Lydia, is very clever. Comes from a very educated family, she does. If you ask me, she married beneath herself. Oh, our Bernard's as daft as a brush and thinks the world of her, but he's not as bright as she is.'

'Didn't you get anything? It doesn't seem very fair.'

'No. I didn't want anything. When I married Ben I was cut off. Mam was dead and the owld uncle from Ireland ran everything, us included. Ben's not a Catholic, you see, so I was thrown out. We went to the Registry Office on the tram.'

'There were some people down our street who were like that,' Abbie had replied, thinking of Bridie and Edward Chatterton. 'They got married in the Registry Office, too.'

'I still go to mass and the girls are Catholic, Ben says he'll change – one day. Father Murphy just got his back up, you see. He's got a right temper has Ben, mind you, and so have I. Sometimes I think it's a good thing we're not together for too long.'

'Oh, don't say that!' Abbie had laughed, seeing the twinkle in her neighbour's eye.

She was just coming out of Nell's front door when the postman turned the corner with the last delivery of the day. Abbie's heart turned over.

'Sorry Mrs Hayes, nothing from himself, I'm afraid, but there's one here for you, well, for your hubby.'

Abbie nearly snatched it from him, noting the seal bearing the Liver bird on the back.

'That's it isn't it, Abbie?'

'Yes. It's addressed to Mike.'

'Oh, go on, Abbie, open it. It concerns you both.'

'Oh, Nell, I couldn't.'

'How long will it be before he gets in then?'

'About an hour. I can't wait that long. I can't. I'm going to catch a tram and go up to Burlington Street now.'

'You will let me know how he's got on, won't you? The suspense is killing me!' Nell called after her.

She ran all the way to the tram stop and waited impatiently for a tram to come along. The minutes seemed like hours, and the journey seemed to take for ever. She'd never realized just how many stops there were between County Road and Scotland Road, and she wanted to scream at people to hurry up, they seemed to take for ever boarding or leaving. When she alighted at the Rotunda she quickly crossed the road, dodging between the carts and lorries, and ran down Burlington Street.

'Abbie! What's wrong, you look a mess!' Hilda cried, alarmed. The girl was red-faced, perspiring, and her hair was slipping from its pins.

'Nothing. Mike . . . Letter.' Abbie gasped out, trying to get her breath back.

'Michael! Michael come here quickly!' Hilda yelled.

The look of consternation on Mike's face changed to anxiety as he caught sight of his wife, but she was feverishly waving an envelope at him.

'Is that it?'

'Yes. I . . . I ran—'

He took it from her, his hand shaking a little. Their future was contained in this letter.

'Well, go on, open it. The girl's exhausted herself tearing up here with it.'

Mike ripped it open and scanned the lines of neat writing. His face split into a wide grin and he caught Abbie up in his arms, twirling her around.

'I'm in! I'm in!'

She shrieked with joy and relief, while Hilda looked bemused.

Frank appeared in the doorway to see what was going on. He'd heard the noise from the back yard.

'I'm in, Dad! They've accepted me. I've to go for training next week!'

Frank shook his hand. 'I'm proud of you, lad, and so is your mam. I'd never thought I'd see a son of mine as a police officer.'

'It's a step up, that it is, and we are proud of you – both,' Hilda added, thinking for the first time that her son had indeed made a good choice when he'd selected Abbie Kerrigan for a wife.

'This calls for a drink. Hilda, is there any sherry left?'

'A drop. I'll get some glasses.'

'None for me, thanks, I'd prefer a pint.'

'Oh no you don't, Michael Burgess. Frank, you go and get a small bottle of whisky from Red. This is a family celebration.'

Frank nodded. She was right, and besides, he doubted there would be much in the way of congratulations from most of the customers of The Black Dog.

'We should go and tell Mam,' Abbie said firmly. If it was a family do then Sal and Pat had to be included.

'I'll call in, Abbie, I'll send your da down here.'

'What about Mam?'

'Oh, don't worry. I think Joan will let her up for an hour, don't you? There's no party without Sal, is there?'

Abbie laughed. Mam would be so proud of her now. A policeman's wife, and with her own home; she just hoped Mam wouldn't start on about babies again. When they got home she'd take Nell in a drink, for she knew that she'd be spending a lot of time on her own, too. There would be long hours when Mike was working shifts; and besides, she liked Nell Hayes.

Abbie was very surprised when, two days later, Phil Chatterton turned up on her doorstep.

'Phil, it's great to see you. Come in.' As she shepherded him into the kitchen she wondered what had brought about this visit, for she didn't know him that well. Dee had been her friend, and Phil was Dee's brother, but that was about the extent of their acquaintance. 'It was good of you to come. It's not a bad little house is it? Look who's come to see us,' she informed Mike, who was sitting at the table ploughing his way through the *Liverpool City Police Manual of*

General Orders and Instructions, only one of the many books he'd been told to read and digest. It was hard going and he was glad of the interruption.

'Phil, it's great to see you!'

'I'm sorry for barging in, Mike, I didn't know you were studying.'

'Sit down. I was going to take a break anyway, my head's in a whirl with all these long words and rules and regulations. It's damned hard work. I'm not used to having to study all the time and have to go to evening classes three times a week at Everton Terrace. That's the training school. I start there full time on Monday.'

'For how long?' Phil asked. It didn't sound that bad, but he'd always been a great reader and had done well at school.

'Two months.'

'Oh, he looked ever so smart in his uniform when he was sworn in. I was so proud of him. Mind you, I don't know where I'm going to put all the stuff they gave him, and those capes weigh a ton. It's a good job we've got a spare room upstairs,' Abbie laughed as she put the kettle on.

There was a lot of stuff, she thought. Two dark navy serge tunics with high buttoned collars, on which was attached the city's emblem, the Liver bird, and Mike's number, 746. There were four pairs of serge trousers, the thick heavy cape with the metal clasp, a shorter black rubber cape, two helmets, each topped with a silver-coloured metal spike rising from four tiny feet, and the silver badge, again depicting the Liver bird. There was a whistle and a short truncheon, but you had to buy your own boots, although the police paid an allowance of three pounds ten shillings a year for those. The pay wasn't bad either. One pound sixteen shillings a week to start with, but it went up to two pounds and four shillings after two years. It had been increased at the end of last year.

They had both been astounded to learn that police officers were subjected to fines.

'Can you credit it? I never thought they got up to things like that. I always thought they were pillars of respectability,' she'd said, leaning over his shoulder to read the list.

'Ten shillings for being drunk on duty. Ten for neglect of duty, whatever that means, and a whole pound for being asleep on duty,' Mike had read out.

'Five shillings for "accepting improper passes for goods leaving the docks". I think that means bribery,' she added.

Abbie could see Phil was on edge about something. 'I'll pour this tea for you both, then I'm going next door to see Nell.' She could see Phil was relieved, and she was intrigued as to the reason for his surprise visit.

When Abbie had gone, Phil stood up and thrust his hands deep into his pockets.

'You're not going already?' Mike asked.

'No, I . . . I wanted to ask you something.'

'I thought you did, you've been like a cat on hot bricks since you got here. What is it?'

'I've been thinking. I hate my job. I hate being stuck in that office all day with all those old bores. I thought I might apply for the police, like you.'

Mike was a bit taken aback. Phil had always seemed so content and he was a quiet, bashful lad. 'There's no harm in trying, Phil, but is it really what you want?'

'It's a good career, Dad said so. I know I haven't any Army service like you, but I'm tall enough, I'm fit and I did get my Leaving Certificate, and with good marks. If there had been the money I would have gone to college, maybe even university.'

Mike knew how he felt. He'd also wanted to further his education, but there hadn't been the money. 'I know you're bright enough, Phil,' he was still trying to find the right words, for he didn't want Phil to think he was being dog in the manger. 'It's a tough job. You've seen how the police have to break up fights in the pubs along the dock road.'

'I know all that and I know I might seem . . . a bit soft, but I'm not.'

'Your age might be against you.'

'I'll be too young? You were only sixteen when you joined the Army.'

Mike sighed. 'That was different, Phil, everyone was enlisting, and they didn't really ask too many questions about age.'

Phil felt deflated. He'd thought that if he joined the police then Chrissie might look at him in a different light. 'I want to try anyway and if . . . if they won't have me, then that's that, I will at least have tried.'

'Have you talked about this with your dad? He's educated, sensible.'

'No, not yet. I came straight to you.'

'Maybe you should talk to him first.'

'I will, but will you give me the address?'

'Yes. Put as much in the letter as you can. Say you are looking for a career, not just a job.'

When Phil had gone Abbie came home. 'I saw him leave. What on earth did he want? It wasn't just to see the house, I could tell that by his attitude.'

'He wants to join the police.'

'Phil? He's too quiet, and he's so young. He's only nineteen.'

'I know. I told him that.'

'Do you think they'll have him?'

'I don't know. He's clever enough, but he's got no Army service. I don't think he's up to being a copper on the beat. Maybe in the Criminal Investigation Department, but I've got a feeling that our Chrissie is at the bottom of this. He worships her, he follows her around like a lap dog, but she won't go out with him. I know Mam would approve of Phil.'

'But Chrissie won't entertain him. She's a fool. He's a nice lad, too nice for her. She can be a madam and a half can your Chrissie,' Abbie added. In her opinion Phil would be better not to get involved with Chrissie at all, she'd only hurt him.

All the way home on the tram, Phil had studied the name and address Mike had given him. It was a good career. Steady wages that meant a good standard of living, nothing extravagant, still working class, but there was also the chance of promotion. He'd never get much further up the ladder in the shipping business, and he wasn't even sure if he wanted to. He could at least offer Chrissie hope for the future. A better future and a position of respect in the community. He knew that she didn't consider that he had any prospects at the moment. Maybe that was why she was always refusing him. Yes, that must be it. Once he could tell her he'd been accepted for the police, she was bound to look at him in a new light.

When he finally arrived home it was to find Bridie looking very anxious.

'What's the matter? You look upset.'

'I'm worried about David.'

'What's he been up to now?' David was his younger brother, and always up to something or other. His great friend and accomplice from the age of eight was Bertie Kerrigan, and Phil knew he missed Bertie.

'He went out to see Bertie.'

'I didn't know the *Aquitania* was in.'

'She's not, well at least she won't be now. She was due to sail at six.'

Suddenly Phil caught the drift of what Bridie was implying. 'You don't think Bertie's smuggled him aboard?'

'I don't know what to think, you know those two and their hair-brained schemes. A right pair of divil's imps they are. "I'll only be half an hour", he said.'

'Has he taken anything with him? Clothes, things like that?'

'I don't know. Oh, I wish Edward would get back.'

'Where is he?' Phil suddenly noticed the absence of his father and his half sister, Elizabeth.

'He's taken Elizabeth to the library, but he shouldn't be long now.'

'Go and have a look in our room, see if anything of David's has gone.'

Bridie headed for the stairs while Phil took the piece of paper Mike had given him and smoothed it out. There wasn't much chance of him trying to compose a letter of application now, as he'd been determined to do. If David had stowed away on the *Aquitania* the whole house would be in an uproar for days, maybe even weeks. He cursed his brother, who had always been something of a free spirit. He knew David didn't enjoy his job, he was more or less only a tea boy, although his proper title was Office Boy in the establishment of Lamport and Holt, yet another shipping company. But if he'd been so determined to go away to sea, then why couldn't he have gone through the proper channels, he thought irritably.

He looked up hopefully as the door opened, but it was Rose, his ten-year-old sister. 'Oh, you've decided to come home then, have you?'

Rose's blue eyes widened and she tossed back the mane of thick, light brown curly hair. 'What's up with you? I've only been to see Aunty Sal, like I always do.'

'Didn't Aunty Bridie tell you not to be going there

all the time? Aunty Sal's not well, Rose, you know that. She really is sick.'

Rose raised her chin determinedly. 'She's not that sick. You're just like Joan, always moaning about me. Aunty Sal likes me to go and see her. "Yer always cheer me up, Rosie. Give us a song then, Queen."' She mimicked Sal's voice expertly.

Phil began to lose his temper. 'Rose, can't you get it into your stupid head that she's very ill? If she has another one of those turns, she might well die.' He was in no mood for euphemisms tonight.

Rose said nothing. His words had shocked her. Ever since the day they'd come to Burlington Street she'd called Sal Kerrigan 'Aunty' because Sal had immediately taken charge of the seriously ill Gwendoline Chatterton's three-year-old daughter. From that day Rose had looked on Sal as her mother. She couldn't remember Gwendoline at all now. Most of her life had been spent with the Kerrigans. She'd become one of Sal's large and often obstreperous family. She'd only come home to sleep and then she'd often had to be dragged home, protesting and screaming, by Dee.

The tense atmosphere struck Bridie immediately, and, catching sight of Rose's stricken face, she frowned. 'What's going on now?'

'Phil says Aunty Sal's going to die,' Rose blurted out, close to tears.

'I didn't!'

'You did!'

'I didn't. I said she might die.'

'Oh, stop it the pair of you, haven't I got enough on my plate? Why did you say a thing like that to her?'

'I told her off for running up there all the time and annoying everyone.'

Bridie sighed heavily. 'Look, Rose, luv, Aunty Sal is very sick, that's why she has to rest all the time. But everyone has to die at some time, it's the only thing we are all certain of in this life. But don't you go getting upset over it. Sal's not ready to go to heaven just yet, she's as stubborn as a mule, but you have to stop popping in and out all the time.'

Rose's tears dried; basically she was a pragmatic child, and very like Dee in some ways. 'Will it be all right if I go and see her straight from school? There's only Joan there then, and Aunty Sal likes me to go, she says I cheer her up. I went tonight to show her my new dance and to sing.'

Bridie uttered another sigh, and Phil raised his eyes to the ceiling. From a very early age Rose had been precocious and had often amused both families with her theatrical antics. Where she got such talents – and she did have talent – Edward was at a loss to know. Rose's greatest treat was to be taken to the pantomime or a matinée at the Rotunda. She learned all the words of the latest songs and was always dressing herself up and dancing around the house.

'As long as you don't make a nuisance of yourself.'

Phil's attention returned to the subject of his brother. 'Has anything gone?'

'Not that I can see. Mind you, that room is such a mess I wouldn't know.'

'It's David's fault, he never hangs anything up.' Phil had always been tidy, it was a trait instilled into him in the years, so distant now, that he'd spent at boarding school, when they'd had money.

He was still trying to concentrate on what he would put in the letter, if he ever got the chance to write it, when Edward and Elizabeth came home.

'Elizabeth, luv, go and show Rosie your books,' Bridie urged, looking earnestly at her husband.

'She laughs at me, Mam, all she's interested in is singing and dancing and messing around like that.' Elizabeth was a serious child, like her father in many ways, but with Bridie's easy-going temperament.

'Go and ask her to show you her new dance or whatever it is she's going on about,' Phil urged.

'Aye, none of us will get any rest until we've seen her new party piece,' Bridie added. 'Are you sure there was never anyone in your family who was on the stage?'

'I'm certain,' Edward replied, looking concerned. He'd caught the anxious looks exchanged by his wife and son.

Elizabeth shrugged, and when she'd gone it was Phil who spoke. 'David went off to see Bertie.'

'And he's not back?' Edward queried. 'They've probably both gone off somewhere and forgotten about the time.'

'They might well have gone off somewhere! The

damned ship sailed at six o'clock and it's now ten to eight!' Bridie exploded.

'Shall I go up and ask Pat has he seen David?'

'No, give him another half an hour. I don't want to worry Sal.'

Edward looked annoyed. 'I hope he's not been stupid enough to try to stow away. It's a serious offence, at least in Cunard's book. If he's caught, they probably will press charges.'

'I'll kill him if he has!' Phil said with unusual vehemence, seeing in his brother's escapade the end of all his hopes.

'You'll have to get in the queue behind me and your dad,' Bridie said grimly. 'This time he's gone too far.'

'That's if he *has* gone,' Edward reminded them.

Phil sighed. He might as well make a start on his letter. Sitting here just waiting would drive him mad. He found paper and envelopes in the dresser.

Bridie had taken out her mending basket and was too preoccupied to notice, but Edward asked him what he was doing.

'I'm applying for the police force, like Mike Burgess.'

Edward nodded absent-mindedly.

'Let's just hope you don't end up having a jail bird for a brother, that wouldn't go down well,' Bridie commented, then, as a series of thuds and thumps came from upstairs, she threw down the sock she had been attempting to darn and made for the lobby.

'She'll have the damned ceiling down the way she's

going on. I wish to God she'd give over with all this flaming dramatic nonsense.'

Elizabeth was sitting stoically on the bed she shared with Rose, pretending to be The Audience, as she'd been instructed. Rose was executing what she thought were a series of graceful pirouettes while singing 'I'm Forever Blowing Bubbles' at the top of her voice. The fact that she had a strong, clear soprano voice was lost on Bridie.

'Rosie! In the name of heaven will you give over! The plaster's coming off the ceiling down there with you charging around up here like a baby elephant, and Elizabeth, get off that bed with your dirty shoes on!'

Rose was stung. 'I'm not like a baby elephant! I'm very light on my feet, aren't I, Elizabeth?'

'Yes, Rose,' her sister answered automatically. It was always easier to agree with Rose.

'Well, you're making far too much noise, so stop it.'

Rose looked defiantly at her stepmother, then decided that it would be best to humour her. 'All right, but I wouldn't make such a noise if I knew how to do it properly. If I went to dancing lessons they'd teach me, then I wouldn't be annoying you.'

'Rosie, we've been through all this before. We can't afford dancing lessons.'

'But I could pay for them.'

'What with?'

'I could earn the money, doing jobs for people.'

'What jobs?'

'Running messages, cleaning steps and windows.'

Rose shot a glance at her sister and pouted. 'Elizabeth gets more than I do.'

'She doesn't!' Bridie answered defensively.

Rose was a sharp child and quickly saw her advantage. 'She does, and it's not fair! She's never had second-hand dresses, like me. The only nice, new dress I've ever had was the one I wore when I was Joan's bridesmaid when I was three, and that had to go back to the shop. Da takes her places, the library, the museum . . .'

'He offered to take you, too, but you said you hated places like that.' Bridie ignored the reference to second-hand clothes. Rose had grown up when times were hard and they'd all had second-hand clothes.

To her consternation, Rose flung herself on the bed and started to cry noisily. 'It's not fair! It's not fair!' she sobbed.

'Oh, Rosie, stop it! I'm upset enough as it is.'

Rose sobbed louder, sensing Bridie's weakness. 'It's not fair! I want to go to dancing lessons. I've never asked for anything, and she gets more than me. She gets everything!'

'Oh, all right, Rosie, I'll see what we can do. Stop whingeing for heaven's sake. You'll have to help out, though.'

Rose wiped away her tears, hiding the triumphant light that had come into her eyes. She'd learned how to manipulate people almost from the day she'd been thrown into Sal's household.

The front door slammed and Bridie heard Edward's

voice. 'I hope that's David!' she cried, rushing towards the stairs, Rose and Elizabeth forgotten for the moment. 'Oh, thank God! Where've you been?' she cried as she entered the kitchen.

David was looking sheepish. 'I told you I was going to see Bertie off.'

'You didn't. You said you were going to *see* Bertie.'

'Well, I watched the ship leave. I waited until she was out of sight, then I had a wander around the Pier Head. I wish I could go to sea. Bertie says it's great. It's hard work, but there's great times to be had.'

Bridie felt as though she were sinking under the weight of all the worries of the evening. 'What's the matter with this family? You want to go to sea, he wants to join the scuffers, and madam up there wants dancing lessons, if you please. Real cut up about it, too, she is. Saying she gets nothing.'

David seized the opportunity. 'If I were away, you would have less meals to cook, less washing, less shopping. I'd leave you an allotment, and if Phil joins the scuffers he'll be on good money. You'd have loads more money in your purse and Rose could have all the dancing lessons she wants, and you'd get some peace.'

Bridie looked helplessly at Edward for rescue and was thankful to see he was deliberating on David's words.

'Well, if you're so set on going to sea maybe we can ask around to see if there are any vacancies.'

'I could go to the Pool,' David offered.

'You're not going to sign on as a stoker or trimmer or anything else in the stokehold.'

'I don't mind.'

'I do, David. Anything else but the stokehold. It's a brutalizing job, and the conditions are appalling.'

'So, I can go?'

'If you can get a job then, yes, you can go.' Having sorted that out, Edward turned to Bridie. 'How much are these dancing lessons Rose keeps going on and on about?'

'Sixpence a week. They have them on a Saturday morning in Our Lady Immaculate's church hall. She says she'll help to pay for them herself. Run messages for people and the like, but it's not just the sixpence. It's special shoes and clothes.'

'Well, I think between us we can manage sixpence, it will be worth it for a bit of peace. Now, put the kettle on, dear, and we'll take our tea in the front room. Phil wants to get on with his letter and he needs to concentrate fully.'

Phil was very thankful for this unexpected respite, and he was surprised too. It wasn't often his father was so decisive. In fact, for most of his life, Edward Chatterton had relied on other people to help him make decisions. Well, maybe the ones he'd made tonight weren't exactly of national importance, but at least it meant that now he had the kitchen to himself.

Chapter Seven

———◆———

THE JULY SUNLIGHT STREAMED in through the sash window and Hannah blinked rapidly as she lowered the blind. 'That's better.'

Richard Ashenden smiled at her. Ever since that first full conversation in May, he'd begun to look on and treat her as a friend, not just another nurse. She'd told him that she'd had to lie to Sister on that occasion, and he'd suggested that she make that statement the truth by reading to him.

At first she'd been very self-conscious about her lack of understanding of the books she read and her struggle with the unfamiliar, long words, but as the weeks had progressed she'd become more confident, and she had learned a lot too.

They were about one third of the way through the life of Admiral Lord Nelson, which she found rather tedious, and she was sure he thought it was too, for he often fell asleep.

'Shall we try something else today, Nurse Harvey? Nelson is beginning to pall a bit.'

'It is a bit . . . well, flat.'

'You mean boring. You should say boring.'

'I . . . I didn't want to upset you.'

'You wouldn't have. You choose something this time.'

He watched her as she browsed through the large collection of books that had been sent from his home. She was a restful sort of girl, her voice was quiet, her movements unhurried, and she was far more intelligent than he'd supposed her to be. He enjoyed her company, and sometimes in the evenings, when she was officially off duty, she would sit with him and read, or they would talk. She had sound commonsense and a simple, direct approach to life that was refreshing, and she did much to lift the depression that still claimed him from time to time, usually at night.

It was also very lonely being by himself for much of the time, although he'd not felt like that when he'd first come here. He hadn't wanted to see anyone then.

She had chosen *Oliver Twist* because it appealed to her. Dickens's portrayal of the London slums resembled some areas of Liverpool, she thought.

Before she had settled herself, she adjusted the pillows. 'You're looking much better these last couple of days, Sir, and Sister says you don't have the paraldehyde at night now, either.'

'Please stop all this Sir, your Lordship and my Lord.'

Hannah stared at him aghast. 'Oh, I can't do that!'

He smiled. 'Why not? We've become friends, have we not, Hannah? May I call you that?'

'Yes, of course, Sir. I mean . . . are we supposed to be . . . friends at all?'

'Why not? You've been so kind, so supportive, so amiable.'

'But it's my job.'

'No, not entirely. Your duties don't cover reading to me or sitting with me when your working day is over, do they?'

She shook her head. 'I find it . . . hard at home.'

'Why?'

'Too many memories, I suppose, although it really is better these days.'

He knew a little about her background. Her father was dead, her brother had died quite frightfully of bovine tuberculosis, and now there was just herself and her mother. He'd often thought of her words when she'd first told him that working in the field hospital was an escape, and he wondered again. 'Are they such painful memories then?'

'Yes. Very.'

'Would you like to share them? It might help. You've shared mine.'

She had. She'd calmed his terrified ravings when, in his dreams, he'd ordered his men over the top time and time again and seen them blown to pieces. She knew of the strain there had been between himself and his father, and the guilt he felt because his father had died before they had made their peace. She knew of his arguments with Freddie and Angela who were both extravagant, careless and stubborn; of his great affection for and friendship with his brother Hubert, and the pain and shock of learning that he'd been killed.

Hannah laid the book down, unopened, on her knee. It might help, but would he shrink from her? Ask to have her removed? He'd said they were friends, but she knew it could never be a deep friendship, not with her background. She did like him, anyone would, he was such a quiet, undemanding, well mannered person. But it would be so good to talk to him, and why not? After all, he'd be going home soon and then she would return to the general ward.

'My dad was a very religious man, a Non-Conformist. He was a lay preacher. We used to have to go to service three times on Sundays and a couple of nights in the week, too.'

That was a bit excessive, he thought. The man sounded like a fanatic. 'Did you mind?'

'Not all the time, only as I got older. Jerry hated it long before he'd even left school, but he was afraid of Da, we both were.'

'Why, Hannah?'

'He was strict. Very strict. We often got a hiding for things that, well, other people wouldn't think were bad.'

'Did no one intervene?'

'No, there was only Mam and she was scared of him too, although she wouldn't admit it. I remember, once, some neighbours did stop him beating Jerry. It was after a wedding and Jerry had been drinking. I . . . I was never allowed out to play with the other children.'

'Why not?' He could see she was struggling with memories of a childhood that appeared to be very unhappy. But had his own been any better? It had been different, he thought, for although he'd not seen a great deal of his parents, there had been Nanny and Mason, the butler, and Hubert, until he'd gone away to school.

'I don't really know. I think it was a bit of snobbery. He thought we were better than most of our neighbours. We certainly had a lot more money than most of them, although he kept Mam short. He was a very mean man in a lot of ways, not just with money.'

'Sometimes it doesn't do a person much good to have plenty of money.' He was thinking of Freddie and the hundreds of pounds he'd wasted.

'There was never plenty of it, we just had a bit more than others in the street. As Jerry's sickness got worse, he . . . he felt so awful he tried to hang himself. I found him. I wish now I hadn't.'

'The poor chap,' he muttered, thinking of how he'd often wished he were dead, when the black moods overtook him.

'When I wanted to join the VAD there was a terrible row. Jerry was very ill by this time, but Da hit him and he fell. Then Jerry picked up the poker, I don't know where he got the strength from, and . . . hit Da with it. He killed him.'

He was shocked. 'Good God! You poor girl!'

Hannah wiped away a tear with the corner of her apron. 'It was awful. They took Jerry to Walton

Prison, just down the road from here. He—' the words choked her and she couldn't go on, she dashed the tears from her cheeks with the back of her hand.

He was appalled, but, remembering how often she'd soothed away his torment, he reached out and took her hand in his. 'Stop if you want to Hannah.'

She shook her head. 'No, it's all right. Dr Wallace did everything he could, he tried to talk to the police, but it was no use. There wasn't a trial, thank God, and he didn't—' she swallowed hard – 'hang. He died before that. When it was all over I joined the VAD. Oh, I felt so guilty. I blamed myself. It was *my* fault, but Mam said it was Jerry's gift to me. There wasn't anything else he could give me, except the chance to live a normal life.'

'I would never have called life on the battlefields of France and Belgium normal.'

'No, neither did I, and yet it was in a way. I could be like the other girls, I could choose . . . things.' She suddenly looked at him, her brown eyes swimming with tears. 'Do you believe in God?'

'No. Not any more. Not after what I've been through, not after what I saw.'

'I don't know now if I believe or not. Mam said she prays that Jerry hasn't gone to hell. Da wasn't a good man despite all his pretence. But it *was* murder. I can't bear to think of Jerry having to suffer for ever – for me.'

It was terrible, and she had been tearing herself apart, and yet she had shown no outward sign of distress. She had lived with this awful secret for years.

'I don't think a jury would have found him guilty. It sounds like self-defence. Your father struck your brother, and he was a dying young man. It is reasonable to suppose that he feared for his life if your father continued to beat him. No, I don't think he would have gone to the gallows at all.'

'But the Bible says "Thou shalt not kill".'

'I have killed men, so many of them. The enemy directly, my own men indirectly. A heinous sin – or was it? It was in a just war. There are circumstances, exceptions, exemptions, you have to believe that. It wasn't your fault.'

She felt better, what he said did make sense. The God she'd been taught to believe in was a wrathful, vengeful, unforgiving God, but he was saying that maybe that wasn't true. He was implying that the God she believed in was merciful and understanding. She felt better. 'Thank you. And, thank you for listening to me. It . . . it's the first time I've ever spoken about it properly.'

He smiled at her. 'Now we've no secrets. Or have we?'

She managed a fleeting smile. 'No.' Then she realized for the first time that he was holding her hand, and she withdrew it gently. She pulled herself together. 'You'll be going home soon. Are you glad?'

A frown creased his forehead. 'I don't know. I feel that once I'm there I will have to face all the problems of the estate. I'm going to have to learn an awful lot, too.'

'It's a big responsibility.' She didn't know exactly what it entailed, but she assumed it was a serious burden.

'Maybe too big, but it's my heritage. It's my duty, if you like, to maintain it and everyone connected with it.'

'You will have to take things easy at first, you do know that?'

'How can I do otherwise, like this?' His voice was bitter.

'I meant rest.'

'I know. I'll cope – eventually.' He suddenly felt bereft and strangely afraid. 'Will you come and nurse me?'

'Me? Come to . . . your house?'

He hadn't planned any of this. It had just suddenly occurred to him. 'Yes. I'm going to need a nurse, and why not the one who has tended me so well? I'd also like to have someone who knows me, not someone I've got to get to know, get used to.'

Hannah couldn't think straight. 'But . . . but there's Mam.'

'Will she object?'

'She'll be on her own and—'

'She works, does she not?'

'Yes.'

'What does she do?'

'She cleans offices.'

'I'm sure a place could be found for her.'

'You mean you want us both?'

'If it means I can have my kind and trusted nurse, then yes.'

'Oh, that's very, very kind of you, Sir.'

'No Sirs, and I'm really being selfish. I've come to lean on you for support, Hannah. I can't face the thought of having anyone else around me. And I know my mother: she would engage someone like Sister Marsden, and then life would be unbearable.'

She smiled. 'Mine will be too. It's time for me to tidy things up. Mr Copeland will be around soon, and if Sister sees the state of this room, my life won't be worth living.'

He watched her work in silence. He did lean on her far more than he had realized, and he wasn't looking forward to going home. Not with all the painful memories that abounded there.

Hannah really didn't know how she felt. If anyone had pressed her on the matter, she would have said she was utterly confused. Her mind hadn't been on her work for the rest of the day, and when she finished, she decided she'd go and see Abbie, for her thoughts were scattered to the winds.

Abbie was on the early shift, starting at six and finishing at four; Mike was out.

'Hannah, come in. I've just made a pot of tea. Do you want something to eat?'

'No thanks.'

'Hannah, you look upset.'

'Not really, Abbie, but I'm just so confused.'

'What about?'

'His Lordship has asked me to go home with him, as his nurse, and he says Mam can come too,' she blurted out.

'Good God! What are you going to do?'

'I don't know. We have become friends, you know that.'

'I know that you sit and read to him.'

'We talk, too, about lots of things. He's very nice and I think I'd like it, going home with him, but I'm not sure I could cope, that I'd be able to fit in. I'm . . . well, I'm too common.'

'Indeed you are not! That's something you've never been, Hannah Harvey. You were never even let out to play in the street with us common kids.'

'Oh, Abbie, what I meant was compared to him – them, and the sort of nurse his mother would employ.'

'I see what you mean, but you're good at your job. No one could fault you, not even Sister.'

'I'd have to mix with all the other servants, and I don't know how to treat people like that.'

'They're earning a living just like you, Hannah. When do you have to decide?'

'He didn't say, but I suppose it will be soon. Oh, Abbie, I just don't know.'

Abbie was silent. It would be good experience for Hannah, and after her services were no longer needed, she certainly wouldn't be short of a job, and a good one too. She'd have references that no one could fault; and yet she was concerned for her friend.

'Hannah, you aren't getting too fond of him are you?'

'No, it's nothing like that, Abbie. He's just nice and friendly, and I suppose that because I've been with him day and night for six months, he feels comfortable with me. I don't think he is looking forward to going home.

'With a ma like his, do you blame him?'

Hannah managed a smile. 'Oh, she's not too bad if you treat her properly.'

'Then I think you'd better talk about it with your mam. It will be a big change for her, leaving all the neighbours.'

Hannah nodded and stood up. She'd better go. 'Thanks, Abbie, for your help.'

'What help?'

'Oh, you know what I mean.'

Abbie watched her walk down the lane, still dappled by the evening sun, and she sighed. She just hoped that Hannah didn't get too fond of him – it happened sometimes between nurse and patient – for there was no future for Hannah there. He could never marry her, and if she did love him, that way led only to heartbreak.

The house was very quiet, Hannah thought as she opened the door. It was also very warm, as though the heat of the day had been caught and held within the walls. There wasn't that chilling silence, though, the cold, menacing silence that had pervaded the house when Abe had been alive. She'd hated coming home from school. There had been hours of terrible suspense, wondering what mood he would be in. She'd lived in fear of her father coming home from work in a violent temper, for a beating then inevitably followed; he'd find fault with some trivial thing, no matter how hard they tried to do and say everything correctly.

'Mam, I'm home!' she called, as she placed her hat on the coat stand in the hall and went into the kitchen. Winnie was rubbing her eyes.

'I must have dozed off, luv, it's so warm. I've done you some ham and tomatoes and a bit of lettuce. It's too warm for hot meals. I'll put the kettle on. Have you had a hard day?'

'Not in the way you mean, Mam.'

Winnie stared intently at her daughter. 'Then how?'

Hannah thought it best to get it over with. 'His Lordship has asked me to be his nurse when he goes home, and there will be a place for you, too, Mam.'

Winnie sat down suddenly. 'You mean . . . go . . . and . . . live . . . ?'

'At Ashenden Hall. Yes.'

'Hannah, you're not thinking of agreeing, are you?'

'Yes, I think I am.'

'But how will you manage, girl? They're not just wealthy, they're . . . they're the high and mighty of the land.'

'Mam, it's just a job. It will be the same as I'm doing now, but in a better place.'

'You mean you'll be happy to mix with all those servants? I've heard that some of them are terrible snobs, Hannah. Particularly butlers and housekeepers and ladies' maids and the like.'

'They can't all be bad. Will you come, Mam?'

Winnie looked very perturbed. 'I don't think so, luv. I couldn't cope with it all.'

'I thought you would be glad to leave this house.'

'No. Once maybe, but not now. Things are different, and besides, I couldn't leave all my friends and neighbours. They've always been so good, so kind. Even when things were so awful. I knew I could count on them.'

'You'll be lonely.'

'I won't, there's always someone dropping in, or I can go and have a natter to Sal Kerrigan. And then there's my job.'

'You won't have to work, Mam. I know how you hate it, even though you say you don't. I'll earn enough to send home.'

'You've decided, haven't you?'

Hannah nodded. 'It seems like it. I feel sort of responsible for him, for his health. Sometimes he gets so very depressed.'

'Well, if that's what you want, Hannah, then go, and go with my blessing. You didn't have much of a childhood – you haven't had much of a life at all so far. This might be your big opportunity.'

'Are you sure you won't come? And you really won't mind me going?'

'No, Hannah.'

'I'll get some time off so I can come home and see you.'

Winnie smiled. 'I said go, luv. If you can cope with it all, good luck. I think it's what Jerry would have wanted for you.'

Tears started in Hannah's eyes as she remembered her conversation with Richard Ashenden that had resulted in the post now being offered. Yes, Jerry had wanted her to escape from here, to live her life to the full.

She hadn't mentioned it, and neither had he, but two days later Sister Marsden called her into her office.

'You're to go to Matron's office at once, Nurse Harvey.'

Hannah's heart turned over. What had she done? Had Matron somehow found out about her conversation with his Lordship? 'Me, Sister?' she stammered.

'Of course I mean you, Nurse. There is no one else here, is there?'

'I don't think I've done anything wrong, Sister.'

'I'm sure I don't know anything about it,' Sister Marsden sniffed. 'Just get along there now.'

Her heart was thumping against her ribs, and there seemed to be thousands of butterflies dancing manically in the pit of her stomach as she knocked on the door. She was told to enter but, to her surprise, it wasn't Matron, but Lady Ashenden, who sat in Matron's chair.

'Sit down, Nurse Harvey, I wish to speak to you.'

Hannah sat tensely on the edge of the chair. 'Yes, my Lady?'

'I believe my son wishes you to accompany him when he comes home, in the capacity of nurse.'

Hannah didn't look up. 'He . . . he did mention it.'

'He will, of course, need the services of a nurse for a while yet, so I have been informed.' Lady Ashenden drew off her kid gloves, revealing hands adorned with costly rings. 'I had intended to select someone myself, but he is adamant.' She paused, looking round the austere room without much pleasure. 'Have you always worked here, Nurse?'

'No, your Ladyship. I served with the VAD at Zillebeke and at Arras. When the war finished I came here.'

'So you have never worked in a private capacity?'

'I'm afraid not,' Hannah replied quietly, feeling very tense.

The older woman tutted. 'You will, of course, be expected to fit in with the staff. Do you think that will be a problem?'

'I hope not.'

'Indeed, so do I. How old are you, Nurse?'

'I'll be twenty-one in November, my Lady.'

'That's very young. Very young indeed.'

'I don't wish to appear rude, but there were girls younger than me serving in the field hospitals.'

'That is very enlightening, but the war is over. We must all now try to resume a normal life.'

114

Hannah wanted to say that, for some, the war would never be over. Their sightless eyes, their missing limbs, their gas-seared lungs would be a constant reminder to them, as would Richard Ashenden's paralysis; but she remained silent.

'Very well. You shall have one full day off every fortnight, one half day per week, and your salary will be three guineas a month, paid half yearly. I will, of course, provide your board and your uniform. I think a simple grey dress, a white apron and a small starched cap would be more appropriate than that uniform and flamboyant headdress.'

'Thank you, my Lady.'

Honoria Ashenden was trying to remember what else it was her eldest son had insisted that she mention. She was not at all happy with this situation, she considered the girl to be too young and too inexperienced to cope with life in an establishment like Ashenden. She apparently came from a very humble home. Still, Richard was adamant, and the girl appeared quiet, well mannered, and from what she'd seen and had been informed of, efficient. Ah, yes, she'd remembered. 'Your mother.'

Hannah had been wondering whether the interview was over. She didn't know whether she was expected to get up or have to wait to be dismissed, and she'd been so engrossed in her dilemma that Lady Ashenden's words startled her a little. 'Yes, my Lady?'

'She is, I believe, a widow, and you are her only surviving child.'

'That's correct.'

'My son has requested we find a place for her.'

Hannah could see Lady Ashenden didn't agree wholeheartedly with her son's request. 'Thank you, my Lady, but she – it won't be necessary. She . . . she feels,' Hannah was picking her words carefully, 'she is happy where she is, she has friends and good neighbours.'

Honoria Ashenden breathed a sigh of relief. Well, that was a blessing. She had told Richard that they couldn't afford to offer employment and lodgings to all and sundry, and his reply had caused her some consternation. 'It's not all and sundry, it's her mother, a widow, as you are.' She'd been incensed with that remark and had said so.

She gathered up her gloves and rose. 'Then you may go. You may return to your duties here. Arrangements have been made to convey Lord Ashenden home next Wednesday. Can you be organized by then?'

'Yes, my Lady. Thank you.'

As she closed the door behind her Hannah let out her breath in a long sigh. She would sooner have faced Matron.

Chapter Eight

———•———

IT WAS JUST SO DAMNED hot, Abbie thought as she pulled a kitchen chair out into the yard. The leaves on the trees in the churchyard beyond the wall hung limp and dusty, and were not moving even fractionally. There was not a breath of air to cool the humid August night. In fact the air was so dense and heavy that she felt she could cut it into chunks with the carving knife.

She was exhausted, totally drained. All day every single task had been an effort, and Sister's temper had been very short. There were times recently when it had taken all her resolve not to scream at the woman. She was being unfairly victimized. Nothing she did was ever right, but she couldn't afford the luxury of telling Sister Marsden what she could do with her job, not with this threat of a strike hanging over them. She fanned herself with a piece of cardboard. It was so sticky and uncomfortable.

'It's too damned hot to do anything!'

Abbie jumped, startled by Nell's voice.

'Sorry, Abbie, I didn't mean to make you jump like

that.' Nell had also pulled a kitchen chair into the yard. 'The kids are still awake. They're worn out, but it's like an oven in that bedroom. I don't know how Ben sticks the heat. He says it's always like this up that river. It's surrounded by jungle for miles and he has to wear his "tropical" whites. Tropical! They're made of heavy cotton. He might just as well wear a suit made of canvas.'

'It must be a big river if a ship like the *Hildebrand* can get that far up it and still be in the jungle. What's it called?' Abbie asked idly.

'The Amazon, and he says it's big and wide and long. They go one thousand miles up, can you credit that? One thousand miles!' Nell could see Abbie wasn't really listening. 'You look worn to a shadow. Has that one been getting at you again?'

'Oh, I should be used to it by now, Nell. She can't stomach the fact that I'm a married woman. I'm not dedicated enough, and in her book that means everything I do is wrong.'

'Seems to me you've plenty of dedication to put up with her.'

'It's not just her. I'm worried about this strike.'

'I thought that was all over and done with last year, before Mike joined? They got a pay rise and it was back-dated, so what do they want now?'

'A union, and the right to strike like everyone else. Oh, they've got a federation, but whatever the difference is between that and a union, I don't know. I don't understand any of it.'

'I thought it was only the London police that were striking?'

'No, it's all of them. I'm confused, Nell, and so is Mike. All I do know is that he may well be out of a job before the weekend, and then we can say goodbye to all our plans for the future.'

'Will it affect him? He's still a probationer, isn't he?'

'He's just about finished, but still on the low wage.'

'Well, maybe it won't affect him. The way I look at it is this, are the big noises in London going to keep you, Abbie? Like hell they are! Have you talked about it to your mam?'

'No. Da doesn't really approve of Mike being in the force to start with; this will just make things worse, and I don't want Mam upset. Oh, I wish he'd come home.'

'Night shift?'

Abbie nodded. It was to gain experience, so they told him. 'He could well be wasting his time.'

'Does he want to go on strike?'

'I don't think he knows what to do. Thank God I'm off tomorrow, although with this weather everyone will be out for the Bank Holiday.'

'I'm taking our Monica and Eileen to New Brighton. It will be packed solid, and we'll have to get down early for the ferry, but it's a day out. Why don't you come with us? It would take your mind off things.'

'Thanks, Nell, but I've got the housework to catch up on, and we've promised to go to Hilda's for tea, and then I said I'll go and see Mam.'

'Have you heard from your friend lately?'

'Hannah or Dee?'

'Not the one in Canada, the one you worked with, Hannah.'

'I had a letter last week. She can't get over how big the place is, it's like a palace, she said. I think she's a bit lonely. When she was home last she said she doesn't mix with the servants. She said they are a right toffee-nosed lot, all except the scullery maids, and she can't talk to them because her position in the household is so much higher than theirs. She seems to spend her free time reading. She said the library's enormous, like the Picton, she said.'

'Will I nip over to the pub and get us a drop of beer? We can mix it with lemonade and have a shandy.'

Abbie smiled and roused herself. 'I'll go, you keep your eye on those two. I might get something a bit stronger though, something that might help us to sleep.'

'I might give the kids a few drops, too, can't harm them.'

Mike felt the sweat trickling down the back of his neck and ran a finger around the uncomfortably high tight collar of his uniform tunic. Thick serge wasn't exactly the most suitable material for weather like this, and neither was the helmet. He could feel his hair sticking to his scalp beneath it, and the chin strap was uncomfortable. In his right hand he carried his bullseye lamp, the leather strap slipped securely over his wrist.

'It's too damned hot in summer but warm enough in winter, lad,' Albert Owens, his companion, commented drily.

He'd been with Owens for two days now. They'd given him a rest from the text books and lectures, and sent him to Westminster Road Police Station, the station house for E Division. He liked Owens, a quietly spoken man and a veteran of twenty years.

'Pretty much the same as khaki. It's much the same as being in the Army, too, except for all the books.'

'Disciplined forces of men, both. You live by rules and regulations in the Army and the police.'

'At least the enemy here doesn't come at you with machine guns, grenades or flaming gas.'

'Don't underestimate them though, the way everyone did with the Huns. Did you see much action, lad?'

'Enough. I was a bloody fool and enlisted at sixteen.'

'Then it's a bit of a miracle that you got through it in one piece.'

'I know.' Mike glanced sideways at his companion as they walked at regulation pace along the deserted street. Shops and houses were in complete darkness.

Owens was a giant of a man with a deep barrelled chest and a bushy moustache. His reputation and courage were both formidable and legendary. Over the years he'd been involved in most of the riots in the city, mainly between the Catholic and Protestant factions, but also in the more infrequent eruptions between the small black population and the suspicious white dockland community. If it was nothing else, Liverpool was cosmopolitan, Mike thought. A word he'd come across recently. Owens had told him that the police authorities had decided that, after twenty years, he'd taken enough beatings, and had posted him to Westminster Road, a quiet patch. Mike privately thought you'd have to be stark raving mad to take on this colossus. Owens must be six foot six. He himself was six foot, and the man was head and shoulders over him.

'I reckon the officers are much the same as in the Army, too.'

'I reckon they are. I've never set eyes on the Head Constable. I've never seen a superintendent in twenty years. An inspector is the only officer I've ever seen, apart from sergeants, and I don't class them as top brass.'

Mike didn't answer. He'd heard about the tyrannical pettiness of some sergeants who stuck to the Disciplinary Code that was as severe as anything in the armed forces. He'd been deeply embarrassed when Sergeant Lynch had ranted and raved, in front of him, at an officer with ten years' service, all because the top button of his tunic had not been done up. Lynch had a bad reputation, and he'd disliked the man on sight.

Albert Owens seemed to read his mind. 'Lynch let Fred Jarvis go home off night duty last week and then recalled him.'

'What for?'

'Because he'd forgotten to say All Correct before he'd left the station.'

'We had vindictive bastards in the Army, too.'

'Just putting you in the picture, lad.'

'Thanks.'

They walked on in silence, and Mike's thoughts returned to the strike. He'd gone over and over it all in his mind, arguing the point of union solidarity and striking with his colleagues, against losing his job and what that would mean to both Abbie and himself. It would be back to the shop, and they'd probably have to give up the house if Abbie got pregnant. He decided to sound Owens out.

'This strike . . .'

'What about it?'

'I'm confused. What do you think?'

'The way I see it, and I'm not trying to influence you, it's just my opinion, is that it's doomed. What they're fighting over now is union or federation, and seeing as MaCready down in London has improved pay and conditions, I don't think many forces will come out over something like that. The timing's wrong, too. We've just got all our back pay for working seven days a week during the war.'

'But it was the union that got that.'

'I'm not disagreeing with you. I've been a union member from the start – in the days when we had to hold meetings in front parlours, with all the cloak and dagger stuff.' He stepped into a shop doorway and flashed the beam of his lamp over the lock and across the side window.

'Then you'll be happy with a federation?'

'I won't know that until we see if the federation has got any teeth.'

Mike didn't answer and they moved on.

'When I was a young copper like you, I was called to a cellar near where you come from. Times were even harder and conditions were even worse than they are now. There was a young woman there, about twenty, and two kids. She was dead and they were half dead. It was the middle of February and there was no fire, no furniture, nothing except the bare floor and a few rags. She'd starved to death, in fact the rats had chewed her fingers and toes, and they'd had a go at the kids, too. They went to an orphanage and a verdict of Accidental Death was given on her. I tried complaining, but I came up against a wall of indifference. She wasn't important you see, no one cared. I suppose after that you could say I turned socialist.'

'And you stayed in the force?'

'I did. It took me a long time to learn that I couldn't change the system. Only the City Fathers can do that, and the politicians, and all they do is make empty promises. The only way we can help is to try to protect the weak. We're paid to uphold the law, keep the peace and stay impartial. It doesn't matter what your religion or politics are. Are you Church of England?'

'Catholic.'

'Well, you'll be expected to dole out a few clouts to

your own and have them spit on you, swear at you and belt the living daylights out of you if they can, for protecting the supporters of King Billy on the glorious twelfth. That's how impartial you'll be expected to be.' Owens grinned sardonically. 'The force is the only religion you're supposed to have. The Liverpool City Police Manual is the Bible.'

'I've begun to realize that.'

'They don't like you to have friends or even associates outside the force, either.'

'I'm not giving up my friendships, although most of my mates are buried in France.'

The older man stopped in front of a small shop and flashed his lamp across the name over the door. 'He's a nice old feller. He's worked hard all his life in this shop. He never has much money to spare, but he always gives us a few bob at Christmas for the Orphans' Fund. He lost both his lads at Ypres, and his wife in the 'flu epidemic. It's a shop just like your mam and dad's.

'Except it's a chandlers.'

'Have you any idea what would happen to this place and to him if we go on strike? Aye, and maybe your mam and dad too?'

Mike felt suddenly apprehensive.

'Take the cat away and the mice get bold as brass, except mice is too delicate a way to describe them.'

'Rioting and looting?' Mike answered hollowly.

'On a scale that would make all the other riots look like a holiday outing. And being a scouser myself, I know it wouldn't be confined to just the villains. Oh no, the rest will join in just for the hell of it. And can you blame people who can't find the money to feed and clothe their kids, if they help themselves, too? Who'd protect the weak, the poor, the decent people like your mam and dad then?'

'You're not going out?'

'No, I'm bloody well not. I won't turn this city over to mob rule, and that's a decision I made without a thought for the City Fathers, who should make some effort to help all the poor sods who can't help themselves. Besides, I took an oath to keep the King's Peace. The King's mind, not Mayor John Richie's. You've taken two. One for King and Country and the same one I took. You didn't break your first one, and who would trust a policeman who stood up in court and swore to tell the truth, after he'd already ignored his previous promise? I bloody wouldn't for one. But you've got to make up your own mind.'

It was getting a little lighter. The sparrows and starlings had started to stir, breaking the silence with a far from melodious dawn chorus. Owens turned sharply on his heel and they both began to walk slowly back towards Medlock Street and the station house.

Mike was turning things over in his mind. There was a lot of sense in what the older and more experienced man had said. 'You're not paid to be loved nor even liked. You're paid to do a job, and if you can't do it then you should never have joined.' Those words had been impressed upon him many times. Then there was his oath. As Owens had pointed out, he'd been prepared to die rather than break the first oath. Many of his mates had died rather than dishonour it. To him an oath was sacred, not lightly taken or easily broken. Then there was Abbie and their future, his mam and da, and all their friends and neighbours. He also knew his city and he knew he was paid to keep the lid on the potentially turbulent, explosive areas where conditions were far from good: the docklands and his old neighbourhood, where there were more than enough hardened criminals who thrived by exploiting their neighbours and those unfortunate enough to be unable to defend themselves.

They lingered on the corner for a few minutes as Owens checked the time. You never set foot inside the station until the precise minute your shift ended, unless it was to take a prisoner in or when called back. There was a fine of five shillings for any man who strolled in earlier than six o'clock, and Sergeant Lynch took a delight in extracting it.

They were the first to report back, and it was to Lynch who looked like a bad-tempered ferret, and who immediately thrust a piece of paper, stamped with the blue Liver bird, under their noses.

'Read that!'

Owens took it from him, and they both read it.

'"Every member of the force who does not return to work immediately or parade at his divisional office for orders at 8 pm on this first day of August 1919, will be dismissed and will not be reinstated." So?' Owens demanded curtly.

'You do understand it? Or do I have to read it for you and spell it out?'

'It doesn't apply to me. I'm not on strike and I don't intend to be either.'

Lynch sank down in the chair behind the big wooden desk across which were strewn papers, lists, a copy of the *LCP Manual*, the *Report Book*, the *Punishment Book*, which was open, the *Standing Order Book* and various rubber stamps. 'Then parade here tonight as usual.' He ran his pen down a list and ticked off a name.

Mike stared at the far wall, his eyes fixed on the list of habitual drunkards that hung there.

'And you, Burgess?'

'It doesn't apply to me either, Sir.'

'Then you're to parade at Headquarters, Hatton Garden at six. Anything to report?'

'Nothing. All correct, Sir,' Owens answered.

'All correct, Sir,' Mike added, letting his shoulders slump now he'd voiced his decision.

'Straighten up, Burgess! I'll have no damned sloppiness in my station!' Lynch barked.

Mike ignored him. He just wanted to get home now and tell Abbie.

Chapter Nine

S HE HADN'T BEEN ABLE to sleep. She'd tossed and turned in the cloying darkness, her hair sticking to her neck with perspiration. In the end she'd given up and gone down and had a wash in the scullery and put on a loose cotton wrap.

She made herself a cup of tea, wishing it was possible not to have the fire burning in the range, but there was no other source of heat for cooking. She set the table for breakfast although she wasn't in the least bit hungry. Mike would be, though, she mused. She just wished he would come home and tell her what was going on.

She went into the parlour where her new brown leather sofa and highly polished sideboard, on which stood a cut-glass vase, gleamed and sparkled in the early sunlight. The tall plant stand, with its glossy-leaved aspidistra in a china pot, stood near the window. In front of the empty fire grate was a painted screen. The bright colours of the lady in a crinoline and bonnet that decorated the fire screen, and those of the new square of carpet, seemed to jangle on her taut nerves. She couldn't stand being in here, not when all this might have to be sold soon, all her lovely possessions that they'd worked hard to buy.

She closed the door behind her and went to open the front door, just in time to hear Mike's voice as he returned the greetings from Sam Casey, the landlord of The Beehive, who was opening his windows to let out the stale odours of beer and tobacco.

'You're up early, Abbie, luv.'

She returned his kiss. 'Oh, I couldn't sleep. It was too hot and I was worried. You look all in yourself. I'll get your breakfast.'

Mike followed her into the kitchen, unbuttoned his tunic and placed it over the back of a chair. 'I'm starving and I need a bath, but I suppose a good wash will have to do. I'll go over to the baths when they open later on.'

As she handed him a cup of tea, Abbie's hand shook, the result of frayed nerves and exhaustion. 'What's happening, Mike? I went over the road last night for a drop of sherry for Nell and me, and everyone was saying that all the police forces are coming out on strike.'

Mike caught her around the waist and pulled her onto his lap. 'I was out with Albert Owens and he said he doesn't think they'll all come out. He talks a lot of sense, Abbie. He's a really decent bloke, too, and he's got twenty years' service in. When we got back Lynch had an official notice.'

'Saying what?'

'Saying we had to report for duty today or else we'll all be sacked and no one will be reinstated.'

Abbie felt her throat go dry and she laid her cheek against his forehead. *Oh, Dear God, do we have a future?* she prayed. Whatever decision he had made, she would respect it and stand by him. She loved him and she'd promised for better or worse, for richer or poorer. If he'd decided to come out, then she still had her job and there was still Frank's shop.

'I'm not going out, Abbie, and it's not just us I'm thinking of. It's not a totally selfish decision, Owens made me see that.'

Tears of relief welled up in her eyes. 'Oh, Mike. I'm glad. I've been feeling ill, really sick with it all.'

He grinned at her. 'Too much sherry.'

'Oh, don't joke.'

'Sorry, luv. Things are serious. Owens reckons there will be rioting and looting, that's part of the reason why I won't go out. Who will see to the likes of Mam and Dad, and the shop? I can't stand by and see everything they've worked hard for all their lives be wrecked. It's for people like that, and our neighbours, that I'm not going to strike. I reckon we *are* different. We're not like the miners or the railwaymen. If we go on strike the results will be far more serious than coal rationing or no trains. People's lives and businesses are at risk. Soldiers can't strike, can they? And I suppose that in peace time we're on the same footing as them. I'll be going in tonight as usual.'

She kissed his cheek and wiped her eyes. 'I'll get your breakfast, then you'd better get some sleep. What time will you have to be back?'

'By six o'clock, and by the look of you, you could do with some sleep yourself.'

'Thank God I'm off today. I don't think I could have stood it. I'd probably have murdered Sister Marsden if she'd looked sideways at me. I want to go and see Mam and your mam, then maybe I'll have a rest this afternoon. Nell's taking the girls to New Brighton, so it will be quiet.'

There was something different about Burlington Street, she thought, as she alighted from the tram. There was something different about the entire area. It seemed to be holding its breath, waiting. Front doors that were normally open, and more so in this heat, were firmly closed. There were no women on their doorsteps and no children playing in the street. She glanced fearfully at the boarded-up windows of her mother-in-law's shop, and had just crossed the road when three figures stepped out from Vauxhall Road. She drew her breath in sharply as she recognized Billy Hodge and the MacNamaras.

'Eh, Billy, it's the scuffer's judy!' Marty Mac jeered.

'I'm his wife!' Abbie snapped.

'An' where's 'e then? On strike, like the rest of them?'

They'd been drinking, she could smell it. She glared at them. She was afraid of them, but she wasn't going to show it. She was near enough to the shop to dash in if need be. 'No, he's not!'

'Is that right, girl?' Billy Hodge was mocking her. 'Shame that, eh, Marty? Might 'ave ter change our plans with that big feller on the loose.'

Abbie's eyes narrowed. 'What plans?'

'Now wouldn't that be tellin'? You just tell that bleedin' scuffer yer married to, to watch 'isself.'

'An' you too,' Marty Mac added.

'Get out of my way! Go on, sod off the lot of you before I call Mr Burgess and my da out here!'

'Oh, God, Billy lad, I'm terrified!' Fergal Mac cried theatrically, grabbing Billy Hodge's arm.

'Gerroff!' Billy shoved him hard and he fell against Abbie. She raised her foot and kicked him hard on the shin, and he yelled in earnest.

'Yer bitch! Yer bloody little bitch!'

'Clear off! Go on!' she yelled and was very relieved when they moved away.

'You wait! You bloody wait!' Fergal Mac yelled back as, limping, he and the others walked away.

She ran the short distance to Sal's house, her heart pounding. She took deep breaths before she went in. She didn't want Mam to get worried.

'Mam, it's deserted out there. It's so quiet.'

'How would I know what it's like, stuck up here? And it's like a flaming glass-house. It's too damned hot to be in bed,' Sal replied irritably.

'I know, I'm just praying it will get a bit cooler. I couldn't sleep at all last night.'

'Have you been to Hilda's?'

'No, I came here first.'

'So, what's he going to do then? Has he decided?'

'He's not going out on strike.'

Sal sucked in her breath. 'Yer da won't be very pleased about that. He says everyone should be in a union, and they should all stick together otherwise the bosses will walk all over you, and he's right. All the flaming bosses are interested in is their profits. They don't care if the men haven't got enough to keep body an' soul together. Look at the posh houses they live in, while we're stuck in these flaming hovels.'

'I know, and it was the union that got them their pay rise last year, but it's different for the Police, Mam.'

'Why? The Mayor an' Corporation are their bosses, and look what they've got. Their wives don't even know what a pawnshop is, never mind have to use one.'

'It's different because, if they all go out, do you know what will happen?'

'You'll be short of his wages.'

'He'll get the sack, he'll have no job. But it's not just that. There'll be rioting and looting.' She thought fearfully that that was no doubt what Billy Hodge had meant by 'plans'.

'Says who?' Sal demanded.

'Albert Owens, a copper with twenty years' service. He knows from experience.'

'That's not gospel truth. Who do we know down this street who'd go rioting and looting?'

'Well, there's that lot in number forty for a start, and there's plenty of others.' Again she thought of Billy Hodge and his mates.

'You're changing, girl, do you know that?'

'We all change, Mam, it's part of life.'

'You're getting like one of them.'

Her nerves were already on edge, and she lost her patience. 'Mam, will you stop all this "them" and "us" nonsense! You sound like Da. Mike was a soldier, that was a job, and now he's a copper, and that's a job too. He's not changed. I nursed in battlefields, now I nurse in a hospital. I'm doing a job and I've not changed. I don't want to hear any more of this rubbish. I want to ask you something.'

Sal's belligerent expression changed to one of curiosity. 'What?'

'I haven't been feeling well lately. I put it down to the heat and Sister flaming Marsden always getting at me. I never thought I'd see the day when I'd say I hated my job, but I do now, and it's all her fault.'

'Well, what do you expect from a bloody-minded spinster? Her work is all she's got in life, take that away and what's she left with – nothing.' Sal scrutinized her daughter closely, then a slow smile spread across her face. 'You're pregnant! I can see it in your face. There's always a certain something, a sort of pinched look around the nose.'

'That's what I thought. I haven't seen anything for two months either. I haven't told Mike yet, he's got enough on his plate.'

Sal instantly changed tack. 'All this worrying over strikes has got to stop now, girl. It can be a dangerous time, any shock, too much worry, and you can miscarry. Go and tell that Marsden woman to stick her job! You've got a more important one as a wife and mother, an' tell 'er that, too. Eh, wait until I tell yer da. I'm made up for you Abbie.'

Abbie thought of the shock she'd just had. 'Mam, don't tell anyone yet, at least give me time to tell Mike.'

Sal hugged her. 'All right, but don't go telling Hilda, or the whole street will know in half an hour.'

'Well, don't you go saying I told you first or there'll be trouble and then I'll get upset.' She managed a wry grin.

'That's different, I'm your mam. It's only right I should know,' Sal said with some satisfaction.

'But not before I've told my husband. So for heaven's sake, Mam, keep your mouth shut for at least a day or two.'

At twenty minutes to six Mike walked through the doors of Police Headquarters in Dale Street. All the way on the tram he'd been aware of curious and suspicious glances from the other passengers. He'd noticed that there were no police on point duty at busy road junctions, and the traffic was congested. Neither were there any on duty along County Road, Walton Road, Kirkdale Road or Scotland Road. When he entered the parade room, he realized why. The austere room was packed. It looked as though everyone who had not heeded the strike call was here.

Men were standing or sitting in groups, talking. He heard snatches of conversation. Some had been stopped by pickets, others had noticed that the shawlies and street urchins, always the testers of police strength, had been out in force. He caught sight of Albert Owens and made his way over to him.

'I thought you had to report to Lynch at Westminster Road?'

'I did. He sent me down here.'

'Who else is there?'

'Just Barnes.' Joe Barnes was another veteran of long standing and with a reputation second only to Owens'.

'They're obviously expecting trouble, although it was quiet on the way down here.'

'Too quiet, and why do you think they've got us packed in here like bloody sardines? Look around lad, there's not many old faces here. They're mainly like yourself, recruits.'

Mike glanced around. Owens was right, there were many faces he knew from training school.

'What's the latest?'

'There's nothing very clear. The London bobbies are out, I don't know about the other forces. Bootle and Birkenhead have refused to go out, although how long that will last is anyone's guess. I heard that a ferry full of pickets went over to Birkenhead to try and get them to come out. If you ask me, it's a bloody shambles. A strike's no use unless its "one out, all out".'

'That's what I heard, too.'

'Eh up, we've got a visitor.'

The room fell silent, Mike folded his arms across his chest like Owens, and waited. There was a shuffling at the other end of the room and then a small man, who appeared to be standing on a chair, looked over them and cleared his throat.

'Bloody hell, I've seen everything now. It's his Worship the Mayor in person. Things must really be bad,' Owens muttered.

The bespectacled little man, whose chain of office seemed to be something of an encumbrance, started his speech. It soon became clear to Mike and everyone else that this was no well rehearsed patter. The appeal for loyalty during this 'incredible crisis' sounded like the words of a much troubled man.

'The whole community relies on you, on your loyalty, the loyalty you've given freely of over the years, and on your sense of duty. The security of this great city depends on you,' he finished.

'Our loyalty's been paid for on the cheap and grudgingly over the years, too,' someone muttered from behind Mike, but the appeal did bring some applause and the Mayor climbed down from his rickety perch and hastily departed.

The buzz of conversation filled the room, and Albert Owens rocked back on his heels. 'Seems they underestimated the reaction to the strike call,' he remarked cynically. 'Looks like there's only us.'

Mike looked around, a sense of deep gravity dawning on him, and not only him. 'We can't do it! There's not enough of us.'

'I thought you were in the Army?'

'I was,' Mike replied sharply, stung by Owens' question and its implication. 'But how the hell can we keep the whole city under control?'

'God knows, but we'll have to try or it will be God help Liverpool.'

Before Mike could speak, an inspector called for silence.

'All training has been cancelled for the next few days, and no one is to leave the building. No one, understand? No nipping out to the pub for a quick one or nipping off home to see the missus. You're to be split into two groups, I'll post the names when I've finished. These groups are to be mobile, you won't be restricted to any particular area. You'll go wherever you're needed and do whatever is needed.' He paused. 'I repeat, you'll do whatever is needed. So for the moment you can stand down and deliberate on his Worship's speech.'

'Confined to barracks,' Mike said, thinking of Abbie. 'How long do you think we'll be here?'

'Who knows? Will she be worried, your wife?'

'She's bound to be, but she's not the hysterical type, she served in the VAD, and they often worked in the thick of it.'

Owens nodded. 'If you've got to worry at all, lad,

worry about yourself. They've just made us into the Flying Squad.' He sank down onto his haunches, his back against the wall. 'We might as well try and get a bit of rest, it's going to be a long night.'

Mike followed suit, but with a sickening feeling in the pit of his stomach, the feeling that had always been present before the order was given to 'go over the top'.

By ten o'clock the air in the parade room was thick with cigarette smoke, speculation and rumour. Two CID men had come in half an hour earlier to inform the inspector that larger than usual crowds were gathering around pubs on the dock estate. Reports came in of two incidents in Great Homer Street, but all the rest was rumour.

The men of the CID had unanimously refused the strike call and Mike, knowing a little of their work, thought they appeared to be a law unto themselves. From what he'd heard, they were ruthlessly efficient. They were all taciturn, burly men, detested by the criminal element and often disliked by their own uniformed colleagues for their methods, the rules they ignored, and their attitude towards those who had to adhere to the regulations and pound the beat.

Owens was puffing thoughtfully on his pipe and Mike was trying to think how he could get word to Abbie. God alone knew what rumours were flying around the city, and he prayed she wouldn't take it into her head to try to go to Burlington Street to see if everyone was safe and well. Another CID man came in, spoke hurriedly to the inspector, and departed.

Inspector Rigby called for silence. 'Group A into the van, smartish! The mob's on the move towards the Sandon Dock. There's cargo being unloaded there from America, and it's to go into the bonded warehouses. Make damned sure it gets there.'

Mike scrambled with the others into the motorized black Maria, known as the battle taxi. As it jolted and bounced over the cobbles, throwing them from side to side, he looked around with disbelief. There were only a dozen of them in all, including Inspector Rigby: twelve of them against hordes of God knows how many, so how the hell were they going to contain the mob?

Before he could voice his question, he was thrown violently against Joe Barnes as the van stopped. As he jumped out he could see that they'd come into the dock the back way, along Regent Road. The van was left under the iron columns supporting the overhead railway.

As they moved forward towards the heavy doors set in the high stone wall of the dock gate, he could hear the yells and jeers coming from the other side. Inspector Rigby lined them up and shouted something about arrests which was lost in the tumult. There wouldn't be many arrests, Mike thought, there must be hundreds of them out there.

Amidst the yells and howls of rage and derision he heard another sound, a dull thudding noise, and he realized that something was being used as a battering ram on the heavy doors.

While Rigby shouted through a hole in the gate at the crowd, Mike felt himself begin to tremble. It had nothing to do with fear. It was the reaction to the cacophony of noise. He'd always shaken like this before an offensive, it was the waiting that he always thought was as bad as the action that followed. He caught a glimpse of steel beneath the aperture of the massive hinges and then the sound of splintering wood.

'Bloody crowbars,' he muttered. The trembling had stopped but his mouth felt dry, and he gripped his truncheon so tightly that his knuckles were white. Quite unconsciously, he was not holding it straight out as the others were doing, but at the angle he'd held his rifle. The sound of wood being forced and rent grew louder, as did the noise from beyond the doors. It reached a crescendo as the gate began to give and finally fell inwards.

'Come in here and you'll be arrested! I'm giving you fair warning!' Rigby bellowed, but his words were lost in the ensuing shrieks and catcalls, and then those at the front of the mob surged forward.

Mike's apprehension turned to disgust. They were like a swarm of dock rats, the scum of the city's slums. They were drunk and brandishing axes, crowbars and stakes. There were women amongst them, drunken harridans with their hair streaming over their shoulders, and broken bottles and bricks in their hands. At the sight of the line of blue uniforms the mob fell silent for a second, surprised, expecting to see just two policemen, the usual number on duty at the dock gate. Then as Rigby roared 'Charge!' all hell let loose.

Mike couldn't remember the exact sequence of events, everything happened too quickly. It was lash out or go down. Forgotten were the rules of arrest and use of the truncheon, it was every man for himself, with odds of thirty to one. He saw a man, blood spilling from his stubbled head, go down like a pole-axed bull under the truncheon of an ex-soldier. He flailed about trying to avoid the iron bars and broken bottles. To raise his arms to protect his face would be useless and would be seen as an act of submission. No, it was strike out regardless. As he turned to dodge a blow aimed at his head an axe hurled past him, missing his cheek by a fraction of an inch, then burying itself in the cement between the stones of the dock wall. He felt a sharp pain in his leg and stumbled, but the fear of going down and being at the mercy of the boot brigade gave him strength, and he charged forward again.

The mêlée was breaking up and running, but he wasn't giving up. Scum, that's what they all were. Bloody scum! Cowards who derived their strength from looted whisky and sheer force of numbers. He'd risked his life for four bloody years for the likes of them. He was still laying about him at the fleeing crowd when the shrill, prolonged blasts of a whistle brought him to a halt and he turned to see Rigby blowing so hard he was red in the face. Slowly he and most of the others, who had been chasing the fleeing mob, made their way back.

'What the bloody hell do you think you're all playing at? Get these bastards cuffed.'

'Sore, surprised and bloody sorry now, aren't they?' The speaker was Albert Owens. One side of his face was masked in blood from a gash above his eye.

'You look sore yourself,' Mike replied, snapping the handcuffs on the dejected man held in the vice-like grip of Owens.

He spat out a tooth with a mouthful of blood. 'They said you lot were on strike. Bloody lyin' scuffers, all of yez.'

'You're looking to lose the rest of your teeth!' Owens growled.

'Yer lyin' bastards!' was the response.

'So file an official complaint!' Rigby yelled at him as he was bundled into the van.

'Not bad considering the odds, and the fact that we're mainly recruits,' Mike said to Owens as they both climbed back into the black Maria. His leg was starting to throb, and he was becoming aware of aches and pains all over his body.

'Don't think that's it, Burgess. This is just the beginning!' Rigby snapped. He, too, was smarting from cuts and bruises and loss of dignity. It was a long time since he'd had to do anything physical. He usually just issued the orders.

Chapter Ten

———•———

ON THEIR RETURN TO THE Garden they cleaned up their wounds as best they could. Mike used his handkerchief to tie up the gash in his leg caused by a broken bottle. Fortunately the thick serge of his uniform trousers had helped to lessen the injury. Owens and another man were sent, under protest, to the Royal Infirmary to have their wounds stitched.

They'd only just gone when the squad was called out again to the Bramley Moor Dock, and they sat in grim silence in the van, wondering what the odds would be this time.

On arrival, there was no sign of anyone. The dock was deserted. 'Word must have gone around that we're not all out,' he said to Joe Barnes as they climbed back into the van.

'But it won't take them long to realize there's only a few of us,' was the ominous reply.

'Do you think we'll get a break now?'

'Your guess is as good as mine.'

There was no respite. Within minutes of returning

they were called out again, but only six of their unit this time to supplement B Squad.

'Now what?' Mike asked of the sergeant who was a total stranger to him.

'Sturla's Department Store, Great Homer Street.'

Mike didn't answer, there had been no need for its location to be explained. This was his own neighbourhood, and his thoughts were for his mam and dad.

As they climbed out, ready to try to restore order, one by one they all fell silent. Mike shook his head in disbelief. He'd never seen anything like this in a city in peacetime. There was not a soul in sight, but Sturla's was a ruin and it had been thoroughly looted. Not only had all the stock gone, but in an orgy of destruction the mob had smashed light fittings, showcases, dummies, the carpet from the floor had gone, even the window frames and doors had been torn out and smashed. The place had been picked clean, and his boots crunched on broken glass, splintered wood and rubble.

'We only got the call ten minutes ago. For fast workers you can't beat them!' a voice said quietly, almost in awe.

The sergeant looked up and down the dark deserted street.

'House to house, Sarge?' Barnes asked laconically.

'What the hell for? No one will have seen or heard a bloody thing, they never do. Back in the van. You, Moore, stay here. The owner's been informed, he's on his way, poor sod.'

'What if they decide to come back, Sarge?' Constable Moore asked.

'What the hell for? There's only rubble left, and they can't eat, drink or flog that.'

It had shocked Mike more than any of the events of the night so far. The fairly small criminal element couldn't possibly have done something like that alone. There must have been hundreds of people looting. People from the neighbouring houses and streets. He couldn't believe that people he knew had behaved this way. Then he remembered Owens' remarks about those who would join in for the hell of it and those who had nothing taking advantage of the situation.

After midnight things quietened down and they were able to rest and eat. The sergeant went out and came back with food and jugs of beer, something totally unheard of before. Mike slept fitfully on the floor, exhausted like everyone else.

Next morning they were all sore and stiff and were in need of a wash and clean clothes; the latter was out of the question, but they all did get a wash. An office messenger boy who was passing, and who had loitered curiously by the door, was hauled in by Rigby, and messages were written out to wives and mothers. The lad was instructed to send them by telegram, all to be paid for by the City Corporation.

The day progressed quietly enough, but the two squads took it in turns to patrol through the city centre streets, to give local traders and store owners at least a semblance of security.

When Mike got back just after three, he was surprised to see a group of men in civilian clothes in the parade room, and was even more astonished to see Phil Chatterton amongst them.

Phil came over to him. 'Mike you look terrible.'

'Nice way to greet a mate, that is. What are you doing here?'

Phil pointed to the armband on the sleeve of his jacket. 'I've been sworn in as a Special, we all have. They couldn't keep me out this time.' He had been bitterly disappointed when he'd been turned down because of his age and lack of experience.

'You must be mad. Have you seen Sturla's or what's left of it?'

Phil nodded. 'Everyone's terrified. Your mam and dad have got the windows boarded up, and so have a lot of other shops. Your dad's got a four-foot bar of angle iron, he say's he'll use it too, if anyone comes near them. It's hard to believe it's happening.'

'It's hard to believe that it's people we know.'

'Not all of them.'

'I didn't say that, but it's not just the real hard cases.'

'I told you, some will join in for the hell of it, and there's others who've got mouths to feed, kids to clothe and no jobs and no money coming in,' Albert Owens interrupted.

Mike introduced him to Phil.

'Well, when this lot's over, they won't be so damned fussy about age or lack of experience, lad. They're going to have to recruit a whole new force, and none of them will have any bloody experience of a carry-on like this. You will, because you can bet your life they'll go on the rampage again tonight. They know now just how few of us there are.'

'Will they bring in the Army?' Mike asked.

'They'll have to, if they want the city to remain in one piece. It just can't go on and on night after night. Oh, you'll get plenty of experience tonight, lad.'

It was eight o'clock when they were called out. A full-scale riot was raging in London Road. It had started earlier in Scotland Road when the windows of Latarche's jewellers had been smashed; that had been the flashpoint. After that, every shop was a target. When the squad arrived it was to scenes of unparalleled drunken, mindless destruction.

'Take no prisoners! Break them up! Keep them on the move! Keep them away from Lime Street. If the bastards get down there it'll be the beginning of the end for the city!' Rigby ordered.

It was a frightening re-run of the previous night. At first the crowd scattered before the police charge, dropping their loot in the process. Then they became bolder. Cobbles were ripped up and hurled at the police. Twice Mike lost his helmet but managed to retrieve it, knowing that without it a blow from a flying brick or cobble would lay him out cold, and he knew he'd never get up again.

It was hopeless, he thought desperately. As soon as

they had broken up one crowd, another formed further up the road and they were exhausted from the repeated baton charges. Once he had caught sight of Phil, a wooden stave in his hand, grimly laying about him. He had neither the time nor the breath to call out to him. It was every man for himself.

By midnight, London Road was crowded with a seething mass of rampaging humanity. Not a single shop window had escaped. Acres of plate glass were ground to powder under the feet of the mob and the police, and still there was no end in sight. Mike knew that if they didn't contain the rioters and they spilled into William Brown Street and the city centre, then it would be God help Liverpool.

When, at last, the Army moved in two and a half hours later, he hardly had the strength to raise his truncheon. A cordon of steel-helmeted troops from the Notts and Derby Regiment and the Royal Welch Fusiliers advanced, in battle order, from the north and south of the area with bayonets fixed.

Mike couldn't even raise a cheer; he slid down into a doorway, battered, bruised and exhausted. Phil Chatterton sat beside him. His jacket was torn, his face streaked with dirt, sweat and dried blood.

'We've been stood down,' Phil gasped.

Mike could only nod, as an armoured car trundled past and then stopped. The stoning ceased, the noise abated as the turret lid opened and a figure emerged. Not a soldier but a much despised city magistrate.

He cleared his throat and began to read from a

card in a tremulous voice. ' "Our Sovereign Lord the King, chargeth and commandeth all persons being assembled, immediately to disperse themselves and peacefully to depart to their habitations or their—" '

The rest was drowned out by a spontaneous roar of rage.

'God Almighty, it's the Riot Act!' Mike gasped.

'They're not taking any notice.'

'They bloody well will when they start to shoot.'

A volley of missiles was hurled at the armoured car, but the soldiers moved forward, jabbing those nearest with the point of their bayonets, and none too gently, either. The mob began to fall back and then broke, disappearing down the warren of streets that led off London Road.

'Battle's over,' Mike said, dragging himself to his feet while Phil shook his head in disbelief. The street lights shone on the frosted glass that littered the whole area. Doors lay on the pavement along with blinds and shutters torn from shops. Everywhere there were scattered clothes, household goods, shoes and boots, rolls of carpet and dozens of rolls of material, all of which had been abandoned.

Albert Owens and Joe Barnes crossed the road towards them. Both their uniforms were torn and dirty, their faces grey with fatigue and spattered with blood.

'That's it for tonight anyway,' Owens said, while Joe Barnes helped Phil up.

'You gave a good account of yourself, Phil. You'll make a good copper and I'll tell Rigby so, too.' Owens grinned tiredly. 'There's a surprise for us in Lime Street.'

'What kind of a surprise?' Mike asked.

'Four tanks parked on St George's plateau and more soldiers on the way.'

'Tanks! Then it must really be over, apart from the clearing up.'

'Not according to a certain superintendent I heard talking to Rigby just now. They're sending down a battleship from Scappa Flow.'

Both Mike and Phil looked staggered. 'What for?' Mike finally asked.

'They sent a gunboat up the Liffey in nineteen sixteen. It blasted half of Dublin away.'

They had rounded the corner, and before them stretched the neo-classical buildings of William Brown Street and Lime Street. It was starting to get lighter, and the buildings at the heart of the city – the town hall, the cotton exchange, and, further on, the fine buildings on the waterfront – stood out in relief against a sky of soft pewter streaked with silver.

'They'd never do that to . . . to all this, surely?'

'They're not complete fools: They hope just the threat will be enough. HMS *Valiant* is on her way nevertheless. Right now I couldn't care if the whole damned fleet were on the way, all I want is a drink, a smoke and some sleep.'

Mike and Phil looked at each other wordlessly as they limped towards the van waiting to take them back to the Garden.

* * *

Abbie had been worried sick, quite literally, and as she'd retched miserably she remembered Sal's warnings. When the telegraph boy had knocked on her door it was as though that terrifying day of the war, the day Tommy had been wounded and both her brothers had died, had returned. She'd stood staring at the envelope, her hand shaking. Nell had also seen the boy and had rushed around.

'I . . . I can't open it, Nell. I just can't!'

Nell had taken it from her and torn open the envelope. 'It's not bad news, Abbie, it's not. It's from Mike. Here.'

Abbie had scanned the lines. Her first emotion was that of relief. Thank God he was safe, but then close on the heels of that came anxiety. 'Things must be bad, Nell, if they won't let them come home.'

'He'll be all right, he came through the war, didn't he? He's not likely to let a shower of bricks bother him,' Nell said firmly.

After that she had settled down to wait, going over to see Sam Casey in the pub at intervals, to see what news he had gleaned from his customers. There hadn't been much of it, and she'd wanted to go to Burlington Street to see if everyone was safe, but Sam and Nell had dissuaded her. It just wasn't safe, and Mike would be out of his mind with worry if he knew she'd even contemplated it.

As the evening wore on she got more and more nervous, thinking of the likes of Billy Hodge. One of

Sam's customers had got as far as St Anthony's Church on Scotland Road, before the tram driver had refused point blank to go any further. Then they heard there was wholesale rioting, looting and running battles along Scotland Road, London Road and the Dock Estate. When Sam finally put the towel over the bar, they'd heard that the Army was to be brought in.

'Go home and try and get some sleep, luv,' Sam had advised.

She had tried, but she only managed a few minutes at a time, or so it seemed. She'd drop off then wake with a start, remembering what was going on. Then the bells of St Mary's wakened her, and she sat bolt upright in bed, wide awake, the events of the previous night crystal clear in her mind. Well, she'd had enough of just sitting waiting at home, she was going to see what was going on.

When she reached the top of the stairs the nausea overtook her, and she half ran, half stumbled, as fast as she could to the scullery. The bout eventually passed, leaving her weary. She then turned her mind to practical matters. She got Mike's shaving things, some clean underwear, socks and a shirt and then began to make some sandwiches.

She'd just finished wrapping them in greaseproof paper when Nell came in, followed by the two little girls.

'Abbie, what are you doing?'

'I'm going down there, Nell. I can't stay here any longer. I'm like a cat on hot bricks. I just *have* to know what's going on. He must need a shave and some clean things, and I want to see Mam, too.'

Nell was horrified. 'You can't! No one even knows if the trams are running all the way into town.' She glared in the direction of the churchyard. 'Jesus, Mary and Joseph! I wish they'd give over with those damned bells, you can hardly hear yourself speak, and I thought they would have had more sense than to go ringing them today, when they know everyone's been up half the night.'

Abbie was determined. 'Then I'll walk.'

'Abbie, have you looked in a mirror? You look terrible.'

'Nell, I don't care, I just want to know that he's not hurt and that Mam is well. I've been so worried about them all, but particularly Mam, she can't stand shocks, not with her heart. Look, I'll be fine. Even if the whole of the city centre has been flattened it won't be any worse than the places I nursed in, in France. We often had to work with shells and moaning minnies flying everywhere, we wore tin hats and army coats and boots. Nothing can be as bad as that.'

Nell sighed. 'Oh, if you must, but make sure you get back here before evening. You won't be doing Mike any favours if he's got to worry about you getting caught up in a riot.'

The trams were running, but as they neared Kirkdale Road she was tempted to get off and go to Burlington Street first. It was far worse than she had expected, even though the corporation men had started to clear up. She didn't join in the shocked conversations that were going on around her. All she could think of was, if this is what they'd done to one of Liverpool's busiest roads, then what had they done to the men who had tried to stop them?

She got off in Dale Street and crossed over to Headquarters, becoming aware that there were other women, all carrying bags and bundles, going in the same direction. As they nodded wordlessly to each other their presence comforted her and gave her strength. Nothing was said, all signs of worry were hidden, but the shadows beneath all their eyes gave them away.

Inside the building there was some confusion as sons and husbands were enquired about. Edging her way through the crowd, she caught sight of Phil Chatterton. He looked terrible, in fact they all looked terrible – unshaven, dirty, bruised and battered. Then she heard Mike's voice and felt his arm around her.

'Abbie, you shouldn't have come.'

'Mike. I was so worried, I had to come. It . . . it's awful out there.' She wasn't going to add to his anxiety by telling him that Fergal Mac had threatened her.

'I know, but at least I wasn't dodging bullets or shells, just bricks, bottles and cobblestones.'

She was feeling much better now. 'Let me see to that cut on your forehead and clean up any other gashes and grazes before they get infected.'

'Still the efficient staff nurse,' he joked.

'Hold still. What's Phil doing here?'

'He came down to enlist as a Special, and gave a good account of himself, too. They should take him on now. They've sacked everyone else.'

'Have you heard anything about Mam or your dad?'

'No.' He didn't say that their safety was now his main worry. Burlington Street had been in the thick of it.

'I'm going to see them when I leave here.'

'Abbie, be careful, if there's any sign of trouble—'

'I'll go straight home, I promise. Do you know when you'll be able to come home?'

'No. None of us do.'

'But they've brought the Army in, I saw the tanks.'

'I know, and damned glad we were of them last night. I promise I'll be home as soon as I can.'

'I'll take your dirty clothes home, if there's anywhere where you can wash and get changed. Good grief, there's Bridie.'

They both turned and waved to Bridie Chatterton, who was looking very confused.

'Oh, am I glad to see you. Where's our Phil? Is he hurt?'

'He's over there, and no he's not hurt.' Mike called to Phil who came towards his stepmother, grinning.

'You can wipe that grin off your face meladdo, you've had us out of our minds with worry. Your da looks terrible, and I made him stay in bed. Are you sure you're not hurt?'

'I'm not, Aunty Bridie. I can take care of myself.'

'He can, too,' Mike agreed. 'He's certainly got the experience now.'

'I brought you some things.' She shoved a bundle into his arms and Abbie pulled her to one side as both men went to line up for a shave and a wash.

'Abbie, you look as bad as I feel.'

'Is Mam all right? Is everyone? Was there trouble?'

'As far as I know she's fine, and so are Hilda and Frank, Lizzie and Emily O'Brien and Winnie Harvey. But by all the holy saints, I've never known a night like it. Every damn shop has been wrecked and so has nearly every pub, too. Red was laying them out cold with a docker's hook, so he's managed to save something. Frank and Harry O'Brien kept them away with bars of angle iron. They'd cracked a few heads before those . . . those fiends finally got the message and moved on somewhere else.'

'Oh, dear God!'

'Now don't get all airyated, Abbie. Everyone just locked themselves in and shoved the furniture behind the doors and windows.' Bridie had never been so terrified in her entire life, but she didn't want to worry the girl. 'Mind you, Edward looked out after the crowd had passed and saw Mo Cowley staggering up the street, dead drunk and loaded down with stuff. Then Frank and Harry saw him and by, didn't they tear a strip off him. Can you credit it, Mo Cowley! And the times he's hammered away on the presbytery piano at all the do's we've had, and he wasn't on his own either.' Bridie was still outraged. 'Well, I just hope that when it's all over, the scuffers will get warrants to search and confiscate the bloody lot! There'll be a lot of people who won't be spoken to again, I can tell you, Abbie.'

Mike and Phil came back in time to catch the end of Bridie's speech.

'Like who?' Mike questioned.

'Like the flaming O'Sheas and the Hodges from the bottom end of the street, that's who.'

At the mention of the Hodges Abbie bit her lip to stop herself from crying out.

'Take Abbie back with you, will you, and stay together.'

'It's quiet now. Well, people are coming in to have a look at the mess.'

'I want you home before seven o'clock, Abbie.'

'I'll see she is, even if I have to take her myself,' Bridie said firmly.

When they were outside, Abbie clutched Bridie's arm. 'I've been worried about Billy Hodge.'

'Has he been bothering you?'

She nodded. 'I kicked Fergal Mac, and he and Marty Mac sort of threatened me.'

'Take no notice! That lot have never been known for their guts. Most of them spent the war running away. Oh, very good at frightening women and kids, an' they have to be in a gang to do it, too! On their own and against a feller they run a mile!'

'I suppose . . . well, I suppose I should have expected it – the abuse – Mike being a scuffer. I suppose it's something I'll have to get used to.'

Bridie didn't answer, she had no answer. She was surprised something like this hadn't happened sooner.

Abbie was appalled as they turned into Burlington Street. Women were already brushing up the glass and debris, men were repairing damaged doors and window frames. Frank, Hilda and Chrissie were all clearing up, both inside and outside the shop.

She hugged them all in turn. 'Thank God you're all safe!'

'These two are still a bit shaken,' Frank replied, 'but I wasn't going to turn everything we've worked for over to scum like that, and Red said he wasn't going down without a fight, either, and I suppose we've not done too badly. Have you seen the state of Rooney's?'

Abbie nodded.

'Is Michael all right? Have you seen him?' Hilda's face was grey with anxiety and shock.

'Yes, I've just been up there. Just a few scratches. I took him clean clothes, but he's no idea when he'll be home.' She caught sight of Joan with the yard brush, shovel and the dustbin, and, muttering an apology to her in-laws, dashed up the street to her sister.

Joan dropped the brush and hugged her. 'Oh, Abbie! I've been worried. I stayed here last night, I couldn't leave them. I don't know if I've even got a home of my own any more.'

'There was nothing going on in Everton, don't worry. There was nothing round my way either, but how is Mam?'

'She slept through most of it. I gave her nearly half

a bottle of whisky, not all at once. I couldn't think of anything else that would keep her calm.'

Abbie began to laugh. More from relief than mirth. 'Oh, Joan you're a case! I bet Da was furious that you didn't give it to him.'

Joan, too, burst out laughing. 'He was, he moaned all night. Now Mam's got a headache and she's livid that she missed it all, all the excitement, she's calling it!' Joan's laughter died. 'God help us, it was like a battlefield for hours, until the soldiers came charging down the street with rifles and bayonets. Thank God for them. I think that'll be the end of it now. Oh, they're very brave when they're the ones doing the belting, smashing and the throwing, but it's a different tale when the boot's on the other foot and it's rifles, bayonets and men who obey orders, even if they have to wound, maim or even kill. I heard they had to read the Riot Act.'

Abbie felt relief wash over her. Mam hadn't been scared to death, Frank and Hilda had saved their livelihood, and Mike was still in one piece and still had a job. Suddenly she gasped aloud.

'What's up now?' Joan cried.

'I've just remembered something, Joan.'

'What?'

'I should have been on duty at eight o'clock this morning! Well, that's done it now!'

'It's a good job Mike's still got a job, then, isn't it? Anyway you hated it. You'll soon get another job with your experience.'

Abbie suddenly remembered something else she'd forgotten. She hadn't even told Mike that he was going to be a father.

Chapter Eleven

———•———

ABBIE'S LETTER LAY ON the small writing desk that faced the long sash window, enabling Hannah to gaze out. A light covering of snow lay across the grounds and gardens of Ashenden, and it looked just like a Christmas card. Beyond the terraces, at the bottom of the sloping lawn, was the lake, frozen now. She could see the summer house and the boat house, and beyond them the small coppice of trees and shrubs, and the curve in the drive bordered by yew trees. Beyond all that, the distant tower of Ashenden village church was outlined against the December sky.

She would never forget the day she'd arrived here, she thought, chewing the end of her pen. To say that she'd been astounded and amazed was an understatement. When they'd driven up the drive, she had assumed they were in a narrow lane. Large oaks and horse chestnuts stood in groups at the edges of the paddocks where cattle grazed and sleek, thoroughbred horses had sought shade beneath the trees. Then she had caught a glimpse of the lake, the drive curved

163

again and the weathered grey stone walls of Ashenden had risen majestically before her.

She'd gaped at the gables and the profusion of tall, Tudor chimneys, the hundreds of leaded windows sparkling in the sunlight; the long, gravelled terraces and the old, half-ruined wall that enclosed the kitchen garden. She hadn't been able to utter a word when they'd driven through the archway and the ambulance had pulled up outside the imposing front entrance, where the line of uniformed figures standing on the steps awaited the arrival of their new master.

Once Lord Ashenden had been taken into the Hall and made comfortable, she'd been led by a young girl through a maze of corridors, through the enormous kitchens, and finally to a cramped, dark room opposite the back stairs. Its small mullioned window overlooked the courtyard at the back of the house, which was flanked on three sides by outbuildings: stables, storerooms and the estate offices.

When she'd unpacked, the girl Nora – an under housemaid apparently – had taken her through the green baize door into the main hall, with its sweeping staircase. She'd stared around her, daunted by the huge portraits in gilded frames of men and women in old-fashioned clothes.

'The picture gallery. All the old earls and countesses,' Nora had explained off-handedly with a sniff. She had taken on herself the role of guide, and pointed out the gun-room, the ruby drawing-room, the smoking-room, the morning-room, the small dining-room, the large dining-room, until they'd finally arrived, via that tortuous route, back at what were known as the terrace-rooms.

'Because they all face onto the terrace or open onto it. It's not what you'd call a very original name, is it?' Nora sniffed again.

This time Hannah had more time to take notice of her surroundings: the terrace-rooms that would become her place of work and his Lordship's exclusive domain, for they were all on the ground floor.

Hannah's first impressions of the drawing-room had been of a large, light airy sitting-room, with french windows that opened out onto the walled terrace. She was to discover that there was a bedroom, also opening onto the terrace, a bathroom and a small dining-room decorated in shades of green and cream. The suite of rooms resembled a house, bigger than any house she knew, yet it was only a tiny part of Ashenden. She was to discover that there were more than twenty rooms on the ground floor alone, and more than thirty on the second floor: bedrooms, staterooms, drawing-rooms and dining-rooms, many of which she'd never seen.

She hadn't considered the room allotted to her to be pokey, but it was rather on the dark side and smelled musty. She hadn't remained there for very long, though, for after a remark made by Freddie D'Arcy, she had been moved to this room.

It was his practice, when at home, to visit Mason in his pantry, and he'd met her coming out of her room.

They'd almost collided. It had been later that day when she'd been helping Lord Ashenden to bed that Freddie had commented on it.

'Poor Nurse Harvey. They've shoved her in a room at the back that I'm sure must resemble the black hole of Calcutta,' he'd said flippantly.

His brother had then asked her to explain exactly where her room was. The following day Mason had told her she was moving upstairs at the end of the week, to the second floor, to what had been a dressing-room and a store-room. They had hurriedly been converted into a sitting-room and bedroom.

Abbie wrote every week now that she'd left Walton Hospital. Hannah tried to see her for half an hour or so on her day off, but travelling took up so much time that there were always some things they'd not had time to discuss. Hannah thought how long ago August seemed now. The riots had gone on for three nights before the Army and ultimately the weather, in the form of torrential downpours, had finally brought them to a halt. Abbie was very well, she wrote, and looking forward to Christmas. Hannah wished she, too, could look forward with enthusiasm to the holiday.

She'd made no friends here; she'd been so daunted, so unsure of herself that she'd been afraid to. The staff seemed to number hundreds, and were presided over by Mason, the butler, and ultimately Lady Ashenden. Everything ran like clockwork.

She took her meals in her sitting-room, her laundry

was taken away and returned clean, starched and ironed. She had had to apologize, stammering, after she'd made her own bed and tidied up. The housemaid had pursed her lips and shaken her head with disapproval, before wrenching off the bedclothes and starting again. Her cheeks had burned with embarrassment. She was really only at ease when she was in the terrace-rooms with Richard Ashenden. The rest of the time she was nervous about making a social gaffe.

She'd been worried about Mam being on her own for Christmas, but Winnie had told her that she was going to Hilda Burgess's for the day, and she was quite content to do so.

'It's you I'm worried about, Hannah.'

'Why?'

'You don't mix, Hannah. You've no friends, you're the one who is going to be on your own, luv.'

'Oh, I'll be fine. Just give me a nice fire and a book and I'm happy,' she'd answered brightly, hiding her true feelings.

Richard Ashenden had told her she could go home for Boxing Day, but she'd refused. There was no public transport, no trams, no trains, and it would mean someone would have to drive her there, wait for her and then bring her back, and that wasn't fair. It meant that someone else wouldn't have a day off. He'd understood. She was always thinking of others, he'd mused. She didn't appear to have a selfish bone in her body.

Her deliberations were interrupted by a knock on

the door, and Mason entered. Hannah immediately felt agitated; the butler's composed and lofty manner always made her terribly nervous.

'Cook wishes to know if you will be taking Christmas lunch with us in the servant's hall, Nurse Harvey, or are you going home?'

Hannah fought down her panic. 'No. I mean yes, I'll be here.'

'It's quite informal. It is the one occasion in the year when we all relax together, so to speak. Of course the meal is at a later hour than the family's, and we are all officially on duty.'

'Thank you. I . . . I'll look forward to it.' Her heart had sunk like a stone. She was already dreading it. She was bound to make a fool of herself in some way, and they would all stare at her and no doubt laugh at her later. But she'd agreed now, and she really was going to have to do something about her nerves. Life couldn't go on like this. She was so weary of always being in a dilemma, always worrying about her words and actions. She drew on every ounce of courage she possessed.

'Mr Mason, can —'

'Yes?' he interrupted. She was terrified of him, he could see that. She looked like a frightened young rabbit in a trap.

Hannah was picking her words carefully. 'Mr Mason, do you have some time? I mean, can you stay while I ask you for help, advice?'

'Of course, Nurse Harvey.'

She twisted her hands together and fixed her gaze

on the flowered pattern on the carpet. 'I . . . realize that . . . my . . . position here is awkward.'

'Awkward, Nurse?'

She looked up at him pleadingly, all thoughts of a succinct and grammatically perfect explanation had fled. 'Oh, please, can you help me? I know a lot of people think I shouldn't even be here at all. Maybe they're right, but his Lordship insisted. I . . . I come from a very humble home in a poor area of Liverpool, and I just don't know how things are done correctly. I don't want to make a fool of myself, but more importantly, I don't want to let his Lordship down. Please, are there any books in the library that I could read that would help?'

'I don't think you will find anything like that in the library, Nurse.' He felt sorry for her. He was a Liverpudlian himself by birth, although it was many years since he'd lived there. She was a quiet, timid, unassuming girl. Quite often these private nurses were haughty, demanding, overbearing women, full of their own importance. She was obviously out of her depth, and wasn't afraid to say so, or to seek advice. He'd been with the family since before Lord Ashenden had been born; he'd been a footman then, but he was very fond of the young Earl. From what he'd seen and heard, this young girl was very efficient in her duties. Nor was she as inexperienced as he had first supposed her to be. He'd been informed of her war service. The Dowager Countess had instructed him to keep an eye on her.

'I'll try to explain things.'

'Thank you. I don't intend to try to be something I'm not, you understand? I just don't want to show anyone up, that's all.'

'I'm sure you don't, so I'll just outline some of the rules of etiquette for you. Maybe that will help you to adjust, settle in, if you like.'

For the first time in weeks she relaxed. She listened intently to his instructions on the correct forms of address, the somewhat feudal hierarchy of the staff, and a hundred other details, such as the relevance of the gong, that would make life at Ashenden more bearable for her.

'Will you enjoy your Christmas a little more now?' he asked kindly, when he'd finished.

'Oh, yes, thank you so much! You've been very kind. I still . . . prefer my own company. It's such a luxury, you see, to be able to read, to be able to learn. No one will mind, will they? I don't want anyone to think I'm unfriendly.'

'I'm sure no one will think like that at all, Nurse,' he replied. She was very sensible for someone so young. He just wished that some of the other young female members of the staff were as demure and decorous.

Before she left Lord Ashenden on Christmas Eve, she wished him a happy Christmas, and rather bashfully handed him a small parcel.

'I didn't expect this, Hannah.'

'It's not much. I didn't know what to get – you have everything.' She watched as he unwrapped the gift that she'd spent so long searching for on her last visit home. She'd bought it at Solly Indigo's pawnshop.

'It's a photo frame, but a very unusual one.' He examined it closely. 'It's mosaic, of the type usually found in Greece or southern Italy. It's quite exquisite. Expertly done.'

'I . . . I thought you might like it. I suppose with Liverpool being a sea port, lots of foreign things get into the shops.'

'I'll put that photograph in it.' He pointed to a small sepia portrait of himself and his brother Hubert that stood in a silver frame on his bedside table. She knew he was very fond of it. 'I was going to wait until tomorrow to give you your gift, Hannah. It's on the tallboy. Will you pass it to me, please?'

'Oh, you shouldn't have bothered to get me anything. I never expected . . .' She was flustered and a little embarrassed.

'Nonsense. Here you are. A happy Christmas, Hannah.'

Slowly she undid the coloured twine and took off the paper that covered the box, then as she opened the lid she gasped. 'They're beautiful! Oh, you shouldn't have, really. They . . . they're lovely.' She wished she had a better command of English: neither 'lovely' nor 'beautiful' were adequate. Inside the box, nestling in layers of tissue paper, were a hairbrush and hand mirror, the backs and handles of which were silver with a pattern of Acanthus leaves engraved on them. They were obviously expensive.

'Yes, I should. I'm very grateful to you. Not just for your nursing skills, but for the companionship, the friendship you give so freely, and without a thought of recompense.'

'But I like being here. For me, it's wonderful. I love to walk in the gardens and the grounds. Everything is so . . . beautiful,' she finished, wishing again that she could find a better description.

'Are things any better? Do you still spend much of your time alone?'

She looked startled. 'I . . . I didn't think—'

'Oh, nothing gets unnoticed here, Hannah. You think it does, but the walls have ears, and not only the walls.'

'Mr Mason has been very kind to me. He explained a lot of things. But, as I told him, I enjoy being alone. I love to read, and I have so much to learn about . . . everything.'

He smiled at her; her thirst for knowledge amazed him. 'But you will be having your Christmas lunch with everyone else?'

She suddenly saw his hand in the reason why Mason had come to see her himself, and had not delegated the task to one of his underlings. She smiled. 'Yes, I will.'

'Good, Christmas is a time to be with people.'

'My mother is going to her friend's house for the day, so I won't worry about her, but . . .' a frown creased her forehead.

'I know. There are people absent, their dear,

172

familiar faces missing, and we always remember them at Christmas.'

She nodded, thinking of Jerry. She knew his thoughts were of his brother and his father. 'At least your brother and sister are here.'

Her reference to the Honourable Freddie and Lady Angela D'Arcy didn't seem to please him. 'Yes. Angela won't stay long, though, she gets very bored here. Freddie will stay only until the January steeplechase is over.'

She placed the box on a chest of drawers. 'I'll get you into bed now, if you don't mind.'

'Yes, we have an early start tomorrow. Church, and then the gathering of friends and acquaintances.'

He sounded as though it were going to be something of an endurance test, she thought, as she folded the bedclothes over his legs.

He was thinking along the same lines. It would be the first time since his injury that he'd visited the Church of St Ambrose at Ashenden. There was a private chapel on the ground floor of the Hall, but at Christmas and on St George's Day, it was the custom for the family to attend St Ambrose's. He would be the object of everyone's pity, and he knew he would hate every minute, every well-meaning condolence, every enquiry after his health. Suddenly he reached out and caught her hand. 'I'm so glad you're staying here for the holiday, Hannah.'

'Thank you.' She knew she should withdraw her hand, but she didn't. His grip was strong and comforting in a way. 'I couldn't spoil someone else's day off. It would be very selfish of me.'

'You're very thoughtful and kind. Good night, Hannah.'

She slipped her fingers from beneath his. 'Good night, sleep well and don't get too upset tomorrow.'

She had gone with a few of the other servants to Church in the village. She hadn't joined the family party. Richard Ashenden had been pushed down the aisle by his brother, and she'd felt deeply sorry for him as she watched from the back pew. Heads turned, glances of pity were exchanged, looks of shock and curiosity had come over the faces of the parishioners. She'd returned on foot with Nora and Jessie, who'd kept up a running commentary on the fashions of the ladies of Ashenden village. It was a conversation she didn't take part in.

She had enjoyed her lunch. She'd felt very shy as Mason had indicated her place at the table.

'You sit with Jessie and me, Nurse Harvey,' Nora had said kindly. 'I'm starving. I thought they'd never get finished upstairs.'

'That's enough of that, Nora,' Mason chided.

Nora made a moue with her mouth. 'Oh, Mr Mason, you know what I mean. It seems like hours since their soup went up, doesn't it Jess?'

The level of noise dropped as the thick brown Windsor soup was eaten with relish.

'I thought you might have gone home for Christmas?' Jessie said companionably.

Hannah had glanced around the table at the friendly but curious faces. 'There's only Mam . . . my mother and me. She's gone to friends for the day.'

Mason was carving the enormous turkey and was fully occupied by the task.

'And of course you put your duty to his Lordship first, how commendable,' Bancroft, Lady Ashenden's maid said sweetly, too sweetly, shooting a sour glance at Cook.

Hannah blushed furiously.

'It *is* commendable, and what's even more commendable is that she had the chance to go home and refused because she wouldn't have you working on Christmas Day, Bert. Is that sufficient meat for you, Letitia?' Mason asked, thereby denying Bancroft any further comment.

'Spiteful old cow,' Nora muttered under her breath.

'I know, Mr Mason. I've already thanked her, haven't I?'

Hannah blushed again and nodded.

'And where is "home" Nurse Harvey?' Cook asked.

'Liverpool.'

'I know that, dear, whereabouts?'

'Burlington Street, off Scotland Road.' She stared at Cook steadily, wondering if the woman was being unkind, but the older woman just nodded as she passed the bowl of crispy golden roast potatoes to Letitia Bancroft who was sitting next to her.

'I was in the Army with a couple of lads from Scotland Road,' Henry said. 'Good blokes they were, too.'

'We heard you did your nursing in France, on the battlefields. Did you? Weren't you scared stiff?' Jessie asked.

'Jessie, it's Christmas. No one wants to be reminded about the war, not today,' Cook said firmly.

'I did, and I was scared stiff,' Hannah replied quietly as Henry passed her the tureen of sprouts.

All the female members of staff had glasses of sherry or Madeira wine and the men beer, whisky or port, and Mason looked around with satisfaction at the festive scene: the table groaning with food, the branches of holly and mistletoe that decorated the room, the flushed, eager, happy faces of the staff. Raising his glass of port, of which he was particularly fond, he smiled. 'Well then, I wish everyone here a very happy Christmas. Let's not leave this veritable banquet to go cold.' And so the merriment had begun.

She had been returning to her room, passing the large formal blue drawing-room, when she heard the sound of raised voices, and stopped at the foot of the main staircase. The doors were open slightly, and Richard and his brother Freddie were arguing.

'For God's sake, there isn't a limitless supply of money for your debts, Freddie! Why do you frequent these places? Why is it necessary to attend every race meeting in the country, no matter how small or insignificant, and get into debt with so many bookmakers?'

'I don't go to every one and it's not much, Richard, old chap. It's just a couple of hundred. Well, four to be exact.'

'Four hundred pounds, you owe four hundred pounds?'

'Guineas, to be precise.'

'And you've exhausted your allowance. You had an extra two hundred pounds last month.'

'It doesn't go very far. I have standards to keep up.'

'It should do. I can manage on far less.'

'Well, you don't have . . . er . . . an active lifestyle, do you?'

'You mean a cripple doesn't need much to exist on?'

Hannah winced at the words.

'No, I didn't mean that.'

'Oh yes you did.'

'Oh, stop it both of you.' Angela D'Arcy's bored voice cut in.

Hannah hadn't realized she'd even been in the room.

'And I've a few words to say to you about your extravagance.'

'Oh, Richard, must you be so tiresome, so petty-minded? It's Christmas, for heaven's sake. It's bad enough being stuck here in this ghastly pile as it is, without you lecturing me on economy.'

'What neither of you realize is how much debt there is. Father was too interested in breeding and racing his horses to be bothered about other things. He left too much, too many decisions, in the hands of others, some of whom are far from competent or honest. The upkeep of this "ghastly pile" as you call it costs a fortune in heating, lighting and repairs alone. Never mind anything else.'

'Then why don't you get rid of some of the servants?' Angela retorted. 'As there are only you and mother here, on a permanent basis, you don't need dozens of servants. You're much better now, you don't really need a nurse. That would be one wage less.'

Hannah stiffened and clutched the ornate bannister rail tightly.

'I need Hannah – Nurse Harvey, and I won't economize on the staff, Angela. You can't just throw people out of work like that. Most of them have been here for years. We have obligations.'

'Then for heaven's sake stop moaning about Freddie and me.'

'She's right, old man. It is Christmas. Season of good will and all that.'

'You can have the money this time, Freddie, but it's the last time I'm bailing you out. This irresponsible gambling has got to stop. You're going to have to be more prudent, and don't go complaining or begging to Mother, either.'

Hannah breathed deeply again and went upstairs, thinking how utterly selfish and callous Angela and Freddie D'Arcy were.

Chapter Twelve

———◆———

THE SNOW HAD GONE, but the weather had grown bitterly cold in January and even now, in late February, it was still freezing. All day a thick hoar frost covered the fields, hedges and gardens, barely thawing in the weak sunlight. Icicles hung like diamond pendants from the balconies of Ashenden Hall and the bare branches of the trees in the coppice and paddocks.

Huge open fires of logs burned in the hall, the ruby drawing-room, the small dining-room and the morning-room. Most of the rooms that were not in use were simply left without heat, and in many of the bathrooms the water in the pipes had frozen.

Hannah had a fire in her sitting-room, but had refused the offer of one in her bedroom. She remembered Richard Ashenden's words to his brother.

As she looked out over the frozen grounds, she longed for the warmer days of spring. The gravel on the curve of the drive caught the rays of the winter sun and gleamed like a ribbon of malachite.

She glanced again at the clock on the overmantle: half past one. Just ten minutes since she'd last looked at it. Any minute now her mother and Hilda Burgess would arrive at Ashenden for the first time, to take tea with her. It hadn't been her idea, and she was still rather dubious about it all.

She had mentioned, in passing, that it took quite a long time for her to get home to see Winnie on her day off. It was two miles to the station, three quarters of an hour by train into Exchange Station, and then a tram ride to Burlington Street.

'Why don't you ask her here for tea?' he had suggested.

She'd been astounded. 'Here?'

'Why not?'

'I couldn't! I couldn't impose, like that. People would think I was getting above myself.'

'It's not an imposition, Hannah, and as for "getting above" yourself, that's utter nonsense. I've never met anyone so reticent. It would be no trouble at all for someone to fetch her from the station and take her back again. It's certainly not going to cause a major disruption in the kitchen, now, is it?'

She hadn't replied, she'd been thinking of the comments that would be made beyond the green baize door.

'Are you ashamed of her, Hannah?' he'd asked quietly.

'No! No, of course not, but she might feel . . . uncomfortable.'

'Surely not in your sitting-room? Would it help if she brought a friend?'

'A friend?'

'For company. Didn't you tell me she'd spent Christmas with a friend?'

'Yes, but she still might feel overcome.'

'Your sitting-room can't be called ostentatious by any stretch of the imagination,' he urged.

Although he found it difficult to move about the house, one of her main duties was to push him from room to room, and he had insisted on seeing her new rooms. It had meant that Harold and Charles, the two footmen, supervised by Mason, had had to carry him in the Bath chair, up two flights of stairs and back down again, but he'd been resolute.

'Would they be able to stay just there? I mean, not have to go anywhere else?'

He'd smiled. 'Not if they don't want to.'

There had been no other reason to prevaricate.

She wandered around the room, plumping up a cushion, straightening one of the many small pictures that hung on the walls, moving one of the ornaments. They were not priceless heirlooms and, although the room was cheerful and cosy, lacking nothing in the way of comfort, it was far grander than any room at home.

She poked the fire that burned in the tiled grate, the flames reflected in the polished brass of the fender. She'd asked Henry to bring them up by the back stairs. She didn't want to put Mason to any trouble. She had asked Cook for just the usual sandwiches and small cakes that constituted her afternoon tea. She wanted nothing fancy, so there could be no complaints about people getting 'fancy notions'. She had in fact once heard Cook mutter those words under her breath. The comment hadn't been specifically directed at her, but she had assumed the worst and had been upset.

She looked at the clock again. They would be coming up that part of the drive that veered off to the left, then cut through the gap in the ruined wall to end near the stables. She wished the room overlooked the back of the house, she could have seen them arrive.

When she'd first mentioned it to Winnie, her mother had been dumbfounded, then horrified. It had taken a lot of persuading on her part to get Winnie to agree, and that only if Hilda would accompany her. She was glad now that he had suggested this, she hadn't liked the thought of her mother travelling back alone to Liverpool in the winter dusk.

A sharp rap on the door interrupted her thoughts, and Henry entered, followed by Winnie and Hilda.

'Thank you, Henry. It was very kind of you.'

He smiled at her. He often felt sorry for her. She had very little to do with any of them, but she was shy, not snooty, according to Nora and Jessie, and she was thoroughly nice.

'Mam, did you have a good journey?' she asked, taking their coats and noticing that they both wore their Sunday best.

'Aye, it's a fair way, though. No wonder you're tired when you get home and can only stay a couple of hours. Oh, this is very nice, Hannah,' Winnie said looking around with amazement.

Hilda's dark eyes had quickly taken in the good furniture, carpet and curtains. Not new, indeed the furniture looked well worn, but it was all good, solid stuff. There were some lovely bits of china, and a fancy gilt framed mirror over the fireplace.

'Come and see my bedroom,' Hannah urged, 'then we can settle down.'

'It's bigger than my two put together,' Winnie commented, although by the standards of Ashenden it was small. Again it was well furnished, comfortable and quite pretty, she thought, feeling the thickness of the towels on the wash-stand. Oh, yes, Hannah had more comforts here than at home and was more than well looked after.

Hilda peered out of the window. 'By, Hannah, that's a great view. Does all that belong to him?' she waved a hand indicating the grounds and fields that stretched as far as the eye could see.

'Yes. I couldn't take it all in at first, and the house is so big. There must be over eighty rooms. I haven't seen them all, and I still get lost.'

Winnie and Hilda both settled themselves in fireside chairs, and Hannah pulled a long settle stool up to the hearth so she could give them her attention.

'I've asked for tea at three o'clock, so you'll have plenty of time for the train back.'

'Hannah, you don't mean someone is going to have to bring it up all those stairs?'

'Mam, I couldn't go for it myself.'

'Why not?'

'It's not "done". Oh, there are so many things I've had to learn. So many things that are not "done".'

'You *are* happy here, luv?'

'Yes, of course I am. I spend my spare time either going for walks – the gardens are beautiful in summer – or reading in here. There's a kitchen garden, too, and the gardeners are friendly.'

'What about his Lordship?'

'He's coming along very well, Mrs Burgess. His speech is back to normal, and he has a little feeling in his right arm. Mr Copeland, the specialist, comes about every three weeks, but his right leg is paralysed and there's no chance he'll ever walk again. I don't really have much to do, not compared to being at home and nursing in Walton. I'll have even less soon.'

'Why?'

'He's having a special Bath chair made for him. It will have a motor, like a car. Then he won't need me or anyone else to push him around. He keeps busy. He often goes to the estate office to keep his eye on the managers. He says he's going to make the estate and the farms his life's work. I think his father left debts. I know most of the horses have been sold. There are only a couple of hunters left now, and the carriage horses. Lady Ashenden prefers the carriage, she says motor cars make her feel ill. Sometimes he still gets upset. He has headaches and nightmares and moods of depression, too. Not as often now, though.'

Hilda tutted sympathetically.

'What about his ma?' Winnie asked.

'Lady Ashenden. I don't see much of her, she goes out quite a lot, mainly in the afternoons. She pays calls on friends and she has her charities to supervise, when her health permits.'

Hilda sniffed. 'It must be nice to have time for all that, Winnie.'

'I suppose it's what you're brought up to Hilda. Have you seen much of the other two, Hannah?'

'I've only seen the Honourable Freddie twice, and Lady Angela has only been home once, at Christmas. She spends most of her time in London. There are other houses.'

'Is she the one our Chrissie sold some underwear to?'

Hannah nodded, smiling at the expression on Hilda's face and remembering her remarks about Angela D'Arcy.

'Hannah, I just can't get over you living like this.'

'I thought I'd never get used to it, Mam. I thought I'd never be able to cope, that I'd always be a bag of nerves. I was when I first came here, but I didn't tell you that. But I have coped, I'm happy here. It's lovely and it's so peaceful. I've learned so much. There are books in the library on everything under the sun.'

'Oh, I wish poor Jerry could see you now, Hannah. He'd be so proud of you.'

Hannah smiled sadly. 'I know, Mam. I'd never have come here, never gone anywhere or done anything, if it hadn't been for Jerry.'

The logs crackled in the fireplace and the clock ticked softly. They were the only sounds in the room for a few seconds, until Hilda thought it was time to dispel this air of despondency.

'Did you know that our Michael and Phil Chatterton are going to the town hall next month?'

'No. What for?'

'All those who didn't strike are to receive a special truncheon with a silver band around it – as a token of thanks for their loyalty. Mind you, Frank says they deserve a medal, never mind a fiddling bit of silver. We're all going: me, Frank, Chrissie, Bridie and Edward. Bridie said she's had a letter from Dee, wishing she could be there, too, and asking for photographs. Bridie said she'd not even thought about that. No one has a camera, or even knows anyone who has one, so unless there'll be an official photographer, there won't be any pictures to send to Dee.'

'That will be a great day out, but like Mr Burgess, I think they deserve a medal.'

'It's terrible the way they've treated the men who went on strike, though. A lot had ten or more years' service in. They've lost all their pensions, and can't even go over the doorstep of any police station.'

Hilda tutted. 'Well, just look at the damage there was, Winnie. Downright irresponsible, that's what they were. And it wasn't even over wages. They'd got a rise and improved conditions. It took the Army two days to quieten things down, and Frank says it wasn't them alone. He says that the fact that the heavens opened and it poured with rain for hours on end was what finally put the damper on the carry-on out of them.'

Their conversation was interrupted by the entrance of Nora with the tea-tray. No one spoke until she'd set it down on the low occasional table, then Hannah thanked her and said she could collect it at any time that suited her.

'Oh, Lord! Would you look at the china!' Winnie exclaimed, holding out a cup. 'It's so delicate I'm frightened I'll break it.'

'Mam, stop that. You'd be surprised just how strong china is. Jessie dropped a whole tray one day, at the top of the stairs, and only two saucers broke.' She poured the tea from the large china pot, thankful that the silver was only used for the family and their guests.

'What exactly do you do, Hannah?' Hilda enquired, making a note of everything, including the tiny cucumber sandwich, minus the crusts, that she was enjoying. It was only a mouthful, Frank wouldn't even have called it a sandwich. No, he'd call it a butty and show everyone up, she thought.

Hannah sighed. 'I get him up in the morning, he can manage to shave himself now. I give him his medication. We do the exercises Mr Copeland advised, although they don't achieve much. I take him to the study, or the estate office, or the drawing-room, or wherever he wants to go, then I come back here. He rings for me.' She indicated the bell above the door. 'Mr Mason or Charles come for me. After dinner – lunch they call it – I take him out for a walk if the weather's fine. Then I bring him back for tea. Sometimes he has people, visitors, so we don't go out. Then I help him change for dinner. After that he likes to read or listen to the gramophone. Then I get him ready for bed. He has a bell pull in his room, near the bed, if he needs me during the night.'

'It's not a lot really when it comes down to it, is it?'

'No, Mrs Burgess, that's what I mean. Anyone could push him around. Mason could get him up and help him at night, but he insists he needs me, and Mr Copeland agrees, in case there is an emergency.' She paused. 'There was one.'

'Really?'

'He got upset, it was one of his bad days. I could hear him cursing and swearing and then there was a crash. He'd got so annoyed, so frustrated with himself that he'd tried to get out of the chair and walk, and had fallen.'

'Did he hurt himself much?' Winnie asked.

'He caught his forehead on the corner of a table. It was a small gash, but I insisted the doctor come and see it. Oh, Mam, I feel so sorry for him sometimes. He just sits and stares out of the window. He used to ride horses, and play tennis and golf, and go boating on the lake. It's very hard for him now.'

'It's a crying shame, that's what it is,' Winnie agreed.

'But I try to cheer him up. At least he's alive. He can see, and there's nothing wrong with his lungs. A lot of the lads were gassed. He has all this and he'll never want for money or comfort or care. Last time I was home, I saw three ex-soldiers begging by the station. Young men. One was blind, the others had lost a limb each. When I told him about it he said it was wicked, it was criminal, that soldiers be reduced to that. He said there should be good pensions for those who'd put their lives at risk for their country.'

'He's right. It's not just at the station that you see them. There are men on the streets now selling matches, bootlaces. It's a disgrace. A land fit for heroes! It's flaming diabolical.'

'So, telling him how fortunate he is does sometimes help, but not all the time.'

'How long do you think you'll stay here, Hannah?'

'I don't know. Until he finally realizes he *can* do without me.'

'You'll have no trouble getting another job, not with the references you'll get from here. It's almost as good as working at Buckingham Palace. It's nearly as big, anyway.' Winnie had only ever seen pictures of the palace, she'd never been outside Liverpool in her life.

Hannah didn't reply. She didn't want to think about it. She knew the day would come, but she always pushed that thought to the back of her mind. 'Would you like to come for a walk? I can show you around the gardens. If we wrap up well and keep moving, it's not too cold.'

'We'd like that, wouldn't we Winnie?' Hilda urged. An opportunity like this was certainly not to be missed, despite the cold.

Hannah had donned coat, hat, gloves and a thick scarf, but, as they were about to leave, there was a knock on the door.

'That'll be Nora for the tray,' Hannah informed them, going to the door.

To her horror it was Mason, Charles and Richard Ashenden.

'Thank you, both, I'll only be a few minutes.' Richard dismissed his helpers.

Hannah was terribly flustered. 'I . . . I'm sorry . . .'

'No. I'm sorry for intruding. I wanted to meet your mother, Hannah. Is she leaving?'

'No. No, we were just going for a walk.'

'Then I won't detain you long. Wheel me in, please.'

Hilda and Winnie both stood as stiff as ramrods, and neither knew whether to bow, curtsey, speak or remain silent.

'Good afternoon, Mrs Harvey. It's a pleasure to meet you.'

'Thank you . . . Sir. It's . . . very kind of you to have . . . us . . . here.'

Hannah had partially regained her wits. 'And this is Mrs Burgess, my Lord. A close friend and neighbour.'

Hilda nodded and smiled.

'I'm sure you will feel more at ease in your mind now that you've ascertained that Hannah is comfortable.'

'Oh, yes, Sir. I mean, I knew she was, but it's nice to see for yourself.'

'I rely on her a great deal, and I'm certain that she has played no small part in my recovery.'

'I was . . . am . . . just doing my job,' Hannah replied, her cheeks still tinged with pink.

'Well, Ladies, I won't detain you from your outing. It has been a pleasure.'

Hannah duly opened the door and wheeled him out, leaving him with Mason and Charles in attendance. 'They won't be very pleased about that. They've had to carry him up and back down,' she said as she closed the door.

'He . . . he's very pleasant.'

'What did you expect, Mam?'

'Fancy that! I can't believe it! He came especially to see you, Winnie, and him a lord or whatever he is.' Hilda for once in her life was completely overcome.

'He's got very good manners. A very thoughtful young man, wanting me to see how she's treated here.'

'He's an earl, Mrs Burgess. One step down from a duke, but he does have good manners and he is thoughtful. I don't think there are many of the gentry like him.'

'He's been through a lot, Hannah, and something like that either makes or breaks a man. He was a real gentleman to start with, don't forget.'

'Not like most of the lot around our way,' Hilda added cuttingly.

Hannah said nothing as she led the way downstairs.

It had been very thoughtful of him, but she wished he hadn't done it. It would only cause eyebrows to be raised. All she wanted was a quiet life.

After she'd seen Winnie and Hilda safely into the car that was to take them to the station, she walked along the terrace and down into the sunken garden where, in summer, the roses bloomed in profusion. There was a rustic bench at the far end and she sat down on it, looking up at the grey stone walls of the Hall. She loved it here. It was like heaven on earth, especially in summer when all the flowers were in full bloom, and the sunlight sparkled on the surface of the lake, where the long, slender drooping branches of the willows dipped almost into the water. And she had spent so many happy hours in the small domed summer house.

She wished she could remain here for ever, but knew that was impossible. She wasn't indispensable. She'd seen him through the worst part of his suffering in the hard days and even harder nights. They were good friends, although she was very deferential and strictly polite to him in front of everyone. Only when they were alone, and there was no possibility of being overheard, did she drop the formal address. Even now she frequently called him 'Sir', and most of the time she tried to avoid using his Christian name at all. She was fond of him. In a way, in the latter days at Walton, she'd come to care for him and treat him as she had Jerry, like a brother. Since she'd been at Ashenden all that had changed. This was his home, he was more confident in this environment, whereas she still wasn't, and probably never would be. What she felt for him now was affection tinged with reserve. She sighed heavily and got up. Dusk was falling already and it was bitterly cold to sit for very long.

From the window of the dining-room of the terrace, Richard Ashenden watched her. A stranger seeing her, and come to that her mother, would never have guessed the terrible things that had happened in both their lives. He knew she was his rock, his support, even though most people didn't realize it. He supposed that those same people were saying her services could be dispensed with, but he knew otherwise.

She'd become so much a part of his life, a vital part. Hers had been the face he'd seen as he'd slipped in and out of consciousness, when he'd woken, shaking, sweating and screaming, from the nightmares. He had shared all the terrible experiences of his life with her. How could he possibly think of sending her away? No one understood him the way she did. No one understood how much he'd changed. She'd saved his sanity, something else they didn't realize. He couldn't envisage a life without her.

Chapter Thirteen

'**D**O I LOOK ALL RIGHT?' Abbie twisted and turned in front of the long mirror on the wardrobe door. The visit to the town hall for the presentation of awards, for loyalty and bravery during the strike, should have taken place earlier in the month, but had been postponed. Now it was the end of March, and she was due any day. She looked awful, she thought. What a time to have to go anywhere so important. She was the size of a house.

She wore a three-quarter-length coat in pale blue linen over a loose-fitting, cream-coloured dress. It looked like a tent, she thought, even though it did match her wide-brimmed hat, with its two huge cream roses. She'd wanted to look her best, but how could you when you couldn't even see your feet?

Mike grinned at her. 'You look wonderful, Mrs Burgess.'

She pouted. 'Oh, I just wish they could have had it when it was supposed to be, then I wouldn't look so big. What time is it?'

'Stop worrying about the time. Mam and Dad aren't here yet.'

'Why didn't you say we'd go up there?'

'Because I'm not dragging you all over Liverpool, that's why. We can all go together in the taxi cab.'

'Will we all fit in?'

'Of course we will. Chrissie's going with Phil and Mr and Mrs Chatterton.'

He didn't know whether he was glad about that or not. He knew Phil was highly delighted that Chrissie had agreed to it, and it would have been a terrible squash if she'd had to come with them, but he just hoped Chrissie wasn't leading Phil a dance. She had been out with him a couple of times lately, but he suspected that that was only because there was no one else on the horizon, and Mam let her stay out later when she was with Phil.

'Can we afford to go by taxi cab? I mean, do you think it will look—'

'What?' Mike interrupted her. 'I don't care how it looks, I'm not having you waiting about at tram stops in this cold wind, nor being bounced and thrown around all over the place. It's a special occasion, too. Are you sure you'll be warm enough?'

'Yes.' She smiled at him and patted his cheek. 'I'm having a baby, I'm not ill.'

The arrival of Hilda and Frank put a stop to any further discussion.

'Oh, don't you look great,' Abbie greeted her mother-in-law, who was wearing a new dark green coat and a black hat trimmed with dark green feathers.

Hilda patted the hat with satisfaction. 'Frank said I had to have something really smart. I got it in Blacklers. You look very well yourself, Abbie.'

'I look awful. I look like a balloon, that's how I look.'

'Oh, stop that! That colour suits you, it always has done, and look at the roses in your cheeks. This is a great day for us all.' Hilda removed an imaginary speck of dust from the shoulder of Mike's tunic. 'We're proud of you son. I think they should be giving you a medal, but never mind.'

'At least they're getting something out of that shower of skinflints,' Frank added, running his finger around the neck of the starched collar of his shirt.

'Frank, stop doing that! You'll get dirty marks all over it.'

'It's too tight.'

'Have the others gone?' Abbie intervened, pulling on her gloves.

'Chrissie went down to Bridie's when we left the house,' Hilda informed her. She was very pleased that now at last Chrissie seemed to have seen sense about Phil. He was everything she could want in a son-in-law and she'd said so to Frank.

'Right, there's the taxi. Mam, will you help Abbie in while I lock up?'

Out in the lane with Hilda fussing over her, Abbie waved to Nell, who was standing at her parlour window mouthing the words 'Good luck'.

Phil looked like a cat with a bowl of cream, Abbie thought, as they arrived outside the ornate building whose domed roof was crowned with the figure of Minerva. Chrissie wore a deep pink costume, the skirt of which was shorter than anything she'd had before, and which had caused an argument at home. Her dark hair was swept up and covered with a fetching hat that sported a huge pink bow.

Bridie greeted them, wearing her best coat and a new hat. 'Don't we all look the bees knees! Grand enough to take tea with the gentry.'

'Just stop that Bridie Chatterton! Just because we went to see Hannah and happened to be introduced to his Lordship, doesn't mean you can keep harping on it, making sarcastic comments like that.'

Abbie suppressed a grin. Hilda had been so full of it for weeks now that Sal had commented acidly that everyone would be having to bow and scrape to Hilda next, and she'd probably want a tiara for Christmas.

None of them had ever been inside the Town Hall and were quite staggered by the magnificence of its interior. There was a huge fireplace in the hallway and they stood close to the dancing flames, for the March wind was cold. After a few minutes they were ushered into a large room with deep sash windows that over-looked Exchange Flags. The room seemed full of policemen and their wives and families.

'Is there a chair or something she can sit on? If we're to be here for a while she can't stand,' Hilda hissed to Mike.

He looked around, but there didn't appear to be anything suitable.

'Oh, stop fussing over me. I'll be fine. I don't want anyone flapping and drawing attention to me.'

Hilda tutted, thinking it was very remiss of them not to have provided some sort of seating. God knows how long they were going to have to wait before the proceedings even started.

After twenty minutes, Abbie was thinking along the same lines. The ceremony had started about a quarter of an hour ago, but the Mayor seemed to be making a meal of it. Mike had already received his truncheon with the silver band inscribed '1st August 1919', but they were being called in alphabetical order and when the presentation was over, someone was bound to make a speech. She prayed it wouldn't be a long one.

When it was at last over and Chrissie was examining the official scroll of thanks that each man had been presented with, Abbie clutched Mike's arm tightly. 'Can we go home now, please?'

'What's the matter?'

'I . . . I've had a few pains.'

Hilda instantly took charge. 'All this standing about, that's what's done it. How bad is the pain?'

'It's gone now.'

'How long was there between each pain?' Bridie asked, remembering the hours she'd spent in agony having Elizabeth.

'I don't know. How long should there be?' Abbie

was becoming very apprehensive. Oh, she'd read all the books when she'd been training. She remembered Ginny, Bertie and Seb being born. She knew what was supposed to happen, but when it actually happened to yourself it was frightening.

'Never mind, let's get you home right away. Michael, go and get a taxi. Chrissie, alter your face, you look as though someone has shoved a dead rat under your nose. You and Phil take your da, our Michael and Mr Chatterton home and get them something to eat. Bridie and me will go with Abbie.'

Abbie gasped as a pain tore through her.

'All right, luv, just hang on to me. It'll pass,' Bridie said, gripping Abbie's arm tightly.

'Oh, in the name of God, what's our Michael doing? Why doesn't he get a move on? Does he want her to have it here on the Town Hall steps?'

'Hilda, it won't help anyone, you going off the deep end like that. He's coming back now.' Bridie pointed to Mike who was threading his way through the traffic in Dale Street.

The contraction had passed and Abbie breathed deeply, still clutching Bridie. 'Chrissie, will you go and tell Mam I've started?'

'And what good will that do? Sal will get all airyated. She might even create and make Joan bring her down to your house, and that won't do anyone any good at all.'

'Oh, I want my mam!' Abbie cried as she was once again gripped by pain.

'Holy Mother of God, Hilda, they're coming very quickly! We've got to get her home,' Bridie hissed.

'Chrissie, on second thoughts, you come with us. When it's all over you can go and tell Sal.'

Chrissie looked horrified but was bundled into the taxi before she could protest or argue.

'You lot can see to yourselves,' were Hilda's parting words as the cab pulled away rapidly, leaving Frank, Edward, Phil and Mike standing staring at it.

'Hoy! Wait! What about me?'

'Oh, you'd be no use, Mike. You'd have to wait in the parlour or the yard anyway, you might as well come home and wait until Chrissie gets back.'

'I can't wait that long! I'm going home. I'll sit in Nell's kitchen if I have to, but I want to be there.'

He did wait in Nell's kitchen, but Nell had gone next door to help Hilda, Bridie and the midwife, but he didn't wait alone, for Ben Hayes was home.

'I missed all this. I was away when each of my two were born.'

'You were lucky.' Mike walked up and down the small kitchen.

'That's not going to do any good. Sit down and have a smoke.'

Mike accepted the cigarette but resumed his pacing.

'I'll go over to the pub and get something in, to wet the baby's head.'

'No thanks, not for me. I'm on duty tonight.' Mike

stopped pacing. 'Do you think she'll have had it by then? I mean, I can't stay at home.'

'Of course she will. It doesn't take that long, so Nell says.'

'She started at the Town Hall, and Mam said the pains were quick, so why is it taking so long now?'

'I don't know, but she's in good hands.'

'Should I go for the doctor?'

'What for? If he's needed they'll come and tell us. There's no sense in adding to his bank balance when there's no need for it.'

Mike sat down at the table and rubbed his eyes. He was tired. He'd done a tour of nights and would still have been asleep but for the presentation.

As Chrissie appeared in the doorway he jumped to his feet.

'Oh, sit down! Mam sent me in to make you some tea.' She was very thankful for her release, for Abbie's screams terrified her.

'Thanks, but I don't want anything.'

'He's even refused a drop of the good stuff,' Ben said.

Chrissie looked without much interest at the dapper sandy-haired man in whose kitchen she stood, and thought with annoyance that Mam could have let her go home. She couldn't see much point in her being here at all, and these two were capable of making themselves a drink.

'Well, I'd better go and meet the girls from school. I don't see them very often, so I always treat them to sweets on the way home. You've got to spoil them a bit. I spoil Nell, too. I bought her a lovely fox fur stole with head, tail, legs – the lot – and an oil painting for the parlour. She's a brick is Nell, there's not many who would put up with being on their own for nine months at a time. Maybe there'll be some news by the time I get back.'

'What will you call it?' Chrissie asked her brother when they were alone.

Mike wasn't concentrating. 'What?'

'I said, what name will you give it?'

'Oh, Liam if it's a boy and Leah if it's a girl.'

'I've never heard that name before.'

'Which one?'

'Leah.'

'Oh, Abbie said Hannah Harvey knew someone or had read about someone called Leah. She liked it, it's different.'

Chrissie wondered whether her niece, if it was a girl, would like it. Of course you never got consulted about your name for obvious reasons, but she hated hers. Mam could have been a bit more adventurous. Even Sal Kerrigan had managed to come up with Abigail, Virginia and Sebastian. She would have liked Veronica or Helena.

They both sat in silence until Hilda opened the door, her eyes shining with pride. 'It's a boy! A fine healthy boy!'

Mike leapt to his feet. 'And Abbie? What about Abbie?'

'She's great. She's tired out but that's usual. Go on in and see her and your son.'

'Liam. Liam Burgess,' Chrissie said, smiling at her brother.

'And you, lady, put that kettle on. We're all parched. But first go and ask Nell where she keeps her cups, we can't go rooting through her cupboards without a by your leave. She's been a good help has that girl.'

'Well, she's had two herself,' Chrissie retorted.

'Aye, and not a sight nor sign of her husband home from sea for either of her confinements. Get a move-on Chrissie.'

Chapter Fourteen

SPRING HAD COME AT LAST. The trees, shrubs and hedgerows burst forth with new buds. Beneath the trees in the paddocks, the east wood and the coppice, the ground was carpeted with bluebells. Although she'd longed for the warmer days and had welcomed them, Hannah was miserable. He didn't need her now, the new motorized Bath chair had arrived, and they had been like two children with a new toy. Through the rooms and corridors and along the terraces they'd gone, laughing when he'd collided with doors and furniture until he'd got the hang of steering it.

'It's a bit like a car, Hannah!' he'd laughed.

'Then it's a good job they provide roads to drive on, or there would be chaos if everyone drove like you. Mind that table!' she'd replied, deftly removing the obstacle from his path.

Where there were flights of a few steps, a piece of board was placed over them. In fact, as he'd become more skilful in negotiating the doorways, the boards became permanent features. It was no hardship for everyone else to surmount the gentle slopes. The last time Mr Copeland had come to Ashenden he'd told Hannah in so many words that her services would no longer be required. There was nothing more he, she, or anyone else for that matter, could do now for Richard Ashenden. There were servants to help him, whenever they were needed, and there was talk of installing a lift at the back of the house, by the back stairs, which would enable him to get to the upper floors without having to be carried.

Hannah sat again on the bench in the sunken garden where the first new shoots had appeared on the rose bushes, and looked across at the house and grounds she'd come to love. What would she do now? Go home and then start to look for another job? Oh, she'd miss all this so much – but most of all she'd miss him.

Ever since Christmas her affection for him had grown. She was doing the very thing Abbie had warned her against. She was falling in love with him, and she couldn't help herself. That was what really hurt the most. Knowing she loved him and always would, and yet having to leave him. She wiped away her tears with the dab of cotton and lace that was a handkerchief. She must be mad. There was only one solution, one direction in her life she could take, and that was to leave. To maintain her dignity and self-respect, she must hand in her notice. The longer she stayed the worse it would be. She had to be resolute, she had to go and write the letter, every word of which would be a lie, and would cause her aching heart even more pain. But it was the only solution.

She got to her feet slowly, half-blinded by tears, and was half-way up the slope to the terrace before she saw him.

'Hannah, I was looking for you. What's wrong?'

'Oh, nothing. Just some dust in my eye, I think. I was going in to write you a letter, but maybe it's better if I speak to you.'

He looked at her with concern. 'Then let's go down into the rose garden. It's more sheltered, there's still a nip in the wind.'

She didn't reply, but followed him as he steered himself down the ramp and along the path to the bench she had just vacated.

'Sit down and tell me what's the matter. I know there's something troubling you.'

She swallowed hard. Oh, this was going to be so hard. She *had* to keep control of her voice, her tears, her emotions.

'I'm . . . I'm going to have to leave you. Mr Copeland said as much to me on his last visit. You don't need me any more now. You're fit and well. Mason and Henry and the others will be here if you need them.'

'I'll never be fit and well Hannah, you know that. And I don't want "the others".' Her words had come as a terrible shock. He couldn't imagine life at Ashenden without her. Mother had her own circle of friends, her own interests. Freddie paid occasional visits, Angela's were less frequent, but he had very little in common now with either of them. True, he could get around by himself and there was help on hand should he need it, but he couldn't let her go. He'd grown not only to rely on her, but to love her.

When he'd first realized that that was what he felt for her, it had shaken him profoundly. He'd fought a battle with reason and commonsense, but it was a battle neither of those faculties had won. Then he'd become morose, thinking there was no future for his love. How could anyone as lovely, as young, as full of compassion as she was, possibly love him? He was only half a man, a cripple, a burden. Someone who would be dependent on her for life. He was very loathe to tell her, ask her. He was afraid of rejection, but if he didn't speak now it would be too late. He realized she was crying and that hurt him deeply.

'Hannah, you don't have to go.'

'I . . . I love it here so much. The space and the sheer . . . loveliness of it all, but I have to go. I really do.'

His body was tense and he gripped the sides of the chair tightly. 'Does your mother need you at home?'

'No.'

'Then what is it, Hannah? Don't worry about saving me the cost of your wages. Angela spends more on hats in a year than you earn.'

'No, it's not that either.'

'Then what, for heaven's sake?'

'I can't tell you.'

He reached over and took her hand. 'Do you remember when you told me about your father and brother?'

She nodded.

'Can there be anything worse than that?'

'No. But I can't . . .' She looked up at him, her eyes swimming with tears.

What he saw in her eyes moved him profoundly. It was as though he'd been physically struck. 'Hannah! If you love me then stay. Please!'

She ducked her head, cursing herself. Why had she weakened? Why had she looked at him? She'd betrayed herself. He'd seen the love and the longing in her eyes.

'How . . . how can I?' she whispered.

'Because I love you. I think I've probably loved you for a long time, but never realized it until recently. I have so much time to think these days.' He longed to take her in his arms. He thought of the courage that had carried him through the war, when he'd been whole. He'd declared his love, but dare he ask her to marry him? He took her other hand in his. 'Will you marry me, Hannah?'

She gasped aloud. Her heart had leapt when he'd confessed he loved her, but this! 'I can't! I love you, I'll always love you, but I can't marry you.'

'Why not? Because I'm a cripple?'

'No! It has nothing to do with that. I don't even think of you as . . . as being crippled. I'm too far beneath you, socially. I'm just a common working-class girl. I didn't even have a very good education. I had to beg Mr Mason for advice—'

'None of that matters to me. You're a very uncommon girl. You have so many graces and wonderful attributes that I've never found in anyone else. Please, Hannah, I love you. I don't want to spend the rest of my life here without you.'

The tears were falling rapidly now and her heart was beating with odd little jerks. 'I couldn't cope.'

'You wouldn't have to. We'd lead a very quiet life, just you and me . . . together.'

'Her Ladyship . . . your mother . . .'

He could see she was weakening, and joy and determination filled him. He'd fight tooth and nail to keep her. He'd fight everyone, society, public opinion and convention to keep her at his side. 'Don't worry about Mother. Please, Hannah, say yes. You do love me?'

She nodded, she wished with all her heart to spend the rest of her life here with him, but she knew others would intrude, that was an inescapable fact.

She looked into his eyes and knew she couldn't deny him any longer. Suddenly a great tide of happiness surged through her. 'Yes, I'll marry you, Richard.' She slid down and knelt on the stone flags beside him.

He leaned towards her and lifting her chin he kissed her gently on the mouth. 'Oh, Hannah! I love you so much. I never expected to love anyone. I never expected to be loved, not the way I am.'

She touched his cheek. 'That doesn't matter to me.

To me, you're someone special. So kind and thoughtful and . . . loving.' She slipped her arms around his
neck and buried her face against his shoulder. 'Oh,
Richard, I do love you.'

When they finally went indoors she felt as though
she were walking on a cloud. He was insisting she go
home straight away and tell her mother. He didn't
want her to be here when he told his mother their
plans. He knew just what the Dowager Countess of
Ashenden's reaction would be.

He wasn't disappointed. She stared at him blankly for
a few seconds, shaking her head in disbelief.

'Richard! Richard, you can't . . . can't possibly be
thinking of doing something so, so crass, so utterly
stupid!'

'I don't see it like that, Mother.'

Honoria Ashenden struggled for words. 'She's . . .
she's . . .'

'Common? Yes, by birth she is, but no one, not
even you, can say she's been ill mannered, loud or
uncouth in any way while she's been here.'

'It's been her place to be well mannered and docile.'

'She's kind, sensitive, gentle, intelligent and she
understands me and what I've been through. I would
probably have been locked in an asylum by now, if it
hadn't been for her. I don't intend to subject you to a
great social occasion, a large formal ceremony. There
will be no announcements in the press, no engagement
party.'

Lady Ashenden shuddered at the mere thought of such things.

'We have discussed everything. She is quite content to live as she has been, very quietly and without any pomp. She has never mixed freely with the staff.'

His mother continued to shake her head, aghast. 'I don't believe I'm hearing this. Your father – your poor father—'

'Father is dead,' he interrupted. 'I have to live out the rest of my life in this damned chair, always dependent on people. Do you think it's a prospect that fills me with pleasure, Mother? I have little to look forward to. Left to face the future alone, I would probably degenerate into madness. I need Hannah and I love her.'

She could see further argument now was useless, and besides, she felt quite faint. 'You do realize that half the servants will leave rather than have her as mistress of Ashenden? Dear God, Richard, I think you must already have started to lose your mind for this is total lunacy! A nurse from . . . Liverpool as Countess of Ashenden!'

'Mother, the title means nothing to her. I don't think she even fully realizes what it does entail. She has no social ambitions whatever.'

'What am I going to tell Freddie and Angela?'

'I don't care, Mother. In fact you needn't tell them anything, I'll inform them.'

'Oh, Richard! Richard!'

'Mother, you'll get used to it. Even the hardest

things become acceptable in time. Hannah wants nothing to do with the running of the house or any social occasion that may arise. She views that entirely as your domain and prerogative.'

Lady Ashenden was unmoved, her attitude cold, her face set in harsh lines of fury and disapproval. 'That really makes no difference. I will never accept her, Richard. You'd better send for Mason and ask him to inform the staff and to be ready to contact the agency for replacements. I want nothing at all to do with it.' She rose and walked quickly to the door and slammed it behind her as she left.

He sighed heavily as he pulled the bell sash. This was exactly what he had feared and why he'd sent Hannah home.

'My Lord?' Mason was puzzled, although there was no outward expression of his feelings. He'd seen her Ladyship go upstairs with a grim, set look on her face. She was obviously furious about something.

'I'm afraid I have upset her Ladyship and I fear I might be going to upset you, too, Mason.'

Mason raised an eyebrow.

'You will be aware, because I know nothing escapes you, that I have become very fond of Nurse Harvey – Hannah. I have asked her to be my wife, and she has accepted.'

It took all Mason's years of training to keep his composure and not reel with shock.

'My mother expects that the entire staff will tender their resignations. Is that likely, Mason?'

Mason's emotions were in utter turmoil, although his facial expression had hardly changed.

'I . . . I . . . don't think so my Lord,' he managed at last. 'There will be . . . comment.'

'I expect there will.'

Below stairs would seethe with comment and gossip, Mason thought. It was a situation that would need a firm hand.

'Mason, you've known me from the day I was born. It was you who kept me amused with those tricks involving bits of coloured paper. You slipped me half a crown each time I went back to school. You taught me how to catch fish in the lake with a bit of string, a bent pin and a piece of bread. You covered up for so many of my scrapes and escapades – Hubert's too. You saw me off to war with a handshake and cheerful words when I went to join my regiment. It was you who welcomed me back here with more cheerful words. Well, the damned war left me like this, half a man, unable to pursue any of the pastimes I once enjoyed. With nothing left to look forward to in life except the running of the estate.' Mason had recovered a little. All his Lordship had said was true. He was indeed very fond of Richard Ashenden, and he could see just how little life did now hold for him. The girl was quiet, unassuming, thoughtful, but she was not well bred by any stretch of the imagination. He could well see why her Ladyship was so upset.

'She'll need help, Mason. Even though she won't have anything to do with the running of the house, that will still be my mother's function, there will be times when Hannah will get out of her depth. We intend to live very quietly, she shies away from all contact with Society as both Mother and I know it.'

Mason was thinking rapidly. He was much relieved and heartened by his Lordship's remarks. If the Dowager Countess was still going to be the chatelaine of Ashenden, and Hannah was going to live much as she had been doing since she came here, then it might not be too bad a situation to contend with. He did think highly of the girl. She had never once, by word or deed, upset or affronted anyone. 'The young . . . lady seems to take a very sensible attitude towards things.'

Richard breathed deeply, very relieved. Having won Mason over to his side, maybe the rest of the staff could be persuaded to accept Hannah too. There only remained Freddie and Angela to contend with, and he really didn't care what either of them thought. He held the purse strings, which was what counted most with those two.

Hannah found her mother entertaining Hilda, Abbie and baby Liam.

Winnie was surprised to see her. 'Hannah! What's wrong? You didn't tell me you were coming home.'

'I didn't know myself, Mam. I'm glad you're here Abbie.'

'Here, you hold him. You're his godmother.' Abbie smiled as she passed Hannah the baby.

'He's growing. Even in a couple of weeks I can see a difference.' Hannah sat down and gently rocked the baby in her arms. That was the one aspect of her future she hadn't thought about. Would she and Richard ever be able to have children?

'Well, we're all waiting,' Abbie said, her eyes full of laughter and curiosity.

'I'm going to be married.'

Three faces turned towards her, their expressions totally bemused, and Hannah handed Liam back to Abbie.

'Who to? You've never mentioned anyone ever.'

'I have, Abbie. Often.'

Winnie and Hilda were still looking baffled, but Abbie's eyes widened. 'Hannah, you don't mean? You're not going to . . . ?'

'Marry Lord Ashenden. I am, Abbie. I love him.'

Winnie was utterly speechless, and Hilda's mouth had dropped open.

'Hannah, how . . . how on earth will you manage?'

'We're going to live very quietly, there will be no fuss. His mother will take care of everything, and I'll have Richard to help me, to explain things, and Mason. He's a very kind man when you get to know him.'

'Oh, Hannah, I don't know what to say!'

'Mam, it would be nice if you said, "Congratulations. I hope you'll be very happy."'

Abbie unceremoniously dumped her son on his grandmother's lap and threw her arms around Hannah and hugged her. 'If anyone deserves to be happy, you both do. You've always put other people before yourself and he . . . well, he's been to hell and back.' Abbie suddenly began to laugh. Peal upon peal of mirth that filled the room, dispelling the stunned silence.

'What's so funny?' Hilda demanded.

'Oh, could you just picture Sister Marsden's face, Hannah! "Nurse Harvey, remove that bedpan at once!"' Abbie mimicked. '"I'm so sorry, Sister, to have to correct you, but it's my Lady now."' Abbie sank onto the sofa, suddenly serious. 'Hannah, Countess of Ashenden.'

The full impact of her words hit Winnie. 'Oh, my God! Hannah, what's got into you? You can't marry him! You can't! They're nobility, and your da was only a labourer really, on the tugs. Hannah, they'll never accept you, girl, not in a million years.'

'Mam, I don't care. I love him. I don't want anything to do with the way "they" live.'

Hilda too was shaking her head.

Abbie rallied round. 'Times have changed, Mrs Harvey.'

'No they haven't, Abbie, not that much! Oh, I know young girls are all working, having their hair cut and hitching up their skirts, but there are some things that will never change. Hannah, don't be upset if her Ladyship puts a stop to it and throws you out.'

'She can't do that, Mam. He's twenty-eight, he runs the whole estate, with help of course, but he is the one who deals with the financial side of things.'

'What about – well, the other side of things – the marriage bed?'

'Mam, I don't know. We . . . we've not spoken about . . . that, but it doesn't bother me, though, really.'

Winnie and Hilda exchanged glances and Abbie looked worried. 'It might well do in time, Hannah,' Hilda said quietly.

Abbie decided that this subject was one that had nothing to do with anyone except Hannah and Richard Ashenden. 'Oh, for heaven's sake, let's look on the bright side of things,' she urged, smiling at Hannah. She'd meant what she said. Hannah Harvey had had a rotten life so far, she deserved something better.

'Look on the bright side of what?' Chrissie asked. She'd arrived unannounced and unexpectedly. No one had seen her come in.

'What's up with you? Why are you even home at this time of day?'

'I've got a terrible headache and I feel sick, so she sent me home. Da said to come and get you, he can't find the aspirin or that kaolin stuff.'

Hilda passed the baby back to Abbie and rose. 'Get yourself home. I don't want you spreading germs near Liam. That's all we need, the poor little mite catching something nasty from you.'

Abbie thought this was a bit harsh. Chrissie didn't look at all well, but she supposed Hilda did have a point. 'I don't think he'll come to any harm, Chrissie.

It sounds like migraine. Just sleep. That's all you can do for it.'

'Put a damp cloth soaked in vinegar on her forehead, Hilda, I always found that worked well for really bad headaches.'

At the thought of the smell of vinegar, Chrissie went even paler.

Hilda turned to Hannah. 'Congratulations, Hannah, I hope everything goes well, I really do mean that, luv.'

Hannah smiled, but Chrissie looked puzzled.

'What for?' she asked. Despite what appeared to be sledgehammer blows inside her skull, Chrissie hadn't lost her consuming curiosity.

'Hannah's going to marry Lord Ashenden. She'll be a countess, isn't that something?'

Chrissie swayed and leaned heavily against the door for support. Hannah Harvey a countess! God, didn't that beat all. And didn't she have all the luck.

'You'd better get her home, Hilda, she looks as if she's going to pass out,' Winnie urged.

Hannah took her mother's hand. 'And there's no one like your mam when there's a crisis.'

Mike walked along Walton Lane at regulation pace, his hands behind his back. It was a fine spring day and he glanced into Stanley Park as he passed, noting the unfurling new green leaves on the trees and shrubs. For a city with such desperate slums, it had many fine parks. It was lunch time, the shops were closing, business was winding down. Housewives were on their way home, the morning's shopping and gossiping over and done with. He felt a bit peckish himself, but it would be another hour before his shift ended.

He was enjoying the job. There was always something going on, sometimes challenging and sometimes run-of-the-mill. He grinned to himself; in a city of this size, with such a diversity of races and creeds, eight miles of docks and no less than one thousand five hundred and sixty-one licensed premises, it was never dull. The fact that four hundred and sixty children had street trading licenses saddened him. Kids shouldn't have to roam the streets at all hours, trying to earn money.

As he approached the junction of Fountains Road, he glanced briefly at a man bent over a motor cycle. He'd pulled it into the kerb, out of the way of oncoming traffic and was fiddling with the spokes of the front wheel. This part of Fountains Road was narrower and less busy than it was further up at its junction at Walton Road. His gaze remained on the figure; surely there was something familiar about it? He never knew why at this moment he looked away and into the branch of the Liverpool Trustees Savings Bank on the corner. Instinct, premonition or just a sheer fluke. But he did recognize the figure inside, and he saw the looks of terror on the faces of the cashiers. He wrenched open the door and hurled himself at Billy Hodge who staggered, lost his balance and fell sprawling on the floor. Only then did he see the service revolver Hodge had been holding. It clattered noisily across the floor and was picked up by the branch manager, ashen-faced but in control of himself.

Hodge was stunned, and Mike snapped on the handcuffs; as he did so, he remembered the man and the motor cycle. Marty MacNamara!

'Keep him here!' he yelled at the manager as he dashed back into the street. There was no sign of MacNamara. He should have known he wouldn't hang around. He was long gone. Mike cursed himself for a fool. If he'd taken more interest, looked more closely, acted more promptly, he'd have had them both, and that would have eased his mind considerably. He went back into the bank and relieved the manager of the gun.

'On your feet, Hodge, while I read you your rights!'

Billy Hodge had gathered his wits. 'Gerroff youz! Don't yer touch me, yer effin' turncoat! 'E lived in the same street as me, went to the same school, an' I wouldn't trust 'im with that gun, mister!' Hodge's remarks were directed to the manager and were uttered in a tone of menace.

Mike ignored him and addressed the older man. 'Would you phone Westminster Road Station, Sir, and tell them the situation?'

'Right. Fine. Miss Mayberry, I think we all need a strong cup of tea, if you can manage it?'

The thin-faced and obviously badly shaken female clerk nodded and disappeared through a door with a frosted glass panel.

'You're looking at a long time inside this time, Billy. Marty will be halfway to Birkenhead by now. He didn't hang around waiting for you.'

'Marty who? I dunno no Marty.'

'Suit yourself.' Mike knew there was no evidence against Marty Mac, and obviously Billy wasn't going to admit his mate had been in on anything – yet. 'I'd say you're looking at twelve years' penal servitude. Armed robbery, very serious. I had a revolver like this in the Army. I gave it them back, I'd had enough of guns. Where did you get this one Billy? Kept it? Bought it?'

'Mind yer own effin' business, turncoat!'

'Any more language like that in front of ladies and decent people, and I'll forget all about the rules and regulations for the treatment and restraint of prisoners.'

'I'll 'ave you, Burgess! I'll bleedin' well get you, one way or the other!'

Mike ignored the outburst. Billy Hodge was going to be out of action for quite a while. He felt a bit shaken and he was hungry, but it would be hours now before he got off duty.

Chapter Fifteen

———◆———

LADY ASHENDEN HAD REFUSED to see Hannah, or even to discuss the situation with Richard, until Angela and Freddie arrived home. She had asked for tea to be served on the lawn, the weather was fine and there was far less chance of being overheard by the servants. She was fully aware that voices were going to be raised, her own included, and she wanted no gossiping below stairs that this family discourse had degenerated into a common shouting match.

She presided over the teapot, but remained silent until Mason, Charles and Henry had disappeared along the path by the kitchen garden.

'Well, Richard, are you going to tell them or shall I?'

'I'll tell them.'

'Tell us what? Why all the bally rush and secrecy?' Freddie demanded, annoyed that his plans had been disrupted.

Angela examined her cream leather shoes, to see if the damp grass had marked them. She was even more annoyed than Freddie at being summoned home, having to miss a very lavish birthday party.

'I'm going to marry Hannah, and before you both get hysterical and start breaking the china, nothing, *nothing* is going to make me change my mind. You can argue until you've no breath left, but that's my avowed intention. There will be no formal announcement and only a simple ceremony. We intend to live very quietly here. Mother will, in fact, remain as chatelaine.'

No one spoke at all, and the silence began to lengthen until Lady Ashenden, fiddling impatiently with a silver teaspoon, took it on herself to speak.

'Won't you even consider a period of engagement?' Given time, she might well be able to wear him down, she thought.

Richard pondered her suggestion, thinking that at least she was prepared now to talk about it, which was an improvement. 'I don't know. Perhaps Hannah would like some time.'

'Oh, for heaven's sake let's get it over and done with, and the sooner the better!' Angela snapped. He was mad. Totally, utterly mad, but that was his affair. His plan had given her a valid excuse to avoid the duty visits home after the ghastly wedding ceremony was over. It would suit her very well just to come home once or twice a year. If it wasn't going to be announced, then very few people would know including, most importantly, the people who mattered to her. 'I suppose it's too much to ask that it be kept a total secret?'

'Worried in case your friends drop you, Angela?' Richard's tone was biting.

She didn't answer him.

'Well, have you been struck dumb, Freddie?'

He had been, but the main thought occupying his stunned mind was, would they have children? Would he ever inherit Ashenden and its wealth? He had never thought about it until recently. As a younger son, it had never been a viable proposition. But with Hubert dead and Richard so crippled and so parsimonious, he'd begun to think more and more about it as a possibility. Now it looked as if those hopes would be dashed; but he wasn't going to betray that.

He shrugged. 'It's your life.'

'Exactly. It *is* my life. It's my decision. I would, of course, like you to attend the ceremony, but if you don't, I won't lose much sleep over it.'

Lady Ashenden gazed first at her youngest son and then at her daughter. She had not thought she could be capable of such anger. She wanted to shake them both, to yell at them that they were not taking this shocking state of affairs seriously enough. That they had made no effort at all to support her views, or even try to persuade Richard to change his mind. Freddie in particular didn't seem to give a damn.

'Then I'll leave you to enjoy your tea. I have some appointments.'

They all watched in silence as he steered towards the pathway.

Lady Ashenden poured herself another cup of tea

and wished she had some brandy near at hand. She knew Freddie always carried a flask, but she wasn't going to ask him to oblige her. 'I am appalled, utterly appalled by your behaviour! By your utter lack of concern for me, my position, your positions . . . or Ashenden.'

Angela did care about her position, and she was seething. 'Really, Mother! You could have written and told us, or even telephoned. Now people are going to ask why I had to drop everything and dash up here. What was the grave family crisis all about, they'll ask. What lies am I expected to tell them? He's determined to marry her and you know what he's like when he's made his mind up about something. He's just like Father. There's absolutely nothing we can do except try to keep it quiet. He'll regret it, I'm certain, but . . .' she shrugged.

'Angela!'

'What? Oh, get it over with, Mother! Install them in the terrace rooms and forget about them. The place is big enough for you not to have to see her – them – if you don't want to.'

Her mother's hand was shaking as she replaced her cup on its saucer.

Freddie finally spoke. 'Do you think they'll have children?'

His mother dropped her head into her hands. 'Don't! Don't! I can't bear to even think—'

'Oh, of course, now I understand why you've been so quiet! If they can, you'll never get your hands on

225

the Ashenden money, will you, Freddie?'

Freddie stood up and glared at his sister. 'Shut up, Angela! You'll not do very well out of such a situation, either. I'd be more generous with you than Richard, so just concentrate what little brains you have on that fact!'

Angela flung down her napkin. 'Oh, you're insufferable, Freddie! I've had enough of all this! I'm going back to London. I hope Bancroft hasn't unpacked my cases yet.'

Lady Ashenden felt as though the very ground beneath her feet was moving and crumbling. They were both insensitive, selfish monsters. How had she ever managed to bring up such dreadful offspring! She automatically drew herself up and steadied her nerves as she saw Mason approaching. She would retire to her rooms and ask him to send Bancroft up with lavender water and her laudanum.

It was no longer fitting or necessary for Hannah to travel by public transport. She had wanted to go to see Abbie, and was prepared to take the train, but Richard had insisted Roscoe take her.

'But it means he'll have to wait all afternoon,' she'd protested.

He'd smiled gently. 'Hannah, that's part of his job. Something he's paid to do.'

'I'll feel as though I'll have to hurry up.'

'Then stop feeling like that. What else would he be doing? Mother hates the car, and I've got Mr

Baldwin, the new rural property agent, coming at two thirty.'

So she'd agreed. She had to admit that it was far more comfortable than the train and the tram, and she leaned back against the leather upholstery and enjoyed the view of fields and hedgerows and finally the groups of houses that then merged to become the suburbs of the city.

When they reached Abbie's house and Roscoe had opened the car door for her, she turned and thanked him.

'If there is something you would like to do, or somewhere you want to go Roscoe, I shan't mind.'

Herbert Roscoe knew better than to go traipsing all over the place, wasting his Lordship's petrol, but he wouldn't mind a quick half pint of beer. 'I'll stay here. But if you don't mind, Miss, I wouldn't mind something to drink.' He nodded in the direction of The Beehive.

'Of course.'

'Don't go thinking I'll have too much, Miss. Just a half is my limit when I'm on duty. Mr Freddie doesn't mind and I dare say his Lordship won't either, but—'

'Then we won't tell him. I think you deserve some refreshment, it's a long drive.' She knew it was impossible to ask him in for a cup of tea, and he would have been horrified had she done so.

Abbie came out to greet her. 'You'll have people flocking from miles around just to see the car, Hannah. Is he leaving it there?'

'He's just going for a drink. It seems such a waste to drag him all this way and have to wait for me.'

'Well, that's what life will be like now. Take your hat off, sit down and tell me everything. But first of all let me see your ring.'

Hannah held out her left hand for inspection. On the third finger she wore the ring she had chosen herself from a collection that had been Richard's grandmother's, rings which Lady Ashenden had spurned. The Dowager Countess had never seen eye to eye with her mother-in-law, for her husband's mother had made it very clear that she considered only the daughter of a duke or an earl to be suitable for Aleric, not the Honourable Miss Honoria Parker-Graham.

Hannah had picked the least ostentatious ring, but it was still very expensive. It was shaped like a teardrop, the centre stone a flawless emerald surrounded by eleven diamonds.

'Oh, Hannah, it's gorgeous! It must be worth a fortune.'

'It probably is. It frightens me when I think about it. What if I lost it? I had seven rings to choose from, Abbie, and some of them were so heavy, I felt my hand was being weighed down, and the diamonds were so big and bright that they would blind you. This was the prettiest and the least showy.'

'If I'd have had a choice like that, I'd have picked the biggest and the flashiest, just to annoy Chrissie and dazzle Hilda, Mam and everyone else. But that's me, you've never been pushy.'

Hannah settled herself in an armchair with the baby on her lap. 'I can't say everyone is overjoyed. Her Ladyship hasn't spoken a word to me, and Bancroft gives me looks that would kill you stone dead. Cook kicked up a bit, so Nora informed me, but Mason has firmly quashed any speculation and gossip.'

'Oh, Lord. What happened?'

'Nothing. Nothing at all. Nora said she for one was delighted for me, but I think part of that is because Bancroft is very put out. She doesn't like Bancroft one bit.'

'I can't say I blame her, from the sound of it she's a madam and a half. So when is it to be?'

'At the end of May, in the private chapel. The vicar from St Ambrose's will marry us. It's usual for a bishop to officiate at an Ashenden wedding, but Lord Ashenden said if I wanted the vicar, he wouldn't mind. He's being so considerate, Abbie. He says that despite everything, he wants it to be the happiest day of my life.'

'So who will you ask?'

'Mr Burgess is going to give me away. Then there's Mam and Hilda. Freddie has agreed, very grudgingly, to be best man, and I was wondering if you'd be my matron of honour?'

'Oh, Hannah, are you really sure about that? I mean, won't his sister want to be the bridesmaid?'

'I don't even know if she's coming. No, I want you, Abbie, you're my closest friend.'

'Will we always be friends? I mean our lives are

so . . . different now. I can't just call in to see you the way I would if you lived in an ordinary house in Liverpool.'

'Abbie, you'll be welcome at any time. I'm not going to change, and you'll always be my friend. We've shared so much together.'

Abbie smiled. 'So what will you wear?'

'That's what's been worrying me. I don't want a formal wedding dress with a train, or a headdress and veil. I think it would look overdone.'

'You're entitled to wear both, and I bet there's a few tiaras where that ring came from.'

'I don't know and I don't care. I don't want anything like that. I thought of a dress in satin, maybe. Pale pink or pale blue with a matching hat and just a small bouquet. Lord Ashenden has given me money – a monthly allowance he calls it – that will pay for my clothes, and that's what is worrying me.'

'It's worrying you! Nearly every girl in this city would give their right hand for something like that.'

Hannah sighed. 'I know. What I mean is, I've never been in any of the better shops in town, those in Bold Street or the Bon Marché or George Henry Lee, they were always far too grand and far too expensive for me. I don't know how to go about it. I can "charge" things apparently.'

Abbie looked perplexed. She had no idea how such shopping was done either. 'I hate to have to say this, Hannah, I really do, but there's only one person I know who can give us advice about that.'

'Who?'

Abbie pulled a face. 'Chrissie. She works in that posh shop in Bold Street. She'll know how things are done.'

It was Hannah's turn to pull a face.

Abbie laughed at her. 'I know, isn't it awful? She'll go giving herself all kinds of airs and graces, she'll be insufferable, but we don't know anyone else. I suppose you wouldn't consider asking her Ladyship?'

'I wouldn't ask her the time of day.'

'Then we're stuck with Chrissie.'

'I suppose, seeing as she's going to have to come with us and advise me, she'll have to come to the wedding. I was bothered that because Mr and Mrs Burgess are coming, and you and Mike, that it seemed very rude to leave her out.'

'You've got a point. Oh, I wish Dee were here. She would know all about things, she had a nanny and servants when she was young, she'd be bound to remember. We could write to her and ask.'

Hannah shook her head. 'There's no time. I have to buy new clothes, I've nothing suitable. Lord Ashenden won't hear of me wearing my nurse's uniform now.'

'I'll ask Chrissie. Well, I'll ask Hilda to ask her. I'm going up to see them later on. Mam complains I don't take Liam up to see her often enough, and it's because I moved away from Scotland Road, you know what she's like. Shall we say a particular day, as Chrissie will have to ask for time off work. I can't see that being a problem, not when she explains why. That Clara Unsworth sounds a bigger snob than Chrissie.'

'What about Tuesday, will that suit you?'

'Oh, any day will suit me. Hilda or our Joan will mind Liam if Mike's working. Yes, I think Tuesday will be fine, they can't be that busy in Lingerie de Paris early in the week, if ever they are rushed off their feet.'

'Then I'll collect you about ten on Tuesday.'

'I'll tell Chrissie to be here. You don't want the whole of Burlington Street out gawping at you. Now let's have a cup of tea. I'm afraid I haven't got any china cups, but—'

'Oh, stop that Abbie Burgess! You sound like your mother-in-law!'

'Oh, God forbid!' Abbie cried, throwing up her hands in mock horror.

By the time Abbie got to Burlington Street it was half past four. Mike was on nights and she'd left him a note to follow her up to his mother's. Hilda liked nothing more than what she called 'a family meal', which gave her yet another opportunity to spoil her grandson. Liam had a crib at Hilda's too.

'It's very good of Hannah to ask me to give her away, it's a privilege and an honour really, but I am dubious about it,' Frank revealed, chewing thoughtfully on a piece of liver.

'It's only going to be in a small chapel with a few friends and even fewer relations. What's so awful about that? When our Chrissie gets married you'll have to walk her up the aisle of Our Lady's with the church packed out with friends and neighbours.'

'I know, but this will be so different. For a start, I haven't been inside a Protestant church, except for Abe Harvey's funeral.'

'Neither has anyone else, and I wouldn't class that room as a church. It was like a drill hall, not a flower or a candle in sight.' Hilda pursed her lips with annoyance. He was being offered the experience of a lifetime, an honour, and he was turning up his nose and getting cold feet. Well, she'd have a few words with him later. She'd soon put a stop to him being 'dubious'. 'Who exactly is going, Abbie?' she asked.

'Both of you, Mike and I, Joan's going to mind Liam for me. Chrissie. His Lordship, his brother and I think his sister has finally agreed to condescend to come. Her Ladyship and her sister, Lady Julia something-or-other who lives in London, and that's all.'

This was the first Chrissie had heard of her being included and she stared, open-mouthed, at Abbie.

'Chrissie shut your mouth, luv. You look like a dead haddock on a fishmonger's slab,' Hilda instructed.

'She's asking me? I'm . . . I'm going, too?'

'She wants you to help her choose some clothes as well, and apparently they pay for things differently. You "charge" it, whatever that means.'

'You establish an account with the shop, you "charge" whatever you buy to it. We send you a bill at the end of each month, and then you pay it. Mind you, there's some who have to be virtually threatened with the bailiffs before they cough up.'

'It's not that different to putting things on the slate, is it?' Abbie commented.

'Except that it's respectable and the way things have been done for years. Hardly anyone pays cash on the nail, although Lady Angela D'Arcy did when she bought those slips. I suppose all her accounts are at shops in London.'

'You can ask Miss Unsworth for Tuesday off. Hannah is picking us up in the car at our house at ten o'clock. Make sure you wear your best coat and hat and gloves. Everyone decent wears gloves,' Abbie stressed.

Chrissie glared at her. She didn't need reminding about such things, but she said nothing. She pushed her meal away, her mind was in a whirl, she was far too excited to eat now. She was being asked to go and help Hannah shop, choose her wedding outfit. It was almost as good as being able to shop in the exclusive stores for clothes for herself, and wouldn't it get right up Miss Unsworth's nose. She'd make sure Hannah bought her new underclothes at Lingerie de Paris. And then there was the wedding itself. Not much of a 'do' according to Abbie's description of the plans, but one not to be missed. Her mind was racing ahead. She'd managed to save some money, and she knew exactly what she was going to do with it.

Abbie and Chrissie were both waiting, decked out in their finery, when Hannah duly arrived.

'Chrissie says it's best to visit one of the dress-makers in Bold Street and order your dress,' Abbie informed Hannah as they were driven towards town.

'It's more exclusive,' Chrissie added.

'It's more expensive, I would think,' Abbie muttered *sotto voce*, mindful of Roscoe.

'Cripps, Bacon's and Sloan's are very good for other things, dresses, blouses, jackets and coats. Millicent and Company for millinery, and of course Lingerie de Paris for underclothes.' Chrissie whispered the latter, glancing cautiously at Roscoe's back.

Abbie raised her eyes to heaven. She'd known it. She'd just known it. This was going to be Chrissie's moment of triumph over Clara Unsworth.

'Then you can have something to eat in Lyons or the Chester Rooms, if you prefer.'

'What are the Chester Rooms like?' Abbie asked.

'Posh.' Chrissie mouthed the word.

'Lyons,' Hannah stated firmly.

'What's all this "You can have something"?' Abbie asked. 'Aren't you coming with us?'

'I want to do some shopping myself. It's my day off, remember. I had to take it today instead of tomorrow. I won't get another one this week. I want to look for something for the wedding.'

'Chrissie, it's not supposed to be a shopping trip for you.'

'No, she's right, Abbie. It is her day off and she's entitled to some time to herself.'

'You never change, Hannah. Always putting other people first.'

When both Hannah and Abbie were exhausted and the boot of the car was full to bursting, they both sank down at a corner table in Lyons Tea Shop and asked for the menu. Chrissie had duly disappeared, promising to be back in an hour.

'Oh, Abbie, I'm frightened to even think how much I've spent. Some of the prices – how can they justify them? I know seamstresses and milliners get paid buttons compared to what the shop actually charges.'

'I know. It doesn't seem fair, does it?' Abbie sighed. 'That oyster-coloured corded silk dress with the lace was beautiful, though.'

'I wasn't going to waste fifteen guineas on a dress. It's more than a lot of people earn in a year. It was extortion.'

'Still, what you've ordered will look just as gorgeous.' Hannah had chosen a very pale blue duchess satin for her dress. She had clung tenaciously to a traditional style, but had been persuaded to have the skirt six inches above her ankles. It was cut very plainly, the only decoration being bands of white lace set into the sleeves and skirt. The hat she had chosen was white silk trimmed with pale blue ribbon bows and braid. White silk stockings, white gloves and unadorned white leather pumps with an hour-glass heel, completed the ensemble.

As she sipped her tea she thought of the dresses,

blouses and skirts, shoes and stockings, gloves and underwear she'd purchased. By Angela D'Arcy's standards it probably wasn't much, but to her it was sheer extravagance.

'I wish you'd let me buy you a frock.'

'Oh, Hannah, don't start again. I've got my wedding outfit, it's very smart and it's only been worn twice. I don't go anywhere to wear anything as fancy as all the dresses we looked at. You bought me the hat, that's enough – at that price, too.' Abbie's own wedding outfit hadn't been the traditional white with a train. She'd been a war bride, and it had been difficult to get things.

'Would you like some more tea? We can get a fresh pot.'

'No, thanks.' Abbie had eased her aching feet out of her shoes and was now praying she could get them back in, when Chrissie arrived and made her way over to them.

'Oh, my God! Your mam is going to kill you Chrissie Burgess!' Abbie cried, too taken aback to lower her voice.

'Hush! I don't care. I'm not going to look a frump beside Lady Angela.' Chrissie's thick dark locks had been cut into a short bob, over which she wore a raspberry pink cloche hat adorned with a huge rosette of navy blue ribbon. She also had a large box under her arm with the name 'Lewis's' emblazoned across it.

'I dread to even ask what's in the box.'

'If you must know, Abbie, it's a dress. It matches the

hat, and it's in the new fashion, with a short skirt and a dropped waist with a sash of navy blue ribbon around it.'

'You'll be murdered, Chrissie, you will. I'm not joking.'

'I don't care!'

Abbie shrugged. It was done now, though Hilda would undoubtedly create a terrible fuss, and might even make Chrissie take the dress back. But there was nothing to be done about her hair.

'Oh, Chrissie, you had such lovely hair.'

'But it was so old-fashioned, Hannah. Now it's . . . it's so light. You wouldn't believe how much better, how great it feels, and they said it won't take hours to do, just a quick flick with the hairbrush. I'll have to keep going back about every six weeks to get it trimmed, so it will keep its shape.'

'Now I've got over the shock a bit, I have to say it suits you, Chrissie. Yes, I definitely think it suits you. I suppose we'll all end up with short hair, although Mike would have a fit if I so much as mentioned having mine cut.'

'Oh, I must be terribly staid then because I'll never have mine cut, it's too boyish, unfeminine. Not that it makes you look like that,' Hannah hastily added, seeing Chrissie's expression change. She didn't want to upset the girl, she had been very helpful, she would have been lost without her, and she did have good taste. But in her opinion, Chrissie's hair had been her most attractive feature.

'I suppose we'd better be getting back. I told Roscoe to go and have something to eat, and that we'd be back at the car for two thirty. I promised I'd be back no later than four.' Hannah gathered up her bag and gloves.

'Are you coming home with me, Abbie?' Chrissie asked, feeling far less confident or defiant now.

'I am not. I've got a husband and baby to see to, I've been off gallivanting for too long as it is. And I certainly don't want to be dragged into a row and maybe even be blamed for letting you out of my sight. No, you can go and face your mam on your own.'

'Never mind, Chrissie. She just might like it, you never know. After all, we're both getting used to it,' Hannah said encouragingly, although she doubted that Hilda would agree.

Chapter Sixteen

———◆———

THE CHAPEL AT ASHENDEN faced East, and the May morning sunlight streamed in through the stained glass window depicting the Virgin and Child. Prisms of red, blue, green and gold light fell on the small group of people gathered inside.

At the altar rails Hannah stood beside Richard, her eyes glowing with love and happiness. She had been so nervous as she dressed earlier that morning. Her hands had been shaking as she'd tried to do up the row of small buttons on her dress, and Nora had finally completed the task. Abbie had had to secure her hat with a pearl-topped pin, but her nerves had disappeared as soon as she'd seen him waiting, smiling at her, as she'd taken Frank's arm and walked up the short aisle. She had told Richard she would prefer 'Guide Me Thou Divine Redeemer' to the traditional entrance music. It was one of Winnie's favourite hymns.

Winnie, Mike, Hilda and Chrissie stood in the pews on the left hand side of the chapel. Lady Angela,

Lady Ashenden and her sister, Lady Julia Fitzmaurice, in the pews on the right. From the staff, only Mason and Bancroft were present, and Letitia Bancroft had made it quite plain to both Mason and Lady Ashenden that she was only going out of deference to her mistress.

Winnie was so proud and so happy that her eyes had been misted with tears nearly all morning. Hannah had insisted that she buy her outfit from Cripps. She had argued that it was a shocking waste of money, the prices were sheer daylight robbery, but Hannah had been firm.

'Mam, I'm not having any of them looking further down their noses at us,' had been the reply. So the amber wool suit with the russet velvet trim, and the amber and russet hat, had been purchased and packed, and Hannah had said she could match anyone for style and cut now. It was a triumph of good taste.

She was still feeling very nervous when Lord Ashenden had welcomed her, but now, as she watched Hannah looking so serene, so dignified and so happy, she had to dab her eyes again. Oh, never in a million years could she have foreseen anything like this for Hannah, her once timid and cowed daughter. Today she was glad, actually glad, that Abe was dead. She knew it was wicked, but she was thankful that Jerry had found enough strength to lift that poker. He'd done it for Hannah and for herself, because now life for them both held nothing but good fortune.

Hilda had glanced quickly around before fixing her

eyes on the vicar, a pleasant-looking, middle-aged man. She was very surprised how like a Catholic chapel it was. Of course there were no Stations of the Cross, no statues of the Virgin, the Sacred Heart or any of the saints, but there were flowers and candles. The altar clothes were richly embroidered, there was a tabernacle and a sanctuary lamp, even a small confessional box. She pondered these facts and came to the conclusion that the Church of England seemed to operate a class system. The higher your status in life, the more trappings of the Church of Rome you were entitled to. Of course she'd only heard what Protestant churches were like.

She then turned her thoughts to the luncheon that was to follow the ceremony: it was going to be very fraught indeed. Her Ladyship's face was set in lines of disapproval, as was that of her sister, Lady Julia, a stout woman with iron-grey hair, whose features resembled those of a horse, Hilda thought unkindly. Lady Angela looked bored and irritable, and was fidgeting with her gloves.

There was a moment of heart-stopping tension when the vicar had uttered the words 'If any man can shew any just cause, why they may not lawfully be joined together, let him now speak, or else hereafter forever hold his peace.'

Abbie had glanced surreptitiously at Lady Ashenden and then Freddie, and had uttered a short prayer. The moment passed, with those on the bride's side of the chapel breathing a sigh of relief. Hannah's voice was quiet but steady as she repeated the words of the marriage vows.

Freddie was thinking bitterly that if only he'd been able to find some legal objection, he could have stopped this misalliance. Still, it might not be a physical marriage. Richard might not be able to consummate it. It was a recurring thought, and it comforted him a little, but there was no way he could voice that speculation, except to Angela.

Chrissie wasn't taking any notice at all of the proceedings. After first, like her mother, noting all the details of the chapel, her gaze had alighted on Angela D'Arcy; Chrissie was priding herself on her foresight, for her clothes were as smart, if not as expensive, as those of Lord Ashenden's sister. In fact, she thought her appearance was, if anything, superior. Angela had a 'washed-out' kind of beauty, as her mam would put it. She had forgotten the row there had been when she'd returned home with her new hairstyle and outfit. She'd ignored most of what her mam had said anyway. She was twenty, not sixteen.

Angela D'Arcy wore a royal blue wool crêpe dress with a short pleated skirt, long sleeves and a V-neckline. A matching hat, its narrow brim edged with black satin ribbon, covered her hair. She hadn't wanted to come at all, but Aunt Julia had insisted she support her mother through this débâcle. Grudgingly, she had to admit that Hannah looked well. Certainly not very fashionable, but not gaudy, or tasteless. So did the girl who was her matron of honour. The other girl with the short dark hair, wearing a pink-and-navy dress seemed vaguely familiar. She was dressed in the height of fashion. Not expensive, definitely not haute couture, but very stylish. There was to be a cold collation, a buffet of sorts, after the ceremony. It promised to be a ghastly affair and she was wondering how soon she could escape and go back to London. She knew Aunt Julia would stay for at least two days with her mother, but she had no intention of remaining that long. As she watched Hannah bend down and kiss Richard on the cheek, she realized it was over.

Hannah's eyes had filled with tears of happiness as she kissed him. Nothing mattered now, not her Ladyship's barely concealed disapproval and coldness of manner, nor Freddie and Angela's chagrin, nor the open hostility of Letitia Bancroft. She loved Richard and she loved Ashenden, and the years ahead stretched like a beautiful dream come true. It came as a shock when Mr Rowles, the vicar, said, 'Congratulations your Ladyship', and she realized that now she was no longer Hannah Harvey. She was the Countess of Ashenden.

The buffet was laid out in the small dining-room, and it had been Angela's idea. 'They are the latest thing now, Mother, for informal receptions. There's no need to sit down and dine together.' Lady Ashenden had been very relieved, for the thought of a full meal had appalled her. She had no wish to sit at table with these people. In fact, had it not been extremely rude and hurtful to Richard, she would have gone straight to her own suite of rooms.

It was an awkward situation, in fact a very awkward one, Abbie thought. Over by the window Lady Ashenden was deep in conversation with her sister. By the buffet table, Hannah and his Lordship were talking to Winnie and Mike. Hilda, Frank, Chrissie and herself formed a group by the fireplace, and the tense, frigid atmosphere was so strong it was almost tangible. It seemed as though everyone was on pins, waiting for some sign, some signal to escape. Well, nothing was going to spoil Hannah's day, she thought resolutely. Someone had to make the first move and she decided it would have to be herself. She took another sip of champagne from the tall crystal flute and walked purposefully across to Angela and Freddie, who were lingering by the door.

'How do you do, Lady Angela, I'm Mrs Abigail Burgess. Lady Ashenden and I served together in the VAD.'

'Really?' Angela replied with obvious lack of interest, but she shook the hand Abbie held out.

'How splendidly noble of you. I'm Freddie D'Arcy, Richard's brother.'

Abbie wasn't sure whether he was being sarcastic or not. 'I know. What do I call you?'

Angela pursed her lips, but Freddie managed a polite smile. 'Oh, I suppose Mr D'Arcy and, seeing as you're a friend of my new sister-in-law, may I call you Mrs Burgess, Madam is so formal, don't you think?'

Abbie smiled back; at least the ice was broken.

'Please, it's just Abbie. That's my husband, talking to your brother. He's a police officer in Liverpool.'

'How fascinating,' Angela replied in a tone of voice that made it obvious that she was devoid of any interest or fascination whatsoever.

It was left to Freddie to keep the conversation going. 'That must be interesting.'

'I don't know about interesting, but he was involved in the riots when the police all went on strike. He wasn't one of the strikers, though.'

'A shocking state of affairs. Letting the riff-raff take over the city like that.'

'He wasn't badly hurt, just cuts and bruises, but it was a very worrying time for me.'

'Who is that girl?' Angela interrupted imperiously. She'd had quite enough of listening to the problems of the Liverpool City Police and their wives.

'My sister-in-law, your Ladyship. Christine Burgess.' Abbie inclined her head towards Chrissie, who needed no further encouragement to escape from her mam and dad.

Freddie looked at her with interest. She was an attractive girl, of the working class of course, but very stunning to look at. He'd been eyeing her favourably all morning.

'How do you do, er . . .' Chrissie shook his hand but foundered on the dilemma of how to address him.

'Freddie. It's the Honourable Frederick, but that's too much of a mouthful.'

'I'm Christine . . . Chrissie.'

Abbie had noted the look of admiration in Freddie D'Arcy's eyes and wished Chrissie wouldn't simper in that idiotic way.

Angela looked speculatively at Chrissie as they shook hands.

'We . . . we've already met once, your Ladyship.'

'Your face is familiar, but I can't think why.'

'You bought some things from the shop I work in. Lingerie de Paris in Liverpool.'

Angela suddenly remembered the little shop girl who had been so complimentary, so flattering. 'Yes, of course. That shop in Bold Street. It was when I was up visiting Richard when he was in that dreadful hospital,' she informed her brother.

'I took your advice. I found the courage.'

Angela looked puzzled.

'I had my hair cut.'

'And very fetching it looks too,' Freddie interposed, smiling.

Chrissie blushed and simpered, and Abbie felt like hitting her. He was handsome, with a very charming manner – at least on the surface, she thought.

Chrissie wanted to ask Angela if she'd managed to get the garment she'd been looking for, but she couldn't mention such things in front of Freddie.

Abbie had had enough of this, she wanted to get Freddie away or before long Chrissie would be fawning over him. 'Shall I introduce you to my husband?'

'Yes, do.' Freddie thought a brief chat with a representative of the law might pass a few minutes;

hopefully the bride's party would soon depart.

'Did you ever find that . . . that cami thing you wanted?' Chrissie asked Angela in a low voice.

'Oh, yes. I got it in a shop in Bond Street.'

'And is it . . . comfortable?' Chrissie would never have asked such a question as a rule, but the champagne had emboldened her, and she thought she was doing rather well.

'Yes it is. Very.'

Chrissie made up her mind to seek out and buy one. Clara Unsworth still did not stock them. 'I think the modern fashions are so much nicer. No more long skirts to get dirty or trip you up. No awful corsets to stick into you. No big awkward hats always getting knocked, and best of all, no long hair that takes hours to dry and hours to put up.'

Angela thawed a little. At least the girl was company and they seemed to have some things in common. Superficial ones of course, but better than none at all. The alternative was to sit and look at her watch, and the girl had been very flattering, and was gazing at her with a mixture of admiration and awe.

Angela D'Arcy was an example of the upbringing of her class. A product of a system that entrusted her formative years to first a nanny, then a governess and finally a finishing school. She was self-confident, self-centred and arrogant. Her ego had been bruised, first by her Aunt Julia and then by her mother, both products of the same system, and Chrissie's reverential manner was balm to a deflated spirit.

'I agree. I can't understand why so many girls and women are clinging to the old styles.'

'Your outfit . . . er ensemble, is very smart and flattering.' Chrissie had quickly rejected the word 'nice' as inappropriate and ordinary.

Angela smiled. 'So is yours. I must admit I never thought that anyone in the . . . wedding party . . . would be quite so fashionable.'

Chrissie beamed. 'Thank you. I was looking forward to coming here today. I knew you'd look absolutely stunning, your Ladyship, your clothes being so well cut.'

Angela ignored the sycophancy but basked in the flattery. She was a pleasant little thing. Quite a stunning girl herself with those huge dark eyes, long thick eyelashes and pale skin. She looked well in the fashionable but cheap dress, being slim. There wasn't anything better to do, or anyone more diverting to talk to, so she might as well continue the conversation. 'Do you visit the theatre?'

Chrissie wasn't quite sure what she meant. 'Not real theatre. Music Hall, at the Rotunda or the Hippodrome, and I love going to the cinema. I saw Rudolf Valentino in *The Four Horsemen of The Apocalypse*. Oh, he's gorgeous!'

'Isn't he just,' Angela agreed. 'Of course Douglas Fairbanks is handsome, too. Have you seen him?'

'Oh, yes.'

Mason appeared bearing a tray of glasses. 'More champagne, my Lady?'

Angela helped herself. 'Have another glass, Chrissie. It's rather good. It's Bollinger.'

Chrissie had never even had champagne before, so the name meant nothing to her. 'Thank you.'

'Of course I saw *The Four Horsemen of the Apocalypse* when I was in New York. They have such wonderful shows there and wonderful places to go, like night clubs. And all kinds of new music – and the dances! Some of them are quite shocking, so shocking they've been banned as immoral. They're really not *that* bad, it's just the old fuddy duddies' opinions.'

'I've heard of that new music. Is it called jazz?'

'Yes. It's so different, so lively, it makes you want to dance. How did you hear about it?'

'Abbie's brother goes to New York quite a lot, he told me.'

'Really?'

'He works on the *Aquitania*.'

'That's the ship I travelled in. It's just like a floating palace, you wouldn't think you were on a liner at all, except for the weather. It's rather like being here at Ashenden and looking out of the window and seeing the ocean instead of the gardens. They do carry third class passengers as well, though – emigrants.'

'Of course I've never been inside, but she looks very grand and big. I wish I could hear this jazz music.'

'Don't you have a gramophone?'

'No.'

'Oh, I see. No doubt it will eventually find its way from London to Liverpool.'

Richard called for everyone's attention, and the very subdued buzz of conversation ceased.

'If no one has any objections, my wife and I will leave you now. Thank you for your good wishes, we both appreciate your support.'

Hannah hugged her mother. 'I'll come and see you in a day or so, Mam. I promise.'

'Oh, Hannah, I'm so happy for you.' Winnie was again close to tears.

'We all are,' Abbie added, hugging her friend.

'Thank you all for being here, especially you, Mr Burgess. I can't think of anyone, apart from Jerry, I would sooner have had to give me away.'

'Do we have to call you your Ladyship now?' Hilda enquired. She liked to get these things right.

Hannah smiled. 'Heavens, no! It really doesn't matter to me.'

'Do we have to stay and . . . chat to them?'

'No, Mike, that ordeal is over. Roscoe is waiting to take you back, and Mason will show you out. I know both Freddie and Angela are on pins to go. Freddie has his own car.'

'Then I suppose we'll have to go and say goodbye. I mean it's only polite, isn't it?'

'Do we have to? Those two look a real pair of dragons.'

'Yes, we do!' Abbie hissed at her husband.

Hands were shaken very briefly and very stiffly.

'I enjoyed chatting to you Chrissie,' Angela said, relieved, as the rest of the group filed out behind Mason.

'So did I. I hope we meet again.'

Angela didn't reply. Chrissie's company had only been a few minutes' diversion to her. Soon she could leave Ashenden.

'What do you mean "meet again"?' Hilda demanded in a loud whisper. 'What was all that about? And I saw you knocking back that champagne as though it was lemonade.'

'Oh, Mam, for heaven's sake stop going on. You're showing us up.' Chrissie jerked her head in Mason's direction, knowing that just mentioning those four words were enough to silence her mother. She'd enjoyed herself and she had plenty now to tell Polly, Ellen and Miss toffee-nosed Unsworth.

'Why do you only wear that for weddings? You look gorgeous in it, Mrs Burgess,' Mike asked as he turned the key in the lock and opened the front door for Abbie and Liam.

Abbie looked up at him and smiled. 'It's my "wedding" costume. I like to keep it for really special occasions like weddings and christenings. Here, see to your son while I get changed. I'll need this suit for the next christening.'

'Oh, aye, whose?'

'Our son or daughter's.'

Mike's face broke into a wide grin. 'Abbie! Why didn't you tell me?'

'I wanted to be certain.'

Mike took her in his arms. 'Then you shouldn't

have been running around with Hannah and Chrissie.'

'I enjoyed it, I really did. Besides, there's Liam now to see to. I can't just sit back because I'm expecting. Look how Mam had to cope with us all and Da and the housework, not that she really did much and now I know why. I'm just amazed she had any energy at all. But I'm so happy, Mike.'

'So am I, luv.'

'We've got so much, haven't we? More than I ever dreamed about.'

'Not compared to Hannah.'

'Oh, I know, but I'm not jealous of Hannah, and never will be. She's had a rotten life up to now. I just pray she'll spend the rest of it being loved.'

They'd had a quiet family dinner after which they retired to the terrace-rooms, Hannah blushing a little and avoiding the eyes of both Angela and Freddie.

She helped Richard undress and get ready for bed, and helped him into the large, ornately-carved double bed. She had done all this so many times before, but tonight everything was different.

Modestly she took the new white lawn nightdress and négligée into the bathroom and got washed and changed. She stared at herself in the mirror. Apprehension was very evident in her eyes. She prayed there would be no embarrassment, no failure. Mr Copeland had told her that there was no reason why they shouldn't have a normal relationship and eventually children. She took a deep breath to try to calm her racing heart. *For Heaven's sake you were a nurse! There's nothing you haven't seen before, it's just false modesty and nerves!* she said to herself sternly.

'Happy?' Richard asked as she lay down beside him, pulling the sheet over her.

She turned towards him. 'Happier than I've ever been in my life before.'

'You see, it wasn't too bad. At least there were no arguments, and no one was cut dead by Mother or Aunt Julia.'

'No, and Chrissie seemed to get on well with Angela and Freddie.'

His brow creased in a frown. 'Freddie will chase any pretty girl, and I hope Angela wasn't filling her head with . . . nonsense.'

'Oh, you sound just like a stern Victorian father.'

He laughed. 'I do don't I? Well, now there's peace perfect peace, Hannah.'

'It was lovely. Even if things had been different, I wouldn't have wanted a great fuss. The chapel is beautiful, I felt so calm there, and afterwards I suddenly found I was very hungry. I hardly ate any breakfast, I was so nervous.'

'Maybe it was the champagne that loosened people's tongues and kept the proceedings running so amiably.' He levered himself up on one elbow and looked down at her. 'Hannah, this isn't going to be easy.'

She reached up and touched his cheek, her eyes filled with love and concern. 'I know. I know . . .

how . . . what . . . should be done. Mr Copeland said it would be all right.' She drew his head down on her breast and closed her eyes. 'I love you so much, Richard. I'll . . . help if you tell me . . . show me . . .' she faltered.

'Oh, Hannah! I wish—'

'Hush, my love! Everything will be wonderful. I know it will. I love you and I know you're going to make me the happiest woman on earth.'

'It . . . it may take time . . .'

'We have plenty of that. The rest of our lives.'

'I never thought I'd ever be happy again, but it's a miracle. You're my miracle.'

Chapter Seventeen

———◆———

A T LIVERPOOL CROWN COURT ON the 22nd of
November, Billy Hodge was sentenced to ten
years' penal servitude in Walton Jail. On the 30th, a
cold foggy day that brought the traffic in the city
virtually to a halt, Abbie had a visitor.

She was tired these days. She found it exhausting
running around after Liam, keeping up with the
chores and Mike's shifts and visiting Sal, and the
weather didn't help. All day long the thick yellow fog
had lain like a blanket over everything. She couldn't
even see across the road, and all day the ships in the
river had sounded their whistles and fog-horns
incessantly. She'd not ventured over the doorstep all
day.

Mike had gone to work at two o'clock, but it would
be late, very late when he got home. He'd have to walk
all the way. Liam had finally worn himself out and lay
peacefully in his bed upstairs, the nightlight burning
beside him. She'd just sit down and have a cup of tea
before tidying up.

She'd just finished her tea when she heard the knock on the front door and got to her feet, irritably. As she opened the door an inch it was torn from her grasp. She screamed as she was pushed back down the lobby by a figure so muffled up she couldn't see its face. Her thoughts flew instantly to Liam. Oh, God! Her child! Her baby!

'What do you want? Who are you?' She screamed the questions but her cries were silenced as he lashed out at her, sending her reeling against the kitchen door.

'That's for Billy Hodge!' Again he struck out and she staggered into the kitchen, but Abbie had always had guts, and despite the pain and terror, all she could think about was Liam. She snatched up the teapot and flung it as hard as she could in his direction. He ducked and it hit the wall and smashed but she'd already picked up the kettle, still screaming.

'Shurrup! Shurrup that bloody noise!'

'Get out! Get out or I'll brain you!' Her threat was ignored and she hurled the kettle, only to see him duck again and move towards her. She seized the heavy brass poker. Her lips were swelling and she could taste the blood in her mouth. Her vision wasn't very clear either. 'I'll kill you! So help me God I'll brain you like Abe Harvey was brained!'

He checked his progress, staring at her from the folds of the dirty muffler that shrouded his face. She looked as though she meant it. It wasn't as easy as he'd thought it would be. 'I'll sort 'er out, Billy! See 'ow

Burgess likes that!' he'd promised his mate. Now he was remembering other things. She'd been a nurse on the battlefields in the war. Abe Harvey had been done in by his lad, a weak, consumption-ridden feller, and now he'd lost the element of surprise.

Abbie was shaking, the poker still raised. 'Get out! Get out!' she took a step forward, but she was feeling faint. 'Nell! Nell! Come in here!' she screamed.

It was too much for Marty MacNamara. He turned and blundered and crashed his way down the lobby and collided with a well-made young woman.

'Here, you!' Nell had heard the screams and the noises and she made a grab at the intruder, but he twisted out of her grasp and disappeared into the fog.

'Abbie! Oh, my God!' Nell cried, catching Abbie as she fell, the poker still in her hand.

Hannah placed the last coloured bauble on the bottom branch of the Christmas tree, and sat back to admire her handiwork. This was her second Christmas at Ashenden, but her first as Richard's wife. Oh, how much her life had changed in that year. She had never realized that such happiness could exist, nor love become so much deeper.

The tree was a fairly small one and was set in a corner of the drawing-room. There was an enormous tree in the hall that had been decorated by Nora, Jessie and Henry, supervised by Mason, but this was *their* tree.

She had decorated the room herself with holly,

mistletoe and ivy, but Nora had been horrified by the ivy.

'Oh, my Lady, take it down! It's bad luck!'

Hannah had laughed.

'I mean it. Something awful will happen.'

'Nora, don't be so superstitious,' she'd chided, but the ivy had been taken down.

Freddie and Angela were due home tomorrow, Christmas Eve, she mused, and she wondered how they would all progress over the holiday. She hoped everything would go smoothly.

The firelight caught the ornaments on the tree, and they glowed and sparkled. She loved this room. It got the sun on it for most of the day, and through the summer afternoons and evenings they'd sat with the french windows wide open, looking out over the lake, the still air filled with the perfume of the flowers in the gardens.

On Boxing Day she was to go to see Mam. She went every week, but although she had pleaded and begged, nothing would induce Winnie to come to Ashenden, least of all the fact that it was Christmas, a family time. Winnie would spend the holiday as she had done last year, with Hilda and Frank.

The sound of the gong echoed throughout the downstairs rooms and she sighed, getting to her feet. It was time to dress for dinner. Richard had insisted that at least once a week, on Fridays, they all dine together in the small dining-room. His mother kept very much to herself, and it was the one day in the week when they were in each other's company for longer than a few minutes.

Her mother-in-law's attitude had scarcely altered. She was formally polite, but that was all. Hannah gave one satisfied glance around the room before going into the bedroom.

'I've laid out the dark green corded marocain, my Lady.'

She smiled at Nora. Mason had told her she must have a lady's maid, and as there was nothing on earth that would induce her even to consider Bancroft, she had elevated Nora to the position. They had both struggled along together, for Nora was far from *au fait* with her duties, and wouldn't ask Bancroft for help. They had both relied heavily on Mason over the last few months.

Nora helped her change, something she reluctantly permitted. But she insisted on doing her own hair, and she wore no make up.

'Mason has laid out his Lordship's things.'

Hannah nodded. It was not one of Mason's duties, it was that of a valet, but Richard had refused a valet and she helped him, with the assistance of Mason, of whom she'd grown fond. When requested, he never tired of explaining or offering advice. Her toilet finished, she thanked Nora, who opened the door for Richard to come through.

'I'm sorry I'm late again, Hannah.'

'There's no need to be. I'm early. I always am, you know I have a horror of being even a minute late.'

He smiled at her fondly. 'You do have an obsession about punctuality, Lady Ashenden.'

'Oh, stop teasing me.'

'It always makes you blush, and you are even more beautiful when you blush.'

'You be careful I don't choke you with your bow tie,' she laughed, before becoming serious again. 'What time will Freddie and Angela arrive tomorrow?'

'As late as possible, I suppose. They'll be here for dinner. I suppose Angela will return to London as soon as there are trains running again. Freddie will stay for the racing, as usual.' He pulled on his stiff-fronted shirt and she fastened the studs and deftly tied the black tie, one of the many tasks she'd become adept at.

She helped him into his jacket. 'I expect things will go well.'

He caught her hand. 'Don't worry about it, Hannah. It's only a few days.'

'I know. Come on, we don't want to be late.'

'There you go again.'

She laughed. 'I know, but the dinner gong has gone.'

The small dining-room was a very misleading description, she thought. It was far from small, but she supposed in comparison to the crystal dining-room, which could seat sixty guests, it was. It was decorated in pale yellow-and-green silk, in a decidedly oriental style. Many of the ornaments, and indeed the furniture, had been shipped from the Far East by one of Richard's ancestors.

Mason stood ready to seat her. The Dowager Countess was already seated, and Richard greeted her cordially.

'Are you well, Mother?'

'Yes, and you, Richard?'

'Excellent.'

'You must be pleased to have Freddie and Angela home for the holiday,' Hannah said quietly.

'It is traditionally a time for families to be together,' her mother-in-law replied, ignoring the fact that Hannah's mother would not be joining them.

Mason had indicated to Henry that the soup should be brought in.

Hannah had got used to the fact that only limited conversation was carried out while Mason, Henry and Charles were in the room.

'Perhaps Angela will grace us with a week this year, instead of the usual two days, though I doubt it.'

His mother didn't reply.

After the fish had been served, Richard addressed himself to his mother. 'Hannah and I were hoping for some advice.'

'What kind of advice?'

Richard glanced at Hannah, urging her to speak.

'Whenever I go home to see my mother, I notice that there are more and more ex-soldiers being forced onto the streets to beg or sell matches, bootlaces, all kinds of things. Many of them have injuries that make it impossible for them to work, if there were jobs to be had at all. It's a pitiful sight.'

'It's more than pitiful, it's criminal,' Richard interposed. 'After what they suffered, what they endured, what they sacrificed, to be forced into such humiliation is nothing short of a national disgrace.'

'I must agree, although I was not aware of such matters.' Lady Ashenden seldom went to Liverpool.

'Hannah and I were thinking of starting some charitable foundation, some form of relief for them.'

'Such as? And will they not resent such charity?'

'If they have been reduced to such a state, surely help can only be viewed with relief.'

'We don't mean anything like . . . soup kitchens,' Hannah added.

'What do you mean then?'

'Something that won't take away what self-respect they have left, or maybe help for their wives and children.'

'I will offer as many of them as I can work on the estate, but it will only benefit a handful. The need is greatest in the towns and cities.'

'Richard, you can't hope to take on all the ills of society.'

'I know that, but there must be something we can do to help. You have your charities, we thought—'

'None of my charities are connected with men.'

'I know that. Distressed gentlewomen, relicts of the clergy and their offspring, and all very admirable, but can you not think of something?'

Hannah decided to air one of her ideas. 'When I was training as a nurse in Whalley, we used to have to sew calico shrouds and hem linen squares for slings.'

Lady Ashenden shuddered. 'Could the wives of these distressed soldiers not do those things?'

It was what Hannah had intended. 'Yes, and be paid for it. I know many nurses would be very thankful for such help.'

'It's still not enough. I, we should set up a fund for cases of extreme hardship.'

'It would be a bottomless pit, Richard. A constant drain on the resources of Ashenden.'

'But we can't just do nothing.'

'It is the problem of the Government,' his mother stated flatly.

'I'm aware of that.'

'Then use what power you have to change things. Let your voice be heard. You have never taken your seat in the Lords as you are entitled to do. Go and persuade your fellow peers to do something to help.'

Richard smiled at her. 'Mother, you have hidden depths.'

'Then you'll go?' Hannah asked.

'Yes, as long as I have you to help me, Hannah.'

'Me? I . . . I couldn't—' she stammered.

'I don't think he meant in the capacity of your position.' Lady Ashenden still couldn't bring herself to say the words 'Countess of Ashenden'.

'No, I wouldn't inflict that on you. I'd need you more as a nursemaid . . . helpmate.'

Hannah breathed a sigh of relief.

'Well, as the House is in recess until the new year

shall we defer this discussion? In the meantime I suppose you could enquire into the correct avenues for these . . . sewing matters.'

Hannah nodded her agreement. She was grateful to her mother-in-law for her sound suggestion, thinking it would give Richard some other purpose in life if he took his seat in the House of Lords. She didn't really relish the thought of travelling to London, but perhaps after she'd been once or twice, Henry could be detailed to go in her place. At least they were trying to do something for the maimed and injured ex-service-men. Seeing so many of them on the streets and in obvious distress and need, she had begun to ask herself if the lads who had died were the really fortunate ones. They would be remembered for ever as young, healthy, gallant men who went off cheerfully to fight for King and Country. Those who were left, like Richard and the men she'd seen on the streets of Liverpool, would grow old, would degenerate and become bitter, being denied the pleasure and dignity of the life they had once known.

Freddie and Angela arrived at tea-time on Christmas Eve. When Angela had supervised her unpacking, she went down to join her brother in the ruby drawing-room.

'Hitting the cocktails already, I see,' she remarked tartly.

'No, just a scotch and soda. Can I interest you in a gin and tonic?'

She plumped herself down on the large, comfortable sofa and took the drink Freddie proferred.

'Gasper?' he asked, holding out a gold cigarette case.

'No turkish?'

'Sorry.'

'I'll smoke my own.' She withdrew her own cigarette case and holder from her bag. Freddie obliged with a gold lighter.

'Well, here we are again then.'

'Yes. This place gets more like a museum every day, and everyone is so dull.'

'Any sign of the happy couple?'

'No. Apparently Richard is over at the estate office, playing lord of the manor, doling out the Christmas wages, plus "a little something extra" as Mother used to say. On Christmas Eve, I ask you! He could have done it yesterday. I have no idea where Hannah is. Mother is lying down with yet another of her headaches.'

'She will be coming down for dinner though?'

'Oh, yes. She wouldn't miss the great family dinner party on Christmas Eve, which is almost as dire as the great Christmas lunch tomorrow.'

'Oh, don't be so bally miserable. Everyone goes home for Christmas.'

'Not everyone. And some people's homes are in town, too.'

Freddie shrugged. 'Only those who don't have a country seat. I suppose you'll be champing at the bit by Boxing Night?'

'Why not? There's no reason for me to stay, is there?'

Freddie shrugged again.

'Mother informs me that Richard is going to take his place in the House, after the Christmas recess. Something about trying to get a better deal for ex-soldiers.'

Freddie frowned and stared with distaste at his drink. It had suddenly lost its appeal. 'I suppose that's our new sister's idea? Very mindful of the needy is Hannah.'

Angela got up and walked to the window draped with its long, ruby-red velvet curtains. It was a wild, stormy night, the rain was lashing against the walls of Ashenden, driven by a gale that rattled the branches of the cedars nearest the house. 'Oh, it's so depressing here. We have to do something to liven things up, even if it's only for a day or so.'

'What would you suggest? A fancy dress party? A masquerade ball? Hire a troupe of acrobats?'

'Don't be so damned sarcastic!'

'Then what?'

'Couldn't we invite someone for drinks?'

'Who? I thought you wanted this whole situation kept as quiet as possible? Obviously it's no secret, but there's no need to draw attention to Richard and Hannah's misalliance, and throwing a cocktail party would do just that.'

'I was thinking of that girl, what was her name? She was at the wedding.'

'Oh, the pretty one with the huge dark eyes and the willowy figure. Chrissie.'

'Yes, Chrissie. We could have drinks, play the gramophone.'

'Chat? Maybe even dance a bit? She is quite a stunner.'

'Until she opens her mouth. I mean she'll be amusing . . . diverting.'

'Oh, she's that all right.'

'Oh, don't go getting involved with her, for heaven's sake. One in the family is enough.'

'One what?'

'You know what I mean . . . where she comes from. As I said, she's amusing, but you couldn't actually take her anywhere. She'll be flattered and highly delighted to come here.'

'Angela, you're cruel, do you know that?'

A cat-like smile spread across her face. 'Not really. Selfish, yes.'

'But how is she going to get here? And when?'

'Christmas Night, and Roscoe can go for her. Hannah can tell him where she lives. She can stay overnight and go back with Hannah on Boxing Day. I believe she is going to visit her mother then. I don't think we should mention this to Mother.'

'But you'll have to mention it to Hannah.'

Angela shrugged. 'Leave it to me. I'll tell her after dinner.'

'You want Chrissie to come here on Christmas Night?' Hannah said when Angela informed her nonchalantly of the idea, after Lady Ashenden had retired.

'Yes. Why not? I thought it would be entertaining for us . . . all.'

Richard shot a suspicious glance at his younger brother.

'It will mean Roscoe driving all the way to Liverpool, and she won't be expecting to come—'

'We thought it would be rather a nice surprise for her,' Freddie added.

Richard looked meaningfully at his wife.

'Just a social call. A few drinks, some music, a chat. She can go back with you, Hannah.'

'She's to stay overnight?'

'What is so terrible about that? She'll enjoy it. It's only one night, and I'm sure she must get as bored as everyone else. I think all this family Christmas stuff is very over-rated.'

'But only in the country, Angela,' Richard said with a note of sarcasm in his voice.

Hannah wasn't at all happy about this state of affairs, and she could tell Richard wasn't either. Oh, Chrissie would walk all the way if she had to, there would be no stopping her.

Freddie rose. 'So, that's settled then. I'll go and inform Roscoe. Will you give him the address, Hannah?' He also intended to slip Roscoe ten shillings by way of a bribe to keep his mouth shut, at least until he set off for Liverpool.

'I . . . I suppose so.'

Richard was very uneasy, and he told Hannah so later that night.

'I don't trust him, Hannah.'

'Do you mean he'd . . . well, he'd take liberties?'

'I wouldn't put it past him.'

'And Chrissie's so silly, she'd be flattered. She's not used to drink or such illustrious company. She'd be putty in his hands.'

'I wonder whose idea it really was, and what the reason for it is? I'm sure they're only inviting her here to amuse themselves.'

'What can we do?'

'Not a great deal without causing an argument that will upset Mother and cause gossip below stairs. We shall both have to be watchful. We'll have to stay up with them.'

'I'll ask Nora to air that bedroom next to your mother's suite,' Hannah said firmly.

Richard nodded. 'Very sensible. He won't dare try to disturb her with Mother next door, and being a very light sleeper. They obviously haven't informed Mother about this.'

'No. Will you tell her?'

'No. Why cause an argument and upset and spoil her Christmas? She sees precious little of those two as it is.'

When Chrissie arrived the following night, she was still in a state of disbelief and shock. She had hurriedly scattered the entire contents of her wardrobe all over her bedroom floor in her haste to find something suitable to wear and to take. Hilda had been in as much of a flurry to find Chrissie a clean nightdress and under-wear, soap, handkerchiefs and toothpaste.

Initially, Hilda had been very wary and suspicious when Roscoe had been shown in by Frank and had stated the purpose of his visit. It had only been the note that Hannah had written that had eased her mind about this trip. Despite the ten-shilling tip, Roscoe was none too pleased, either, at having to turn out on a particularly bad night to drive to this very shabby street in Liverpool. His Lordship and his brother must be going off their rockers, he thought. A nice state of affairs it was when people who lived in a place like this were invited to wine, dine and stay with the nobility.

'Just you behave yourself, my girl. No nonsense. Don't go drinking and making a show of yourself and us! We might not have much, but we've got our pride. Go on, off with you.'

'At least she'll have Hannah to keep an eye on her,' Hilda said to Frank as the car had moved away.

Chrissie was cursing that she didn't have what she called a 'proper evening dress'. She had bought a new dress for Christmas, but it was a daytime sort of dress. Normally she didn't go anywhere grand enough to warrant an evening gown. Under her best coat she wore the cherry red dress trimmed on the collar and cuffs with black braid. A wide sash of black georgette was swathed around the hips and tied in a loose, floppy bow. She had managed to put on a little lipstick that had gone unnoticed by her mam in the general confusion and haste.

Hannah greeted her in the hall and took her upstairs to the room that had been hastily aired. A fire burned in the small marble fireplace. The deep plum-coloured curtains had been pulled across the windows. The bed with its carved and scrolled headboard and footboard had been made up, a thick bedspread of plum damask overlayed with a pattern of oriental design was draped over it. The carpet was thick and heavily patterned. The china ornaments were expensive, and a large jug of evergreens and Christmas roses had been placed on a rosewood chest.

'This is for me?' Chrissie gasped.

'Yes, there is a bathroom next door on the left and Lady Ashenden's rooms are on the right, so no noise. She's a very light sleeper.'

'I thought you were Lady Ashenden?'

'We both are, confusing isn't it?' Hannah smiled wryly.

Chrissie had placed the small and decidedly shabby case on the bed. It was the only case they had, for no one ever went anywhere for longer than a day.

'Nora will unpack for you.'

'I can do it. It won't take long, I've only got my nightdress and some underwear.'

'Leave it, Chrissie. It's how things are done here.'

'Why was I asked?'

'I've no idea, but I don't want the whole of Burlington Street to be treated to a detailed account of every single minute, or every single stick of furniture and its value.'

Chrissie was stung. 'I won't do that!'

'You forget I've known you all your life, Chrissie Burgess.'

'Well, this is different. It's special to be asked here. I know how to behave.'

'I hope you do. But we'll all be together, all evening.'

'You mean you'll be watching me like a hawk?'

Hannah smiled. 'Something like that. Come on, and I'll take you along to the ruby drawing-room or you're bound to get lost.'

Her initial pessimism had been unfounded, Hannah thought. It had been quite a pleasant evening. Oh, Angela and Chrissie had got a little tipsy, but she'd managed to limit Chrissie's drinks. Freddie had drunk far more than anyone else, but it didn't show and he was very good company, but she'd seen the looks that had passed between him and Chrissie, and was very glad that she'd organized the sleeping arrangements.

Chrissie surprised her, too. She got on very well with both Angela and Freddie, although she did think Angela's attitude to Chrissie was patronizing in the extreme. She was tired and she knew Richard was, too, but they were both determined to stick it out.

Chrissie was enjoying herself. She felt a little light-headed and knew she was laughing too much, but she didn't care. This was wonderful. She was being treated just as a close friend. Freddie liked her, in fact she knew it was more than that, she had quickly inter-preted his glances and innuendoes. She was glad that there was no sign of her Ladyship. She'd gone to her rooms apparently.

By midnight Freddie realized that his brother and sister-in-law were determined that he should have no opportunity to get Chrissie alone, and altered his plans. He yawned expansively.

'So sorry, it's been a long day.'

Angela too had had enough. Chrissie's company, her shrill laughter and often fatuous remarks were beginning to pall. 'Yes, I think I'll retire, too. You look exhausted Richard.'

'I am, but it's been a very pleasant evening. Quite a change really.'

Hannah had risen. 'I'll show Chrissie to her room, she's bound to get lost otherwise.'

Chrissie was disappointed. She'd been having the time of her life. 'Thank you. It's been really great. I've enjoyed myself so much. It was so good of you to ask me. I really do—'

'That's enough, Chrissie,' Hannah said sharply.

'Good night then.'

When they reached her room, Chrissie sat down on the bed.

'What do I do in the morning?'

'Nora will bring you a cup of tea at eight. You can come down for breakfast, I'll come for you or Nora will show you the way. We're leaving at ten. I doubt either Freddie or Angela will be up,' Hannah replied, dashing Chrissie's hopes of any kind of tryst with Freddie.

'You're really lucky Hannah. All this: servants, money, everything!'

'I know, but I didn't marry Richard because of all that. I would have been just as happy in a small house, with a little money and no servants. Like Abbie or Dee.'

Chrissie was becoming argumentative. 'Oh, it's easy to say that when you've got all this.'

'Will you stop that, Chrissie!'

'It's not fair – life I mean.'

Hannah thought of her childhood, her nursing days, of Richard's blighted life, obviously none of which Chrissie was giving a thought to.

'No, Chrissie, it's not. Compared to a lot of people you've got a good life. You've got loving parents, a brother, sister-in-law and nephew, a good home and a job.'

'It's boring. I hate working in that shop. When I get home I'm lucky if I can get out to enjoy myself.'

'Phil takes you out.'

'Yes, at least Mam lets me stay out later then,' Chrissie replied, missing Hannah's point intentionally. 'Oh, I wish I was like them. Lots of money, no need to work, enjoying myself all day and all night like Angela and Freddie.' She had had a brief taste of how 'the other half lived' as her mam would have said. She had had champagne and bits of food called canapés, and listened to jazz music on a gramophone, and she'd had a cigarette. She hadn't liked it much, in fact it had made her feel a bit queasy, but it was all so exciting . . .

so glamorous. She felt grown-up, what was that word that Angela used a lot? Sophisticated, that was it. She felt grown-up and sophisticated now.

'They lead very shallow lives. They don't achieve anything.'

'I wouldn't mind leading a shallow life,' Chrissie said mutinously.

'Well, it's something you're not going to get offered the chance to do.'

'Why? He likes me. I know he does. He kept smiling at me and making remarks . . . compliments.'

'Don't take that seriously.'

'Why not? If he falls in love with me, I can't help it.'

'Chrissie, you've had too much to drink. He was just flirting with you. It didn't mean anything.'

'How do you know how he feels? I could be like you. His Lordship fell in love with you, and he married you. Why shouldn't Freddie love me and marry me?'

'Oh, don't be stupid, Chrissie! It's totally different!'

'Why is it different?'

'Use your brains, Chrissie! Do you really think that if Lord Ashenden had come through the war without being wounded that we would ever have even met? Of course not. Our paths would never have crossed. He would never even have met me, never mind loved me. He would have married the daughter of a duke or someone like that. Just get that into your stupid head. Freddie will be going back to London soon and in a week he won't even remember you. He was flirting. You amused him, that's all. Now get some sleep.'

When Hannah had gone, Chrissie tore the red satin band from around her hair and threw it across the room. Hannah Harvey was just being spiteful! Oh, she knew what she was up to. She had everything, but she didn't want anyone else to be as fortunate. If Freddie fell in love with her and married her, she would have everything that Hannah had, except a title, and she wouldn't mind about that.

She'd always been ambitious. She'd always known the best means of getting her own way. Well, why shouldn't she move up in life the way Hannah had done? She didn't love Freddie – yet, but she was sure she would, when she knew him better. If she was ever going to be allowed to get to know him at all. If she ever got the opportunity to come here again, or even see him, then she was going to set her cap at him, and she didn't care what anyone thought or said.

She lay back on the bed, staring at the ornate plaster ceiling. What a life it would be: no more housework, ironing or cooking; no more having to dash into the shop to help out; buying all the clothes she wanted, going to night clubs and dances, the theatre, and drinking champagne all day and night if she felt like it. For all that, it wouldn't matter if she never loved Freddie, just as long as she could make him love her.

As Hannah left Chrissie's room, she caught sight of Lady Ashenden standing in the doorway of her drawing-room.

'Would you come in here please and kindly enlighten me as to what is going on?'

Hannah sighed, followed her mother-in-law and closed the door. She should have known that Bancroft would inform her mistress, and her mother-in-law must have heard her arguing with Chrissie.

'Who is that person in the room next door?'

'Christine Burgess, you may remember she was a guest at my wedding. I can assure you, your Ladyship, her presence here is nothing to do with me. I did not invite her and neither did Richard.'

'Then who did?'

'I believe it was the joint decision of Freddie and Angela. She is leaving in the morning, your Ladyship.' Hannah was always formally correct with her mother-in-law.

Lady Ashenden was furious. This was intolerable. She remembered the girl well. A precocious, hard, brassy-looking chit. 'And Richard did nothing to stop them?'

'No. He thought . . . he thought that as it was only for a short time—'

'Oh, that I should live to see this day! Servants sent all the way to Liverpool for . . . for . . . a girl like that!'

Hannah remained calm. She certainly had no intention of becoming embroiled in an argument on Chrissie's behalf. 'I'm sorry you are upset. I wish you had been informed.'

'Upset! Upset! I knew Frederick was something of a libertine, but to send for his . . . his paramour, and have her entertained and accommodated under this roof! It's intolerable!'

Hannah was not going to let that pass. Frank and Hilda had been insulted as well as Chrissie by those remarks.

'Chrissie is not a person like that. She's not a bad girl. She comes from a very respectable family. Not wealthy or with any degree of social standing, but decent, honest, hard-working people.'

'Then that is even worse!' Lady Ashenden glared at Hannah. 'I hope she doesn't entertain any ideas that she can ensnare Frederick and come to this house as a bride.'

Hannah stiffened and her manner became cold. Lady Ashenden must have heard what both she and Chrissie had said. Or more likely, Bancroft had been listening at the door. 'That is absolutely out of the question.'

'It most certainly is. Have you this girl's mother's address!'

'I have.'

'Then please write it down for me.'

Hannah wrote Hilda's name and address on the top sheet of a pile of crested paper that lay on the writing bureau. Her mother-in-law had every right to be annoyed. She should have been informed of the invitation to Chrissie. She'd resented Lady Ashenden's remarks implying that Hilda and Frank were lax parents, but a curt note to Hilda would put a stop to Chrissie's idiotic notions.

'I am going to visit my mother tomorrow. Do you wish me to take a letter with me? Roscoe can hand it in.'

Her mother-in-law looked at her less coldly. 'Thank you. That is very considerate and sensible of you.'

Chapter Eighteen

———◆———

CHRISSIE HAD A HEADACHE. She hadn't slept very well at all. She had been too preoccupied, her head full of ideas and plans that whirled around her brain and kept her in a mood of high excitement.

She had envisaged herself, dressed to the nines in expensive clothes, sitting beside Freddie in his car driving to London. Then she had imagined herself in the chapel downstairs, dressed in yards of white satin and lace, a tiara on her head and filmy tulle floating behind her. It was after three o'clock before she'd dozed off.

She had had breakfast in a dining-room full of exotic furniture and pictures. She hadn't felt hungry, but the array of food under covered silver dishes, set on the mahogany sideboard, had tempted her. To her intense disappointment, there was no sign of either Angela or Freddie, and she and Hannah had hardly spoken in the car all the way home.

She had derived some satisfaction from the stares of sheer amazement from the neighbours as she'd got out of the car, turning to wave to Hannah and to thank Roscoe. She did think it was stupid of Hannah not to get out and walk the remaining fifteen yards to Winnie's house.

As the car moved off, Hannah leaned forward and spoke to the driver.

'Roscoe, I have a letter her Ladyship wants delivering to Mrs Burgess. It does seem ridiculous for me not to have handed it in myself, but there is a reason. Would you please take it down?'

'Of course, my Lady.'

'Thank you, then go off and see your father and brother. I'll be ready to go home at about half past two.'

He nodded his thanks. When she'd found out that what family he had left lived in Aigburth, she'd told him that instead of just hanging around waiting for her, he must go and visit them. She might not be born to the gentry, but she was far more of a lady than Lady Angela was, he thought, as he reversed the car down the street.

Chrissie was chatting excitedly and very enthusiastically about the events of her brief sojourn at Ashenden to Hilda, Frank and Mike. Mike had called in to give his parents the good news that he was to be promoted to the ranks of the CID as from February. He'd had it confirmed that morning when he came off duty, and had broken his journey home. His good fortune had been put in the shade somewhat by Chrissie's experiences.

'I'll go,' he offered, for the sharp rap on the side door hadn't had any effect on Chrissie's flow of words. It was bound to be someone who had run out of tea or bread. When he came back into the room he looked puzzled, and handed a letter to Hilda.

'It was that bloke who drives Hannah around. He must have forgotten to give it to Chrissie to bring in.'

Hilda felt the thick, crested envelope and was just as mystified. Things were made crystal clear to her when she opened it and scanned the brief lines of hand writing.

'Just what have you been up to, madam?' she demanded grimly of Chrissie.

'Nothing! Who's it from?'

'Hannah's mother-in-law, that's who. Saying she doesn't ever want to see you in her house again, and that if you've got any designs on her son then you can forget them, or words to that effect.' Hilda was fuming with temper and smarting with humiliation. 'What have you been doing, Chrissie? And I want no lies!' she yelled.

'Nothing, Mam! I didn't even see her. I was with Hannah all the time. I was! You can go and ask her!' Chrissie now realized that Hannah must have known all about this letter, but had said nothing. Maybe she'd even had a hand in it. Oh, she was so sly.

'You must have done something to upset her, and what's all this about you and the Honourable Frederick?'

'Nothing!'

'Don't lie to me! There must have been something going on. You've been making a show of yourself and us, that's what you've been doing.'

'Mam, I haven't! We had some champagne, we all did, Hannah as well. We talked and played the gramophone until midnight. Hannah showed me back to my room and it was next door to that old witch's, so what could I get up to?'

'Don't call her Ladyship names like that – it's disrespectful.' Suddenly a thought occurred to Hilda. 'That's it! You were drunk, loud-mouthed and disrespectful! I shouldn't have let you go.'

'I wasn't drunk! I had a bit of an argument with Hannah in my room, that's all. Oh, she makes me sick. The airs and graces out of her now, and she only came from down this street.'

Hilda caught her daughter by the shoulders and shook her hard. She could just imagine it. Chrissie yelling at the top of her voice and Lady Ashenden being able to hear every single word. God knows what the stupid young madam had said. 'Yes, she did, but at least she knows how to behave. She always has done, not like you! Where did I go wrong with you, Chrissie?'

'I'm twenty, Mam. I'll be twenty-one in a couple of months.'

'And high time you stopped acting like a hard-faced sixteen-year-old. There's Phil Chatterton, a nicer, more steady and reliable lad you couldn't wish to meet. He worships you, and what do you do? You turn up your nose because you think you can be like Hannah. Well you can't, you were born common and you'll stay common. That's the end of your hob-nobbing with the high and mighty of the land, madam.'

Chrissie jerked herself from her mother's grip. 'I haven't *done* anything! It's not my fault if Freddie D'Arcy thought I was attractive and . . . liked me. I didn't encourage him. I'm fed up with all this. I'm going upstairs, I've got a headache.'

As she flounced out Hilda turned on Frank. 'Did you hear her? Did you? Freddie! Freddie! She's getting too big for her boots, is that one, Frank. You're her da, you go and talk some sense into her.'

'When have I ever been able to do that? She's like you, stubborn. What exactly does that letter say?'

Hilda read it out while both Frank and Mike looked grim.

'As far as I can see, she didn't know Chrissie was even in the house. It doesn't sound as though anyone consulted her. No wonder she's mad.'

'That's as may be Frank, but the bit about Chrissie having designs on this Frederick must be true.'

'If Hannah was with her all the time she can't have got up to anything much. You know Hannah is very careful about things, very sensible. It sounds to me as though Chrissie had too much to drink, maybe there was some larking about, then when Hannah got Chrissie alone there was a row and her Ladyship must have heard it.'

'Well, she's not going there again, and that's that.

I'm not having her playing fast and loose with poor Phil, and the sooner she gets it into her head that she's got to settle down, the better.' Hilda turned to Mike. 'Now, lad, tell us more about your promotion. You'd hardly got the words out when she barged in and started sounding off like the *Mauretania*'s steam whistle.'

Hilda calmed down and made a bit of lunch, after which Mike said he was going home to spend the rest of the day with Abbie and Liam.

'She'll be delighted,' Frank enthused, proud of his son.

'She might not be after a while. The hours are even longer. It won't come as a complete surprise, she knew it was on the cards, and we did talk it over.'

The calm was suddenly broken by a frantic knocking at the door.

'Oh, damn and blast! Are we to get no peace at all? Why can't people cater for the holiday and not go running out of things!'

'I'll go,' Frank offered, for the knocking had continued without a break. As he opened the door, young Seb Kerrigan burst into the room.

'It's me mam! Me mam's bad! Our Joan sent me to see if our Abbie was here.'

Mike took charge. 'How bad, Seb?'

'Real bad. Terrible pains in 'er chest, an' she looks awful, our Joan said.'

Hilda had snatched up her jacket.

'Mam, go up and get Hannah, she was a nurse. Seb,

get round to Dr Wallace, no on second thoughts I'll go, you go for Father Fitzpatrick.'

A sob escaped Seb, he was frightened now he knew his mam might be dying.

Hannah hadn't even paused to get her coat, she'd run up the street and straight up the stairs to Sal's bedroom. When she saw Sal she realized she was too late. With tears in her eyes she laid Sal's hand gently on her chest. There was no pulse. As she pulled the sheet up over Sal's face, Joan sank down on her knees beside the bed and began to sob. Pat, Seb and Ginny were all downstairs in the kitchen.

'It would have been quick, Joan. Apart from a bit of pain, she wouldn't have known anything.' It wasn't strictly the truth, the pain would have been acute, but Joan was so upset it didn't hurt to bend the truth a little.

'I tried to keep her calm, Hannah, she would insist on getting up yesterday and staying down for the day. Oh, Mam! Mam! Why did you have to be so stubborn?' Joan sobbed.

Hannah put her arms around her. 'Stop that. You have absolutely nothing to be sorry or guilty about, Joan. No one could have done more for her than you. No one.'

Joan raised a tear-streaked face. 'But she . . . she went without being absolved. Without a priest. She'll never forgive me for letting her go like that.'

'Joan, I don't know very much about the Catholic religion, but I do know that she was a good Christian woman, a caring wife and mother. What possible sins can she have committed? And if there were any, they'd surely be forgiven.'

'But she should have had Extreme Unction. I was in such a state, I couldn't think straight. I should have sent Seb for Father Fitzpatrick first.'

'Well, he's here now with Dr Wallace.' Joan dissolved once more into tears as the elderly priest placed the purple stole around his neck and made the sign of the cross. Hannah went to greet the doctor.

'She was dead when I arrived, Doctor. There was nothing I could do,' she said quietly, leading him back onto the tiny landing.

'A heart attack?'

'I think so.'

'Then I'll wait until the priest has finished his ministrations. I can't say I'm shocked. I've been expecting this to happen.'

Hannah nodded. 'It would have been much sooner if it hadn't been for Joan. She devoted herself to her mother, and Mrs Kerrigan wasn't the easiest of patients.'

'Do the rest of the family know yet?'

'No, but I suspect that seeing the priest, they will have guessed.'

'That may not be the case. I have heard that occasionally and in some circumstances, the Catholic sacrament effects a recovery. But not from a heart attack, that would necessitate a miracle.'

'Do you want me to break it to them, or should I leave it to the priest or you?'

Dr Wallace thought briefly of the day he'd been called to the Harvey house, to find a scene of shocking violence. Jerry Harvey had been in a state of collapse, his father dying from a massive blow to the head, and Mrs Harvey and Hannah had been in an advanced state of shock, clinging together, trembling and crying. He had felt dazed himself. But how this girl had changed. He had heard that she'd gone to France, and of course he'd heard about her marriage. There was no vestige now of the terrified little creature she'd been that dreadful day.

'You have known them for a long time, your Ladyship, I think it would perhaps be better coming from you.'

Hannah nodded and went slowly downstairs. Dr Wallace would issue the death certificate before he left.

Pat looked like a wizened old man, she thought. He was hunched up in his chair, his face grey and drawn with worry. What hair he had left was now snow white. Ginny's eyes were red and swollen from crying. Hannah was surprised by Rose Chatterton's presence, but was thankful to see that the girl had her arm around Seb, who was staring at Rose with wide, frightened eyes. They were like brother and sister, had been bosom friends since the age of three, when Rose had first come to Burlington Street.

'I'm so very sorry . . . but Mrs Kerrigan, your wife, your mam, is dead. God rest her soul.'

Seb buried his head against Rose's shoulder and

there were tears coursing down Rose's cheeks too. Sal Kerrigan had taken the place of Gwendoline Chatterton, and Rose had loved Sal far more than the aloof woman she only vaguely remembered. Ginny had laid her head on her arms and was sobbing, but Pat just sat staring at Hannah. Shock affected people in different ways, she thought. Then she remembered Abbie. She wasn't aware that she'd spoken the name aloud, but as Dr Wallace came into the room, followed by Mike Burgess, she turned to them.

'Mike, someone should go for Abbie.'

'I'll go. Dad says he'll take care of all the official things.' He could see that Pat was incapable of doing anything at the moment.

Hannah was calmer now, her mind on practical matters. 'Roscoe will be back soon, so we'll wait. He can drive us and bring Abbie back here. Rose, take Seb and Mr Kerrigan down to your house. Your dad will help you – all.' She went and put her arm around Ginny. 'She wouldn't have wanted to go on year after year as an invalid, Ginny. You know how she hated not being in charge, not being able to get out and see people. Why don't you wash your face, and we'll take you round to Alfie's house?' Hannah thought time spent with Alfie Taylor, Ginny's fiancé, would help the girl. What she was trying to do was get everyone, except Joan, out of the house before Sal was laid out. It was not a pleasant task: necessary, but very upsetting for the family.

Joan at last came downstairs, looking far older than

her thirty-two years, Hannah thought. Mike had seen both the priest and the doctor out. Hannah busied herself making a pot of tea.

'Oh, Hannah. I'm . . . stunned . . . I feel awful.'

'It's the shock, Joan. Even though you all knew it could happen at any time, it's still a shock. Here, drink this, it's got plenty of sugar in it. I've sent your dad and Seb down to Bridie's house with Rose. Mike and I will drop Ginny off at Alfie's, then we'll go for Abbie.'

'Our poor Abbie, she's going to be so upset that she wasn't here.'

'What could she have done?'

'I know. I shouldn't ask you this . . . not now that you're who you are.' Joan was struggling with her tears.

'What?'

'Will you help our Abbie to . . . to lay her out? I don't want Mrs Malloy, Mam never liked her.'

'Of course I will, Joan. It's the least I can do. She was always very kind to me and Mam.'

Mike had been standing at the front door, waiting for Roscoe to return. He'd noticed that, one by one, curtains in the front rooms of the houses in the street had been drawn over: a mark of respect. Bad news spread quickly. He knew Abbie was going to be devastated. He was upset himself, for Sal Kerrigan had been one of the real characters of Burlington Street. Her rows with Pat when the kids had been growing up were vociferous and legendary. She'd never had much money, there were times when she'd had none at all, but she had always had plenty of generosity of spirit and a heart of gold. She'd loved the bones of every one of her nine children, her life had centred on her large and acrimonious family. Well, she'd be reunited now with the two sons she'd lost at Montauban. Someone was going to have to write to Tommy and Dee in Canada and to young Bertie who was halfway across the Atlantic Ocean. He suspected it would be either himself or Abbie.

Roscoe was hurriedly informed of the situation and nodded gravely as Ginny and Hannah emerged from the house. Mike sat with him in the front of the car until they reached William Moult Street, where Hannah hugged Ginny and saw her safely into the Taylors house.

'Abbie's going to know that something is wrong as soon as she sees the car, Mike.'

'It can't be helped, Hannah, unless you drop me at the end of the lane?'

Hannah nodded. 'Maybe that would be best. Should I stay in the car or come with you?'

'Would you mind staying?'

'No. I'll have enough time to try to comfort her on the way back.'

'Won't his Lordship be worried about you? You're going to be late.'

'No, I don't think so, and he'll understand when I explain everything to him.'

When they reached St Mary's, Hannah sat back and watched Mike walk down the narrow lane. From her small circle of friends, only Dee knew what it was like to lose a mother. Somehow it seemed far worse, far more heart-wrenching than losing a father, even if that father had been generous, kind and loving – unlike her own.

Abbie wasn't surprised that Mike was a bit late, she'd known he was calling at Hilda's.

'Well, did they confirm it? Are you going into the CID?'

'Yes, but, Abbie . . .'

A frown of apprehension creased Abbie's forehead. From Mike's expression she knew something was amiss. 'What's wrong?'

'Oh, Abbie, luv, I'm sorry . . .'

'What? For God's sake, what is it?'

'Your mam.'

Abbie's eyes widened with fear and disbelief. 'Is she . . . ? Has she . . . ?'

'She died about three quarters of an hour ago, luv.' He held out his arms and Abbie fell into them, sobbing.

'Mam! Mam!' And she hadn't even been there! She'd never see Mam again now. Never to laugh, never to joke, never scold. 'Oh, Mam!'

'It's all right, luv. Hannah's here with the car, to take you back, and she'll stay with you. Ginny is with Alfie, and Seb and your dad are with Bridie and Edward.'

Abbie looked up at him through her tears. 'She's not on her own? They've not left Mam in the house on her own?'

'No, luv, Joan's with her. Come on, get your things. I'll get Liam ready.'

'He'll never know her now, Mike. He'll never grow up knowing his nan.'

Mike placed her coat around her shoulders and led her still weeping, out into Hannah's arms. Then he went back for his son.

Chapter Nineteen

———◆———

ABBIE THOUGHT SHE'D NEVER seen anyone so annoyingly sanctimonious as her sister Monica, or Sister Mary Magdalene as she was now called. Not once had she dissolved into tears for her mother since she'd been home. Abbie's eyes were swollen and red from crying. Monica's expression was one of detached, mild sorrow.

The church was packed, for Sal had been a popular figure in the neighbourhood. The coffin was covered with spring flowers, bought out of season and therefore expensive, but both she and Joan were determined that Sal was going to have a good send-off. She certainly hadn't had much from life.

The murmured words and responses of the Latin requiem and the smell of incense soothed Abbie a little, they were sounds and perfumes she had grown up with. Da was like a lost soul, she thought. She'd never really noticed or realized that he was getting old. He had been a real handful in his younger days, they'd always been arguing and fighting, but lately he and

Mam had grown closer. Now he looked as though his sheet anchor had been blown away, his confidence, his vitality, all gone.

She tried to concentrate on the prayers in her missal, but her gaze kept wandering back to the coffin, and her heart ached. She felt drained and very weary. *Oh Mam, what are we all going to do without you? You were always there – always. We brought everything to you, our joys, our hopes, our plans, our sorrows*, she thought miserably.

Joan was dabbing her eyes with a handkerchief, and Abbie remembered the day when Joan had flung herself into her mother's arms and cried brokenly for the loss of her young husband. Sal had been grieving, too, for her sons, but she'd put aside that grief to find words of comfort for Joan.

Ginny was clinging to Alfie's arm. Rose Chatterton held Seb's hand tightly in hers, both their young faces set in lines of mute misery, they looked so lost. Abbie had written to Tommy and Dee in Canada to tell them the news, but of course the letter would not have arrived yet. Tommy would be so upset that his little Charlotte would never see her grandmother now.

She was so thankful that Hannah had come. Over the past days she'd been so grateful for Hannah and Lord Ashenden. After Hannah had returned and explained the situation, he'd been kindness itself. He had made the car and Roscoe available for their use. Hannah had been a tower of strength. It was she who had gone with Frank Burgess to register the death at Brougham Terrace. They had arranged the funeral, she had done everything and anything that could help them to get through the bitter, confusing days.

She had cried the whole time, barely able to see what she was doing, when she and Hannah had laid Sal out. In the end, Hannah had sent her downstairs to sit with Joan and had finished the task by herself. Mam had looked so peaceful, so young, she thought, as friends and neighbours had called to pay their last respects to the woman who lay in the parlour. The walls had been draped with white bedsheets. Candles had burned at the head and foot of the coffin, as custom dictated. Monica had sat, silently saying her Rosary, in a corner of the room.

Abbie had put her foot down about a wake, not that anyone had really been much in favour of one. She couldn't have stood that. They usually ended in a drink- and grief-induced brawl, and Mam was going to have some dignity at least.

Monica had arrived home the day after Sal had died, and her attitude had jarred on everyone's nerves except Pat's. He was pathetically grateful to have a nun as a daughter. Monica must lead the family prayers, he'd stated, and converse with the clergy who seemed to be drifting in and out at all times of the day and night. Abbie wasn't in the least bit grateful, and her overwrought nerves had made her turn on Monica the previous night.

'You haven't said a word about how upset you are.

In fact you don't even seem to be upset at all!' she'd cried.

'I am! It's just that we're trained . . . taught to accept these things. We must pray for her soul in purgatory.'

Abbie had been outraged. 'What do you mean, "her soul in purgatory"? Mam's soul will have gone to heaven. What did she do lately that was wrong?'

Monica had lowered her eyes and folded her arms, tucking her hands into the sleeves of her habit. 'Da said there was no time for her to confess or receive absolution.'

'I know that! But Father Fitzpatrick was here within minutes to give Extreme Unction.'

'You know as well as I do that for a soul to go straight to heaven, it must be as pure as the driven snow, without a stain of sin, no matter how small.'

'Oh, stop that! It's nonsense! Mam hadn't fallen from a state of grace. She'd had Communion on Christmas Day, young Father O'Neil came round here especially. So, you can take your stupid views on purgatory and go there yourself, or better still, go to hell, Monica! You don't care, do you? You're not upset. You were always selfish and callous, even when we were kids.'

'I do care. I just don't show it. Now, if you don't mind, I have my Holy Office to read before I can go to bed.'

Abbie had stormed out of the bedroom, leaving Sister Mary Magdalene to her prayers. Joan was standing at the bottom of the stairs.

'I wish she hadn't come now! I wish we hadn't even bothered to tell her!'

'Abbie, what a terrible thing to say, and you know Da thinks she's a great comfort.'

'Oh, really! Like hell she is, Joan! All you can get out of her is about Mam's soul going to purgatory! To purgatory! She doesn't care. She's been away from Mam for so long that she doesn't care a fig. Nor did it bother her that she caused Mam so much worry before she became a flaming nun.'

Joan had shaken her head sadly. 'Stop shouting, and don't say anything like that in front of Da, Abbie.'

Hannah had left for the long drive back to Ashenden. Seb had gone home with Rose. The Burgesses, the Chattertons, the O'Briens and Lizzie Simcock had all gone, after helping to clear up the remains of the meal. Everyone felt weary, heartsore and on edge.

'What will you do now, Joan?' Abbie asked, more to break the heavy, brooding silence.

'I'll have to find a job I suppose, and I still have a home of my own.'

Pat suddenly came out of his trance-like reverie. 'What about me?'

'Ginny's here, and so is Seb – and Bertie, when he's home.'

'I won't be here much longer Joan. Alfie and me are getting married next month, and we're going to emigrate.'

'Now is a fine time to tell everyone that! When was

this decided? Why didn't you say something about it before, when Mam—'

Ginny shrugged. 'We didn't know, Abbie, not properly. We intended to get married, Mam knew that.'

'Then why can't you stay here and look after me?' Pat demanded petulantly.

'Alfie says there are bad times ahead. There's no work and we'll never get a decent place to live, so we're going to try a new life in Australia.'

'Australia! You couldn't get much further away if you tried!' Pat cried.

Joan and Abbie exchanged looks. Much as Abbie felt sorry for her da and Seb, she also felt that Joan had done more than her duty over the years.

'So, that's you out of circulation. I have Mike and Liam—'

'I've taken my vows.'

Abbie's frayed nerves snapped. She remembered all the letters she'd had from Monica, agonizing over her choice of a religious life, hinting that she'd had enough of it. 'No you don't, or at least you do only when it suits you.'

'What's that supposed to mean?'

'Oh, you've changed your tune all of a sudden. You're forgetting all those long rambling letters implying that in fact you thought you'd made a mistake. You wanted to come out.'

'I did not! I didn't mean that at all.'

'Oh yes you did.'

Joan tried to intervene. 'For heaven's sake, will you two stop it.'

'Joan, you stay out of this, and you too, Da.' Abbie turned again to Monica. 'You forget I'm more than just your sister, I'm your twin, I know you better than you know yourself! You were young, frightened, easily talked into things when you went to that convent. Then when you went to France you suddenly realized that there were other things in life. You've never been cut out for that kind of life, it's just not in your nature. You've been looking for an excuse. I've known something was on your mind ever since you got home, and it wasn't Mam! So you thought you had the perfect opportunity to come out or be de-frocked or whatever it is. You don't care if it's going to upset Da or anyone else. You'd already made up your mind to leave. All that praying and talk about souls and sins and purgatory. You sanctimonious hypocrite! You're as bad as Abe Harvey was, and it's a wonder God hasn't struck you down, Sister Mary Magdalene! And that's a flaming joke as well, you certainly picked the right name. But now that Ginny's leaving and Joan isn't going to stay here and run the home, you suddenly realize that you won't be free to do exactly what you want after all, so it's back to the convent while you think of something else.'

Monica abandoned her pious, serene attitude. 'It's lies! It's all lies!'

Abbie hadn't finished. 'Your duty lies here, at home, looking after Da. You put him and Mam through enough worry over the years. Worry that, added to other things, probably caused her first stroke. So now you can do something for them . . . him . . . for a change.'

Monica rose, her face set. 'Leaving the Order is not something that can be done overnight. It takes time.'

'So, you've got time. All the time in the world to make up to Da for the carry-on out of you all those years ago, and the loss of the grandson you gave up for adoption. Whatever the procedure is, you can start it the minute you get back. Joan's done more than her duty, Ginny's going away, I have my family, so everything is down to you now, Monica. If you walk out on Da, Bertie and Seb, Mam will haunt you for the rest of your life!'

Pat looked from one to the other, not really understanding everything Abbie had said, but remembering that Monica had been a bold madam who had caused his poor Sal to shed many a tear, and he wondered too, about his grandson.

Monica was livid, and she glared at Abbie. For years now she'd been waiting for a chance, a sound and valid reason, to give up a life she found more and more unbearable. Abbie could read her mind, but she'd never forgive her for putting her into this position or showing her up in such a bad light.

'So?' Abbie demanded.

'Oh, go to hell, Abbie!' Monica yelled, storming from the room.

'What have you done?' Joan cried aghast.

'I've made her face facts and her duty. You've done enough Joan, it's time you had a life of your own. It's what Mam wanted, she told me on no account were you to give up your home and come to live here. I wish Ginny had told us her plans earlier, but there it is. There's only madam there left.'

'She won't go back to being . . . well . . . the way she was . . . ?' Pat asked tremulously. Life had never looked more bleak, and he had no Sal to help him now.

'We'll make damned sure she doesn't, Da,' Abbie said firmly.

Later that week, Phil came to see Mike, and as she opened the door Abbie could see he had something important on his mind.

'How are you Abbie?'

She managed a smile. 'Not too bad, Phil. I suppose I'll eventually get used to Mam not being around. I heard you've applied for the CID?'

He nodded, and yet he didn't look very pleased about it, she thought, as she ushered him into the kitchen.

'Mike, I don't know if Abbie should be here for this.' Phil looked grim, yet there was a gleam of something else in his eyes, Mike thought.

'Oh, it's work.' Abbie wasn't really interested.

'No. No, it's nothing confidential.'

'Nothing is confidential in this house.'

'It's about Marty Mac.'

Abbie sat down suddenly, looking strained and upset.

Mike's eyes narrowed. 'What about him?'

Phil hesitated. He didn't want to cause Abbie any more distress.

She motioned to Phil to sit down. 'Now what?'

'He's just made his mistake. The only trouble is, he's going to take a few coppers down with him.'

'How?'

'You know Earnie "Chalkie" White from the top end of Benledi Street?'

'Yes. He pays his runners well so they don't grass on him and he doesn't do a stretch in Walton.'

'Marty Mac is one of his runners.'

'And?' Mike queried. Running for a bookie was a crime, but only small-time stuff.

'The bloody idiot only approached me to join the club.'

Mike looked dumbfounded. 'He knows you!'

'He knows of me, Mike. He knows I'm a copper, but he can't fit the face to the name. I suppose I've always been a bit of a loner, and I don't hang around the neighbourhood much now. I haven't since I joined. In fact I'm looking for lodgings, what with hoping to join the CID and all. I wasn't in uniform. I was walking down the back jigger when who should I see coming towards me but meladdo. Bold as brass, comes up to me and asks do I want to earn a bit of extra cash. Doing a few favours for Chalkie, like. Chalkie is always on the lookout for extra help.'

'Are you sure he didn't know you?'

'Yes. He's as thick as the wall, I told you that. So, I

said maybe. "It's dead easy. It's all squared with Chalkie and his scuffers," he said.'

'What scuffers?'

'I asked him that, and he said "no names", so I said he was lying and I wasn't interested. He said if I didn't believe him I was to go and ask Chalkie.'

'Did you?'

Phil shook his head. 'I don't know if he was lying. I don't know if it's a fantasy from start to finish.'

'He might be setting you up, Phil.'

'He's not bright enough for that.'

'Was he drunk?'

'No. I came to you first. I don't like the sound of it at all, but if I can nail him for anything, I bloody will!'

Mike, too, didn't like the sound of it.

'What will you do?' Abbie asked quietly.

Phil shrugged, but Mike was on his feet. 'Come on, let's go and see my inspector. See what he has to say. I can't say I'm happy about setting up colleagues, but . . .'

'A few rotten apples spoil the whole barrel,' Abbie interrupted.

'She's right.'

'What if it's all lies?'

'No harm you going to see Chalkie and finding out, one way or the other. I'd give anything to put MacNamara inside, you know that, and trying to bribe a copper will put him away.'

Phil nodded.

'If it's true, and we're both in on the ground floor,

so to speak, it won't do our chances of promotion any harm.'

'I'll get in the CID?'

'Bound to and I might even get made up to sergeant. All courtesy of Marty Mac's stupidity and big mouth. I'll enjoy seeing his face.'

'If it's true,' Phil reminded him. The prospects of promotion, higher status and more money was something he hoped would impress Chrissie, show her he had something to offer her – prospects, a good future – but he wasn't happy about pointing the finger at fellow officers. But as Abbie had said, corruption rubbed off on them all. It tarnished the image of the force and all those who wouldn't take a bribe to save their lives.

It had all been arranged with Inspector Burrows. Phil went to see Chalkie and came back with the names of no less than ten constables. Chalkie had a good set-up. It was known about.

Phil was stunned. 'I never realized! I never bloody realized!' he said to Mike as they sat in an interview room at Hatton Garden, having been interviewed themselves and given statements.

'I know. It makes you feel sick. There's only one who's an old timer, though. The rest were taken on after the strike.'

'Like me,' Phil reminded him. 'Still, they got Chalkie and MacNamara.'

'Chalkie won't do a long stretch.'

'But Marty Mac will. Illegal gambling, and trying to bribe a police officer.'

'If I had my way he'd get life. He was responsible for Abbie losing the baby, you know.'

'They've finished with us now so let's get out of here! It's bloody depressing.'

As they went out into Dale Street, Mike turned to Phil. 'Do you think you'll like CID work?'

'I think it'll be better than pounding the beat, and I was never very happy sorting out drunks and domestics.'

'You've more intelligence than most, Phil, but you're quiet.'

'I get things done – my way.'

'I'm not criticizing. You're a good copper, although God knows what you see in our Chrissie. She's a madam and a half.'

Phil grinned. 'Well, she won't be able to shrug all this off, will she?'

Angela D'Arcy slammed the drawing-room door shut behind her and threw her hat and purse on the sofa. She wanted to scream, but Nichols would hear her. She stared malevolently at the sullen March sky beyond the windows. It suited her mood exactly. Her interview with her aunt had been far from pleasant. She'd been annoyed when Aunt Julia had telephoned and demanded she go immediately to see her, but to be ordered home like a child of ten had been far worse.

'Your mother is ill.'

'Mother's health has never been good since father

died,' had been her reply. Mother seemed always to be ill lately. She was becoming a hypochondriac. She was sure it was all done for attention.

Her aunt had been very firm and very scathing about where her niece's place should be, and Aunt Julia was a formidable old harridan who brooked no disobedience. So, despite her chagrin, Angela knew she had no alternative but to go to Ashenden.

She got up and mixed herself a drink, an idea taking hold of her. She'd telephone Freddie: if she was going to have to go home, then he could accompany her.

'Freddie, it's Angela.'

'Yes?'

'Mother is ill and Aunt Julia has more or less ordered me home, so you can come too.'

'Me? What do you want me for?'

'It's just as much your duty as mine to go.'

'You'll be there, Richard's there and Hannah, she's a nurse. What do you want me to come up for?'

Angela smiled smugly to herself. 'You always go up for the Grand National, don't you? Were you thinking of missing it this year? Out of funds are we?'

Her brother's tone changed. 'No! I'd not forgotten, you just caught me off-balance that's all. Right then, we'll drive up. I'll pick you up in the morning.'

As she replaced the receiver she smiled; it wouldn't be too bad with Freddie there, he was good company and they might not have to stay too long. Maybe just the weekend. She was sure there wasn't anything seriously wrong with Mother.

* * *

Hannah met them in the hall, Richard was busy with paperwork that had to be completed. 'Did you have a good journey?'

'Yes. How is Mother? Aunt Julia led me to believe she is at death's door.'

'She's a bit better today, Dr Fortescue called in this morning, and she's eaten a light lunch.'

Angela pursed her lips. Trust Aunt Julia to overreact. 'Well, I'll go up and see her.'

'I was coming home anyway, for the races at Aintree,' Freddie informed Hannah as she led the way to the ruby drawing-room.

'Really? Then it won't be an inconvenience for you, will it?' Hannah just couldn't understand the selfishness and callousness of Richard's siblings.

He was so different and, from what he'd told her and what she'd gleaned from Mason, his brother Hubert had not been like Freddie and Angela either. She'd always been close to her mother, and to Jerry. She made sure she visited Winnie every week. She stayed all day. Sometimes they went into town, sometimes to the lovely parks that Liverpool possessed. She also made sure Winnie lacked for nothing. Good carpets covered the floors of all the rooms, new curtains hung at the windows. Winnie had plenty of linen and towels, thick, soft blankets, good china, even one of the new gas cookers, and she'd told Hannah she didn't need any more clothes or hats for the rest of her life.

Conversation at dinner was a little strained. Richard was worried about his mother, for despite the fact that he knew her ailments were often imagined or blown up out of all proportion, and that she still hadn't accepted Hannah, he was very fond of her – something that couldn't be said for either Freddie or Angela. He'd had a long talk on the telephone with Aunt Julia, and she had told him to leave everything in her capable hands.

'You'll be off to the races at Aintree, I suppose.'

'Of course, wouldn't miss the Grand National for the world. Actually I've got a strong tip – Derby's Lad. I mean, Derby – D'Arcy, and from a good stable too.'

'I hope you can afford to lose whatever you plan to put on it.'

'Oh, please! I've only just set foot in the place, and besides I'm not going to lose any money on this one.' He was confident that he was going to win a tidy sum on Derby's Lad. He had heard that Kershaw's Music Hall was also strongly favoured, but he didn't like the name, a crazy name to give a horse in his opinion. Besides, depending on the going, it was anyone's race. Thirty-two had been entered so far. It had been very wet of late, and Derby's Lad was a horse that liked the going soft.

'Will you be going with him?' Hannah asked of Angela.

'I suppose so, there's nothing much else to do, although if it's raining I may not bother. I absolutely defy anyone to look smart in a mackintosh and boots.'

Hannah tried to turn the conversation away from

fashion and gambling. 'Dr Fortescue said her Ladyship is improving, but she must take more care of her health. She is not a strong woman, and she's had many shocks to contend with over the last years.'

Angela raised her eyebrows but said nothing, thinking that Mother could have done without the shock of her eldest son and heir to Ashenden marrying a labourer's daughter. Even if that labourer's daughter was as quiet and docile as a field mouse.

'What was it officially, Richard?' Freddie asked.

'A light seizure, so he said.'

'A mild stroke. Her speech will improve and hopefully the paralysis will lessen as long as she rests,' Hannah explained.

'Well, we won't be disturbing her, Hannah. No wild parties, etc., etc. That reminds me, while we're here, will we be seeing that little friend of yours?'

'You mean Chrissie?'

'As if you'd forgotten her name,' Angela laughed.

'I don't think her Ladyship would like that at all.'

'She doesn't have to know. She didn't last time.'

'She did. Bancroft told her. She was most upset and very annoyed. She wrote to Chrissie's mother.'

'What for?' Freddie thought a few drinks, a little music and conversation, wasn't that bad. He'd known Mother wouldn't approve, she didn't approve of anything he did. If Bancroft hadn't poked her nose in she'd never have known, then she wouldn't have got upset. No harm done to anyone, except for that blasted Bancroft woman.

'Because she wasn't consulted, Freddie. This is her home.'

'And ours, too, dash it! Are we not supposed to have friends here now? Can't even do a bit of entertaining? It's a bit thick.'

Hannah thought that for the very short amount of time they spent at Ashenden they could at least defer gracefully to their mother's wishes. It wasn't much to ask. She certainly didn't want Chrissie here again.

'Oh, drop it for heaven's sake, Freddie,' Richard instructed tersely.

His attitude and the even higher-handed one taken by his mother annoyed Freddie D'Arcy intensely. He was an inveterate gambler and womanizer, and he decided that they were both flinging down the gauntlet, and he wasn't a man to ignore a challenge. He decided he'd speak to Angela about Chrissie later.

Both Hannah and Richard retired immediately after dinner. Richard did not enjoy port these days, it seemed to lie heavily on his stomach. Hannah had no desire to sit with Angela, so Mason served the coffee in the ruby drawing-room.

'A bit high-handed of Mother to write to Chrissie's parents,' Freddie said after Mason had departed and Angela passed him the cream jug. 'A bit imperious. Do you know what I've a good mind to do?'

'What?' Angela asked, hoping it was something that would lighten the mood. Ashenden was bad enough, but Ashenden beneath grey, leaden skies from which descended soaking, needle-fine rain was even worse.

'Ask Chrissie to come to the National with us.'

'You mean take her with us? Meet people we know? Freddie, are you mad? Oh, she would look very ornamental and positively charming on your arm, but once she opens her mouth we'd be a laughing stock!'

'She doesn't have to open her mouth. As long as she just smiles and says "yes" or "no" in the right places.'

'Freddie, you're becoming impossible. You've taken a fancy to her, haven't you?'

'What if I have?'

'Richard will be furious.'

'Won't he just.'

'So will Hannah and so will Mother. She'll tell Aunt Julia, and no one will get any peace. We'll never hear the end of it. Oh, leave her alone, for God's sake, you'll just cause more trouble. Mother may have a relapse and we'll have to stay here for ages.'

'Don't be such a stick-in-the-mud, Angela. I'm not going to marry the girl, it's just a passing fancy. A penchant for a pretty girl. They don't have to know about it.'

'Are you suggesting we send Roscoe to pick her up and take her there? It would be all over the servants' hall in minutes, and Bancroft will set a new speed record in her haste to inform Mother.'

'No. I'll go for her in my car.'

'You *are* mad! This will all end in tears, Freddie, and what for? So you can have a few hours . . . well, doing whatever it is you intend to do. I'm not having any part in this, and if Richard or Hannah find out – you know how she runs to him with everything – he'll stop your allowance.'

'So what? I expect to win a tidy sum running into the thousands on this race. I won't need his damned money, at least not for a while. He'll cool down – if he finds out at all, that is. I'm going to write to her and post it from the village.'

'On your own head be it, Freddie, if her ghastly father comes storming up here with a shotgun, looking for you!'

'They don't have shotguns,' he interrupted.

'Who don't?'

'People like Chrissie's father,' Freddie laughed. He was looking forward to his time at Ashenden.

Chrissie had bought a new spring two-piece costume and a matching hat. She was intending to wear them for the presentation ceremony. Phil had been awarded the Humane Society's medal for bravery, for stopping a runaway horse from trampling half the pedestrians in Lord Street.

Runaways were not uncommon, often no one was hurt, or a couple of people sustained minor injuries, but this had been different. Lord Street had been crowded with shoppers, and many people would have been trampled and killed. Stupid horses took fright at the least thing and then took off, at least motor cars weren't like that. You controlled them entirely. If a lumbering great cart horse decided to take it into its idiotic head to bolt because of a sudden noise, there was very little in the way of brakes, reins, bits or anything else that could stop it. Hilda was very gratified that Phil was going to be honoured, and even more so that Chrissie had at last shown good sense in agreeing to accompany him to the Town Hall and had even bought a new outfit. In her opinion Chrissie spent far too much on clothes. But she did seem to be more content with Phil lately. Of course that could be Chrissie's way of lulling her into a false sense of security. She was crafty, was Chrissie, and had been since the day she could talk.

She hadn't enquired about the letter her daughter had received. She'd been busy helping out up at Pat Kerrigan's. She'd promised Joan to take a turn with Abbie and herself getting Pat and Seb's meals now that Ginny had gone. Monica had made the first move to leave the Order, a fact much speculated about and the cause of a fearful row between Abbie and her twin, or so she'd heard.

When Chrissie came down all dressed up on the morning she was to accompany Phil, and announced she wasn't going to the Town Hall, Hilda was at first stunned and then she flew off the handle.

'Why not? You promised! Why are you all dressed up like that if you're not going?'

'Because I'm going to Aintree instead. To the races.'

Hilda was speechless.

'Who the hell with?' Frank demanded.

'With Freddie D'Arcy. He's picking me up by the Rotunda.'

Hilda found her voice. 'Oh no you're not, madam! You're not going to make a fool of Phil like this, and you're not going running off to no races with . . . with *him*!'

'I am and you can't stop me. I'm twenty-one. I can get married if I want to, and without your consent. You can't stop me, I'm going. I don't want to go to a boring ceremony at the Town Hall. When we went last time we were hanging around for hours. I'm going to the races. It's the biggest social event around here, everyone will be there.'

'Frank, stop her! She can't do this to Phil.'

'I'm not going to listen to anything, Da!'

'Chrissie, he's a fine, decent lad,' Hilda interrupted. 'And he's going to join our Michael in the CID next month. He's well thought of after that betting scandal, and he'll go far, he's got brains. Michael says so. He'll have a good wage, he'll be able to afford a nice house like the one Michael and Abbie are moving to on Queen's Drive. How can you do this to him Chrissie, when he thinks the world of you?'

'Mam, he's so quiet, so boring, and I don't want a rotten house on Queen's Drive.'

'Oh, I see, this Freddie isn't quiet or boring and he can offer you more. A big posh house, is that what you're thinking? Well, you're a fool Chrissie Burgess, a stupid little fool! He doesn't care about you, he's using you, he's laughing at you. You're just a pretty bit of fluff he can take out for a few hours!'

'How do you know what he feels for me? How do you know what he's like?'

'Because why else should he bother with the likes of you? All he's after is . . . is what he can get! Don't think for a moment that you'll be like Hannah, because you won't. He's not like his brother.'

'I'm not staying here listening to all this. You don't want me to have the chance of a good time, or something better in life than a stupid, piddling little house on Queen's Drive!'

As Chrissie turned towards the door Hilda caught her by the shoulder and shoved her into the street. 'Look at it, Chrissie! Just take a good look down there at the factory chimneys, the docks, the kids with their dirty faces and tatty clothes! This is what you come from, Chrissie Burgess. This is what you are, and the sooner you realize it, the better it will be for everyone. This is Burlington Street, not Bold Street or Bond Street. This is where you belong!'

Chrissie wrenched herself free, her cheeks burning with anger and humiliation. She straightened her hat, squared her shoulders, set her lips in a tight, determined line and marched purposefully up the street.

Chapter Twenty

———◆———

OH, THIS WAS THE LIFE, Chrissie thought. The morning had been cloudy. There had even been some spots of rain, and she'd been worried that her new outfit would be ruined and she'd look a mess, should it rain in earnest. But the clouds had disappeared and the spring sunshine washed over Aintree Racecourse, making everything appear fresh and newly washed.

It shone on the county stand, making the white paintwork look dazzlingly bright. It picked out the rainbow-coloured stripes of the marquees, the brilliant array of coloured silks the jockeys wore. It gleamed on the smooth, well-groomed coats of the horses that were the result of hours of work with brushes and curry combs. There was excitement and expectation in the air, so strong you could almost smell it. In fact, the whole place had a unique air, probably something to do with the fact that there was only one race meeting a year held here, and the Grand National was the world's greatest steeplechase. And she was here.

Actually *here* in the thick of it, amongst the noisy but good-humoured crowd.

As soon as she'd seen Freddie waiting for her at the junction of Stanley Road, she'd firmly pushed all thoughts of her mam and Phil to the back of her mind. She was going to enjoy herself today and no one was going to stop her. The traffic had been heavy, and the further along Walton Vale and Warbreck Moor they'd got, the thicker it had been.

He'd informed her that he had already dropped Angela off, and they were to meet up in the Owners' Bar. He didn't own a horse, but his father had had many a runner in the National, and both he and Angela were well known.

Angela had been surrounded by a group of quite obviously wealthy young men, most of whom Freddie introduced to Chrissie. Of course she had been very overwhelmed and reticent and hadn't entered into the conversation very much at all. But that hadn't stopped her feeling as though she was one of them, that she belonged to this set. She was confident that, to be accepted, all she needed was a pretty face, a slender figure and fashionable clothes.

Freddie had won ten guineas on the first race, but she'd lost ten shillings and wasn't going to run the risk of losing any more. She couldn't afford it. It was all she had left from her savings, after she'd bought her outfit, for which she'd paid more than she had budgeted for.

'What do you fancy for the big race?' Freddie asked her as they studied the race card.

'Oh, there's so many to choose from that I don't really think I'll bother. It's just as exciting to watch as it is to bet.'

'Chrissie, that's a sacrilegious thing to say! Not bet! Here on the hallowed turf of Aintree, on one of the most prestigious races of the year! Tut! Tut! What am I to do with you?'

She laughed a little nervously, feeling reckless. 'Well, I might be persuaded . . .'

'I know what we'll do. We'll go and place the bets together. Here, have this, put it on any horse you like, but if you've got sense you'll go along with me on Derby's Lad.'

Chrissie was taken aback as he pressed a crisp white five-pound note into her hand. 'Five pounds! I couldn't!'

'Only a fiver I'm afraid. I'm putting my shirt on this one.'

She was about to say that it would take her months to earn five pounds, but she bit back the words and accepted the money with a smile. She must remember she was moving in different circles now, she told herself. Five pounds to Freddie D'Arcy was nothing.

She picked Kershaw's Music Hall at twenty to one.

'Chrissie, it's money down the drain!' Freddie laughed.

'I like the sound of it and there's a family called Kershaw in . . . near where I live and I've often seen them at the music hall.'

'You'll regret it, my lovely. I'll regret it, but if that's what you fancy, go ahead. We're going to have a wonderful day and a wonderful night.'

Chrissie looked at him with surprise.

'There will be a big party at the Adelphi tonight. It's traditional, everyone will be there. The winning owner stands drinks all round. I happen to be well known by the winning owner – well, he will be that by tonight. Oh, yes, Chrissie, the Bollinger will be flowing freely tonight.'

She hadn't expected anything more than a great day out, but a party was an added bonus, and at the Adelphi Hotel of all places. That was where all the very wealthy people and the cinema stars stayed. Then one realization arose to mar her delight. She didn't have an evening gown, and everyone was sure to be dressed to the nines. Neither could she go home to change into something different, because there would be another row. Then she smiled. If she won some money, maybe she could persuade him to take her into Liverpool before the shops closed to buy a dress. Something long, flowing and elegant.

They finally settled themselves into their seats in the county stand. Freddie had binoculars, and he'd need them, she thought, you couldn't see all the course. You could see in the distance as far as Melling Road and the Canal Turn, but no further. You had a very good view of the railway sidings, though, and the clock tower of the local orphanage, known as the Cottage Homes, she thought with mild amusement.

She knew the horses had to go round twice, so it would be a while before she knew if she could afford an evening dress.

The atmosphere was electric, as though everyone was holding their collective breath. Suddenly there was a shout. Everyone stood up and began to cheer, and she realized they were off. In a blur of colours she saw the leaders take the first jump, followed by the rest of the field, quite a few of which didn't get over it, or fell on landing. Before long she had forgotten her carefully maintained composure and was yelling and shouting like everyone else.

When they came into sight again there were very few horses left from the original thirty-two. Freddie looked very down, but she could see the colours of Kershaw's Music Hall still out there running, then they were gone again.

'Is your horse still there, Freddie?'

'No. It's fallen,' came the curt reply. 'Here you'd better take these.' He handed her the binoculars.

Chrissie didn't really notice just how upset he looked. She focussed the binoculars on the course, and then the spectators were on their feet again and she started yelling and jumping up and down, for her horse was one of only three left.

As they pounded down the last crucial stretch she screamed her encouragement.

'Come on! Come on Kershaw's! Kershaw's! Kershaw's!' Then she fell against Freddie laughing, her cheeks flushed, her eyes dancing. 'Freddie!

Freddie! I won! I WON! I'm rich, that's one hundred and five pounds, Freddie!'

'Chrissie, stop making a spectacle of yourself and us!' Angela snapped. She had taken Freddie's advice and had lost five pounds.

Chrissie couldn't believe it. One hundred and five pounds! Then some of the exhilaration faded. 'Oh, Freddie, you lost. You've lost all that money.'

Just how much, she couldn't even begin to realize, if she was overwhelmed at winning a hundred and five, he thought bitterly. And he'd borrowed money. He'd been so absolutely certain that by the end of the afternoon he'd be well in funds, to the tune of a couple of thousand. Now he didn't even dare to contemplate just how much he was down. He managed to shrug, refusing to meet Angela's eyes.

'Easy come, easy go.'

'But you gave me the money to bet with. If you hadn't done that I wouldn't have won. It was your money, you must have the winnings.'

Freddie had pulled himself together outwardly, inwardly he felt sick and depressed. 'Good grief, I couldn't do that. Can't take money off a lady . . . girl,' he amended, seeing the look his sister flashed at him. 'It's out of the question, Chrissie. Let's go and collect your winnings.'

The sun had gone, covered by the thickening cloud that threatened a downpour. The crowds were beginning to leave. The Owners' Bar was packed.

'Lord, what a crush!' Angela exclaimed, although

there was no note of annoyance in her voice and she quickly moved into the crowd, laughing and calling to friends. She'd had enough of Chrissie for one day.

Freddie smiled vacantly at those acquaintances who commiserated with him in an off-hand sort of way. 'Oh, bad luck old chap! Bit of a bad show, what?' 'I'm a bit down amongst the wines and spirits myself', were the type of remarks addressed to him. He was still stunned, and accepted the drinks offered to him until Chrissie tugged at his sleeve.

'Freddie, don't drink too much now, there's the party, remember?'

He looked mystified. 'What party?'

'At the Adelphi.' She pouted. 'We *are* still going? Oh, don't say we can't go, please, Freddie. It's been a really great day for me.'

He wondered if she had any sensitivity at all. The last thing he wanted to do was go to a celebration.

'Oh, please, Freddie?'

He shrugged and nodded reluctantly.

'There's a bit of a problem.'

He looked exasperated. 'Now what?'

'I'll need to go into town – Liverpool. For a dress.'

He finished his drink in one gulp. That's what he needed, some fresh air and to get away from this crowd. 'Fine, let's go.'

Chrissie hadn't expected such enthusiasm and had been prepared to do more coaxing. 'What about Angela?'

'Oh, don't worry about her. She'll find someone to take her home and to the party.'

She had to admit he'd been very patient. He'd dropped her at the top of Bold Street, saying he'd come back for her in half an hour, and had then gone to install himself in the splendidly Edwardian Philharmonic Hotel, opposite the Philharmonic Hall. She would have preferred longer, as this was to be her first evening gown. In the event, time hadn't mattered. She bought the first dress she tried on in Cripps. It might have been made especially for her – scarlet and black chiffon lined with taffeta. The back plunged deeply. The bodice was embroidered with black bugle beads and scarlet sequins. The skirt was cut on the cross and draped beautifully, ending in handkerchief points that floated around her ankles. She also purchased a scarlet satin headband, studded with diamanté stones and sporting two black ostrich feathers. A pair of black patent leather pumps completed the ensemble. She looked stunning, even the sales assistant said so.

It was all packed carefully and she walked up to the Philharmonic and found him propping up the bar.

'I said I'd meet you.' He sounded annoyed.

'I know but I'm early. Can I have a small port and lemon, please?'

He nodded to the barman while thinking what a desecration of fine port it was to mix it with lemonade.

'I hate to be a real pain, Freddie, but where am I going to change? I'm not going home.'

'Oh, for God's sake, Chrissie!' He was facing ruin and all she could think about was herself.

She looked hurt and the barman intervened. 'There's a bit of a room at the back, if the lady doesn't mind a bit of clutter? Or there's the ladies . . . er . . . toilets.'

Chrissie smiled at him. 'Thanks, I'll get changed in the back.' She could have a wash and do her hair in the toilets, there was bound to be a mirror.

Despite the leaden feeling that had settled over him, on which the drink seemed to have no cheering effect, Freddie couldn't help but think she did look gorgeous. Every head in the room turned in her direction.

'Do you think we should go for something to eat?' she asked, pleased at being the centre of attention.

'No, we'll go straight there.' He couldn't afford to give her dinner, and besides there would be canapés provided.

The hotel was very busy, and Chrissie glanced around in awe at the magnificent foyer and public rooms. It was like a palace. She knew she was causing a stir. Openly admiring glances from the men, openly envious ones from the women. She didn't care. She had a great deal of money in her purse, she looked stunning and she had Freddie.

As the evening wore on, the drink flowed freely and they both drank too much. Chrissie's laughter became louder. Freddie's mood morose, then increasingly irritable. At ten o'clock Angela caught her brother's arm.

'For heaven's sake take her home! Get her out of here, Freddie, she's making a perfect spectacle of us both! She's drunk and she's so common!'

'I will. I've had enough. Are you coming home?' he snapped.

'Not yet, it's too early. Charlie Sefton is going to drop me off at Ashenden. His chauffeur's round the back somewhere with the car. Just get her home, Freddie!'

Chrissie was annoyed. She'd been enjoying herself, surrounded by admiring young men who seemed fascinated with her. Freddie ignored her protests, steering her firmly through the crowd.

She settled herself in the car and glanced at him from beneath her lashes. He looked annoyed, and a wave of sympathy washed over her.

'I'm sorry, Freddie. It can't have been much fun for you in there. I'm really glad you took me. I'm very grateful.' Her words were slurred.

He hadn't attempted to start the car or switch on the lights. It was dark in Bolton Street, at the back of the hotel, so he couldn't see her face clearly.

She reached over and laid her hand on his cheek. 'I really, really am grateful. It's been great.' She was concentrating hard on the words.

He felt anger well up inside him. Couldn't she see how devastated he was? Was she really so stupid, so self-centred? He just wanted to get rid of her and get back to Ashenden. He'd had nothing from her all night but vapid, fatuous remarks. No real sympathy, no understanding, no support. Well, he was going to get something before he took her home. He leaned over and took her in his arms, none too gently, and began to kiss her passionately.

She responded, the champagne making her dizzy and giving the impression that she was floating on a cloud. His hands moved over the soft skin of her back, exposed by the low cut dress. Then his fingers closed over the firm flesh of her breast. He pulled her closer and began to pluck at the folds of chiffon that covered her legs.

'Oh, Freddie, don't!' she pleaded in a breathless, half-hearted way.

'Chrissie, I want you!' His hand was moving up her leg and she could feel him hard against her. She shivered with longing. Oh, she wanted him, but it was wrong. What about God and sin? What about Mam? An image of Hilda's face, then that of Frank flashed across her mind. Oh, God! What was she doing? She struggled against him, jerking her head away.

'No! Stop it, Freddie! Stop it!' Her voice became shrill. 'No!'

'Chrissie! Chrissie!'

Nausea washed over her. 'Freddie, I feel sick! I think I'm going to be sick!'

Freddie's ardour died. He pulled away and released her. 'Oh, for God's sake don't throw up in the car!' He got out, went round to the passenger side and hauled her to her feet. 'Take deep breaths! Let's walk for a while, then I'll get you a taxi.' This was the final straw!

Why had he agreed to take her to the bloody party in the first place? Why had he taken her to Aintree at all? Well, as soon as she'd sobered up a bit he'd put her in a cab and be rid of her. Then maybe he'd go down to the river and walk, let the salt air clear his own mind and try to think about the future.

Angela had just arrived home.

'I got her a cab. She said she felt ill.'

'Oh, she didn't cap it all by throwing up?'

'Not while I was with her, she didn't.'

'Well, what's the damage?'

'Oh, God! I don't even want to think about today! I used my entire allowance, and I borrowed on the strength of it too.'

'How much did you borrow, and from whom?'

'Five hundred pounds from Roderick Lansdowne.'

Angela exploded with temper. 'You fool! You stupid, moronic imbecile!' she cried. 'Including your allowance.' She did a quick mental calculation. 'My God! That's nine hundred pounds, Freddie! On a horse! On a blasted horse!'

'I know. I know. But I was certain I was going to clean up.'

'Nothing is ever certain in a race like that. Oh, don't you ever learn? Richard is going to be furious!'

'I can't tell him. He won't bail me out, you know he won't, not for that much.'

'Then what in the name of heaven are you going to do?'

'Emigrate.'

'Don't joke!'

'I wasn't,' he said grimly.

'I'm down myself this month, but I can let you have two hundred. It will mean I'll be destitute until next month, but—'

'You're a brick, Angela. If I can just get enough to pay Lansdowne back, I can live at Elmsford Square quietly, very quietly, for a few months. Maybe if I explained to Mother—'

'No! I couldn't stand another interview with Aunt Julia, and I couldn't face being stuck here and being short of funds.'

'I could buy a ticket and sail to New York. Cunard run a regular service from Liverpool.'

'Don't be so stupid! How long do you think you would last there with no money?'

'What about Hannah, then?'

'She tells Richard everything.'

'Maybe if I asked her not to.'

'What would you do if she refused you and insisted on telling Richard? You'd be up the creek without a paddle then.'

'Well, it's a chance I've got to take!' he snapped. 'You don't think I'll enjoy it, having to ask *her* for money?'

Angela threw her hands up in despair and went up to her room, leaving her brother with his bitter thoughts and the whisky decanter.

It wasn't until after lunch the following day that

Freddie managed to get his sister-in-law alone and away from the house. She was sitting in the sunken rose garden, reading. It was a mild afternoon for the time of year and she wore a lilac alpaca jacket over her warm dress.

'Ah, Hannah.'

'Hello Freddie. You look edgy. Is anything the matter? I noticed that you didn't eat much at lunch.'

He sat down beside her. 'This isn't easy, Hannah.'

She laid down her book. 'What's the matter?'

'I want to ask you something, but I don't want you to speak to Richard about it.'

She looked gravely puzzled. 'Why can't I tell Richard?' She suddenly remembered Chrissie. 'It's nothing to do with Chrissie, is it?'

'No, nothing like that.' He managed a wry smile. 'Your little friend won quite a packet on the National yesterday. On a horse named Kershaw's Music Hall, of all things.'

Hannah, too, remembered the Kershaw family who lived at the top of Dalrymple Street by the Rotunda.

Freddie fidgeted with his watch chain, hating every minute of this. Raw humiliation gnawed at his insides. 'She did, but I . . . I didn't.'

Understanding dawned on Hannah. 'Oh, Freddie, how much did you lose?'

'You must promise you won't tell Richard? I was assured it was a certainty, Hannah, I put everything on it.'

She wasn't happy about not telling Richard of

Freddie's plight, but he looked so down, so utterly miserable. 'How much?'

He knew she would faint if he told her the exact amount. 'Three hundred pounds.'

She was shocked. 'Three hundred pounds! That's an awful lot.'

'I know, but if you could lend me it, I would live quietly in London until I've paid you back.' He was having to bite his tongue. He was so mortified at having to beg her for money. 'Please, Hannah? I really wouldn't ask, but I'm desperate.'

She sighed heavily. She didn't use more than a fifth of her allowance per month. She wanted for very little, and she had no extravagance; she did have quite a bit saved up. 'Well, I suppose so. I can't see you reduced to being penniless. If I lend you three hundred and fifty, that will give you something extra to live on.' She was aware that, for Freddie, living quietly in London was an almost impossible feat. He'd just have to try, that's all.

'Hannah, you're an angel! You're a saint! You're the best sister-in-law a man could ever have!'

'Stop that. I'll go in now and write you a banker's draft.'

'And Richard?'

'I won't say a word this time. I promise.' She smiled at him, he could be so charming, and he did look very relieved. It wouldn't do him any harm to live on a budget for a while.

He watched her as she walked towards the house.

The money Richard gave to her would, in addition to his allowance, have made all the difference in the world to his bank balance. Why the hell had Richard ended up in that blasted hospital! Mother should have had him removed. He would never have met her. Without her, his brother might not have recovered so well, and he would have had more sway over him and Mother, to loosen the purse strings. It could be worse, though. What if she had a child: a boy, an heir to Ashenden? He'd never get his hands on the real money then. But could they have children? Was Richard capable? It wasn't something that could be asked about. He kicked moodily at a small stone and cursed Hannah. Now his allowance would have to go to her and Angela. It would be months before he had any money in his pocket to call his. As he turned, he glared at the grey stone walls of Ashenden and cursed Hannah, his brother and their misalliance.

Chapter Twenty-One

HANNAH WATCHED THE LEAVES falling from the trees onto the lawns beyond the terrace. October. Golden October, Mam always called it. It was a mellow time, she thought. The harvest was in 'ere the winter storms begin', as the words of the hymn sung at the Thanksgiving Service at St Ambrose's had reminded everyone.

The pathways through the gardens to the coppice and the east wood were covered in the golds, ambers and russets of the fallen leaves. The air was misty with the hint of frost, the sun hazy. She smiled happily to herself. Before summer came again, Ashenden would have an heir or heiress. She'd had it confirmed by Dr Fortescue before she told Richard, and when she had told him he'd been so happy, so proud and thankful.

'Oh, Hannah, this is wonderful! A child! I never expected . . . I never thought . . .'

She placed her arms around his neck. 'Mr Copeland always said there was no reason why we couldn't.'

'Not only am I overjoyed, I'm very relieved.'

She'd been bemused. 'Why?'

'Because Ashenden won't end up in Freddie's hands. He'd sell it, and the estate too.'

'Surely not?' She'd been thinking that Freddie had learned his lesson. At least she had hoped so.

'Gambling is a way of life with him. It's like a drug, he can't stop. At least now I know that when I've gone Ashenden will be in safe hands.'

She had kissed him and they had sat making plans for the future – all their futures – until well into the autumnal dusk.

She caught sight of a car as it rounded the bend in the drive. Freddie had been to pick Angela up from Liverpool. She'd come up on the train, at Richard's behest. Lady Ashenden was ill again.

She turned away from the window, thinking how beautiful, how tranquil the summer had been. There had only been one small dark cloud that had marred her peace of mind. Freddie had come back to Ashenden at the end of August and had begged her to try to understand why he hadn't been able to pay off all his debts. It had shaken her to learn that he also owed money to Angela and to a friend. She realized, too, that he hadn't been truthful with her. Now he was once again short of funds.

Her mother-in-law's condition hadn't improved much after her first stroke. Her speech was still a little slurred, she was still partially paralysed. Bancroft hovered over her ceaselessly, flapping like a mother hen until once, in a fit of sheer exasperation and annoyance, she had turned on the woman and told her to leave her mistress alone for once. The poor woman got no peace at all with her hovering over her hour after hour. It had not improved relations between herself and Bancroft, but she had been amazed how well Lady Ashenden had taken her outburst. Her mood had softened a little.

'Fussing around like that! She's enough to make anyone ill. I know she has served you faithfully, but there is a limit to everyone's patience, and she's pushed me to the end of mine.'

'She's getting old, like me,' her mother-in-law had said slowly and thickly.

'You're not old and you'll get over this, with rest. Every day you should have a complete afternoon's rest, without any disturbance at all until tea-time,' she'd stated, and thought the ghost of a smile had lifted one corner of Richard's mother's mouth. 'I know. I'm reverting to my nursing manner. I'm sorry.'

'You have changed since you came here,' had been the unexpected reply.

She had smiled at her mother-in-law, for that was praise indeed.

Mason entered the room, followed by Charles and Henry, and she realized it was tea-time.

'Lady Angela is just arriving, Mason. I'm sure she'll be glad of some tea.'

Mason nodded, and Henry went to fetch more dishes.

'Her Ladyship will have her tea at five, as usual.'

'Henry will take it, my Lady, or would you prefer that Bancroft . . .' he left the question unfinished.

'Between you and me, Mason, I would prefer Bancroft to retire – permanently – but I suppose that's being unkind. She had better take it.'

Mason's features remained impassive, but there was a spark of amusement in his eyes.

'Tea! I'm parched and it's raw outside. I hate to think that winter is nearly upon us.' Angela shivered as she entered the room, having left her coat, hat and gloves with Jessie, and told the girl to inform Bancroft to attend to her unpacking.

'How is Mother?' As she took the cup Hannah proffered, Angela thought she was beginning to sound like a parrot. Mother's health was the topic always first discussed, whether it be on the phone or in a letter or as now, in person.

'There hasn't been much improvement and Dr Fortescue has told us she may well suffer another, more severe stroke at any time. I believe him. I've seen cases like this before.' Hannah thought of Sal Kerrigan while she sipped her tea. Angela seemed genuinely perturbed. 'I'm sorry, but we all have to be prepared for it,' she added.

Freddie and Richard arrived together.

'Have you been upstairs, Angela?'

'No, I've only just arrived, Richard. At least give me time to catch my breath.'

'You've told her?'

Hannah nodded.

'How long will you stay?'

Angela bit her lip. 'I don't know.' She glanced at Freddie for support, but he was staring past her, out of the window.

Angela sighed heavily. 'I'll see how things progress. Aunt Julia will come up as soon as she possibly can.' She was thankful that she hadn't had her aunt to contend with all the way from Euston to Lime Street.

'Good, then before she arrives and while we're all here together, Hannah and I have some news – good news.'

Hannah blushed as Richard took her hand. 'I – we're going to have a baby.'

There was complete silence that, to Hannah, threatened to stretch into infinity.

'Well?' Richard said brusquely.

'Oh, congratulations, I suppose!' Angela managed to get out, still stunned. 'Have you told Mother?'

'No, not yet.' He had wanted to tell her immediately, but Hannah had been more cautious. There was no way of knowing how her Ladyship would take the news. She might welcome it, she might not. 'We'll tell her when she is a bit stronger. Dr Fortescue advised us to wait, as it may be a shock.'

'Oh, it'll be that all right!'

Richard stared hard at his brother; he had been wondering how Freddie would take it. 'There's no need to use that tone, Freddie. I understand how you must feel . . .'

Freddie felt as though he'd been struck a blow in

the solar plexus. He felt winded and physically sick. He'd assumed that they wouldn't have children. They'd been married well over a year and there had been no sign of Hannah becoming pregnant. But now! His anger and outrage burst forth.

'How the hell can you understand? You understand nothing! Nothing!'

'I see. You're in debt again, or is this outburst because you realize that now you'll never inherit?'

Freddie was in the grip of a violent fury. 'I'm in debt because of you! You and your blasted economies. I'm entitled to my share in all this!' he stormed, throwing his arms wide.

'You're not entitled to any part of Ashenden.' Richard's voice had also risen with anger. 'Father's will was very explicit on that. He knew you'd squander whatever you got your hands on. He was a man who enjoyed gambling, but not to excess, like you.'

'For God's sake stop shouting, do you want the whole house to hear you?' Angela interrupted.

Richard turned to his wife and sister. 'Hannah, Angela, I think it best you leave us.'

Angela, too, was becoming angry as the situation dawned on her fully. 'How dare you speak to me like that, Richard. I will not be sent out of the room like a naughty child!'

Freddie was beside himself. He felt cheated, robbed of all status and inheritance by this child Hannah was carrying. 'I'm entitled to more than you deign to give me!'

'You're not! You can take it up with the solicitor – Wilding – if you wish. But don't labour under the illusion that you can make me feel sorry for you and relent, or give you a lump sum as some form of compensation. Do you think I'm a fool? I might just as well sign a cheque over to some bookmaker! I've no intention of doing that, wasting my son's or daughter's inheritance.'

Angela intervened. 'You really aren't being fair to him, Richard. He does have a position to keep up. How can he do that on such a pittance of an allowance? It's barely enough for *me* to manage on.'

'You both live in comfort – in luxury – in two London properties that I maintain. I pay the bills, I pay the wages of the staff. I have only just sorted out affairs here, paid the debts. I have been forced to sell Father's horses, some land and some property, but for once, and since God knows when, Ashenden is now in the black.'

Freddie kicked a footstool out of his path as he paced the room. 'You're obsessed! You're obsessed with this damned place! It's a mausoleum, a bottomless pit, a millstone.'

'It's my inheritance! My children's and yours too!'

'Oh, it will never be ours, we'll not see a penny from it now,' Angela cut in.

'If it was left to you two in a couple of years everything would have gone! Sold, mortgaged, squandered! You are both a disgrace to the name of D'Arcy!'

Freddie slammed a fist down hard on the mantle-

340

piece. 'Oh, to hell with Ashenden, the D'Arcy name and the bloody family! And to hell with you both and your flaming brat!'

Hannah's face was white with rage. She could see that Richard was both angry and hurt, as she was herself. She had never imagined that Freddie could be so callous or so malicious. What he owed her didn't matter, but she saw now how he'd used her, playing on her sympathy to dupe her into not telling Richard. But there was another matter of more importance than wounded feelings to be attended to now. She got to her feet.

'If you'll excuse me, I'll go and make sure your mother has her tea and that no word of this . . . this . . . argument reaches her ears. It could kill her.' She looked pointedly at Freddie before she turned and walked slowly from the room with as much dignity as she could muster.

'Go back to London Freddie, before I say something I'll regret. I'll send for you if Mother needs . . . asks for you,' Richard said coldly.

Freddie walked to the door. 'And what about my dear sister? Is she to follow me into exile?'

'Don't be so dramatic. Angela must make up her own mind!' Richard snapped.

Angela looked from one to the other. 'I'll stay, for a few days.'

Neither Angela or Freddie were at Ashenden when Lady Ashenden died. October had given way to November, and on the eve of Armistice Day she sent for Hannah, who was beginning to feel the first effects of pregnancy.

Lady Julia had sent Bancroft to fetch her, and the woman looked tired, her skin sallow in the lights on the staircase. Her dark dress made her look old and Hannah felt sorry for her. For over thirty years she had served her Ladyship. She'd had no other life, and derived very little enjoyment from it either. She looked exactly what she was – a tired, ageing spinster. Hannah noticed the time on the huge ormolu clock that was set in a niche on the wide landing. It was ten minutes to ten.

'Why don't you go to bed, Bancroft, you look worn out.'

'I might be needed,' came the tart reply.

'Lady Julia and I are here, should she need anything.'

The woman inclined her head stiffly. 'Thank you, my Lady, but I'll decline, if I may.'

Hannah gave up. She was too tired to stand and argue. Lady Julia met her at the door, and Hannah braced herself. Her mother-in-law's sister was a formidable woman who always made her feel inferior.

'You sent for me?'

'I didn't. Honoria wants to see you. Alone, apparently.' She looked pointedly at Bancroft who turned wordlessly and retraced her steps.

Hannah was surprised when Lady Julia turned away too. She thought the word 'alone' had meant without Bancroft. Lady Julia disappeared into the room next door. The one that Chrissie had slept in.

Her mother-in-law's bedroom was dark, the heavy curtains pulled across the windows. A dim bedside lamp threw out a feeble pool of light. The room smelled of sickness and another odour that Hannah recognized. Decay and death.

She approached the bed and was shocked to see how her mother-in-law's appearance had deteriorated. She was worried, seriously worried. 'How are you feeling? Didn't Dr Fortescue leave you some paraldehyde?'

Lady Ashenden looked fractious, and Hannah had to lean over to catch her words. She really didn't look as though she should be exerting herself at all.

'Bancroft told me . . . about the argument.'

Hannah pursed her lips in annoyance. She was going to have to speak to Richard about that woman; she was becoming far too meddlesome. 'Between Richard and Freddie?'

'Yes.'

'I'm sorry it happened. I'm even sorrier that you found out. We didn't want to upset or worry you.'

'They've always been headstrong and wilful, both of them.'

'It's no excuse for the way Freddie carried on, or the things he said. I knew Angela was sometimes insensitive, but I had never expected Freddie to be so malicious. It hurt us both, but particularly Richard.'

'Richard is like Aleric, my husband.' The words were becoming more laboured, the effort to speak more of an exertion.

'What did you want to speak to me about?' Hannah felt this interview should be concluded as soon as possible and the paraldehyde administered. She was also debating as to whether to call Dr Fortescue out.

'The child. I am pleased, of course, about it. It's a shame I won't be here but I'm content that there is to be one.'

'Please don't talk like that. You are only a year older than Lady Julia, and she has excellent health.'

'Julia has always been strong. She's always had a robust constitution. I was never like that.'

'You had excellent health when I first came here. You've had shocks, losses; they tell . . . in the end.'

'I wished you dead, amongst other things, when you first married my son. I freely admit that. But you have surprised me. I'm not saying I approve of you. You will never be suitable, but neither have you behaved badly or indiscreetly. You are a good wife to Richard, I hope you will be a good mother and bring up the child . . . children . . . as befitting their station in life.'

'I'll try to do as well as you have with Richard.' She didn't add 'and Hubert'. She dismissed all thoughts of Angela and Freddie from her mind.

'God forbid that you should ever have to live through a war, or lose your sons, or see them maimed, as I have done.'

'I pray God I won't. I know hundreds of mothers who feel like you, especially now.'

Lady Ashenden moved her head slightly. 'There

will be a minute's silence tomorrow, a minute that lasts a lifetime for mothers. You will know what I mean in time.'

'Don't get distressed.'

There was a moistness in the older woman's eyes but she maintained her composure. 'Nothing can change the fact that you *are* the Countess of Ashenden.' She reached out and touched the chest beside the bed.

'What is it?'

'In the top drawer, there's a box.'

Hannah opened the drawer and lifted out a large, satinwood box inlaid with mother of pearl and ivory, and placed it on the bed.

Her mother-in-law produced a small key and handed it to her. 'Open it.'

Hannah did so, and her eyes widened as her gaze fell on the contents. There was a fortune in diamonds, emeralds, sapphires and rubies. These were the legendary Ashenden jewels. She'd read about some of the pieces in books in the library.

'They are to be kept in the safe in the study, but they are yours, at least you will be their custodian. They must remain in your possession, to be passed on, in time, to the wife of your eldest son. Do you understand me?'

Hannah nodded. Her fingers holding the lid of the box trembled as a strange feeling crept over her. Even though she had been married for eighteen months, it was the very first time she had ever fully understood what the title that had been bestowed on her really meant. She felt very humble and honoured. She also realized that her mother-in-law knew her time was running out.

She took Lady Ashenden's hand. 'Thank you, I'll try to live up to them and my position. I promise I'll always try to live up to your example, too – in everything.'

Her mother-in-law tried to smile, but it was a twisted grimace. 'They will also be safer . . . from Freddie.'

'I'll send Lady Julia in, then you must sleep.'

There was an answering nod and so, carrying the box under her arm, Hannah let herself out. She tapped quietly on the door of the room where Lady Julia waited and went in.

'Your Ladyship, I really think we should send for Dr Fortescue at once, and also for Freddie and Angela.'

Lady Julia glanced at the box and then looked away. 'I think you are right. I'll see to it.'

'Thank you. I must go and tell Richard.'

The doctor arrived fifteen minutes later. Ten minutes too late. A composed but stricken Lady Julia met him and then took him to her sister's room. Richard sat staring at the telephone in the hall, waiting for both Freddie and Angela to ring back. He had insisted that Hannah at least rest.

'I won't sleep,' she'd protested.

'I know, but you can rest. I doubt whether anyone will sleep tonight.'

She'd caught his hand. 'At least she accepted me and she . . . was pleased about the baby.'

He nodded. As soon as he'd seen the box Hannah had carried into the drawing-room of the terrace-rooms, he'd realized that. Perhaps to others it wasn't much of a gesture. Personally passing on family heirlooms, not waiting for them to be handed over by a lawyer, but to him it meant a great deal.

'Not more clothes!' Hilda cried in exasperation as Chrissie staggered in through the door laden with parcels and boxes.

'No, not all of them! Some are Christmas presents.'

'Money just runs through your fingers like water.'

'Mam, I haven't spent that much. I've still got a lot left.'

'It's a wonder,' Hilda replied grimly. She would be glad in a way when all the damned money had gone. She'd never forget the evening Chrissie had come home from a party at the Adelphi, given by the owner of the winner of the Grand National, half-cut and with a fortune in five pound notes in her handbag. Her windfall hadn't made any difference to the way she felt about Chrissie's conduct that day – she'd been livid. He'd tried to hide it, but Phil had been very upset, and she'd soon put the damper on Chrissie's exuberance by giving her the sharp side of her tongue. At least there had been no more visits to Ashenden and no more letters from *him*.

Winnie kept her up to date with the news from

there. Hannah had told her there had been arguments between herself, Richard and Angela and Freddie. She'd said to Winnie that it was no wonder her Ladyship had taken ill and had then died, what with the carry-on out of them.

Of course she'd been as delighted as Winnie that Hannah was pregnant, and so was Abbie. Abbie said that when Hannah had last visited her she looked positively glowing with health. She was in mourning for her mother-in-law, but even sombre black didn't detract from her clear skin and shining eyes.

'Are you going out tonight?' she asked when Chrissie at last came downstairs.

'Yes. I think we're going to see *The Sheik*. Phil promised that as soon as it came to Liverpool we would go.'

Hilda raised her eyes to the ceiling. These modern girls. No wonder they were all so flighty and frivolous, being led up the garden path, given all kinds of mad ideas about love, by men like that Valentino. Of course he was handsome, in a foreign sort of way, and if you considered black oily hair and dark eyes attractive, but one look from him certainly didn't make her swoon. She'd read in the newspapers that his performance in this moving picture was making hundreds of impressionable girls faint. Actually faint! The very idea of such nonsense!

'I think he needs a medal for taking you and for sitting through all that tripe,' Frank commented.

'He's got medals, proper ones,' Hilda replied.

Chrissie said nothing. Mam was trying to impress on her Phil's sterling character. She had bought a new dress, but she didn't intend to wear it until Christmas Day, for Mam went on and on about her clothes. Instead she wore a pale green pleated skirt and loose, hip-length sweater in pale green and cream. It was a much cheaper version of the plain, fashionable sweater suits being advocated by Gabrielle 'Coco' Chanel, who stressed that 'even knitwear can be smart'. Over this she wore a bottle-green coat with velvet cuffs and a wide shawl collar. Her hat was a small confection of bottle green velour and pale green satin ribbon.

'You look like someone out of a fashion magazine,' Phil said admiringly as they walked towards the tram stop.

'How do you know? You don't read magazines – or do you?' she laughed.

'Well, you know what I mean. You look great.'

She glanced up at him from beneath her long lashes. He wasn't a bad-looking lad, she thought. She'd been so downhearted and moody when the weeks had passed and she'd heard nothing from Freddie D'Arcy. Phil had been very cool with her, but she certainly didn't blame him for that. If she were really honest with herself, she would say that she'd treated him abominably, for he was a decent lad. But gradually he'd come round and gradually her chagrin had faded.

It hadn't helped to have Mam saying things like 'That Freddie person thinks he can just pick you up when it suits him and then drop you. And, I told you he was just amusing himself.' But she'd gritted her teeth and said nothing. Yes, Phil was very nice, very ordinary, even a bit staid, but as it was nine months since she'd last seen Freddie, she had more or less resigned herself to the fact that he'd forgotten about her. On the few occasions when she'd seen Hannah, she hadn't mentioned either Angela or Freddie, and neither had Hannah.

'We expect to be busy over Christmas, apparently we always are. It seems to be a good time for thieves, fences and villains in general,' Phil had informed her. 'Mike said he hopes to get some time off on Christmas Day.'

Chrissie had nodded thoughtfully. 'Liam will be able to understand it more this year.'

'It's a nice house they've got.'

'It's all right. It's better than the last one, anyway. Abbie said she thought she would really miss Nell, but apparently she's moved, too. Some new houses in the back of beyond, further out than Aintree even.' As soon as she'd said the word Chrissie regretted it, for she felt Phil stiffen.

He was sure she hadn't done it on purpose. It had just been a slip of the tongue, part of the conversation, but the name triggered off the images of that day. He could still remember how he'd felt. He'd been looking forward to the ceremony, but even more so when she had agreed to accompany him and had bought a new outfit. When Hilda had told him of what Chrissie had done, he'd felt desolate. Somehow he'd managed to keep up appearances, laughing and joking with Mike and Abbie, but he'd been very hurt and very disappointed.

He hadn't gone near Hilda's house or shop for three weeks. He'd heard that Chrissie had won a lot of money, but he'd also heard that *he* had given her the stake money.

Bridie said he was a fool to even speak to Chrissie again, and she'd gone on and on about it. How she'd known Chrissie from the day she'd been born. How selfish, how crafty, how sly she was and always had been. She'd always been causing trouble of one kind or another, even as a child. And he wasn't to forget that she'd been so cruel that Abbie had slapped her face the day of poor Nancy's funeral. But he just couldn't help himself. He loved her. You never really knew where you stood with Chrissie, maybe that was part of the attraction, and she was a very pretty girl. She was young, spoilt and headstrong. He was sure that in time she'd settle down, and he told his stepmother that.

'In time she'll just get worse, you mark my words. You're too good for her, Phil. Give her up, you'll find someone else.' But he didn't want someone else. He wanted Chrissie. Each day he thanked God there had been no word from Ashenden, and it was nine months now. He was sure she was over Freddie D'Arcy and the mad ideas that mixing with the likes of him had put into her head.

Chrissie pulled the collar of her coat higher up

around her neck and shivered. 'I wish this flaming tram would get a move on, it's so cold.'

'You know what they say? They always come in threes.'

'Why don't you get a motor car?' she asked suddenly.

'Me? I couldn't afford a motor car.'

'Mam is always telling me how good a wage you earn, and Abbie doesn't seem to be doing without much these days.'

'Yes, it's not a bad wage, and we do have allowances for boots and clothes, but it's not enough to buy expensive things like cars. Mike only rents that house, he's not buying it.'

'How much are motor cars?'

'I don't really know. I suppose about a hundred pounds.'

'How much have you got saved up?'

'About ten pounds, and it's taken me years.'

'I've got fifty left, so that's sixty.' She looked up at him, excitement glowing in her dark eyes. 'We could save a bit more and buy one – between us.' She quite fancied the idea of herself at the wheel of a car. She had seen women driving them. Lots of girls had learned to drive during the war. Wouldn't that be something to look forward to. Wouldn't that cause a stir. And there'd be no more waiting about in the cold for trams.

He was staring at her with a mixture of amusement and incredulity. 'You're joking, Chrissie.'

'I'm not!'

'Us? Buy a car?'

'Why not?'

'Because people like us don't have cars. Can't afford to run them. Petrol isn't cheap. There's only two CID cars and two patrol wagons in the entire force. I know that because I was at the Seel Street garage the other day.'

'You sound just like Mam! You're so boring at times, Phil, you really are.'

'I'm not. It's just plain daft to think we can go around buying cars.'

She pursed her lips. She knew Mam, Da, Abbie, Bridie – in fact everyone – would side with him. She would be accused of getting above herself again, and she'd never hear the end of it. It wasn't a daft idea. If you had the money, why shouldn't you have things? But it was no use going on about it, she would be faced with derision and censure on all sides. At least there was now a tram in sight, but she felt very disgruntled, and her evening had been spoiled by his attitude and his refusal to see things her way.

Chapter Twenty-Two

———•———

SUMMER HAD BEEN LATE arriving, but from the end of June the sun had shone almost continually and now, in mid August, Hannah found the heat fierce and tiring. Edward was feeling the heat, too, he was fractious and whimpering. Roscoe had the car windows open, but it was still stifling. At least when she got to Abbie's it would be cooler, hopefully.

She stroked the soft cheek of her baby son. He was so precious to both herself and Richard. She looked back now to that night in May and still remembered vividly how exhausted but happy she'd been when, after an afternoon and evening of often excruciating pain followed by utter weariness, Dr Fortescue had placed her son in her arms.

Remembering her mother-in-law's words, and despite her own personal desires and misgivings, she had agreed that he be brought up in the traditional manner. He had a nanny and two nursery maids, a suite of rooms – a day nursery, a night nursery, a bathroom and even a tiny kitchen – but she was dreading the day when she would have to let him go away to school. Of course Richard intended that Edward should go to Eton, as he had himself. It would break her heart, but she had to remember that no matter how much she loved him, he wasn't a little boy who would grow up in Burlington Street. He wouldn't play cherrywobs or ollies on the dusty cobbles, or kick the can or football in the maze of narrow streets. He was a viscount, and was addressed or spoken of as Lord Edward. One day he'd be the eighth Earl of Ashenden.

'Oh, Hannah, let me look at him!' Abbie took the baby from Hannah and led the way to her parlour. 'It's cooler in here, I've kept the blinds down and I'll get us a drink when you've settled him. It's great that it's been such a good summer, but it's exhausting. It's been so hot at night that I can't remember when I last got a decent night's sleep.'

'It's too hot for him, too, the poor little mite.'

'Then why have you got him bundled up like that?' Abbie removed the light cashmere shawl, the satin and lace matinée coat, the embroidered lace dress beneath it and the petticoats. 'There, let him kick. Let the air get to his little body, poor little lamb.' Then she clapped a hand to her mouth. 'Oh, Hannah, I'm sorry. I forgot. I mean, he's not just a baby is he?'

Hannah interrupted her. 'Abbie stop it. He *is* just a baby to me. He's *my* baby. How long have we been friends? I won't let you drive a wedge between us. It makes no difference.'

'But Hannah there *are* differences, and they will

come between us, at least between our children. Especially as he gets older.'

Hannah knew she was right, but the knowledge saddened her. 'It was Nanny who dressed him, and she comes so highly recommended that I don't like to disagree with her. She knows best. Well, better than me anyway. I never had any younger brothers or sisters, so I don't know much about babies. Where's Liam?'

'Oh, he was so crabby that I put him to bed for a sleep. He was wearing me out. Mike has been on a murder case for weeks now, I've hardly seen him. Phil has too, and that hasn't gone down well with Miss High and Mighty Chrissie.'

'But she is still walking out with him?'

Abbie laughed. 'She'd have a fit if she heard you.'

'Why? I thought they had an understanding.'

'I mean she'd say how old-fashioned you were. They don't say "walking out" now, apparently. We're getting old, Hannah. Look at us, two staid old matrons with long skirts and long hair. I have to admit, though, that when it's as hot as this, I wouldn't mind short hair or loose, short dresses. Oh, I forgot, I've had a letter today from Dee and a photograph of Tommy, herself and Charlotte. But best of all, Hannah, she's coming home!'

'When?'

'Next February or March, before they get busy. They seem to be doing well. They've got more land and that means more fruit trees.'

'Does she say why she's coming? Not that she needs a reason I suppose.'

'Yes, you know that when Mam died they were so upset? Well, Dee says her own da is getting older and he's not been well lately, so she wants to bring Charlotte to see him and my dad. Tommy can't come, though, he's got to keep an eye on things. Here, read it for yourself.'

Hannah skimmed the lines of small, neat writing and smiled, then she took the photograph from Abbie. It was a very formal group. Tommy was standing very stiffly, one hand resting on Dee's shoulder. She was seated with the toddler on her knee. 'Tommy's hardly changed but Dee looks better, different. More relaxed, more attractive.' Dee Chatterton had been a very plain girl who wore glasses. She still wore the spectacles, but her hair was different, it was short.

'Oh, she's had her hair cut!'

Abbie laughed. 'I told you we were old-fashioned, but it suits her.'

'She's a bonny little thing,' Hannah commented, looking more closely at Charlotte Kerrigan.

'Isn't she. She seems to have inherited all our Tommy's and Dee's best features, thank God. Mam would have been thrilled to bits with her. She'd have spoiled her something rotten. She's going to be a very pretty girl, she's blonde like me and our Monica.' Abbie looked sharply at Hannah. 'And don't mention *that* one to me. I'm sure she's slowing down the leaving process just to be awkward.' Abbie turned the conversation back to its former topic. 'I remember in one of her letters Dee said she and Tommy had had a bit of a row. Apparently he kept calling Charlotte "Lottie Liverpool".'

'Oh, that's awful, the poor child. These things have a habit of sticking.'

'I know, he's changed it to Lady Liverpool. Now don't go getting airyated Hannah, but he says if your baby can be a viscount, then his can be a lady.'

Hannah laughed. 'That sounds just like Tommy.'

'Dee's taking Rose back with her.'

'Why?'

'Because Bridie's worried about her. She's stage mad. Ever since she started those dancing lessons Bridie says you can do no good with her. She'll be leaving school soon and she keeps saying she's going to be an actress or a dancer. Bridie said she's worn out telling her she's got to get a proper job, she's afraid that Rose might run off to London. She's had her hands full with Rose ever since that dancing class was part of the chorus in the pantomime at the Empire. So she'll be out of harm's way in Canada with Dee. Apparently Grimsby is only a small place, nearly all farms and orchards, although in summer Dee says it becomes like a seaside town. "The Chautauqua of Canada", though God knows what that means. They get boat loads of people arriving from Toronto, and even Buffalo, which is across the border. I suppose it must be a bit like going to the Isle of Man from here.'

'Don't seaside towns usually have theatres and music halls?'

Abbie looked perplexed. 'I never thought of that. I'll

have to write and mention that to Dee. She could end up in the same situation as Bridie, if Rose knows that.'

'What I came for, Abbie, was to ask a favour.'

'What kind of favour?'

'Edward is being christened at the end of this month, in the chapel at Ashenden. I'm Liam's godmother, so will you be Edward's? Aunt Julia is to be the other godmother and a cousin, Austin something or other, is being godfather.'

'What about Freddie and Angela?'

'Richard refuses to have Freddie, and I don't want Angela. Godparents have duties, and neither of them know what the word even means.'

'Is Aunt Julia the old dragon who was at the wedding?'

'Yes. She is a bit of a dragon, but at least she has values and standards. I've no idea what this cousin Austin is like. I didn't even know he existed. Apparently he's the son of Aunt Julia's brother-in-law. He's a barrister, so that's the legal side taken care of.'

Abbie was apprehensive. 'Oh, Hannah, I don't know. I mean there are problems.'

'What problems?'

'Religion to start with. You know I had to go down on my knees to Father Fitzpatrick when Liam was christened. And then . . . won't they all be put out that I'm, well, not one of them?'

'I want my best friend to be godmother to my son, I don't care what they all think. I've got beyond that now. What exactly do you mean about religion?'

'I think I'll have to get a dispensation, and you'd

better ask your vicar if it's possible, from their point of view.'

'It's not the vicar, it's the bishop. Aunt Julia is insisting, and I suppose I do agree with her in a way, it's traditional. Well, anyway, you go and see your priest and I'll make inquiries at my end. I really do want you to be there, Abbie.'

'I know you've called him Edward, but does he have another name?'

'A string of them: Edward Aleric George Gerald Francis.'

'Good grief!'

'Aleric is after Richard's father. George after the King, Gerald after poor Jerry, and Francis after Mr Burgess.'

'What's Edward for?' Abbie laughed.

'Because we both liked it. So I don't want to hear any more reasons why you can't be godmother, Abbie Burgess. I want you in your best frock in the chapel at ten o'clock on Sunday the twenty-sixth of August.'

Hannah was far from pleased to learn that Freddie and Angela were to come up for the christening. 'Why are they coming?'

'Because Aunt Julia said they must be invited,' Richard replied. 'I suppose she's right, to exclude them would only cause gossip, but I suspect that the weather has something to do with them agreeing to come.'

'The weather?'

'You've never been in London in August have you?

It's stifling, and so most people head for the country. All their friends will have left the city and gone home to the family seat or managed to get themselves an invitation to one.'

Hannah thought she didn't really mind Angela. It was Freddie she objected to. He hadn't set foot in Ashenden since his mother had died. They were both coming up on the train, and Roscoe was going to Liverpool to meet them. Angela had said it was quicker, but she was covering up for Freddie. He'd sold his car three months ago.

They travelled in a first class compartment paid for by Angela, and so they had complete privacy, for the train was far from full.

'Why did you agree to come, Freddie? It wasn't because of Aunt Julia's summons, that I do know.'

'I had to get out of London, as simple as that.'

'Escaping creditors?'

He nodded. 'I've sold everything I can sell, apart from the furniture, and I've even been tempted to do that.'

'Good God, it's that bad? Are you hoping to cast yourself on Richard's mercy? I'm afraid I don't think it will work. Now he has a son neither of us will get a penny more. I can help you a bit. How much do you owe, in total?'

'I daren't tell you. God, what am I going to do? I seem to owe everyone.'

'Start by giving up going anywhere near a racecourse or a casino.'

'I have. I've just told you I owe everyone.'

'Aunt Julia?'

'No! She'd haul me before Richard.'

Angela was really concerned. There had been cases of young men blowing their brains out because they'd been unable to meet their debts. 'Haven't you got any ideas about where you can raise funds?'

'If I could get my hands on a couple of pieces of jewellery . . .'

'Are you really serious?'

'Of course I'm flaming well serious!'

'Well I've got a few bits, I suppose you can have them.'

'It won't be enough.'

'Freddie!'

'I told you, things are as bad as they can be. If I can just get enough to pay some of them a bit on account and promise to pay the rest later.'

Angela was thinking. 'The Ashenden jewels are now in Hannah's possession, so we can't get our hands on them.'

'Couldn't we try?' he urged. A necklace or a couple of bracelets would wipe out all his debts.

'No. She is bound to find out and realize.'

'We could blame that girl, Nora.'

'I think Hannah would believe the girl before she'd believe us. Besides, they're probably locked away somewhere, she never wears any of them. She never goes anywhere to wear them.'

Freddie was disappointed but too desperate to give up. 'What about the silver?'

'I suppose that would be easier. It won't be so noticeable, not if we take only a few pieces, but what do we do with them then?'

'Sell them or pawn them.'

'Who to? I wouldn't even know where to find a ghastly pawnshop.'

'I can't go back to London without some money, Angela, and I can't lug a suitcase of silver down with me either. It will have to be got rid of up here. There's bound to be pawnshops in Liverpool. The place must be full of them.'

Angela suddenly had an idea. 'Chrissie! She'd know where there were such places.'

Freddie was all eagerness. 'She would. Maybe I could even persuade her to take the stuff for me.'

'You haven't seen her for ages and you were rather off-hand with her last time. She might be engaged or even married by now.'

'I'll write to her. I'll do it now and post it when we arrive at Lime Street. Have you got your writing case with you?'

'I have. Nichols is obsessive about it, she always packs it even though she knows that Ashenden is crammed full of paper and envelopes. Do you really think she'll do it?'

Freddie smiled confidently. 'Of course. I can twist her around my little finger. I'll lay it on thickly and she'll feel sorry for me. I may have to dangle some sort of carrot under her nose, but . . .' He shrugged and took the leather writing case from his sister.

* * *

The letter came with a bundle of mail and fortunately Chrissie managed to slip it into her pocket before Hilda saw it. She took it upstairs to open it, and a thrill of excitement and pleasure ran through her. He hadn't forgotten her. He'd been so ashamed and he was terribly sorry he'd been such a cad when they'd had to leave the party. He knew she would understand how upset he'd been, although that was really no excuse. He wanted to see her again. For a moment she thought she was being invited to the christening, but then realized that wasn't the case. She was to go the following evening. Roscoe would pick her up from the station. Freddie needed her help desperately. She'd already begun to think what she would wear, what she would say.

She deduced that she was being given another bite of the cherry, and she'd do whatever it was he wanted. Then he'd be in debt to her. She was the only one he could turn to, he wrote, and he knew she wouldn't let him down. Besides, he was longing to see her again. She wondered why he had no car and what it was that was so desperate, but the words 'I'm longing to see you again' pushed all such questions from her mind.

It had been stuffy on the train, the air heavy and sultry, and she hoped there wouldn't be a storm. She had bought a new dress especially for the occasion. It was cream linen with a short pleated skirt, short sleeves and a sailor collar edged in navy blue ribbon. A length of the same navy ribbon passed under the collar and tied in a floppy bow in the front. Her hat was cream, edged with navy, and sported a bow on the side.

Roscoe had said nothing to her apart from 'Good evening, Miss', and now he was stopping the car at the lodge gates.

He got out and opened the door. 'I was instructed that Mr Frederick would meet you here, Miss,' he replied in answer to her look of mystification.

She got out, still puzzled, and Roscoe resumed his journey. He had been paid to keep his own council about all this by Lady Angela, but he wondered just what those two were up to now.

There was a small wooden bench set against the wall of the empty lodge-keeper's cottage, so Chrissie sat down and waited, trying to reason things out.

She didn't see him until he was almost beside her. He'd walked across the sloping parkland. He was very relieved that she had turned up, and hardly noticed what she was wearing.

'Chrissie, it's lovely to see you again.' He smiled broadly at her.

'Freddie! Why all the mystery?'

He sat down beside her and placed his arm on the back of the bench behind her shoulders. 'I'm going to explain everything, but I'm so glad you came. And you look as beautiful as ever.'

'I thought you'd forgotten all about me, Freddie,' she said petulantly.

'How could I do that? I really was so ashamed of my behaviour, and I've been terribly busy, all kinds of appointments and duties, you wouldn't credit half of the things I've had to do. But when I knew I was coming up for the christening, I immediately thought of you. As to the mystery, well, I want you to help me, Chrissie.'

'How?'

He looked pensive. 'I've had a bit of bad luck lately, on the horses again, amongst other things.'

She was very disappointed. 'Oh, you want me to lend you money?'

'No! I wouldn't dream of asking you for money, Chrissie. I do need it, but I couldn't borrow from you. It's very bad form, that, nor would I deprive you of the means to purchase life's little luxuries that you work so hard for.'

She was mollified. 'Then how can I help?'

He moved closer and took her hand. 'You know, I've always been fond of you, Chrissie. I know I can rely on you, on your tact and generosity.'

She smiled at him, her heart beating faster.

'Can I trust you? Not a word of this must get back to Richard or Hannah by any means.'

'Of course you can, but what is it?'

'I'm really in trouble this time. I owe a chap rather a lot of money and he's not the patient sort of chap I thought he was. Funds are very low, Angela has helped out but she can't let me have any more. Richard is very parsimonious and even more so now. Father, in his wisdom, stipulated in his will that I was only to be given an allowance, and a paltry one at that.' He tapped the end of her nose very gently. It was a gesture of affection. 'You see Chrissie, younger sons are an encumbrance. We usually get shunted off into the Army or the Church, but I refused to enter either.'

Chrissie felt sorry for him. It was humiliating for him to have to tell her all this. 'That doesn't seem very fair of him. I mean, to leave your brother everything: the house, land, the properties and all the money, while you just get an allowance.'

'I know. It's not fair, but I knew you'd understand, Chrissie. You're so perceptive, so sympathetic.'

She didn't know what perceptive meant, but it was obviously a compliment.

'Freddie, I just care about you.'

'I know, and it really upsets me to have to ask you such a favour, but I am forced to – much as I hate myself.'

'What is it?'

'I have, er, purloined some pieces of silver. They have tons of the stuff up there at the Hall, no one will miss a few bits. They're not important pieces. But I've no idea how to go about selling them, you see.'

Chrissie was taken aback and stared at him blankly. He was asking her to sell stolen silver.

'You . . . you want me—'

'To take it to a pawnshop or somewhere like that.' He put his arm around her. 'Chrissie, believe me I wouldn't do this unless I was absolutely desperate. And I am totally, utterly desperate. I trust you Chrissie and I'm very fond of you. I know I haven't treated you very well, but that doesn't mean I don't think the world of you. I do. If you do this for me, I'll get matters sorted out and then, who knows? We might spend more time together, far more time.' He smiled and stroked her cheek. Behind the smile was a ruthless determination to say or do whatever was necessary to gain results. 'In fact, Chrissie, we might spend the rest of our lives together.'

All thoughts of stolen silver vanished from her mind. What was he saying? What was he implying?

'Oh Freddie, do you mean what . . . I think you mean?' she stammered.

He took her in his arms. Let her think whatever she liked. At this moment in time he would sell his soul to the devil, just as long as he got the money to at least pay off some of his creditors and be able to go out, to frequent his usual haunts without forever glancing over his shoulder.

'Will you do it for me – us – Chrissie?' he pleaded.

She was so overcome, she couldn't speak. All those wonderful dreams she'd secretly harboured but had come to accept as fantasies, rose up before her eyes, and now they would become fact. She *would* be like Hannah. She would live in a huge house in London, have servants, exquisite clothes. She'd be invited to all the smart places, in fact she'd be the toast of the city. 'Oh, Freddie, of course I will.'

Chapter Twenty-Three

———— ◆ ————

CHRISSIE FELT VERY PLEASED with herself. She had managed to get Freddie one hundred and twenty-five pounds. She had been a nervous wreck though, after she'd agreed to help him. He had gone back to the house and she'd waited for him to return. When he did, it was with a black leather Gladstone bag. He'd kissed her and then he'd driven her to the station himself.

All the way home on the train she racked her brains as to what she was going to do with the bag. The euphoria that Freddie's words had produced had faded somewhat. Mam would instantly demand to know what the bag contained, where it came from and where it was going. She felt ill as she contemplated the consequences of that line of interrogation. Mam would send for Mike, who would cart her off to the nearest police station and then . . . Dear heaven! It hadn't borne thinking about! In the end she went to Polly's house and begged her to keep the bag for her until the following day. She'd told her friend that it was a gift from Freddie, and Mam would be furious. She said that she daren't take it home now, but tomorrow would be all right because Mam went to her Union of Catholic Mothers meeting and Da would have his usual hour in The Black Dog.

'It's heavy, Chrissie. What is it?' Polly had asked.

'I think it's a solid silver dressing-table set. You know – brushes, mirror, trinket boxes and trays. Promise you won't peep at it. I haven't seen it yet myself and it wouldn't be fair if you saw it first, now would it?'

Polly agreed with her and, much relieved, she went home, thankful that Polly was a gullible girl who admired her greatly.

She collected it the following night and hid it in the yard under a pile of boxes. The next morning she managed to get it out and took it to Maclean's. They were a small but high-class jewellers and pawnbrokers. If they wouldn't buy it then she would pawn it, she thought determinedly. She wore her best coat over her shop dress and affected what she hoped was a middle-class accent.

'Are these yours Madam?' the jeweller asked.

She looked him squarely in the eye with far more confidence than she had felt. 'Of course they're mine. I haven't stolen them, if that's what you're implying. Would you prefer me to bring you a letter of explanation from my mother?'

'Not at all, Madam,' he replied.

He examined the pieces closely. 'They are all exceptionally fine.'

'I know that. They have been in the family for years, but now things are so difficult, so hard, that my mother has reluctantly decided to part with some bits and pieces. It's very distressing for her. It was the war that caused us so much pain. I'm sure you understand.' She bestowed on him her most dazzling smile and held her breath.

He accepted her story. The bag had contained some small boxes, two larger boxes, an oblong tray and a pair of small, but delicately wrought candlesticks. She was amazed when he offered her one hundred and twenty-five pounds. She accepted it gracefully and sauntered out. Once in the street, though, she quickened her steps and once around the corner in Whitechapel, she ran and then began to laugh. Laughter that had a ring of hysteria in it, and also relief.

Freddie had been delighted. He kissed her and hugged her. 'Oh, Chrissie! Chrissie! I knew you'd do it. You're wonderful! Truly marvellous! Here, I've got something for you.'

She was surprised. 'For me?'

'Well, I can't let you take such risks and not have any reward, can I?'

He took a box from his pocket and opened it. Inside was a ring. In the centre was a pearl surrounded by stones that were a turquoise colour.

She looked at him with shining eyes, her cheeks tinged with pink. 'Freddie, for me?'

'Of course.' He slipped it on her finger, her engagement finger. It was no more than a trinket. It was only worth a couple of guineas, Angela had picked it up from some admirer or other, but he hoped it would keep Chrissie quiet. He took her in his arms, but mentally he was working out how much he would give to each of his creditors, on account.

'Oh, I'm so happy, I . . . I could cry!'

He dragged his thoughts away from the money. 'Please don't do that. I hate to see a pretty girl in tears.'

She hugged him tightly.

'There's just one thing, Chrissie.'

'What?'

'We can't tell people about this . . . not yet.'

She looked up at him disappointedly. 'Why?'

'I have to clear things up, get matters sorted out. You remember I told you about the position?'

She understood. 'The, er, financial matters?'

'Yes.'

'But when can I tell people, Freddie?'

'Oh, maybe in the new year. These things take time.'

'Well, can't I even tell Mam – my mother?'

That was the last thing he wanted her to do. 'Particularly not your mother or father. Hannah would hear about it, and then Richard would make the most awful fuss.'

'But he married Hannah,' she cried petulantly.

'I know, Chrissie, but he's so unreasonable these days. There appears to be one rule for him and another for me. No, we'll present him with a *fait accompli*.'

'What's that?'

'I mean when things are all sorted out and back to normal, we'll go off and get married. The deed will be done, accomplished – *fait accompli*. Then he can't say anything, can he? But until then, well, I'm afraid no announcement or wearing of the ring.'

She agreed, very reluctantly, but comforted herself with the thought that now she was really engaged and had a ring. It was tangible proof that a glamorous and exciting future was waiting just around the corner.

He'd had to go back to London; for a while there was no word from him at all and she began to get worried. Then letters, no more than notes really, started to arrive. Not in crested envelopes, but in plain white ones. She understood, or at least she thought she did. Matters were taking longer to resolve, he wrote, but she wasn't to fret. He loved her and he'd be back as soon as was humanly possible. The delay regarding the announcement was unavoidable, he explained, and begged her to have patience. It upset her that the ring must remain in its box. Sometimes, in the privacy of her bedroom, she would slip it on and admire it and daydream about the future. When eventually reality invaded those dreams she became annoyed and frustrated.

Before Christmas she deliberately picked an argument with Phil. It was better to end this now, she had reasoned to herself. She was really being kind to him in a way. If they parted now there would be a period of time before her engagement was announced.

It wouldn't be nearly so bad for him to bear. As a result, Christmas had been ruined.

She had argument after argument with her mam. Her da refused to be drawn into these rows, but was very distant and disapproving towards her. Oh, how she longed to tell them the real reason behind the break with Phil, but she had to keep quiet. She was getting impatient with Freddie. How much longer would it be? How much longer was she going to have to bear the awful atmosphere at home? Surely it didn't take this long to pay off some debts, she questioned in her letters.

In the first week of February she received the note that seemed to indicate that the waiting and the secrecy was over. Freddie was coming back to Ashenden, for how long he didn't say, but she felt certain that it was because he was now in a position to organize their wedding. He also wrote that she was to visit Ashenden, in the same manner as before, on the Friday evening. Roscoe would meet her from the station.

Last time it had been a warm summer evening, now it was cold and dark, and she was disconsolate as she watched Roscoe drive away towards the house. She just hoped this was the last time she would be forced to hang about like this. It was all so sordid, and she hated the secrecy. She hated sneaking in and out in the darkness like a thief. It was an unfortunate comparison, and she hurriedly dismissed it from her mind. She wasn't really a thief. She hadn't stolen the silver, all she'd done was sell the pieces. She was still an accomplice, though, she reminded herself. These thoughts made her edgy and irritable.

'Chrissie!'

She jumped, for once again she hadn't heard him approach. She threw her arms around his neck and clung to him. 'Oh, Freddie I've missed you so much!'

'I know, darling, but all this subterfuge will be over soon, I promise.'

She snuggled closer to him, his body shielding her from the icy wind.

'When can I wear my ring and tell people? It's been awful at home. I hate all this sneaking about. I want to tell everyone. I want to be happy and respected and envied. When can I come up to the house? I hate having to wait here.'

He became wary. She was becoming disenchanted, and that was fatal. He had to keep her happy for another few days. 'Very soon, Chrissie, I promise. I swear, darling, that it will all be over soon. I still have one last piece of business to attend to. I'm afraid I'm going to need your help again, my darling girl.'

She looked up at him with annoyance and exasperation. 'Oh, Freddie, no!'

'It's the very last time! There is just one chap who is being very persistent. Won't wait any longer, keeps talking about bringing in the police.'

'Oh, not the police, Freddie!' she cried in panic.

'Oh, he's just throwing these idle threats around to try to scare me. Don't worry about it.'

'Will it definitely be the very last time?'

He disentangled himself from her embrace. 'Of course. I brought the pieces with me, but I'll go back and get the car to take you to the station.'

She watched him disappear quickly in the darkness, feeling annoyed and hurt, and she glanced at the Gladstone bag with pure venom. He hadn't even kissed her properly, and she hadn't seen him for so long. It was all so rushed. Oh, she wasn't at all happy about the way he was treating her. Maybe she was too submissive, maybe she should start to put her foot down, she thought, as she walked up and down hoping he wouldn't be long.

When he returned she was markedly cool towards him as they drove through the dark lanes to the station.

'Chrissie, you seem upset.'

She didn't turn her head. 'I am, Freddie. I feel that you are just using me.'

'Oh, Chrissie, how can you think such a thing? You know I idolize you. I couldn't get along without you. I know things have been difficult, I really do appreciate that, but once this is over, then I'm going to whisk you away. Maybe to Paris, we could be married there. Would you like that? A wedding and a honeymoon on the Champs Elysées, you'd love the shopping.'

It was a dazzling prospect and she smiled, all her petulance and doubts gone. 'Oh, I'd love that, Freddie! Paris! Oh, it's so . . . so romantic!' She'd never been anywhere outside Liverpool.

'Then Paris it will be, my pet. Will you come up to Ashenden in two days, like last time?'

'Yes.'

'I'll send Roscoe down to the station.'

'Oh, can't I come to the house, Freddie?'

He sighed inwardly. She was becoming a real pain in the neck. He didn't really care if he never saw her again, but she would have to be placated, humoured, for a couple more days.

'Of course,' he smiled. He took her in his arms and gave her a farewell kiss, then watched with annoyance as she walked into the station building. Still, he thought as he pressed his foot down on the accelerator, he would soon be rid of her. She had served her purpose and he'd be off to London, or maybe he would go to Paris or Monte Carlo. The further away from Chrissie, the better.

Mason was upset and disturbed. It was quite a few months since his attention had been drawn by Jessie and Emily, one of the tweenies, to the fact that four of the snuff boxes, two cigar boxes, a tray and some candlesticks had gone missing. He had checked carefully and then questioned everyone, but it appeared to be a mystery. He had of course reported it to Richard, who admitted it was odd and asked did he suspect anyone.

'I honestly don't know what to think, my Lord. All the staff have been with us for so long and there has never before been a single instance of pilfering.'

'They couldn't have been moved? Put away somewhere?'

'I suppose they could have been, but it appears unlikely. I'm sure someone would have remembered.'

Richard, too, had been troubled, but there seemed no obvious solution, apart from calling in the local police and having everyone questioned and the whole place searched, and that would prove a mammoth task. Angela and Freddie had been in London, so no blame could be apportioned there. 'Well, we can only trust they will turn up, Mason.'

Mason had thought that that was the end of the matter. His Lordship's attitude seemed to indicate that the disappearance should not be pursued. However, he'd been more watchful, more alert to the movements of the junior servants. It had remained in the forefront of his mind and now, despite his vigilance, more pieces were reported missing.

'I'm afraid this time, Mason, it will have to be investigated thoroughly,' Richard said seriously when Mason had finished speaking.

'I agree entirely. Shall I inform the staff?'

'Leave it with me for a few hours.' Richard had an uneasy feeling that Freddie's presence had something to do with this. Of course he hadn't been at Ashenden when the first pieces were missed, he mused. But maybe it had been some time before their loss had been realized and reported. It was a large house, with many artifacts. He sent for Freddie.

'Mason has just informed me that certain things seem to have been mislaid.'

'What kind of things?' Freddie asked nonchalantly, helping himself to a drink. He had a feeling he was going to need it.

'Silver. Snuff boxes, cigar boxes, goblets, candlesticks, trays, oh and a silver statuette presented to Father for some event that must have included Sun King, that Morgan stallion he bought in America. It was inscribed on the bottom of the base. I believe the words were "Lord Aleric Ashenden, Sun King. 1912".'

Freddie's heart lurched sickeningly and he cursed himself. Why hadn't he been more careful? He hadn't known about that inscription, nor had he seen it, but he should have examined the statuette.

'Are you accusing me, my dear brother, of pinching the family silver?' he asked in what he hoped was a remorseful yet slightly jocular tone.

'No. I'm just asking you, have you seen any of those pieces?'

'I can recall seeing a variety of all such items scattered about the place, but nothing like that statuette, it sounds a ghastly piece of bric à brac.'

'Ghastly it may be, but it's worth a lot of money. It's made from a particularly pure ore.'

Freddie went on the offensive. 'I say, this is definitely off! Now it seems I can't come home without being accused of theft.'

'I'm not accusing you. If you haven't seen it, you haven't seen it. I'll have to take the matter up again with Mason. Would you be good enough to open the door, please?'

When he'd gone, Freddie sat down and began to bite his fingernails, trying to reason things out calmly. Maybe Chrissie would notice the inscription, she was a sharp little minx. Even if she didn't, what was the worst thing that could happen? No one could accuse him and make it stick, there was no evidence. If Chrissie was caught with that blasted statuette she would be accused of the theft. He would deny all knowledge of having seen her since the Grand National last year. Roscoe knew of her visits of course, although the man had never seen Chrissie and himself together. If Roscoe informed Richard or the police, then he would deny any involvement. He could even accuse Roscoe of being in it with Chrissie.

He could imagine what his barrister would say should the case go to court. 'Does anyone seriously believe that this girl, from a slum area of Liverpool, was engaged to the brother of the Earl of Ashenden? No, she is a scheming opportunist who has colluded with Roscoe, a mere chauffeur, to rob the Earl and to drag the ancient and honourable name of D'Arcy through the courts.' It would be their word against his, and who would possibly believe them? Even Hannah wouldn't take Chrissie's part, she didn't like Chrissie at all. With some persuasion, should it be needed, he could convince them all that it was Chrissie who was the thief; but he hoped it wouldn't come to that.

* * *

She used the same method as before, telling Polly that this time Freddie had asked her to take care of a few personal things for him. There was not much privacy at Ashenden, with all those servants forever nosing about. She was very thankful that Polly didn't have a suspicious nature, her gullibility verging on idiocy as far as the D'Arcys were concerned.

She didn't want to have to trail it into town either, it was so heavy that it made her shoulders ache. She'd have to take it somewhere nearer. Then she had a brain-wave. She'd take it to Solly. He'd known her all her life, he certainly wouldn't suspect it was stolen. She'd tell him they were gifts from an admirer, one that Mam didn't approve of, so she couldn't have the pieces scattered around the house. Now she wanted to sell them because she had fallen out with him and would sooner have the money. She knew she could make it sound plausible, after all she'd fooled the man in Maclean's.

She waited until half past six, when she knew he would be slack, and everyone would be indoors having their tea.

Solly looked up and smiled as she entered his cluttered shop.

'Hello Chrissie, I haven't seen you in here for years. I heard you'd come into some money.'

'No, I won the money, Solly.'

'And you've spent it all already?'

She laughed nervously. 'Not all of it.'

'Then what can I do for you? You want to buy something?'

With an effort she heaved the bag onto the shop counter. 'Solly, can you help me? This is a bit difficult, a bit delicate, like.'

'Why?'

'Well, I've been going around with this chap and Mam doesn't like him. She can't stand him actually. She won't have him over the doorstep. He keeps buying me things, presents, and she's been getting very suspicious. He's rich, I don't know where he gets his money from, and I don't care now because I've told him I don't want to see him ever again. He's . . . he's . . . well a bit flash, if you know what I mean.'

Solly nodded his agreement. He'd heard that she'd had a falling out with Phil Chatterton over something or someone. He liked Phil, so maybe now Chrissie would go back to him and there'd be wedding bells.

'So, I want to sell everything he gave me. I would sooner have the money, Solly. I can't even bear to look at the stuff. Here, I'll take whatever you can give me.' She pushed the bag across the counter. It had all come out so pat that he *must* believe her.

He opened it, gazed at the contents, then he pursed his lips and emitted a low whistle. 'This is good stuff, Chrissie.'

'I know it is, but it's no use to me, and Mam would go mad if she knew I had it.'

'He must be rich. Anyone I might know of?'

'No. I met him ages ago at Aintree. You see what I meant about being flashy?' She pointed to the small collection with a look of distaste.

Solly was uneasy. He had begun to feel suspicious, but surely not of Chrissie, he told himself. The Burgesses were a very respectable family and always had been, even had a son in the CID. Surely Chrissie wouldn't be lying to him? He shook away his doubts.

'I'll give you one hundred pounds, Chrissie. It's all I've got here at the moment.'

She was disappointed, she'd expected at least two hundred, there was more stuff this time; but she couldn't say that or show her true feelings. 'Fine. I told you I'd be happy with anything. I'm just glad to be rid of them. Yes, one hundred is great, thanks.'

'Wait there until I fetch it.' Solly disappeared into the room at the back of the shop.

Chrissie felt the anxiety drain from her. He had believed her story. She'd pulled it off, but it was the very last time. She'd go to Ashenden tomorrow, give Freddie the money, and then it would all be plain sailing – to Paris. She smiled to herself. Wouldn't Hannah be furious when she came back as Freddie's wife, with every right to be entertained at Ashenden!

She thanked Solly and put the money in her bag. A cold gust of wind buffeted her as she closed the shop door and, pulling her coat more closely to her, she bent her head and hurried home.

'Where are you off to now, Madam?' Hilda demanded when, the following evening, Chrissie came downstairs wearing her best coat and hat. Hilda was still fuming that the romance between Chrissie and Phil was off and remained off despite everything she had tried to do to revive it. Privately she'd told Frank that what Chrissie needed was a damned good hiding.

'She's not a child, luv, she's a woman, and there's nothing we can do to make her care for Phil,' he'd replied.

'Well, she needn't come crying to me when he up and marries someone else and she suddenly finds she's twenty-six and left on the shelf,' she'd retorted acidly.

Chrissie felt strangely elated. Now she could drop all the pretence, all the secrecy.

'I'm going to Ashenden, if you must know.'

Hilda dropped the basin she'd been drying. 'You're WHAT?'

'You heard, Mam. Freddie has invited me, Roscoe's meeting me at the station. I don't know what time I'll be back.'

Hilda sat down, suddenly weary of the constant battling with her daughter. 'I thought all that nonsense was over and done with. I thought we'd heard the last of *him* too. Oh, Chrissie, for heaven's sake use your head. He's just using you. How long is it since you heard from him? Nearly a year, and as soon as he crooks his little finger you go running!'

'Well, that's where you're wrong. He's been writing to me for months.'

Some of Hilda's fire returned. 'You've been hiding letters? You sly little madam!'

'If I'm sly then it's because I've had to be. If I'd have told you, you would have created merry hell, just like you're doing now.'

'Chrissie, I don't want you to become just a play-thing! For heaven's sake consider what you're doing.'

'I won't be a plaything!'

'I wish you'd see Phil.'

'Mam, stop it! I'm not going to see Phil Chatterton ever again! Freddie is—'

'Is what?' Hilda demanded.

'Freddie's the one I'm really in love with, and he loves me, and don't tell me I'll never be like Hannah.'

Hilda lost her temper completely. 'Oh, go on then. Do what you like, but don't come crying to me when you get hurt, and you will. He doesn't love you! You'll come a right cropper from that high horse of yours, Chrissie Burgess!' she yelled.

'You're going to eat those words, Mam, before long!' Chrissie yelled back.

Frank had had enough. His patience had been stretched to the limit.

'I want you back in here at half past eleven, Chrissie, over twenty-one or not. While you live under my roof you'll abide by my rules. If you're not back then that door will be locked and bolted and I mean it.'

After Chrissie had slammed out, Hilda sighed heavily and dropped her head in her hands. 'I just don't want to see her hurt, Frank, and he's going to hurt her badly.'

'I know, luv, he'll drop her again. I don't think she fully realizes that, or just how hurt she'll be, because he won't marry her. But there's nothing we can do, they're both adults. I'll put the kettle on while you clear up that mess.' He patted her shoulder and indicated the pile of fragments lying in the hearth. The remains of the pudding basin she'd dropped.

It was an hour and a half later when a surprised Frank opened the door to Solly.

'Solly, what brings you here at this time? Have you shut up shop?'

'No, young Eli is minding it for me.'

'Come on in then, don't stand there on the step.'

Solly followed Frank into the kitchen and placed a large box down on the table.

'What's all this?' Hilda asked.

'I've come because I'm worried, Mrs Burgess. I hope I'm doing the right thing. I've been worrying since last night. What to do, I ask myself over and over. They are good people. I want no trouble. They want no trouble.' He'd examined every piece carefully, and when he saw the inscription he knew that they were stolen. He also knew he should go straight to the police, but he'd known the Burgesses for over twenty years.

'What's the matter? What's all this about trouble?'

'Well, Chrissie brought these things to me. She said they were gifts from a young man, one you didn't approve of.'

Hilda suddenly thought of Freddie D'Arcy. 'What young man?'

Solly shrugged. 'That, I don't know. But she said

she no longer wants to have anything to do with him and she asked that I buy these from her.'

Hilda looked from Solly to Frank. 'What kind of a story is that? I don't know anything about any gifts.'

'No, she said you didn't know. So I believed her and I gave her a hundred pounds.'

Hilda clutched Frank's arm. 'God Almighty!'

'They are good quality silver. Very, very good quality, but when I examine them closely, well . . .' he reached into the box and drew out a small silver statuette of a horse. Turning it upside down, he passed it to Frank.

Frank peered at it, then a slow flush crept up from his neck and his eyes filled with fury. 'This belongs to Hannah's husband's father. It says here Lord Aleric Ashenden. She's stolen it, or someone's stolen it.'

Hilda stared at him in horror.

Frank turned to Solly. 'Will you leave them with me? I'll sort this out. Don't worry – you'll get your money back.'

Solly nodded his agreement and made a helpless gesture of apology as Frank showed him to the door.

He reached for his coat and cap.

'Frank! Frank! What's going on? Where are you going?' Hilda begged.

'I'm going for our Mike. This has got to be sorted out Hilda, and now! Maybe he can handle things better than anyone else.'

'Oh, Frank! What's she done?'

'I don't know, but I'm damned well going to find out!'

'She'll be there by now.'

'Well she'll be coming home even if I have to drag her all the way, and she won't ever be going near that damned place again! I'll kill her first! That Freddie is at the bottom of this, you mark my words, but by God, Mike and I will sort the pair of them out!'

Hilda shut the door behind him and for a few minutes she stared at it, then leaning her forehead against it, she burst into tears.

Chapter Twenty-Four

———◆———

PHIL WAS AT MIKE AND Abbie's house. Quite often he called for a drink before going home. Abbie would go and get a jug of ale from The Beehive, and the two men would discuss the day's work while she got supper ready.

Abbie opened the door to Frank. 'Come in. Is mother-in-law all right?' She could see by his face that something was wrong.

'She's worried sick, like me.'

'Dad!' Mike cried, getting to his feet.

'Mike, it's our Chrissie! Your mam and I are at our wits' end with her.'

'What's she done now?' Abbie asked.

'She sold Solly some silver. Oh, she told him a cock-and-bull story, but it's stolen. It's come from Ashenden Hall. One ornament was inscribed "Lord Aleric Ashenden". Solly brought it to us. Thank God he didn't go straight to the police. Mike, what the hell are we going to do?'

'Where is she?' Mike asked grimly.

Abbie's hand had gone to her mouth, her eyes wide. Phil looked from Mike to Frank, not knowing what to say.

'She's gone up there. Bold as bloody brass!'

'Why did she do something like that? She doesn't need money.'

'No she doesn't Abbie, but I'll bet that Freddie D'Arcy does. He's at the bottom of all this.'

'I told your mam we'd go and bring her home.'

'Too flaming right we will, and him, if he's pinched the stuff.'

'It's not our patch, Mike,' Phil reminded him, unable to believe what he was hearing.

'Maybe not, but she's my flaming sister.'

'How will you get there? It takes hours, and there's no trains back after ten o'clock.'

'She's got a point, Mike.'

Mike was shrugging on his coat. 'There's a motor cycle and sidecar at the station.'

'It's not police business,' Phil interrupted.

'Maybe not entirely, but I'll square it with Sergeant Morris. We're acting on information received, and let's hope to God we don't have to arrest the pair of them.'

'You can't lock your own sister up, Mike!' Abbie cried.

'I don't want to, Abbie, believe me. I'm hoping to sort everything out. I'm hoping Lord Ashenden doesn't know – hasn't missed the stuff. I can give the pair of them a fright and return the things.'

Abbie pushed the casserole back into the oven and

slammed the door. 'It's about time your blasted Chrissie grew up and started to behave herself!'

'Oh, she's for it this time and no mistake,' Frank said darkly, following his son and Phil Chatterton out.

As they reached the lodge gates, Chrissie had waited to see whether Roscoe would slow down. If he did then she was going to instruct him to take her to the house; she was in no mood to be fobbed off with remarks about what his orders did or did not include.

On the train she had gone over everything in her mind and was determined that when she went back home it would be as the fiancée of the Honourable Frederick D'Arcy, with a ring on her finger to prove it. Then wouldn't they all have to eat their words. Freddie was going to hang back no longer. If necessary, she would force him to tell Hannah and his Lordship, even if it meant revealing all the facts.

As the car swung through the lodge gates it picked up speed, and she leaned back with some relief as they continued up the drive until the walls of the house were visible through the bare branches of the trees. Not many of the rooms were illuminated and she was glad of this. She wanted to see Freddie alone first.

Mason opened the front door to her and inclined his head in a greeting of sorts. His manner was frigid and she could tell he was not pleased by her arrival.

'I've come to see Mr D'Arcy. It's very important and he is expecting me.'

'Mr Frederick is in the games room, Miss.'

'Thank you, I know where that is,' she replied sharply. He was another one who would be very surprised before the night was over, and he could then treat her with more respect.

The hall and the corridor were dimly lit and it was depressing, she thought. It had all seemed so bright and richly decorated the last time she'd been here.

Freddie was sitting in a winged armchair beside the fireplace, a glass in his hand. On a small table beside him was a cut-glass decanter, almost half-empty, and an ashtray full of cigarette butts. The room was off the main corridor, towards the back of the house, and was dark and gloomy at the best of times. A billiard table dominated the centre of it, the cues, rest and markers were in a rack on one wall. There were various other smaller tables and cupboards set around the room, and the walls were adorned with prints depicting all kinds of sporting activities. Tiffany lamps, which jarred with the rest of the furniture and décor, gave out sparse light, for the main chandelier was unlit. She thought the whole room was dismal.

Freddie had been dreading this moment all day. He'd been trying to devise by what means he could induce her to part with the money and then go home, without making a scene and demanding to tell the entire household about his promise of betrothal. It had all been in vain. As usual he'd left it until the last minute. He thought airily that he would come up with something, but he hadn't, and he was now irritable. He needed a few stiff drinks to concentrate his mind and to deal with Chrissie, but he'd had more than a few.

'Oh, there you are, Chrissie.'

She stared at him hard: he'd been drinking, but she couldn't estimate how drunk he was just yet. She took off her hat and coat and went to stand by the fire. 'I've got it, Freddie.'

He looked up at her and reached for her hand. 'I knew you would, Chrissie. How much did you get?'

'How much have you had to drink? You smell like a distillery!' she snapped. 'Oh, of all the times to get drunk!'

'Oh, I've not had that much. I've been drunker. Did you have any trouble? I mean . . . did anyone ask about things?'

'No, I had no trouble. I took it to someone I know. A pawnbroker in Burlington Street, where I live.'

The implication of her words penetrated the mist of whisky fumes that fogged his brain. 'You did what?'

'Oh, don't go getting all airyated – all upset! He didn't suspect anything. He's known me for ages.'

'You fool!'

'Don't talk to me like that! And stop drinking.'

Freddie ignored her and refilled his glass. 'How much did he give you?'

'One hundred pounds. I was expecting to get two hundred, there were more things this time. That's all he offered, all he had in the shop, but I couldn't argue about it, could I?'

He'd forgotten about the statuette, the inscription, the suspicion she may have aroused.

'That's all you got, one hundred? One hundred measly pounds?'

Chrissie was getting annoyed and resentful. She'd done all the hard and dangerous work. She was the one who had taken all the risks and had had to lie to everyone, not him. She'd had to come dragging out here in the darkness and the cold, and now he was belittling her efforts. 'I suppose you could have done better? You couldn't have done anything without me, Freddie.'

He suppressed his sarcastic retort, he must keep her pacified for a bit longer. 'I know. I know, Chrissie. I'm sorry I said that.'

She opened her bag and handed him the money. 'Oh, I'm so thankful it's all over, I really am. I had a terrible row before I left home. Da . . . Dad is going to lock the door if I'm not back by half past eleven. Can Roscoe take me back, and can I tell them now?'

Freddie wasn't listening to her. He was concentrating hard. It wasn't enough. It wasn't nearly enough. She'd have to be persuaded to sell some more for him; it was now all so risky, so tiring. Despite all the problems that beset him, he felt his eyelids drooping.

'Oh, for heaven's sake Freddie, don't go to sleep! Did you hear me? I said Roscoe will have to take me home. Why did you have to get drunk? You're ruining everything!' Chrissie jerked him back to awareness and slipped her arms around his neck.

'Can we tell everyone now, Freddie?' she asked, determined to salvage something from this evening, despite the fact that she was annoyed and disgusted by his drunken state.

'I . . . I'm not sure . . . we should.' His words were slurred. He disentangled her arms and poured himself another drink.

She snatched it away from him. 'You've had enough!'

He felt anger rise in him. Who the hell did she think she was, snatching his glass like that? He'd expected at least two hundred and fifty pounds, not that pittance, and now she was getting high-handed and very much above herself. And what was she? A shop girl, and not a very bright one at that either.

'We can't tell yet.'

'Why not? You promised. You promised me Freddie!'

He realized she was shouting. 'Chrissie, it's not as easy as that. I'd expected more – at least two hundred and fifty.'

This was the final straw. Disappointment and rage washed over her. 'You lied to me! You got me to do all the dirty work, and I could have been arrested. Now you're breaking your promise and it's not fair, Freddie! You swore to me that that was it. That we could tell them now and I could wear my ring. I want to be able to tell people!'

He lost his battle with his temper. 'Oh, shut up, Chrissie! For God's sake stop harping on and on about bloody rings! I can't do anything with a hundred pounds, I—' he fell silent as he caught sight of Hannah standing in the doorway.

'What are you doing here, Chrissie?' Hannah asked sharply.

Chrissie spun around, her hand going to her mouth, her eyes wide, and then she pulled herself together. What did it all matter now? What if she told Hannnah all about it, in fact it just might make Freddie keep his promise. 'He promised he'd marry me. We're engaged. He gave me a ring, but he said I couldn't tell anyone yet.'

Hannah walked towards her, shaking her head. It came to her in a dreadful moment of realization that Freddie had stolen the silver and Chrissie had helped him to sell it. 'Oh, Chrissie, you little fool! You stupid little fool!'

Chrissie's cheeks burned. 'I'm not a fool! He loves me, don't you, Freddie?'

He didn't answer, he was past caring. A dull lethargy was creeping over him. He could see his future ebbing away. Now things would have to be explained. Now his plans to pay off some of his debts and then leave the country were turning to ashes. He refilled his glass and took a deep swig.

'Freddie, you love me, don't you? We're going to get married, aren't we?' Chrissie appealed, feeling the stirrings of panic.

'What's going on now, Freddie? Mason informed me that you had a visitor.'

Hannah stood aside to let her husband enter the room. He manoeuvred the chair until he was in front of his brother, while Hannah held Chrissie's arm.

'Freddie has been promising marriage to Chrissie, or so she says.'

'He did! He did, Hannah!' Chrissie forgot all decorum. She was frightened now, realizing that she could be blamed for stealing, and she had a horrible suspicion that Freddie would deny all knowledge of theft. 'I came because he asked me to. I did something for him – a favour.'

'So it was you?'

Freddie helped himself to another drink. 'What was me?'

'Put that down, you've had enough, Freddie. It was you who stole the silver and talked this foolish girl into selling it for you.'

'*I* didn't steal it! I wouldn't have had anything to do with it, but he gave me a ring.' Chrissie was close to tears. Her glorious future, her grandiose dreams, were fading and she was in deep trouble.

'One you no doubt purloined from Mother's jewellery box, or was it Hannah's?' Richard asked cuttingly. He'd been right in his assumptions. Freddie he could have dealt with. Given him a lump sum and forbidden him ever to come near Ashenden again. But he'd involved Chrissie, involved her in a cruel and cowardly way.

A mist of anger was swirling in Freddie's mind. 'No, it wasn't.'

'Of course you had no intention of marrying her. You were just using her. What did you intend to do? Run away? Desert her? Let her take all the blame when whoever she's sold that statuette to goes to the police?'

Chrissie uttered a cry and clung to Hannah.

'He didn't tell you, did he, Chrissie? That statuette was inscribed on the base with my father's name.'

Chrissie went pale and swayed, and for a moment Hannah thought she was going to faint.

'I took it to Solly! Oh, God, I took it to Solly!'

'A local pawnbroker. He'll know. He'll have gone to the police.' Hannah looked at Richard in dismay.

'You're despicable Freddie. This is the end. This time you've gone too far. You'll leave Ashenden now and you'll never return – ever! And you can say goodbye to your allowance. You can work for a living. You can stay on at Elmsford Square. I won't throw you out on the streets, although you deserve it. Get out of my sight and my house!' Richard barked.

Freddie lashed out at the decanter, sending it crashing into the hearth, where it shattered into thousands of fragments. A fierce rage consumed him and he shook like an aspen in the wind. He was penniless, hunted by creditors, and now that stupid bitch had let him down. He'd lost his allowance and was to be banished from Ashenden. He hated his brother and his plain, mealy-mouthed common wife.

'You pompous miser! You miserable cripple. Your life has been ruined and you want to ruin mine too! It's all your fault! If you'd given me a decent allowance I wouldn't have had to steal. Anyway, it wasn't stealing, I've as much right to things as you have.'

Richard's eyes blazed with anger and hurt, and he gripped the sides of the Bath chair tightly. If he could get out of this damned chair, just for a few minutes, he'd show Freddie how he could really ruin his life, for he'd beat him to a pulp.

'You have no rights! You're an idle waster, a feckless, lying, cheating thief! You've deceived everyone, but most of all Chrissie and yourself, because if you thought I would let you get away with all this, you're mistaken.'

'Go to hell! Go to hell . . . all of you!' Freddie roared, pushing past Richard and lurching towards the door. He knocked Chrissie aside and she burst into tears.

Hannah guided her to a chair. 'Oh, Chrissie, you poor little fool!'

Chrissie raised stricken eyes. 'What will I do? What will happen to me?'

Hannah looked at her husband questioningly. At the moment she felt she could murder Freddie herself. She would never forgive him for what he had said to Richard. 'What can we do?'

'Freddie will have passed out by now. Tomorrow I'll send him packing – forcibly if I have to. This pawnbroker, will he have gone to the police?'

'I don't know. He knows the family well. He knows they are honest and respectable people. Chrissie, what did you tell Solly?'

Haltingly, between sobs, Chrissie told them.

'He might just have gone to see Frank Burgess first,' Hannah said when Chrissie had finished.

Richard looked grim, turning the matter over in his mind. The girl had been stupid, but he harboured no ill will towards her. She'd been duped by the glittering life Freddie had no doubt outlined and promised. He remembered Frank and Hilda Burgess from the wedding. 'Isn't her brother in the police force?'

'Yes. Why?'

'Is there any way of contacting him? By phone?'

'I don't know.'

'Could he deal with it? Could he see this man, Solly was it? And his own parents?'

'I think that if you rang the police station they could get a message to him, if he isn't there. Just ask him to phone us, here. It's Westminster Road Station.'

Chrissie's sobs began to subside as Richard said he would try to contact Mike.

'Oh, Hannah, I'm so sorry! I'm so sorry!'

'Chrissie, did you love him so much?'

'No. I don't think I loved him at all, but he said—'

'You would have everything I have?'

Chrissie nodded.

'But I have never wanted that kind of a life. Money, possessions, position don't mean anything to me, Chrissie. I have jewellery almost as valuable as the crown jewels but I'll never wear it. Don't you understand that I love Richard and Edward. If we lived in an estate cottage I'd be just as happy.'

'I suppose I wanted too much. Mam said he was using me and he . . . he was!' She burst into fresh sobs as she remembered her mam, and how she would greet this news.

Richard came back and they both looked up.

'He wasn't there. They seemed to think he was on his way here. Let's hope he is, and that we can get it all sorted out.'

'I'll ask for some tea to be brought in.'

Chrissie had calmed down and Richard was lost in thought when the door bell echoed through the downstairs rooms.

'Could this be her brother?'

'I don't think so. He doesn't have a car and it takes ages to get here by train.'

'Mason will see to it then.'

Mason was startled to see the three men on the doorstep.

'Good evening. May I be of assistance?' he asked coldly. The events of the past few hours were not to his liking at all.

'I'm Michael Burgess, Chrissie's brother. This is Philip Chatterton, a close friend.'

'And I'm Frank Burgess, her da. Where is the little madam?'

'If you will step inside and wait, I'll inform his Lordship of your presence,' Mason said grimly. Things were at a nice pass when irate fathers, brothers and family friends arrived on the doorstep at this time of night. As he turned, the door of the gun-room was thrown open and Freddie lurched into the passageway.

'That's him! It's him we've come to see!' Frank yelled. 'It's his fault. He's at the bottom of all this.'

'If you would wait here, please,' Mason insisted firmly, but he was alarmed. He had thought that Freddie was in bed or collapsed in a chair somewhere, oblivious to everything with the amount he'd had to drink.

Hannah had come to investigate, and she looked relieved.

'Oh, it's you Mike – Mr Burgess. We tried to get hold of you. Thank you, Mason.'

'Hannah, where is she?' Frank demanded.

'He's the one we want to see. He put her up to it if I'm not mistaken. She's not a thief.' Mike jerked his head in Freddie's direction.

'You know? Have you seen Solly? She's in here, Mike. Come with me, all of you.'

Hannah turned but as she did so she saw the hunting rifle Freddie was clutching, and she screamed. And then it was as though everything happened in slow motion. She ran after Freddie, followed by Mike, Frank, Phil and Mason. Chrissie was cowering in the chair but was screaming. The noise of the shot in the confines of the room was deafening and Hannah heard herself scream as she somehow got to Richard's side as he slumped forward onto the floor. She fell to her knees and gathered him up in her arms. She could feel the warm sticky wetness spreading between her fingers and the room was reverberating with noise. Shouts, curses, screams and a wild hysterical sobbing that she didn't recognize as her own.

Freddie had caught Chrissie's arm and had dragged her to her feet, brandishing the rifle at the group of men who stood just inside the room. Frank was paralysed with fear as he watched the gleaming metal of the gun barrel swing towards Chrissie and then back towards himself. Hannah was sobbing, and he could see the red stain seeping into her dress and onto the carpet.

Mike was thinking frantically of the best way to disarm Freddie, but all Phil could think of was Chrissie. She was hysterical, Freddie was drunk and irrational, and any second he could turn the gun on her.

'I'm a police officer and so is he!' Mike jerked his head in Phil's direction. 'Put the gun down! Put the bloody thing down!' Mike yelled authoritatively.

Freddie swung the rifle towards him and glared at him with bloodshot eyes in whose depths Mike glimpsed insanity. 'What for? What's left for me now? I'll tell you – nothing!'

'Mister Frederick!' Mason intervened.

His voice surprised Freddie, who turned towards him, the barrel of the rifle swinging with him. It was enough for Phil. He rushed forward and wrenched Chrissie away, but at the same time Freddie fired. The movement was jerky and the bullet grazed Phil's arm, embedding itself in the wall, but it had given the others the time and opportunity they needed. Mike,

Frank and Mason rushed Freddie *en masse*. Frank wrenched the gun from his hands, Mike knocked him to the floor and Mason held his arms while Mike snapped on the handcuffs.

There was a moment of complete silence in the room, and then Mike took charge.

'We are police officers, will you phone the local police and the ambulance, please?'

Mason, thoroughly shaken but outwardly calm, left to go to the phone, and to inform and direct those servants who were huddled in the hall.

'Dad, get Chrissie out of here, fast. See if you can get someone to make some tea and find something to staunch Phil's wound for the time being. You bloody fool! Let's have a look at it. He could have killed you!'

Phil managed a weak smile. 'I didn't think about it. What else was there to do? Let him kill Chrissie?'

'You're sure you're all right?'

'I'll live, but will he?'

Mike turned and sank down on his haunches beside Hannah. Her hands and her dress were covered with blood and although she was cradling her husband in her arms, he could see the gaping hole in his back and didn't need to be told that Richard Ashenden was dead.

'Hannah. Oh, Hannah, I'm so sorry.'

She stared up at him blankly as though he were a stranger. 'Richard . . . Richard's hurt.'

Gently Mike put his arm around her shoulder. 'Hannah, I'm sorry . . . he's dead.'

She couldn't take in his words, they were too hideous. She was confused. There had been so much noise, so much shouting and then that deafening blast. 'No! No, he's hurt, he's hurt!'

'Oh, Hannah, you were a nurse, luv, you must know!' Not since his days in the trenches had he felt so sickened, so appalled. 'Let me take him now, Hannah, please. There's nothing anyone can do.'

She looked down at the blood that covered her hands and her dress. At Richard's bloodless lips, his pale skin, the hole in his chest and the blood that was still seeping from it, then she felt a rushing darkness sweep down and engulf her.

Nora and Jessie, both white-faced and shaken, had been summoned by Mason. Jessie and Frank got an hysterical Chrissie out of the room and into the amber drawing-room. Nora, the tears pouring down her cheeks, her hands trembling, helped Mike revive Hannah. He then carried her, with Nora in attendance, to the drawing-room in the terrace suite.

Mason had informed him that both the police and the ambulance were on the way and, with the aid of Henry and Charles, he padded and bandaged Phil's arm, produced brandy for Mike and Phil, and sent Henry down with a shot for Frank.

'Can we move him?' Mason asked, looking down with infinite sorrow at the broken figure of Richard D'Arcy. He'd thought this family had seen enough grief with the loss of Mister Hubert, Lord Aleric, Lady Honoria and his Lordship coming home crippled.

Nothing had prepared him for this, or the dreadful irony that after surviving the war, Richard Ashenden had been killed in his own home.

'Not yet, the local police must see everything first.'

'Can't I bring something to . . . to cover him? It's not . . . decent . . .' Mason was struggling with his emotions, for he'd been very fond of his master.

Mike understood. 'Yes. Bring a rug or a sheet, and keep all the female staff well away.'

Mason stared with disgust and loathing at Freddie, who was half-sitting, half-slumped against the wall. 'What will happen to him?'

Mike glared at Freddie. 'He'll swing for this. By God, he'll hang, and all his blue blood won't save him! Theft, murder, attempted murder of a police officer: he'll dance at the end of a rope.'

Mason nodded, thinking that when the first shock of everything that had happened tonight wore off, the scandal would be enormous. 'Will . . . will we have to stand as witnesses?'

'Of course. You, me, Constable Chatterton, Frank Burgess, Chrissie and . . . and Lady Ashenden.' He saw the pain in Mason's eyes. 'I know, but it can't be helped. How is she?'

'I've instructed her maid to send for the doctor. He will give her Ladyship something. She will then sleep, and arrangements must be made to bring her mother here, to comfort her.'

Mike nodded his approval. The man was proving to be a pillar of strength. 'My mother will have to be told of the situation and Chrissie's safety. Would it be possible for someone to go to Liverpool?'

'Roscoe will go.'

'When the police have taken statements from Mr Burgess, Chrissie and myself, could Roscoe take them home? I'll have to go and inform Constable Chatterton's family, but I'll come back with my wife. She is a great friend of her Ladyship's.'

'Of course, sir.'

The sound of wheels skidding on gravel came to their ears. 'That sounds like the lads now,' Mike said thankfully.

Chapter Twenty-Five

———•———

HILDA WAS SICK WITH worry as the time dragged on, but she leapt to her feet on hearing the knock. It was Abbie and Liam.

'Oh, I thought it was Frank.'

'I couldn't stay at home any longer. I knew you'd be worried, so I got the tram up.'

'Put him to bed, Abbie. I'll make some tea.'

Abbie settled her son in the cot in Chrissie's bedroom and went downstairs.

'What the hell has she been up to now? Dad said something about stolen silver and Solly.'

'It's all his fault, that Freddie! She's stupid where he's concerned. She told Solly some tale about a boyfriend I didn't like. Said he'd given her the stuff as presents. It's all in that box.'

Abbie looked at the collection in horror. 'All this? She managed to take all this to Solly?'

'How, God only knows, or where she hid it. I didn't see her with a box or a bag. I'm going to murder her, Abbie, when I get my hands on her.

I'm going to give her the hiding of her life!'

'You'll make yourself ill. Leave all that to Mike and Dad. I won't have you ending up like Mam, all because of the dance she's led you. Phil's gone with them. They borrowed a motor cycle and sidecar from Westminster Road Station.'

'Oh, Holy Mother! Phil will never speak to her again after this.'

'I can't say I'd blame him.'

'She wouldn't listen to me. Oh, I had such high hopes for them, Abbie. He's such a good lad.'

'Too good for her. She treats him like dirt. He's too soft with her, she needs a firm hand.'

'Oh, it's not his nature, and I doubt he'll change. Not that it matters now,' Hilda finished mournfully.

When it got to midnight they were both very agitated. At five past twelve Bridie arrived.

'Hilda, our Phil's not come home and I was wondering—' She caught sight of Abbie. 'Did he call at your house? Is he still working?'

'He's all right Mrs Chatterton. He's gone with Mike and Dad to Ashenden.'

Hilda glared at her daughter-in-law, silently cursing Abbie for mentioning Ashenden.

Abbie shrugged. 'It's no use lying. Phil will tell her everything.'

'Tell me what?'

Abbie informed her while Hilda fumed in silence.

'A nice kettle of fish, I must say. Well, that's put the kibosh on things. This will be the straw that breaks the camel's back as far as our Phil's concerned,' Bridie retorted acidly.

'Oh, let's not start falling out amongst ourselves. This is no time for rows. All we can do is wait. Will you have a cup of tea, Mrs Chatterton?'

It was twenty to two, and Hilda and Bridie had been dozing when Abbie heard the car pull up outside. She shook them both gently.

'They're here. I've just heard a car.'

Hilda opened the door, but a nameless fear gripped her as she took in her husband's haggard features and her daughter's white face, streaked with tears. Chrissie's dark eyes were wide with shock and red from crying.

'Frank! For the love of the Blessed Virgin, what's happened?'

Abbie sat Chrissie down by the fire.

Frank took off his cap. 'Sit down, all of you, while I get you a drop of brandy.'

'No, I'll get it – you look terrible,' Abbie said firmly.

'What's she done? What's happened?' Hilda demanded, her voice strident, her tone harsh with fear.

Chrissie began to sob. 'It was terrible . . . terrible! His Lordship's dead. His brother shot him. He'd found out about the silver. Freddie was drunk, he . . . he went berserk. He had a rifle.'

Bridie screamed and Abbie swayed, clutching the table for support.

Hilda jumped to her feet and caught Chrissie by the shoulder and lashed out, hitting her hard across the side of the head. 'You little bitch! This is all your fault! You wicked . . . lying . . . little bitch!'

Frank pulled her away. 'Stop it! It's no use screaming and carrying on like that, Hilda! It's done. She wasn't to blame.'

Abbie knew her mother-in-law's reaction was due to anxiety. 'Calm down. Sip this slowly. You're going to have a heart attack, carrying on like that.'

Chrissie broke down. 'I didn't know! I didn't know he'd do that! He was drunk. It was awful . . . and Phil—'

It was Bridie's turn to round on Chrissie. 'If he's hurt our Phil, I'll knock you from here to the Pier Head, Chrissie Burgess!'

'It's all right Bridie. He was wounded, but not seriously. He's gone to Ormskirk hospital, but they won't keep him in long. It's just a graze. That Freddie grabbed Chrissie, after he shot his brother, and when the chance came, Phil rushed him and got her away.' Frank's face was grey with exhaustion.

Hilda sank down, feeling suddenly faint. 'Chrissie! Chrissie, what have you done? Just look at the trouble you've caused.'

'Leave her, luv, she's had a terrible time, and she'll suffer for her stupidity. I asked that Roscoe to go for Dr Wallace, or at least to ask him to give us something to calm her down.'

Chrissie prayed that Roscoe wouldn't be long. She just wanted to curl up in her own bed and sleep, to forget everything and to wake up and feel it was all over. But it wouldn't be. The next days, weeks, even months would be terrible.

411

'Oh, dear God, poor Hannah! Poor, poor Hannah!' Abbie cried, stricken.

Chrissie could stand no more. 'Oh, Mam! Mam! I'm so sorry, I didn't mean it to end like this! I didn't! He said he'd marry me and I believed him! Oh, Mam, he was drunk. Then there was an awful row. Da and Mike came and he . . . he got a gun and he . . . shot . . . his Lordship! There was blood everywhere, all over Hannah, and then he grabbed me and then Phil jumped forward and pulled me away and oh Mam! I'm so sorry!' She flung herself into Hilda's arms, her tears soaking her mother's dress.

'Oh, God help us! How are we going to live with this?' Hilda cried.

Abbie had her coat on.

'Where are you going, luv?' Frank asked. 'Mike will be here soon.'

'To see Mrs Harvey. It hasn't been left for poor Roscoe to tell her, has it?'

'We . . . we didn't think. Mike is going to your house, Bridie.'

Bridie snatched up her shawl. 'I'd best go. Edward and the kids will need me.'

'Can I leave Liam here? I'll go with Mrs Harvey. Hannah will be devastated.'

'Of course you can, luv, but wait for Mike. He'll go back with you,' Frank advised tiredly.

All the way to Ashenden Winnie held Abbie's hand tightly while the tears fell slowly and silently down her cheeks. She knew what it was like to lose a husband to a violent death, to see him killed in front of you. Abe had never been the kind, loving husband his Lordship had been, but she could remember the shock, the full horror of it all. Oh, her poor, poor Hannah. Just when she'd thought her life was free of all misery and worry. Just when she'd been so thankful for the happy future she'd been certain Hannah could look forward to, fate had snatched it all away.

Abbie was stunned. Once she'd been able to cope with violent death, she'd had to, but this was different. It wasn't war, and she knew Hannah wouldn't be coping, either. Somehow, until she had seen Mike and had it from his lips, she hadn't really believed it.

Lights burned in many of the windows of Ashenden Hall, even though it was nearly half past three in the morning. Abbie and Winnie braced themselves. Mike, who had been sitting with Roscoe, had gone to see the police who were still at the house, taking statements.

They were met by Mason. 'Madam . . . Mrs Harvey, I'm so sorry.'

'Where is she?'

'Please follow me.'

'How is she?' Abbie asked.

'The doctor's been, but she won't take a sedative. Her maid is with her.'

'And Edward?'

'He's asleep. Nanny White brought him down. She felt her Ladyship would need him close by her. She's put him in their . . . the bedroom.'

Abbie was shocked by Hannah's appearance. Nora had removed her stained dress, washed the blood from her hands and helped her into a loose morning dress. She was so pale, her skin looked transparent. Her eyes were dull and glazed; there were no tears now and she appeared calm. Too calm. It frightened Abbie far more than tears or hysterics would have done.

She took Nora's hand and led the girl out. 'Leave her with her mam, Nora. If there's one person who really understands all the shock, all the sickening horror, it's her mam. Leave them alone for a while. We'll have a cup of strong tea, then you get to bed. You look worn out, girl.'

Abbie settled herself down in the morning-room to wait for Mike. Later she would be able to try to comfort Hannah, but at this precise moment Winnie was the only person Hannah needed.

When Mike arrived half an hour later, he was accompanied by Mason.

'Have they all gone?'

'Yes. They've taken Freddie with them. He'll be charged in the morning, well, later on, by a magistrate, then sent to prison to await trial.'

Abbie shook her head, thinking that for Hannah it would all drag on and on. 'What about the arrangements . . . the funeral? She can't cope with that.'

'I have telephoned Lady Julia, she will be here at lunch-time. She is shocked of course, but is fully capable of making all the arrangements. She will bring Lady Angela with her.'

'Is that wise? Hannah . . . her Ladyship doesn't like Lady Angela.'

'She is close family, Madam, but if her Ladyship doesn't want to see her, well, this is a big house.'

'Mason, what about all the legalities? Can I help at all?'

'Thank you, Sergeant, but there is a family solicitor.' Mason thought it was about time that Wildings did something for the no doubt sizeable retainer they were paid each year. 'Can I get you anything, Madam?'

'No, thank you. Everyone must be exhausted. We should all try to get some rest. I'll try and doze. I won't sleep.'

'No one in this house will sleep now, Madam. Except of course his Lordship, the little Earl.'

'Oh, the poor little mite,' Abbie said, tears again filling her eyes.

'I've phoned the station, and the local boys are going to give me a lift to the railway station later on, in time for the first train back to Liverpool.'

When Mason left them, Mike put his arm around his wife.

'Oh, Mike. I feel so sorry for her. Hasn't she been through enough? Hasn't life been bloody rotten to her?'

'She's got Edward,' Mike said wearily, thinking of his own son, asleep at Hilda's.

'But it's so distressing to hear him being called his Lordship – the little Earl of Ashenden. He's not even a year old yet!'

'I know, luv, but that's what he is now.'

415

* * *

Winnie felt so helpless. If only Hannah would cry, it would help to lessen the pent-up emotions, the shock. For days after Abe had been killed, she'd wandered around in a trance, not eating, not sleeping, not talking. For Hannah it was worse – she'd loved her husband.

'Oh, Hannah, luv, cry! Let it all out, it's better, believe me.'

'Did you feel like this, Mam? As though everything was happening to someone else? Not really being yourself, not really believing . . . anything?'

'Yes. It's the shock.'

Hannah squeezed her hand. 'I remember it all so clearly, Mam. Da yelling and hitting Jerry. Jerry with the poker and then . . . the blood and Mr Burgess and Dr Wallace coming, and the police. Will I remember tonight like that?'

'Yes, but in time things will become hazy. It won't hurt as much. At least he loved you Hannah, and you loved him, that's something to cling to. Your da made my life hell and had done for years.'

Hannah looked towards the french windows. The first streaks of the grey February dawn were creeping across the sky. The night was over. It was a new day. Her first day . . . alone. She looked down at her hands, and her wedding ring glinted in the pale light.

'Oh, Mam, he's gone! I'll never see him again, Mam!' she cried. Then came the tears.

* * *

It made the front pages of all the newspapers, and, added to grief and shock, came public notoriety. Mason answered all telephone calls and queries at Ashenden. The servants were all tight-lipped at his express command. Frank Burgess closed the shop for a week to keep the curious away, regardless of loss of income. They all needed privacy. Winnie remained at Ashenden.

Angela had been brought home by her Aunt Julia, who had put aside her grief and taken control of everything. She couldn't take in the enormity of it. She'd wanted to see Freddie, speak to him, but her aunt absolutely forbade it. She couldn't believe that Freddie was capable of such a thing. Nor could she face the shame and disgrace: her future looked bleak and depressing. There were very few homes she would be welcome in now, and her prospects of making a good marriage had disappeared. Who would want to marry into a family cursed with the sin of Cain?

Richard's funeral was arranged for the last week in February by Lady Julia. Frank would attend, to support Hannah as he had done on her wedding day, but Hilda and Chrissie were to remain at home. Mike and Abbie would also be there with Phil, whose wound was starting to heal. All the dignitaries of the county would attend, and some from further afield.

It was a grey, bleak February day. A cold north-easterly wind was rattling and bending the skeletal branches of the trees that bordered the drive. Hannah gazed wearily out over the parkland. She was still dazed and weighed down with grief. She couldn't accept that he was gone. She still listened for his voice. She would turn to speak to him, reach for him when she awoke each morning, forgetting for a few blissful seconds that he would never again lie beside her. She had no more tears left now. Her eyes were dry and burning.

She was dressed from head to foot in black crêpe. A veil covered her hat and fell almost to her knees, a veil that mercifully hid her face from the world. Somehow she would have to get through this day with dignity, for his sake and Edward's. She could not break down or collapse. Aunt Julia had told her to bite her lip hard and to concentrate on a single line from a poem or a hymn. To repeat it over and over to herself, to leave no room in her mind for other thoughts. The family was reeling under the scandal. Publicly, Hannah was the tragic Countess of Ashenden, dignified in her grief as all her predecessors had been. It was going to be the worst and by far the longest day in her life. Maybe all the past sorrow, pain and violence had had some point, she thought. Perhaps it had been to prepare her, strengthen her, to get through this day.

In a moment someone would come for her, then she would have to act her part and have to go on acting until much, much later tonight. Only when everyone had gone could she allow the mask to slip, allow herself the dubious luxury of giving vent to her feelings. For only to her mother and to Abbie had she broken down completely. Nora, Aunt Julia and Mason had witnessed her tears, but not the outpourings of a broken heart.

Downstairs half the county were assembled to make the short drive to St Ambrose's Church and then back to Ashenden. Richard would be buried in the crypt beneath the chapel, beside his father and grandfather. All the Ashenden earls were laid to rest there.

She turned away from the window, for she'd caught a glimpse of the black horses as they came slowly up the drive, the plumes in their headdresses waving in the wind. They were slowly pulling the ebony-coloured, crêpe-draped hearse, and the sight tore at her heart. *Oh, Richard. Richard, how am I going to get through it all? How can I see you laid to rest downstairs and not break down? How can I carry on? What's left for me now?*

Both her mother and Abbie were near at hand, she knew that, but she wanted these moments alone, to think and remember. The day she'd first seen him, in Walton. The day she'd moved here with him. The day he'd asked her to marry him, and her wedding day. His joy when she'd placed Edward in his arms. A few brief years of happiness for them both in a world that had used them cruelly. It was a double tragedy because Freddie would hang. And what about Edward? He would never know his father, and he would have to live with the stigma that was now attached to the Ashenden name.

She didn't hear Mason enter, but as he coughed discreetly she looked up.

'It's time, my Lady.' His heart went out to her. She'd loved his Lordship so much, and she'd never wanted anything from life other than to be left to live it quietly with her family.

'Mason, I . . . I'll try not to . . . not to disgrace anyone.'

'I know you will do nothing to invite any adverse comments, my Lady.'

'It's so hard. Twice as hard for me. I . . . I wasn't brought up to be a lady. Aunt Julia is so strong, so composed.'

'You are as gracious as any lady who has ever lived or visited Ashenden. We all admire and respect you, Lady Ashenden.'

'Oh, Mason, you've always been so kind to me. How will I manage? How will I cope, bringing Edward up without . . . without . . . Richard's help and guidance?'

'You have Lady Julia and all of us. You are not alone and never will be. Shall we go? Mr Burgess is waiting on the landing.'

'Mason, I know it's not etiquette, but will you walk on the other side of me? You were so very fond of him, and maybe if I have you to support me, too, I'll get through it all.'

Mason's eyes misted over as he took the black-gloved hand she held out, and guided her towards the door.

Chapter Twenty-Six

———•———

AFTER A GRUELLING DAY, and feeling as though he had aged ten years, Frank returned at six o'clock with Phil.

Hilda got up and went to put the kettle on, but he shook his head.

'No thanks, luv, I could do with some fresh air and a bit of time to sort of wind down. Put your coat and hat on and we'll go down to the Pier Head, maybe take a trip on the ferry to Woodside and back.'

She was about to protest that what he needed was to put his feet up by his own fireside, but saw the quick movement of his head towards Chrissie and Phil.

'Aye, I could do with a breath of air myself. I've had a nagging headache all day. I got up with it and it hasn't shifted.'

'How was it?' she asked as they walked arm-in-arm to the tram stop on Scotland Road.

'She bore up well. She's got a lot of guts.'

'She's had a lot to contend with. Far more than

anyone should have had to bear. She's got courage, has Hannah.'

'She spoke to everyone afterwards, but I could see she was exhausted, there were so many people there, important people, too. The Bishop and half a dozen clergymen took the service. In the end, Lady Julia took charge and chased everyone home. Politely of course. I'll say this much, the high and mighty train their women well. Neither she nor Lady Angela shed a single tear. Very dignified, it all was.'

'And you think that's something to be proud of? Not shedding a tear for their nephew and brother?'

'Oh, Hilda, don't start. It all went very well, that's the main thing. Decorous was how Mason described it. You know, he's a decent bloke under that starchy manner, and he's genuinely fond of Hannah.'

'Did Winnie stay?'

'Aye, although you can see the place unsettles her. She's like a fish out of water. She stuck by my side and wouldn't talk to anyone. Even when the Bishop came over to sympathize, all she could do was nod.'

They stood for a while in silence until Hilda spoke. 'Do you think Phil can ever forgive our Chrissie?'

'I don't know. He's got such a placid, understanding nature, but even a worm will turn.'

'He must think something of her to have risked his life for her.'

'That was before he fully understood how things were. A sort of automatic reflex action. He said he didn't stop to think.'

'Oh, I keep praying that now she'll settle down, that he'll forgive her, and that none of it will matter to his job. I'm laying siege to heaven's gates.'

'I know, you seem to spend more time at church than at home. Oh, I'm not complaining. We'll just have to see how things go now. Maybe it will help them to talk. Thank goodness, here's a tram. It comes to something when we've got to go out in the cold at our age so they can have some privacy. Let's hope it's worth it.'

When her mam and dad had gone, Chrissie turned to Phil, but she couldn't look him in the face. It was the first time they had been alone together, and she felt nervous and ashamed of herself.

'Was it very awful?'

'Yes. Hannah held up well, but I don't know how she got through it. Maybe the doctor had given her something. Abbie and Mrs Harvey sobbed all the time, and so did most of the servants. Lady Julia and Lady Angela didn't cry, but they looked awful.

'Oh, Phil, I wish I was dead, I really do!'

'Chrissie don't say that! You could easily have been shot.'

'I'm sorry. You risked your life for me, and I'll never be able to repay you for that. No matter what anyone says, it's my fault. He's dead, you're hurt and Freddie will . . .' she swallowed hard. It was a foregone conclusion that Freddie D'Arcy would hang, and she was riddled with guilt.

'Chrissie, I won't say it's not your fault, I can't say

something I don't believe. But not all of it is. His gambling, his selfishness, his callousness was at the root of it. If it hadn't been you, it would have been some other girl. You were convenient. You were easily dazzled, easily duped into believing his lies.'

'Oh, I was so stupid, so blind! I wanted to be a real lady like Hannah. To have money, clothes, go places. I was so sure he would marry me, but I didn't love him. I don't think I even liked him very much. All I was interested in, all I could see, were the things he could give me. I didn't intend it all to end like this, to hurt so many people. I know what Bridie's saying, that I've always been a trouble-maker. Oh, Phil, I'm so sorry I was cruel to you. I've been so wicked and selfish, and I'm so ashamed of myself. I wouldn't blame you if you never spoke to me again. If no one speaks to me. It's all I deserve.'

He took her hand. 'Chrissie, you were stupid but it didn't stop me loving you and hoping that sooner or later you'd see him for what he was.'

She remembered how she'd deliberately hurt him in the past and her eyes filled with tears. 'I'm not the person I was, Phil. I've changed. So many terrible things have happened.'

'No one would expect you to remain the same, Chrissie, not after all . . . that.'

'And there's still the trial and everything else.'

He knew she meant Freddie D'Arcy's sentencing and execution. 'It will be an ordeal for everyone, especially Hannah.'

'I know. Can you ever forgive me, Phil?'

'Perhaps in time,' he answered truthfully.

'Oh, Phil, I need someone to care for me, comfort me and help me to get through it. I feel so useless, confused, so frightened.'

'I'll help you, and so will your mam and dad and Mike and Abbie.'

'They really don't understand. They think that I deserve everything. I'm frightened. I'm so scared.'

He squeezed her hand. 'Maybe we can start afresh, in a few months' time, when everything is over. Don't let's do anything or say anything now, while we're both upset.'

'Do you mean that, Phil?'

'Of course I do.'

She buried her face against the sleeve of his jacket. Out of the whole sorry mess of chaos and grief she'd helped to cause, and which had hurt so many people, she saw a glimmer of light, of hope for the future. She felt very humble but relieved and somehow more secure.

'In a couple of months?' she begged.

'In a couple of months, I promise, and I don't break my promises.'

The first days of March were bright and blustery, but Hannah hardly noticed. Pale sunshine spread swathes of aureate light across the lawns and gardens where daffodils were coming into bloom and primulas formed splashes of pale lemon and violet under the trees and shrubs. She felt so empty, so lost, so confused and so unable to even contemplate the future.

'Take one day at a time luv,' Winnie had advised. 'There are many stages of mourning. You'll go through so much pain and heartache, guilt and anger.'

'Anger, Mam?'

'Yes. Even though your da and I weren't happy, there were times when I felt so angry that he'd left me to see to everything, to shoulder all the burdens. I blamed myself too. The guilt was almost as bad. I grew to hate the word "if". *If* only I'd have stood up to him, your da was a bully. *If* only I'd have gone for the police, Frank Burgess, Pat Kerrigan, anyone. At least you'll not have anything to blame yourself for or regret.'

'Oh Mam, I have. If I'd stayed in the room, not gone into the hall, I might have stopped Freddie.'

'And been killed yourself, Hannah? No, there was nothing you could have done. He was beyond reason, beyond sanity.'

She'd sent Winnie home at the weekend. She was worn out, and Ashenden overawed her. She'd never been comfortable here. It would do her good to see her friends and neighbours, to be able to talk about her worries, and relieve the burden a little. Here she saw no one.

Hannah sighed and sat down at her writing desk. She had forced herself to start to reply to all the cards and letters of sympathy that had arrived. It was a task that Aunt Julia had divided equally between herself, Angela and Hannah, according to the rank and status of the writer. Hannah had set herself a target of four a day. Two in the morning, two in the afternoon, but she found it difficult to concentrate, and often had to discard her work because it was blotched with tears.

The task seemed to stretch ahead into infinity as did the empty, lonely years. The responsibilities were enormous, and she was ignorant of so many things. How could she run a house and an estate like Ashenden until Edward was old enough to take over? This was his future, his heritage, and she was afraid that she would let it slip away through inexperience and mismanagement. She knew she could rely on Aunt Julia and Mason, but could she also rely on the managers and overseers? Richard had familiarized himself and understood everything. He'd been intelligent and had had a first-class education. While she was no longer the ignorant girl she'd been when she'd left school, there was still so much she knew nothing about. No, she hadn't a clue about running an estate. It was another burden to add to an already crushing load.

Mason interrupted her thoughts. 'Mrs Burgess and another lady have called to see you, my Lady.'

She got up. 'Did Mrs Burgess say who the other lady was?' She certainly didn't feel up to visitors. She was always glad to see Abbie, but she didn't relish having to make polite conversation with anyone else.

'She said to tell you she has come a long way. Her name is Mrs Deirdre Kerrigan.'

For the first time since Richard's death she smiled. 'Dee! Dee is here! I remember now that Abbie said she was coming home in March.'

'Shall I show them up, my Lady?'

'Yes! No! I'll go down, Mason.'

He didn't know who the rather plain young woman was, but her presence had obviously brought a ray of brightness into his mistress's life.

Hannah ran down the stairs and caught sight of the two women and the two toddlers. Mason had said nothing about children.

Abbie smiled. 'Are you up to seeing people today?'

'Dee! Dee! Is it really you?' Hannah cried, hugging her.

Dee Kerrigan smiled. 'Yes, it's really me. All the way from Ontario, and on the roughest crossing for at least ten years! I never thought I'd get here.'

'Oh, it's so good to see you again, Dee! Abbie said you were coming home. So this is Charlotte – and she's every bit as pretty as her photograph. Come into the drawing-room.'

'Will you require tea, my Lady?' Mason asked.

'Yes please, and can you ask Nanny to bring Edward down, Mason?'

Dee looked around her and smiled wistfully. Once, long ago, she'd lived in a big house. Not as grand as this or as large, but they had had servants until, through gambling and sheer extravagance, her father had been bankrupted, and they'd come to Liverpool. Oh, how much misery obsessive gambling was responsible for, she thought, remembering Abbie's explanation of Hannah's plight.

'I had a nanny once. When you mentioned yours to Mason it all came back so clearly, and yet these days I hardly ever look back to my childhood.'

'You look so well, Dee, so different,' Hannah said.

It was true, Abbie thought. Dee still wore spectacles, but now they seemed to suit her. That rather awkward, self-conscious air Dee used to have had gone. Her light brown hair was cut short and now waved, framing her face attractively. Her clothes were stylish, not expensive, but fashionable. Yes, Dee had blossomed since her marriage to Tommy, although Abbie, like many people, had thought they would have little in common. Her brother had always been a bit of an ignoramus and Dee was intelligent. Tommy was brash and liked the sound of his own voice. Dee was quietly spoken and reserved. Tommy, until he'd joined the Army, had been irresponsible, a real harum-scarum. Dee was serious and had had more than her fair share of responsibilities from the age of fourteen.

'It must be good food, hard work, clean air and open spaces. Canada's a wonderful place. It's so big. There is so much space, I can stand on my porch and see for miles. Houses aren't crowded together, there is no sooty grime, and Lake Ontario is five minutes' walk away. In summer it's beautiful.'

'Then you're glad you went?'

'Absolutely, and Tommy loves it. He works hard, very hard, but he says that at least he can see

something at the end of it and something that's his –
ours. We put as much money as we can spare back into
the farm. Now we've got more land, we feel entitled to
call it a farm. We'll be millionaires one day, Tommy
says.' Dee chuckled. 'He's got big plans, has Tommy
Kerrigan. We had a bumper crop last year, so we had
to hire help for the first time, and we're hoping that
this year's will beat it, aren't we, precious?'

Three-year-old Charlotte Kerrigan hid her face
shyly in her mother's lap.

'She's a little treasure. Mam would have loved her,'
Abbie said wistfully.

'She's getting spoiled, what with Grandpa
Chatterton and Grandpa Kerrigan, Aunty Joan, Aunty
Bridie, Rose and Elizabeth, Phil and David and Bertie
and Seb. She's the centre of attention all the time.
Someone is always fussing over her!'

'And why not? She's a little beauty.'

'At least she's not plain like me,' Dee laughed.

'Oh, stop that Dee, you look very smart,' Abbie
chided.

Jessie arrived with the tea at the same time as
Nanny who was carrying Lord Edward Ashenden, the
eighth Earl. She put him down, and he toddled
unsteadily to his mother who lifted him onto her lap
and kissed him, her expression softening.

Jessie and Nanny exchanged looks that said 'Thank
God she looks a bit better.'

'He looks so much like you, Hannah, I mean your
Ladyship,' Dee checked herself. She of all people

should know better, but she hadn't really been concentrating. She'd been thinking that it was hard to believe that this little boy was the heir to one of the largest estates in the North of England, and that he bore an old and honoured title.

'Oh, please, Dee. No formality. Abbie calls me Hannah.'

Dee looked doubtful, she had always been very precise.

'Just Hannah please? "your Ladyship" makes me sound so old. I always think of Aunt Julia.'

'Well, we're matrons now. Some people would call us old – middle-aged anyway,' Abbie replied, pulling a face. She wanted to keep the conversation going. It was doing Hannah the world of good, and she was glad now that she'd persuaded Dee to come with her. She hadn't wanted to, she'd been very reticent to start with, saying it would be an intrusion on Hannah's grief. Dee was always very sensitive.

'Oh, it seems like only yesterday that we were sitting on the stairs in Mrs Burgess's house at that Christmas party. Do you remember, Abbie? There was me, poor Nancy, Mike and Tommy, Mary Simcock and Sean Doyle.'

'I remember. That was the first time Mike had even noticed me. I had a new pale lilac bombazine dress that our Joan and Mam bought between them from Blacklers. It was just after our Monica disgraced us all—'

'And you looked gorgeous, and we were all bright

green with envy, especially Mary who'd bought that awful magenta-coloured dress from Frisby Dyke's. You put us all in the shade.'

'I wonder what happened to Sean Doyle?' Hannah mused. She had never been allowed to attend such parties. Abe had considered them sinful.

'Chrissie said she saw him going for the Dublin ferry in civilian clothes, before the war ended. She said he was deserting, but enough about Chrissie,' Abbie said briskly cursing herself for mentioning Chrissie at all. Nor was she going to remind Hannah that Jerry had been at that party too.

Dee was watching Hannah closely. 'She's a very subdued girl now,' she ventured, hoping her instincts were right.

'And so she should be!' Abbie shot a warning glance at her sister-in-law.

'Sometimes I feel sorry for Chrissie,' Hannah sighed.

Abbie's eyes widened and she bit back the words that had sprung to her lips, for Dee had shaken her head.

'Why?' Dee asked.

'Because her ambition was responsible for every-thing and now . . . now she's left with nothing.'

'She deserves just that, Hannah. Nothing. She's ruined so many lives.'

Hannah sighed sadly. Abbie tutted to herself in annoyance. This was just what she had wanted to avoid, and they had been doing so well. 'After tea we should get back, Hannah. We only intended this to be a very brief visit.'

'No, please don't go.' Hannah didn't know Dee as well as Abbie did, although for a short time they had served together in the VAD, but she felt drawn to the quieter, older girl who seemed to radiate serenity. 'Abbie, I don't want to upset you or offend you.'

'You won't. What is it, Hannah?' Abbie interrupted.

'Would you mind if Dee stayed here with me, for a few days? If she doesn't mind?'

Abbie was taken aback and gazed in astonishment at them both. She was even more astounded when Dee smiled and said, 'Well, just for a few days.'

'What about Charlotte?'

'I'll keep her with me. I'll go and explain and collect some things. I don't think anyone will begrudge Hannah a few days, do you?'

'Roscoe will take you and bring you back. Abbie, are you sure you're not upset?'

'Oh, Hannah, how could I be? I thought we were friends, and friends aren't so petty-minded. Liam will miss his cousin, though. They were just getting used to each other. Well, to be truthful they were just learning to squabble with each other,' she smiled.

Mason was surprised to learn of Dee's stay, and, although Hannah's instructions were carried out to the letter and he was glad to see some animation in her eyes again, he did wonder about the wisdom of it. He needn't have worried, he thought to himself after

Dee's first evening at Ashenden. He recognized breeding, and the young woman from Canada had it. Her manner was quiet but poised. She knew how to treat the staff. She knew how things were done, but most of all, she seemed to understand Lady Hannah. In fact, he mused, in some ways they were very alike. Dee could have been her Ladyship's older sister. Mason was relieved and impressed.

Nanny White was impressed with Charlotte, who had joined Edward in the nursery. 'For a child of three born and brought up, thus far, in the colonies, she is remarkably well behaved and well mannered.'

'I expect that is because her mother is a lady, Nanny. She may not have a title, but she has good breeding.'

Dee drew Hannah out. She encouraged her to talk about her feelings, about what immediate plans she had, though they were very sketchy. She quickly realized that the worst thing Hannah could do was to cut herself off from the world, immure herself behind the walls of Ashenden. Hannah was young and intelligent, and had a thirst for knowledge which would be criminal to suppress.

They talked long into the night, and eventually there was no need for Dee to encourage her, and she knew Hannah would cope – in time. Hannah had an inner strength, an unshakeable belief that eventually some good would come out of all the sorrow and heartache. She had said that sometimes she felt Richard was with her. That his spirit was beside her, and he comforted her and gave her a little more strength each day.

'Maybe one day I will be able to manage Ashenden.'

'Of course you will, Hannah, but don't lose yourself, immerse yourself in it to the exclusion of everything and everyone else.'

'I will miss you, Dee. Abbie is a dear, and she's been a pillar of strength, I couldn't have managed without her, but you seem to understand – really understand me.'

'We're alike in many ways. We've both known tragedy and hard times.'

'But you have Tommy and Charlotte and your farm.'

'And you have Edward, Ashenden and so much scope. Make the most of yourself. What about all his Lordship's work for the unemployed and maimed ex-servicemen? Oh, I don't say throw yourself into good works immediately, but add it to your plans for the future.'

'I wish you were staying longer, Dee. I really do.'

'So do I, but it's just not possible.'

When Abbie returned to see Hannah, and escort Dee back to Liverpool, she could see that her friend had benefitted from Dee's short stay. Hannah hadn't become her old self, she never would, but she had lost that air of utter dejection.

'How soon before you sail?' she asked Dee.

'You just want to keep her here! You should hear

the moans and complaints in Burlington Street,' Abbie said lightly. 'You do seem to be brighter, Hannah.'

'I feel it. Oh, it will be a long, long time before I feel that things are normal again, and I'll never stop missing him.'

'It would help if you had a change of scenery,' suggested Dee. 'There are too many memories here. I'm not saying leave, just have a break, a vacation. Come back to Grimsby with me.'

Hannah shook her head. It was tempting, but not possible. 'No, I couldn't leave before . . . before the trial.'

'After it's all over?' Abbie urged. It was going to be an awful ordeal for Hannah, to have to relive that terrible night. All the nightmares would resurface, still raw wounds would be re-opened. Nor would it do Hannah any good at all to be here when Freddie D'Arcy was executed. Eventually, everyone would sort themselves out. She and Mike would put it all behind them, as would Frank and Hilda, and it looked as though Phil and Chrissie would find a future together. Phil still loved her, and she was a changed girl. And Hannah must look to the future, too.

'It will be a holiday, Hannah. Take Edward and your Mam with you.'

'You'd all be welcome, you too Abbie.'

'Oh, Dee, we couldn't afford the fare or the time, but thanks. Well, Hannah?'

'Maybe . . . I will.'

Dee smiled. 'And maybe it's as well you aren't going

to come back with me at the end of the month. I've got a second-class ticket, and you will have to travel luxury class. You can't have Edward mixing with the lower orders.'

'Dee Kerrigan you're a snob!' Abbie joked, but she knew Dee was right, class distinctions were still strong. Hannah had crossed the dividing line, and in public at least, she must be seen to stay there, as must her son.

'I'm not, and that's one of the reasons I like Canada so much. There are no class divisions. So, will you come to my little town?'

'Yes,' Hannah agreed. Maybe it was what she needed. A break, a change from Ashenden and its memories. When she returned perhaps she'd feel stronger, able to pick up the threads, make definite plans and carry them out.

'Then come when the blossom is covering the fruit trees, it's so beautiful. Acres and acres of pink and white flowers – an ocean of blossoms.'

'Then that's settled. Now let's get you home, Dee, before they send out the search parties for us.' Abbie was very relieved that Hannah was taking the first, difficult steps to overcome her grief, and she'd begun to believe that Hannah would again find the happiness that had been snatched away.

Hannah wouldn't see Dee again before she sailed. It wasn't fair to deprive all the families and friends of Dee's company, the very purpose of her visit, so the farewells were said on the steps of Ashenden.

Mason and Hannah, with Edward in her arms, saw them into the car.

Hannah kissed Dee and Charlotte goodbye. 'Thank you, Dee . . . for everything. Have a safe trip home, and remember me to Tommy.'

'I'll see you soon, Hannah,' Abbie promised as the car moved off.

Hannah waved, and Edward imitated her gesture with a chubby hand. She kissed her son's soft rosy cheek and smiled at Mason.

'Don't forget, come when it's blossom time!' Dee called as the car rounded the curve of the drive and was lost to sight.

'Will you go, my Lady?'

Hannah smiled and held her son tightly. 'Yes, we'll go, Mason. When it's blossom time.'